# Deception
## in
# Honolulu

## The Bryant Family Chronicles

Eddie R. Hughes

Deep Sea Publishing

Copyright © 2015 by Eddie Hughes

All rights reserved. Published in the United States by

Deep Sea Publishing LLC, Herndon, Virginia.

This is a work of fiction. Names, characters, places, and incidents either are the product of the author's imagination or are used fictionally. Any resemblance to actual persons, living or dead, events or locales is entirely coincidental.

**Deep Sea Publishing ISBN:  1939535999**

**Deep Sea Publishing ISBN-13: 978-1939535993**

**Deep Sea Publishing E-Book ISBN-13: 978-1939535986**

www.deepseapublishing.com

Printed in the United States of America

eBook created in the United States of America

# Chapter 1: *Orange Blur*

Bill stared at his glass of water on the sidewalk table in front of him. He sat mesmerized as the ice sparkled from the moving slivers of sunlight that were filtering through the palm trees above him. He was deep in thought and was oblivious to the sweltering heat that was common on August days in Florida.

It was twenty-three days ago that he had received a call while in Chicago to change his flight and come to Sarasota, Florida. The job was supposed to take no more than two weeks, but he experienced one delay after another since the day he arrived. His employers were impatient for job completion, and they had made it clear they were unhappy with the string of excuses he had supplied on every phone update to them over the last two weeks. The fact that he had to make another excuse today made him irritated. He dreaded making the call.

The heat on his bare arms had caused a light film of perspiration on his skin. Relief from the high temperatures came from ocean breezes or passing cars, which made the hair on his arms move and sent a momentary coolness over his body. A forceful gust of wind made him aware of his surroundings again and he suddenly realized that his waitress was standing beside him. He glanced up to see her holding a notepad and looking directly at him as if she was waiting for him to respond. *Had she said something?*

"I'm sorry, did you say something to me?"

"I asked if you were ready to order sir." The pretty blonde waitress had a broad smile on her face. Her ponytail swung over one shoulder as she looked down at him. She wore the same clothes as the other female waitresses -- khaki shorts and a floral pattern shirt. 'Kelsey' was printed on her name tag.

He reached for the menu and pointed to the Suntanned Merluza. The waitress asked if he wanted anything else to drink or an appetizer. He told her no and handed her the menu.

"That will be ready in about fifteen minutes," said the perky waitress. He could have sworn her bright white teeth twinkled. She turned and walked back inside the restaurant to place the order with the cook.

He scanned his surroundings, a habit he had acquired over the years whenever he was in public places, and noticed there were more people now sitting in the other sidewalk tables just outside the *Mango Tango*. He had eaten at the restaurant several times over the last few weeks. He certainly enjoyed the food here, but the main reason he ate at this restaurant was because of its proximity to the home of his mark. *Mango Tango* sat in the heart of St Armands Circle, which was an upscale island resort connected by a large bridge to Sarasota's downtown district.

The sidewalk tables were starting to fill with both locals and vacationers. Some tables had bright umbrellas to provide shade from the hot summer sun. His table was shaded solely by one of the many tall palms that lined the Circle. Bill blended right in wearing black cargo shorts, black convertible strap sandals, and a light blue fishermen's shirt. The loose fitting shirt hid his handgun, which was stuffed in his shorts in the small of his back. A loud scream from a child at the table to his left drew his attention. He watched the kid squirm to get down.

He let his eyes drift slowly ahead of his table where cars were driving by just a few feet away. Farther away he saw the caretaker of the park in the center of the Circle weeding around the colorful array of planted flowers.  The man looked his way for a second and then continued with his work.

Bill lowered his head and began to stare at the newspaper sitting in front of him.  There was yet another front page article about the Bryant family in the Sarasota *Herald-Tribune*.  Since his arrival here, there had been continual media coverage of this family after their last adventure.

*Rick, Danielle, Nikki and Shelli … America's new, perfect family.*  Bill focused on Rick Bryant's picture and thought how much Rick was like himself.   He was driven and a workaholic, but stopped at the drop of the hat to stay involved with the family.

The words on the newspaper began to blur as Bill slipped into his memories.   Images flashed in his head of his daughter and wife at the park.   It was a beautiful, sunny day and he and his family were enjoying their picnic on the green grass near the lake.  He can remember the giggle of his daughter as he chased her again in his role of tickle monster. He smiled as the memory transitioned into another scene of his deployment day.   It was hard to look back at the front door of his house as his wife with tears on her cheek was trying to appear brave at the same time.   She was holding Sarah as they both waved goodbye.  As he slid into the passenger seat of his buddy's car, he turned to see Sarah throwing kisses in big gestures.  He had to fight back the tears so his buddy wouldn't see him cry.

Another outburst of the child at the table to his left jolted Bill to the present.  He slid the paper aside and pulled out his iPhone.  He started scrolling through his surveillance notes.  He always prided himself on his thoroughness. He had to conduct detailed surveillance on all the family members to determine their schedules, likes and dislikes, who were their friends and enemies. It was important details needed for the successful completion of his task.

The tech-savvy entrepreneur, Rick Bryant, and his family had been flung into the limelight with their role in the termination of a Florida drug ring and the treasure find.  But in spite their popularity, Rick's activities at work were simply staggering. His hours at his office had steadily grown since Bill's arrival to Sarasota.

Rick's company had been working with the local Sheriff's office well before their recent adventures.  But their notoriety and the success of his company's port security sensors now drew visits by the Coast Guard and port directors from around the world.

Two weeks ago Rick received a large shipment at the port in Tampa.  The large containers were then transported directly to his Sarasota dockside offices. There was a lot of secrecy around this shipment.  A few days after the shipment arrived, Bill noted the arrival of a team of people from Italy.  He knew nothing much about them and had only figured out that they were Italian after following them back to their hotel.   Given the timing of the Italians arrival, Bill guessed they may have something to do with the shiny orange SUV that left Rick's facility after midnight over the last few nights.   He suspected the SUV was part of the shipment. The orange SUV took long drives around the area only to return back to the facility. Being it was nighttime, he couldn't tell who was driving. The car made frequent stops and even stopped at shopping center parking lots, but no one ever got out. It was all very strange.

Rick's team of engineers was also working on something new on the water.  They would leave all day in the company workboat and return at dark.   Since the company was a converted boat repair center in one of the Sarasota Bay marinas, the indoor boat slips allowed the engineers to covertly load whatever equipment they were testing on their boats.  Bill tried to follow them several times on a rented fishing boat to see what Rick's employees were up to, but had no luck. They were definitely aware of his presence and would keep moving whenever he or anyone else got within a klick of their position. One day he saw them go out and around the backside of a large vessel anchored offshore, but he couldn't get close enough to tell whether or not people from the workboat boarded the vessel. The vessel's name was the **Amphitrite**. Bill had spelled it out phonetically to remember its pronunciation -- **Ăm • fi • try • tee**. He could find nothing about the vessel when he searched public records. It wasn't relevant to the job at hand, so he stopped trying to figure it out.

With their waterside home full of gunshot holes from their drug-ring case, Rick had enlisted the help of a full blown construction team at his house. It seemed as though there were many more people working at the site than were required for just a remodel, so Bill suspected Rick was making substantial improvements or additions. He could only imagine what state-of-the-art electronic hardware was being installed.

Meanwhile, the girls had been busy with friends. Their summertime happenings were frequent and often with friends, but stayed mostly within the confines of Sarasota County.

Shelli Bryant was a dynamo. The tall brunette was popular in school, and she excelled in dance and kung fu. And her curiosity was apparently the key to finding millions in lost pirate treasure. The recent popularity of the family meant that Shelli was invited to every teenage event imaginable. Summer had reduced the dance team commitments for her, so she spent more time at the beach, boating, and socializing. Her black belt in kung fu demanded lessons several times a week, which kept her fit. Shelli was so energetic that she seemed to vibrate even when she sat down. New technology appeared to come easy to her, and Bill had seen her more than once help her mom or a friend with their phone or tablet. At almost 15, she was becoming noticeably more interested in boys. Almost glued to her side was her best friend Stephanie. Shelli had long straight hair, and a perfectly symmetrical face.

Nikki was the older of the two kids at twenty-something. She was a linguist and operator of all things Bryant, and apparently a mean shot with a spear gun. She also had a keen mind for tactics and seemed a natural born leader. Nikki had long brown hair, like her sister. However, Nikki's hair seemed to have a bit more curl. She definitely turned heads. Her rigorous schedule of exercise – a full two hours per day – kept her well-toned. And Bill had found out when he searched their mail that her newfound popularity coupled with her good looks had garnered her several modeling offers. But what was most interesting to Bill was that she went to her father's company each day. From newspaper articles he knew that Nikki was a rising college senior this fall, so she couldn't be a fulltime employee of her dad's firm. He didn't know what she did for the company, but he had seen her go out on the workboat several times with other employees. While eavesdropping one night at a restaurant, Bill overheard Nikki tell her friends that she couldn't go with them to the beach the next day because she had to go into the office for training. What she was training for was still a mystery. Most worrisome was the ever-present boyfriend, Ryan. Being Stephanie's brother further complicated things.

And then there was Danielle. She was still beautiful at 50, and apparently a great mother and wife. Besides being the frequent chauffer to Shelli, Danielle also had a passion for art and stayed active in it at her job at the Ringling Museum of Art. Her days had also become busier in the last few weeks. Not only was Danielle a docent at the museum, she was their go-to docent. Due again to the popularity of the family, she was being asked for by name by dignitaries coming to the museum for private tours. It didn't hurt that she could speak French fluently. Danielle had also been assigned the job of organizing all aspects of the *SeaFair* art show, which would arrive in town in the mid-spring. The *Seafair* was a massive yacht and mobile art gallery, and it made an annual trip to Sarasota Harbor.

All this activity made it hard for Bill to complete his mission – killing the Bryant family. Due to Rick's hi-tech security sensors and the construction at their house, he had not been able to get close enough when they were at home together. And because of their close ties to government and law enforcement communities, he knew he could not complete the mission by plucking the family off one at a time. It had to be all of them at once and it had to appear like an accident. Not because it was his employer's wishes, but he knew he'd be hunted to eternity if it was believed to be a hit. So he had to watch and wait for his opportunity. Plus he would have to get crucial information out of one family member for his employer prior to the execution of the lot. The job had been far more challenging than he had ever imagined.

He was startled by the vibration of his iPhone on the table next to the newspaper. The unknown ID on the phone indicated it was his employer. He leaned back in his chair to gather his thoughts before answering. The phone buzzed again. He's eyes wandered at the beautiful scenery of the park in front of him until he came upon the caretaker in the park again. This time he noticed the caretaker had his finger on his ear and was again looking in his direction. The man lowered his hand quickly and turned away. *What the hell?*

As his phone continued to buzz, Bill slowly scanned the area and his gaze ended at the pretty waitress, Kelsey, over his right shoulder at the hostess station at the bar. She was talking on the phone and staring at him. Bill locked eyes with her and watched her lips move.

"He's looking right at me," she mouthed. Besides the use of weaponry, many professional hit men at Bill's pay grade acquired various other skills useful in assassination. For Bill, lip reading was one of them.

"Shit," said Bill out loud in a low, irritated voice. He stood and reached for his pistol. His phone buzzed again and with the butt of his pistol he smashed it into silence in one quick jab. The sound of the phone shattering drew gasps from people sitting at nearby tables.

The waitress dropped her phone, which shattered and flickered off, and ran toward the back of the restaurant. Bill heard tires squeal and saw two sheriff cars entered the Circle fast. Their lights and sirens were off, but Bill knew that was only temporary. He took off running with pistol in hand toward the rear of the restaurant. Anyone that saw the pistol leapt out of his way, and those that didn't see him were pushed clear. She could easily ID him, so she was a liability. He needed to catch, then dispose of the waitress once he found out who she was talking to on the phone.

The waitress burst through the rear door. She was fast, but Bill's ritual daily training made him faster. He exited the rear door seconds behind the waitress.

There was a staircase immediately to the right with no one on it. Glancing down the wide alley, he saw a clump of trees to the right side of the alley and a tall bush to the left. The pony tail of the waitress disappeared behind the tall bush. He sprinted down the alley. As he reached the end of the alley he heard screeching tires. He abruptly halted and jumped quickly against the left wall with his gun held in both hands and near his face.

He listened intently and heard a car door open and a woman's voice yell, "Kelsey, get in!" He swung out from the wall and saw Kelsey was standing behind the passenger door with one foot in a deep blue BMW X5. She froze at the sight of him. Nikki Bryant was at the wheel.

*Time to clean up,* he thought. He lowered his gun to eye level and fired directly at Kelsey's chest. The staccato sound, which was muffled by the silencer on the end of the barrel, was barely discernible over the decibels of daily noise of the shopping center. The window fractured and the force of the bullet pushed the door toward the girl as she screamed. *The bullet must have gone through without shattering the glass ... convenient.* Bill walked with determination straight towards the car, with his gun still raised to deliver the next deadly shot at Nikki. *So much for my plan of killing them all together.*

He glanced back to the waitress to confirm she was dropping to the ground when he saw she was still standing, frozen in fear, gripping the top of the door with both hands. He stopped, somewhat puzzled and gazed down at the gun in his right hand. He brought it back up again and fired at her chest again. The glass fractured again as the scene was repeated.

"Get in here now," yelled Nikki.

Bill watched her cat-like reflexes reach for the back of the waitress' shorts and pull her into the car. Bill ran toward the car door just as Nikki stretched over the waitress and pulled the door shut. *I should have gone for a head shot.* In frustration, he fired three rounds at the front windshield and Nikki. Nikki didn't even flinch.

"Damn it, bullet-proof glass," said Bill. *Rick Bryant and his friggin' technology.*

Nikki put the car into gear, and peeled away through the parking lot and out through the rear exit. A quick left and she disappeared down the street – toward the Bryant's home fortress.

Bill stood there with his gun down by his side. *How the hell did they make me? I took all the precautions.* He shook his head as if he was dispelling the thought. *Think Bill. How do we get out of here? You've gotten out of plenty of predicaments in the past...time to do it again.*

He realized he could not go back to his car parked in front of the restaurant, so he did a quick survey of the parking lot. As he glanced to the left, a luxury SUV entered the lot. It pulled into a spot just a few feet from where Bill was standing. As the woman slid out of her seat with her purse in hand, Bill rounded the side of the car. He stealthily slipped behind the woman and placed his hand firmly over her mouth while putting the barrel of his gun to her back.

The lady was startled and tried to scream, but couldn't overcome Bill's hand. He warned her that if she shut up and stepped away, she wouldn't be harmed. But if she screamed, he'd kill her. Fear instantly consumed the woman and she couldn't oblige. So Bill pulled the trigger and felt the lady quickly go limp. He caught her lifeless body in his arms and heard her purse land at his feet. He laid her aside and picked up the purse. He jumped inside the SUV and started to search for the keys in the deep recesses of purse. Then he noticed the pushbutton start, and seconds later he was pulling out of the parking spot.

Since the lady he had just killed had pulled into the parking lot, it meant the police had not had a chance to block all entrances and exits. He still had a chance to get off the island.

Sirens started blaring as he shot blindly across incoming dual lanes of traffic on John Ringling Boulevard. Narrowly missing cars in both lanes, Bill maneuvered the car toward the bridge to the mainland at a high rate of speed.

As he expected, flashing lights and sirens appeared in the distance in his rearview mirror as he approached a tall bridge in front of him. The bad thing about trying to escape an island is that the police can call up reinforcements to block the other side of every bridge and you're trapped. His only chance was to get to the other side and plow through the roadblock before it became impenetrable.

Another check of his rearview mirror and Bill saw his maniacal driving was putting distance between himself and the flashing lights. He smiled for a moment before he saw an orange SUV swerve around a slow car with a "Q-Tip" driver. It was gaining on him. It had a low-profile, white dome on its roof, and some sort of camera on top of that. Its emergency flashers were on, but it didn't have police lights or sirens. The vehicle looked familiar. Then he remembered the strange orange SUV driving at night. *It was Rick Bryant.*

Bill strained to see the driver as it approached at amazing speed, but couldn't. No time to worry about it. He had to focus on the cars ahead.

As he neared the bridge he kept thinking of the number of police that must be building up on the mainland side of the bridge. The sheriff cars from behind him would wait until he was on the bridge and then blockade the island side of the bridge as well. He envisioned himself going back and forth between the police on each end of the bridge as they squeezed inward. Like a runner trapped between home and third base. The catcher and third baseman slowly closing in and eventually making the tag. The runner has to wait for a mistake, because he can't run around them.

Then it dawned on him – a run-around. One more glance in the mirror and..., *Orange!* Bryant's SUV was right on his rear bumper. He swerved in surprise, but kept his car under control. He tightened his grip on the steering wheel and yanked it hard to the left at the last possible moment. The vehicle felt as though it was going to flip and may have even tipped onto two tires. Just as he managed to get the SUV back under control, he had to jerk the wheel again to miss the oncoming car. *Boy, this is going to be fun.*

He sped up as he entered the bridge in the wrong direction. Cars were breaking ahead of him as they tried to figure out what to do. Some moved to one side of their lane or the other. *Thank goodness for a bike lane on the bridge.* But the oncoming cars could only move so far since they were on a bridge. He felt as though he was in a video game, but in this case his real life was on the line. And he had only one of those.

He kept his speed as fast as he could and still maneuver. He barely missed a passenger van and took a chance with a quick glance in his side mirror to see if the van was going to stay on the bridge. It slid to a stop as it crumpled the driver's door of a sedan. Then a flash of orange burst around the van and the Bryant SUV quickly moved up again on his bumper. *Bryant! How is he keeping up with me? He can't be that good of a driver.*

As he crested the bridge he saw cars were backing up on the outbound lane. The police roadblock was undoubtedly interrupting the flow of traffic. Since the road curved to the right at the end of the bridge, there was no way to know exactly what the police were planning. And of course, they had no idea he was coming down the wrong side of the bridge. His rearview mirror confirmed the orange SUV was inches behind him and a bridge littered with accidents. This element of surprise would not last much longer. Emergency calls from motorists would alert the police soon.

Just before Bill rounded the corner past the end of the bridge, the traffic coming toward him thinned to nothing. *They know I'm here.* With the intersection of Route 41 looming ahead, he could see the police moving their roadblock directly in front of him. Several officers were already standing behind their cars with weapons drawn. He hit the brake pedal with both feet and braced for the impact with the orange SUV. Amazingly, the orange SUV stopped short of his bumper. *Rick Bryant's reflexes are impressive*, he thought.

He heard a click on the speakers of the car and then the OnStar phone began to ring. He pressed the blue phone icon on the steering wheel and recognized the voice immediately.

"Bill, you don't have a chance. Stop this nonsense and turn yourself over. Innocent people could die, and you too. There is no way to escape." It was Rick Bryant.

*How did he know my name? There's no way they could have found out my name that quickly. I must have been made days ago.* Bill cursed at himself for being so sloppy.

"You're quite the driver, Rick. I'll give you that. But you're too cocky. Eat my dust!" replied Bill. He hung up the phone and gripped the steering wheel with both hands.

Bill had noticed a sidewalk running along the street. His SUV lurched over the curb onto the sidewalk and then into the rough grass beside it. *Bill's short-cut to US-41 North*, he thought. He heard the popping sound of gunfire from the police and the thud's of bullets along the SUV's side doors. Windows of the new, but still vacant building beside him shattered.

"Good ole American know-how," said Bill. He knew officer's standard issue side arms were no match for the heavy-gauge metal of the mega-SUV at that distance. The rear window on the passenger side shattered, but it didn't slow him down. *They'll stop shooting any second,* he thought. *There's no way they are going to endanger nearby pedestrians.*

Looking to his right side mirror verified what he guessed was happening -- the officers were scrambling to get into their cars. A streak of orange in his peripheral caused him to glance over his right shoulder to see the orange SUV was still directly behind him. *I can't believe they fired with Bryant so close behind. They could have taken him out.*

No matter what time of day or day of the week, there were always vehicles on this section of 41. His years of training told him to keep his eyes on the road, but he couldn't help watching the maneuvers of the orange SUV. It seemed like it was always anticipating both him and the traffic. It was almost like it knew what was going to happen before it did.

He approached a red light at the University Parkway intersection, and cars were stopped in both lanes in front of him. Traffic from the airport moved into the intersection from the right. If he stopped, he would be trapped for sure. The feeling of panic was rare for Bill, but for the first time in a long time he started to struggle with it.

Suddenly, he saw the tree-lined median to his left open up to a turning lane to a street to the west. Without hesitation, Bill whipped his SUV into the turning lane. Bill scanned the oncoming traffic from the north and could see the wide eyes of the drivers as their arms stiffened for impact. By accelerating he managed to make it almost through both lanes before a small VW bug plowed into his passenger rear panel. It forced his SUV to jerk to the north somewhat, but didn't slow him significantly. He could see the street he was entering diverted back to the south, which was not the direction to go. So he jumped the curb to his right onto the sidewalk and headed north.

The Ringling Museum off University Parkway has a large center lawn between the east-west entrance and exit roadways. Mature royal palms line the roadways, and three flag poles stand erect in the center lawn. A hundred yards beyond the flags, the lawn is interrupted by a large circular drive connecting the roadways. To the north and south of the circle are the entries to parking areas. A winged female statue rests on the top of a single Roman column in the center of the circle. The entrance and exit roads join into a U-shape just before the art museum front gate. Roads also branched to the north and south of the U.

The sidewalk Bill was driving on ended at the Ringling exit roadway. His car leapt over the curb and weaved behind cars parked in the three exit lanes. He jumped the curb of the inner lawn, which jolted the car and jarred him. He barely missed the three flag poles as the SUV fishtailed in grass that was wet from sprinklers. His vehicle sailed off the second curb into the wide entrance lane.

He punched the gas pedal hard as he moved passed the circular drive. Sunlight flashing off his windshield made him squint and twist his head slightly to the left. He noticed the orange SUV driving the wrong way down the exit lane that paralleled his. And it was moving faster down the roadway than he was. *I can't believe it. He's going to beat me to the U!*

Bill saw the road off to the right as he approached the U, and grasping the steering wheel tightly, he jerked it hard to the right. The shrill cry of the tires echoed as the orange SUV as it came around the U-drive and pulled alongside of him. It swerved into his side door trying to force him off the road.

"Go to hell, Rick Bryant!" screamed Bill as he struggled to stay on the road. He stared briefly into the tinted windows of the orange SUV and saw only his reflection. Its front fender was crumpled from the impact, and had two bullet holes.

*They had shot at Bryant too? The man had balls,* thought Bill.

Suddenly the orange SUV slowed and pulled in behind him -- just in time to miss a passenger van passing in the opposite direction. Up ahead Bill saw people getting ready to cross. He blasted his horn and watched as a protective mom stretched her arms in both directions to block her family from stepping out. As he drove by them he realized it wasn't a mom protecting her kids, it was Danielle. *That's right, she works here.* He expected Rick to stop and check on her, but he didn't. Rick stayed right behind him.

He couldn't continue driving so slowly through this tourist haven without the risk of the police catching up to him. When checking his speed, he noticed the large LED display in the center of his dash. He pushed the "Map" button and then "Agree" for the legal warning posted on the display. The colorful moving map filled the screen and showed he was on Bayshore Drive. He was relieved to see that the road intersected Route 41 again in a quarter of a mile.

This realization gave Bill new hope. *The only way to lose Bryant is to get him to make a mistake and crash. Get rid of Bryant and I can pull down some side road, car-jack another set of wheels. Then take care of Danielle and the kids, and get the hell out of here.*

A mile and a half and several minor accidents later, the orange SUV was still trailing Bill's rear bumper by a couple of car lengths. He passed the end of the airport property and saw stoplights and side streets coming ahead.

Bill arms and shoulders tensed as he managed to get through two green and then one red light. The stress of the chase was getting to him and he felt a bead of sweat run down his temple. Once he could breathe again after the red light at Pearl Avenue, he glanced back expecting to see nothing but orange. But instead he saw the orange SUV slowing and making a wide weaving pattern. *He's stopping traffic behind him! This could mean only one thing.*

Bill looked ahead and confirmed his suspicions. There was no southbound traffic or traffic entering 41 from the side roads. *They are closing in.* He glanced at the digital map and saw the road curved ahead at the intersection of 69th Avenue. *They'll be waiting for me there.*

Then he noticed the deep blues of the marina on the map. The marina had a long dock that paralleled the shoreline and Route 41. A sidewalk wrapped around the edge of the shore and curved around to the dock's entrance. The map showed a hotel sat in front of the docks.

The hotel was coming up on his left. With no worry of being hit by another car, he veered his SUV into the first entrance to the hotel parking lot beyond Montgomery Avenue on his right. He hastily checked the map and found the entrance to the boat dock was at the back of the hotel just south of his position.

He whipped the car back southbound and around the hotel. He pulled up to the sandy parking lot at the backside of the hotel, jumped out of the car, and sprinted towards the dock. The dock ran mostly north-south, and parking lots were to the south where he had just arrived and to the east. Umbrella tables from an outdoor bar were to his immediate right, and beyond that was a pool. Colorful wooden stools were lined up along the left, near the water. No one was sitting at the tables, chairs, or by the pool. *Probably too hot or too early to be out.* The boats were his only option, but he wouldn't be able to start a boat without the keys. And he didn't see a soul hanging around.

Tires sliding in the sand parking lot behind him meant the police had arrived. His only hope was that someone was on a boat, or had left their keys in one of the boats. He grabbed the top of the locked, chest-high gate to the docks, jumped and swung his legs over. He landed with a grunt, and then bolted down the dock looking to his right and left at signs of either an electric start or pull-start motor. But all the boats were hi-end, expensive ones. They had inboards or several outboards – all requiring keys to start.

As he neared the end of the dock, he glanced back and saw deputy sheriffs taking positions at the dock gate with their guns drawn. Up ahead he saw a man enter a building at the end of the dock. *Maybe he had keys to one of the boats.*

As he got closer to the building, he realized it wasn't a building. It had a sign calling it a floating chapel. Then it dawned on him and he came to a halt. The man might just be a church caretaker. He spun 360 at the last boats on the dock and found they too were all locked.

Sheriff cars pulled up to the east parking lot on the shore adjacent to the floating church, and were followed by the orange SUV. *Rick Bryant, I will enjoy killing you.* As the deputies exited their cars, he knelt and fired two rounds off at the orange SUV. One hit a front light and broke it. The other just ricocheted off the windshield. He cursed, but then heard a shot fired from a deputy at the entrance. They yelled for him to drop his weapon. He looked back at the orange SUV and caught movement of something rising from its roof. He didn't stay and watch.

Bill jumped up and sprinted to the entrance of the chapel. Although he had read and comprehended the sign that this was a chapel, he was taken aback at the appearance inside. The chapel had a carpeted floor with wooden pews lining both sides. Three stained glass windows lined each side and a large one framed the pulpit at the end of the wide center aisle. The bottoms of all the windows were clear and made of thick glass. Undoubtedly hurricane proof. The ceiling was vaulted and was edged with ornate trim over thirty feet above his head. A man stood in front of one of the windows with a bottle of cleaner and a cloth in his hand.

"Get away from that window," shouted Bill with his weapon aimed at the man.

"I'm sorry, Mister. I'm just the chapel janitor," said the man with his hands raised. The cleaner and cloth remained in the man's shaking hands.

"Get down on the floor and don't move or you'll meet your maker," screamed Bill. The man immediately complied.

"I've got a hostage, so at least I have some leverage," said Bill aloud to himself. It was then that he noticed the distant sound of the rotor blades of a distant helicopter. He crouched low and moved to the first window to his left -- closest to the direction of the sound. He peeked quickly around the window and saw a chopper moving into position.

He heard more commotion in the east parking lot. Glancing to the front entrance of the chapel he noticed there were no windows. A large arched door sat in the center of the wall. The door was solid oak. He peeked out of the windows on the north wall of the chapel, which was opposite of the docks, and noticed there was nothing but water. He checked a south side window again and saw the sheriff deputies drawing closer on the dock. Even when he took the chance and placed his face low and directly against the glass pane of the window, he still could not see the east parking area to the front entrance of the chapel. He didn't like being blind in that direction. Bryant was there as well as other deputies. There was no way to know what they were doing. They would likely enter through the front entrance, but the dock he had come down was the only approach to the chapel.

Bill moved to the front door of the chapel, staying as low as possible. He locked the deadbolt. As he returned to the first window on the south wall, he noticed a church bulletin in the last pew. He grabbed it and started reading it for useful information.

"I'll be damned. This has outboard motors and can go out into the bay," he said in a low voice. He moved quickly to the front to the man still sitting on the floor. The man's eyes were averted to the ceiling, and his hands clasped in prayer.

When the man saw Bill moving toward him, he stopped praying and said "Please, Mister. I have a family. I, I..."

"Shut up and you'll live to see them," said Bill in a shouting whisper. "From now on, whisper. They could be listening. Understand?" The man trembling, nodded his head slowly.

"How do you pilot this thing? How does it start up?"

The man pointed to a narrow side door to the right of the pulpit. "The captain goes to the helm through that door to start up the engines," said the man in a low voice.

"Shit," said Bill out loud. Whispering, he asked "Is it a key start?"

"Yes, Sir. And the captain has the key."

Bill shook his head, realizing he had no out. "Stay here and don't move."

He started toward the front window of the south-facing wall, which had the best view of the dock. About half way there, he heard an extremely loud voice. It was crystal clear, but at an ear-piercing level. It caused him to stop and drop to one knee with his hands over his ears.

"William Hawthorne.... We know you are there and we have the place surrounded. There's no way out. Come out with your hands up."

*That can't be a megaphone*, thought Bill. *It's got to be one of Bryant's blamed gadgets.* He moved to the front window and saw that the sheriff deputies were blocking the end of the dock and had taken up closer positions in the boats. He saw one of them talk into their shoulder mike. They all had ear protection on, like the ones he used when target practicing.

At that moment a deafening, pulsating sound came from the front of the chapel. The glass in the closest windows shattered, including the one he sat under. Glass shards rained down on him. He sat with his eyes closed and his fingers in his ears. The sound kept going for a few seconds, but it seemed like an eternity.

When the sound stopped, he opened his eyes and took his fingers out of his ears. His ears were still ringing, but he could still hear the hushed sound of a door close. Bill jumped up and ran to the back, side door. The man was gone. *They tricked me!* He had locked the front door, but forgot to lock this one. He crack-opened the door and immediately he felt the heavy door shutter as gunfire hit it. He pushed the door closed and got down low again.

For the first time in his life, Bill felt defeated.  He got up and began to move toward the front again, but had to stop.  He felt exceedingly nauseous all of a sudden.  He tried to get up when the loud, pulsing sound started again.  Bill felt himself get dizzy and dropped down to his knees and his hands.  He started vomiting violently.  He tried to protect his ears, but he couldn't hold himself up while he continued to empty his stomach.  When he had nothing left to throw up, he curled in a fetal position with his hands over his ears and dry heaving.

The sound stopped, but he couldn't move. He was dizzy and dehydrated.  The ringing in his ears muffled all outside sounds.  A burst of light came from the front of the chapel. They were in.

Minutes later, Bill was escorted out the front door of the chapel with his hands cuffed behind him.  His equilibrium was still off, and the deputies on each side of him kept him from falling as he walked.  When he stepped off the chapel's deck, he looked to the east parking lot that he had been blind to while in the chapel.  The orange SUV was still parked there with its motor running.  On the top of it was a raised two foot wide gray circular object.  He strained to see inside, but because of the sun glint, he still couldn't see the driver.

Parked next to the orange SUV was the BMW X5 that he had fired on earlier.  It had a black octagon-shaped disk on a pedestal protruding from its roof.  There in the front seat of the BMW was Rick Bryant. *What the hell?  Who was driving the orange SUV?*  He watched Rick check for traffic over his shoulder, reverse, and drive off to the south.

As Bill exited the docks he felt his balance return, but the deputies remained at his side. There in the dusty parking lot at the south end of the docks sat a deputy's car with the back door open. Before he made it to the door, he saw Rick Bryant pull up in the BMW. The orange SUV followed behind him. The roof sensors now apparently lowered inside. The BMW barely stopped when Rick leapt out, bullet-proof vest visible over his shirt. He was clearly upset.

"You bastard!" Rick's eyes were aflame with anger and his fists clinched. "You shot at my daughter and the waitress, and killed that woman in cold blood back on St Armands. Your reckless driving endangered the lives of countless more! Tell me…who hired you?  Why were you watching me and my family?  Were you hired to kill me…to kill us?" He continued to yell, but his voice was drowned out by the helicopter that was now hovering low over the docks.

Beyond Rick, Bill saw one of the deputies open the driver door to the orange SUV. There was no one in the driver's seat.  He could barely make out computer screens reflecting in the window of the passenger door. He should have known the car was one of Rick's "toys." *Only a computer behind the wheel could have been "thinking" and reacting that fast.*

He turned his attention back to Rick.  He watched Rick's lips ask a deputy to get their chopper to back away.  The deputy looked up and then mouthed, "It's not our chopper."

A bright dot drifted across Rick's chest.  Rick's eyes got bigger with the recognition of the dot.  And then time stopped.

Bill flashed back to his daughter and wife in the park again.  His daughter was asking him to push her higher on the swing.  He watched her giggling and throw her head back as she pushed the swing higher in the air.  It was always followed by the arms stretched wide. "Catch me Daddy," she squealed.

Rick was moving in slow motion toward him with his arms stretched as if to grab him. Their eyes locked and he could only think of one thing to say before he would be off to see his daughter and wife.

Bill spoke two syllables and then the lights went out.

# Chapter 2: *The Promise*

Rick sat on one of the tables of the outdoor bar that overlooked the small marina. There were people milling around the hotel pool and at the bar behind him, likely attracted by the earlier gunfire and heavy police presence. He was still wiping the blood and bits of frontal matter from his shirt and face as Sheriff Mike Steele walked up to him.

"Hello Mike," said Rick. "Heck of a mess, eh?"

"Hi Rick," replied Sheriff Steele. "Yes it is a mess. How are you?"

"Yes I'm fine, but did you get some officers over to Danielle and the kids?"

"That was the first thing we did when the chase was over. They're all fine and back at the house now, but you're going to have to call them soon. They are not about to stay put if they think you are still in danger."

"Thanks Mike, I'll call them shortly. I just don't want them to see me with blood all over. What about Kelsey, the waitress?"

"Nikki took her back to her apartment. Her twin sister, what's her name, yeah Kristin, is with her. Kelsey is apparently still shaken, but who wouldn't be after being shot at twice. Two deputies are parked outside their building just in case there is any retribution by Bill's associates."

The zip of the coroner's body bag drew their attention. They watched as the body was loaded into the ambulance.

"It's a good thing we knew at least a little about him and what he looked like before he was killed. There's nothing left of his face or head for that matter," said Sheriff Steele.

"You weren't there to see it. Have you ever seen a person's head explode?"

"Sorry Rick. I've seen plenty of deaths, but no, I haven't seen a head vaporize." He paused. "Did he say why he was watching your family for the last few weeks?"

"No. He started to speak just before he was shot, but all he said was what sounded like 'auda' or 'arda.'" Rick spelled it out A-U-D-A and A-R-D-A to the sheriff.

"Auda or arda? Do you have any idea what that means?" asked Sheriff Steele.

"No, I haven't a clue. I was recording everything on high definition audio and video from the vehicle. I'm going to send the audio file back to my office so they can study it. Maybe my engineers can get something out of it using our digital signal processing software."

"Speaking of the vehicles, those performed amazingly well. I knew you had a lot of faith in those scientists from the University of Parma in Italy, but seeing is believing. That orange SUV of yours couldn't be shaken, and the man in the body bag tried awfully hard." Mike casually pointed to the body bag being carried off by the coroner.

"We left nothing to chance, Mike. We've been testing the orange Land Rover for weeks here in the states and for months before in Italy. Remember what I told you? The University of Parma had driven a caravan of vehicles from Italy to China without a driver. It was a well televised event. On my first visit there four years ago, they drove me all over Parma without a driver. I was hooked and gave them a contract to work on a vehicle and vessel for me. After years of work, the Land Rover was the first to be finished. Granted, a high speed chase on the busy streets of Sarasota is difficult enough. But to tell it to follow that car off-road at 75 miles per hour without crashing or hitting someone is a bit more than what even I expected.

And the acoustic and microwave sensors on the Land Rover and the BMW also worked well, I thought. Stopping someone from a distance without lethal force is just as tough an autonomous vehicle. Fortunately, that kind of science is what our engineers at Marine Science Systems do."

"Good job and thanks for helping to get this guy. I've got to get back to the office and start processing his paperwork. The guy had no record on file, but he had to have been either a professional hit man or a mercenary of some sort. I don't think he ever realized until maybe the end that you had detected his surveillance of you from the start. He took every precaution – he used burner phones only once and destroyed them. They weren't cheap burner phones – all smart phones. Probably kept a cloud account somewhere to store his notes and pictures. He wiped down all glassware and eating utensils he touched. His hotel room was spotless and paid for in cash. He wore driving gloves whenever he drove his car. Only now that he's dead will I finally get his fingerprints into the system."

"Well it wasn't actually me that detected him," said Rick. "It was the behavioral surveillance software I use. It reviews the cameras, motion sensors, and communication feeds and learns what is normal and what is not. Fortunately, his surveillance of us was spotted and determined to be abnormal. It took me an hour looking at all the information just to verify there was a real threat. Given the sophistication of that system, his reconnaissance skills were exceptionally good to have taken as long as it did to notice him. And I appreciate that you and your men took the threat seriously."

"I'm glad we got him in time, but now we've got another problem. Where is his shooter? And why did they kill our man? We tracked the helicopter tail number and found it was a rental out of Tampa. We put out an APB and our dispatcher notified all airports in a hundred mile radius. It's not likely they will return to Tampa. Honestly, they could be anywhere by now."

"I hope we find them. I'm still worried about my family, Mike."

"We will be there to watch out for them. You have my word on that," said Sheriff Steele. After a few seconds of silence. "You know Rick, given the distance and the damage done to Bill Hawthorne, you are extremely fortunate the bullet didn't find you."

"Yeah, strange isn't it? If I was a target, how come they didn't shoot me too? Good thing I had on my Kevlar vest," said Rick.

"It would not have done you much good. You would need a military vest with the ceramic or metal inserts to help you with that bullet. And even that might not have done much. Remember where the bullet hit Mr. Hawthorne?"

"Good point. We'll I'm going to call the girls. Do me a favor and keep me informed. We're getting ready to head out of town for a new case in Hawai'i, so you can reach me on my mobile number if you find out anything."

"Right. Good luck on that case. They are lucky to have you. I've already talked with the Chief of Police there. Even though he said he'd known you for a long time, I still gave you a stellar reference. Take care and I'll keep in touch."

"Thanks Mike. And I'll let you know if my engineers find anything out on those audio files. You should find your copy of the audio and video files in your inbox when you get back to the office. See ya."

With that, the two parted. Sheriff Steele watched Rick walk back to the BMW and start it up. Immediately the orange Land Rover started up and followed the BMW away. The two vehicles were for sure going to get some attention going down the road – one with no driver and both with bullet holes.

After a few minutes of instructions to his deputies, Mike walked back to his car, started it up, and headed back to the office. He thought of Rick and the Bryant family as he drove. The man was as honest as they come, and loved his family to a fault. As would most law men, he had no doubt that Rick would do anything to protect them. He certainly didn't mind spending what he thought was required to keep them safe.

The sheriff drove by the entrance to Ringling Museum as he continued on Route 41 South. It was only a month ago that the family had solved a murder, brought down a giant drug cartel, and found a buried treasure. Mike remembered it vividly. The family was lucky to have gotten through it relatively unscathed. Rick's shrewdness, his technology, and the amazing skillset of the three women in Rick's life gave them a superior edge over the ill-fated attempts on their lives.

Although Rick and he were pretty well acquainted before that event, Mike knew that case strengthened their friendship. Rick was easy to talk to and he had many of the same passions as Mike – pretty much anything to do with the water. Although Rick was beyond wealthy, you couldn't tell it to talk with him. Probably because he didn't grow up with money. Rick was green when it came to law enforcement, but he was coming along nicely. Being outside the system, he thought outside the box. It was refreshing.

Mike and the Sarasota community had certainly gained a lot by having the Bryant Family around. Rick's sensor buoys now populated the coastal waterways. Besides being key in the drug cartel case, the buoys had detected and helped catch a few thieves, and detected a couple stranded boaters in the last few weeks. Plus the three boats that Rick had just donated were fabulous. There wasn't a deputy in the force that hadn't already tried them out. Just like Rick's own boat, the **Spearfish**, the self-sealing skin that made the boats difficult to sink, a bulletproof steering console, and a directional, ultra-loud hailing system like the one on the Land Rover would keep his people safe. Rick said he'd let them use his original boat too if it was ever needed, except during the next few weeks. Apparently he was planning to take his to Hawai'i.

He was going to miss the Bryant family. They were getting ready to head out to Hawai'i to help out the Honolulu Chief of Police on a high-profile case. Rick had been getting ready for it for weeks. Rick had apparently got his degree, at least one of them anyway, from the University of Hawai'i. The police chief, who had been a friend of Rick's during his school years, had a weird murder case. Not just "a" case, there were apparently a number of murders. The police chief had read how the Bryants had solved the case the local papers had called "*Death and Gold in Zara Zote*" and thought they could help him.

Mike was sure the Bryants would be able to help. He just hoped they survived. As he came to the intersection of John Ringling Boulevard, Mike looked toward the big arching bridge. Rick was probably already over the bridge and pulling into his driveway. He smiled. Mike could picture Rick's girls running to hug him.

***

Rick arrived home in time to see construction workers leaving. Danielle had probably sent them home early today. The house was damaged heavily on the last case, so Rick had decided it was time for some major renovation and home improvements.

He punched in a command on his car's console to tell the Land Rover to park in the driveway. The garage door opened and the headlights on his BMW automatically switched on as he entered. Without delay the kitchen door flung open. Danielle, Nikki, and Shelli came bounding out.

Rick was barely out of the car before Shelli, the younger daughter, was rounding the front bumper. When the car door closed, she went wide-eyed and her face contorted downward. An "ewwww" left her lips in typical teenage fashion.

Like train cars, Nikki and Danielle collided with Shelli. Nikki followed with an "oh my gosh," and Danielle just covered her mouth and shook her head.

*They look like proverbial deer in the headlights...literally*, thought Rick. *I must look pretty bad. Probably didn't get enough of the blood off me.* "I'm fine," he said aloud. "This is the other guy's, and it's all dried now" continued Rick pointing to the blood smears on his shirt and bullet-proof vest.

The gag reflex kicked in for Shelli. Danielle pushed the girls out of the way and reached her arms around Rick and kissed him hard on the lips.

Surprised, Rick started to say how he should get shot at more often, but Danielle put her finger over his lips to muffle him, "Rick Bryant. You had worried us to death. Not another word from you. You look like a mess. Get to our bathroom, take these clothes off, throw them in the trash, and take a long shower."

Knowing that she meant business, he mimed a zippered mouth and walked around the door to the kitchen. As he passed Shelli and Nikki, they simultaneously stepped back and put their hands up to avoid any contact with him. He paused in front of Nikki and handed her the keys to the Land Rover. He stared at her for a moment, then glanced back at the orange vehicle visible through the still opened garage door. Rick then turned and went into the kitchen. They weren't telepathic; Nikki knew without a word being said what she was to do. Get the Land Rover out of the driveway and back to the office before neighbors complained about the bullet-ridden vehicle.

About an hour later, Rick entered the kitchen with his almost-dry hair combed back. He had donned one of several short-sleeved fishing shirts he owned and a pair of khaki cargo shorts. Danielle and Shelli were sitting at the kitchen island and were texting away on their iPhones when Rick entered. Shelli also had earbuds in – probably listening to Pandora or her iTunes. The smell of fresh coffee caught his attention.

Danielle was about to say something when the door opened to the garage and Nikki walked in. She was back from dropping the vehicle off at the office.

"Thanks, Nikki," said Rick. "Any troubles with it?"

"Nope," answered Nikki. "I got a few strange looks when people noticed the bullet holes, but I made it back to the office fine. It was pulling to the left a little though."

"It jumped a few curbs during the chase, so we're going to have to check the front-end alignment and probably the chassis too," said Rick. "How did you get home?"

"My Audi was ready, so one of the guys at work gave me a ride to pick it up. Oh, and the Audi head mechanic came out and talked to me. He said that if you added any more gadgets to it they weren't going to work on it. He said the other mechanics are afraid to touch it, so he had to do the inspection himself."

"They tell us that every time we bring a car there," said Rick. "But I'm-"

"Excuse, me but we're not going to talk about cars right now," interrupted Danielle. "You almost got yourself killed. And for some reason the person that has been watching your family for three weeks, who could have been a hit man or burglar or who-knows-what, had his head blown off within feet from you. I don't know how his head was blown off, and I'm not even sure I want to know.

Rick interjected, "It was from a –"

"Don't interrupt Rick," said Danielle sternly. Nikki and Shelli traded looks with each other and started to get up from their stools. "Stay right there girls. You need to hear this too."

She turned back to Rick. "The point I'm trying to make is that you can't take chances with your life. Your family loves and needs you. And you have to remember that when you're in danger, you can also put your family in danger. I'm not concerned about me, but what would you do if your girls were hurt?"

Rick remained quiet for a short while. He knew Danielle was right and this was the first time he had seen her truly upset in a while. There had been enough time for her to think back at the danger in their last, and first for that matter, case.

"Danielle, you know that I couldn't stand it if anything happened to you or the girls. And it is because I love them that I have been preparing them...training them for future cases. I thought we agreed this is what we wanted to do. Help people. Help our community. Helping to get these criminals off the streets. There's going to be some danger that will come, and I'm trying to use what I know to limit it. Science and technology are my strengths. I promise you that I will take care of you, Nikki, and Shelli. I will not let anything happen to you. It was my technology that spotted that man, Bill. It was my technology that protected Nikki and Kelsey when Bill started shooting at them. It was my technology that chased Bill through the streets of Sarasota instead of endangering myself or other officers. It was my technology that drew Bill out of the church without endangering the lives of any officer. But the helicopter and sniper were not expected. And I can't anticipate everything. But I try." Rick paused. He sensed that perhaps Danielle's decision to allow the kids to go to the Hawai'i was waning.

"We didn't even know that our first case was even a case. We had a friend that was killed and we wanted to help. My company's technology and our combined skills found the murderer and much more. But we were also lucky. I don't like to rely on luck. That's why I've been working so hard to make sure we're safe in Hawai'i. Some people have died in Hawai'i. Are we going to let their deaths be in vain? Are we going to let their murderers go free? I don't want that, and I promised Kaleho we would help. I need the girls and you to help me on this case. I don't want to do it on my own, and I am positive I can't finish it without all of you there with me. "

Danielle sat down on one of the kitchen stools. She shook her head while staring down at the coffee mug in front of her. She seemed conflicted. Rick knew he was getting to her, but she was still struggling with it. Rick decided to try one last angle.

"Danielle, I know you are having heartburn about this. How about this? How about we try this case with Kaleho? If after this case is over you still feel strongly about our ... early retirement from law enforcement, then I'll stop completely. I won't stop trying to protect us, but I'll will not accept any more cases."

Danielle looked up immediately. "Are you serious? Will you promise me that if we make that decision, you'll stick with it?"

"I promise," replied Rick.

There was long pause with no one speaking.

"Well I guess I am willing to do this if we're all careful," said Danielle.

There was a collected sigh of relief from Rick and the girls. Shelli and Nikki looked at each other and smiled. Shelli was about to high-five her sister when Danielle continued.

"Girls, I know you have been enjoying this wild ride your father has created. I do not like being the bad guy, and you know this. But I want you to know that I am especially wary of this whole investigation business. I know you are smart and quite capable of watching out for yourselves, but that does not stop me from worrying. I need to know you are going to be careful. Do not go off on your own. Do not take unnecessary risks."

Even though Shelli and Nikki were excited about Hawai'i, they knew they were supposed to be seriously listening to their mother. They had learned at an early age that when their mother stopped using contractions, like don't or shouldn't, she was dead serious.

The speech concluded with, "...and furthermore, your adherence to the rules will determine whether we stick with this... this crime-stopping business. I am relying on you to do the right thing. Be safe!"

"Deal," said Nikki holding out her hand. Danielle shook her hand.

Shelli stepped up and held out her hand, and then faked out of the handshake. But then she jumped off her stool and hugged her mom. "I love you Mom, and I promise to be careful."

"Well I've had quite the day and I didn't get to eat lunch," said Rick. "What say we hop in the car and head to The Creek for a fish dinner?"

"Yes!" responded Shelli with a touchdown motion. "I was thinking the same thing."

An hour later the food was arriving at their table at the seafood restaurant on Philippi Creek off US Route 41. The four of them sat cozily at the picnic tables on the outdoor deck, which overlooked the waterway. Palms blew gently in the light breeze. All three girls got the grilled Grouper Caesar salad. Knowing it was not the healthiest thing to get and ignoring the groan of his wife, Rick still splurged for the blackened grouper sandwich, fries, and a Coke.

"Let's start planning our trip for Hawai'i," said Rick after the food was ordered.

"That's all you've been doing for weeks now," said Danielle.

"Yeah, but that was the boat and major equipment shipments we were getting ready for Hawai'i," replied Rick. "That's all gone now. The boat should be well past the Panama Canal and in the Pacific Ocean. It's probably about 4 days away from Hawai'i. What I was referring to was our travel plans. Let me pull up the info on my tablet."

As Rick powered on the tablet and began pulling up information, the girls started chatting about the wardrobes they'd need.

"I need a couple of new swimsuits," said Nikki. "Dad's been keeping me busy and I haven't had the time to do much shopping."

"Don't worry, I'm sure both of you are going to do some shopping once you get there." Danielle was seated next to Rick and across from Nikki. She placed her hand on Nikki as she continued. "Remember all the nice outfits you two bought when we went there years ago? We could go to the shop at the-"

"Shopping?" interrupted Rick. "Remember that we'll be working on a case. I doubt we'll be able to do much shopping until after, or if, the case is solved. If you need some clothes, I'd buy them now."

"Good point, Dad." Shelli was sitting across from Rick. She turned to her sister. "They have some good sales now at the swimwear boutique at St Armands. There were some really cute ones when Stephanie stopped by a couple of days ago. We could go over there after lunch. You too, Mom." Nikki and Danielle nodded in excitement.

"Speaking of Stephanie, she's welcome to come," said Rick. "I know you two have been inseparable for months now. I was going to arrange for two rooms anyway. So there should be plenty of beds."

"Oh, thanks Dad. I had already asked Mom and she said the same thing. But Stephanie can't come. I just found out this morning. Her parents don't mind her hanging out with me, but they didn't want her to come with us if we were working a case. "

"I'm sorry, honey. But I do know exactly how they feel" said Danielle as she turned to give Rick an aloof look. She turned back at Shelli and continued, "Would you like me to speak to them?"

"No need for that," said a voice from behind Danielle. "I just had a discussion with them and convinced them I'd be around to watch out for her. So we're both coming Mr. B."

Nikki sat up straight and smiled. She blushed slightly as she pushed her hair behind one ear. "Hi Ryan. How'd you know we were here?"

"Hi Nikki," he said with a smile. He stood mesmerized at Nikki, with his brilliant white teeth showing in his frozen smile. His dark hair, honey-colored skin, rippling arms, and natural good looks had caught more than one female's attention in the restaurant.

After a few awkward seconds, he continued. "Stephanie told me you were here when I texted her about the talk with Mom and Dad. Oh, and hi Shelli and Mrs. B." He then walked over and shook Rick's hand. "Good to see you, Mr. B."

Nikki pushed her sister over on the picnic bench seat. "Make room for him, Sis." Ryan walked over and sat next to Nikki.

"So she can come then? Really?" said Shelli.

"Yeah. She's kind of excited right now. She told me to tell you to call her after you finished eating."

"Yes!" squealed Shelli. "Forget waiting until I finish eating." She swiped her phone off the table, clicked the screen and put the phone to her ear. She got up and walked off so that she didn't disturb the table – a Bryant family rule.

"So did I hear you say that you're coming too?" asked Nikki.

"Oh yes. It's the only way my parents would let Stephanie come. And there is no way I'm letting you out of my sight for that long." said Ryan. Although she said nothing, it was clear that Nikki was thrilled.

"Well should I book a third room then Nikki?" asked Rick.

Knowing that her father had a hidden message there, she responded, "Yes, Dad." She paused for a moment and continued quickly as if a thought had flashed in her mind. "And make sure it's in the same hotel that we're staying in."

# Chapter 3: *Grab Your Bags*

Rick had his mobile phone to his ear, but he still heard a boat pull up at their home dock. He rotated around in his chair at his desk and pulled the curtains to see Shelli bouncing past the pool and then out onto the dock. Stephanie leapt off the boat as it was still moving, and gave Shelli a hug. After urging from Stephanie's Dad, who was piloting the boat, the girls tied it off. Ryan began transferring luggage from the boat to the dock.

Rick continued talking on the phone as he saw his wife wave hello to Stephanie's dad as she approached the dock. She shook his hand and then paused with her arms crossed as she chatted with him for a couple of minutes. Stephanie then jumped back to the edge of the boat and gave her dad a hug and a kiss on the check. Ryan's arms full of gear, did a head nod and told his father he'd let him know when they arrived in Hawai'i. Moments later Stephanie and Ryan's dad disappeared down the waterway.

"We're going to be heading for the airport soon," Rick said. "I'm really looking forward to seeing you again Kaleho. Take care. Bye." He ended the call and placed his smart phone in his pocket.

"DMT Security System...Arm...15 minutes," said Rick aloud. He watched as the security system he developed years ago now come online on the array of monitors sitting on his desk. "DMT Security System activated. Security system protection engaged in 15 minutes," said a calm, synthesized voice. "And have a good day, Mr. Bryant."

*Siri would be jealous.* Rick then picked up his briefcase and headed out the office door.

He arrived the family room as Shelli, Danielle, Stephanie and Ryan entered the room through the white trimmed glass doors leading to the pool area. Ryan sat down their suitcases on the Italian marble floor and began surveying the room.

"Nikki's loading bags in the company van out front, Ryan." Rick signaled with his finger toward the door to the garage. "If you don't mind, please bring the bags through the garage. Girls, we need to get in the van and head out to the airport. Gather anything else you need quickly – we don't want to be late."

They were on their way to the airport a few minutes later. Rick checked his smart phone to see the home security system engage.

"I didn't hear what airlines we're taking," Shelli said.

"That's because I never mentioned it," answered Rick. "Don't worry, we've got good seats and the flight will be nonstop."

He pulled the spacious company van up to a hangar at the north side of Sarasota Airport. He opened his door and then stuck his head back and said, "Grab your bags."

"What's this?" Danielle asked with a look of confusion.

The group stepped in front of the parked van as Rick placed a call on his phone. "We're here, Pete," was all Rick said.

"What's going on, Dad," asked Nikki. "Why aren't we over at the terminal?"

A deep rumble echoed from the hangar doors. With a slow jerk, the large doors began to open.

"This way," said Rick as he slung his black backpack over his shoulder and grabbed the handle of his bag.   He started walking toward the doors.   The rest of the group timidly followed.

When he reached the threshold of the hangar, Rick announced, "Here we are."

His girls, Stephanie and Ryan all stopped and simultaneously dropped their mouths. In front of them was an all-white private jet with swept-back wings, turned up wing tips, and massive twin jet engines near the large rear vertical stabilizer.   There were eight windows along each side, and the door was open just forward of them with steps extended to the hangar's concrete floor.

"Wow, Dad.  Is this for us?" Shelli asked.

"Yes it is, sweetheart.  We need to be there quickly and I've got too many questionable pieces of hardware with me to go by commercial airplane.  This is the Gulfstream G650.  It can hold up to nineteen passengers, and comfortable sleeps ten.  It's transonic with a max speed is 0.925 Mach, and can easily make it to Honolulu without refueling.   We'll be there less than 8 hours.  It's 2 pm now.  With a six hour time zone difference, that will put us in at Honolulu at about 4pm their time.   We'll be checked-in and in our hotel rooms well before dinner."

"Rick that sounded like a sales pitch.  You didn't-"

"No, Danielle, it's a rental," interrupted Rick.

The family and friends stood shoulder to shoulder before the sleek private jet.  As they started walking to the access stairs up to the plane, Shelli tapped on her phone and a song began to play out loud.

"Like a G6...."

# Chapter 4: *Diamond Head*

Kaleho slid off his board in the shallow surf and picked up his surfboard. He emerged from the water onto the beach at Diamond Head Beach Park with his board under his right arm. He turned and waived to his 15-year-old son, Kai, who had decided to stay for a few more sets. Kai said he'd catch a ride home with a friend.

As he walked through the sand, Kaleho felt the ache in his shoulders from paddling in the surf. He rotated his left arm a few times try to relieve the soreness. He had wanted to stay out longer with his son, but at fifty three he knew he'd regret it tomorrow if he did.

Kaleho walked up to the gnarly, half-dead tree near the path leading off the beach and grabbed his pair of *slippas* hanging in the branches. Others remained like strange ornaments, dancing in the constant trade winds. As he reached the paved path, he threw them down and slid his feet in them. He then walked over to the shower and rinsed off himself and his board.

Slowly he began his ascent up the winding path, gripping the metal handrail that ran the course of the path. As he climbed, he saw the sun setting in the west was haloing the old lighthouse that peered above the low-lying tree line. The brown, dry vegetation on his left was sparse enough for him to see a few doves settling down for the day and the waves still breaking off in the distant surf. The darker coral patches were easily visible in the varying tones of blue and green water. The only sounds were the cooing of the doves, the surf, the muffled sounds of cars on the road above, and the shuffling of his slippas on the path. The paved path was cut into the steep hillside of the park, and the aging high wall of dirt and lava rock to his right was held in place with chicken wire and metal rod. He could remember how much more difficult it was to get down to the beach in his youth. Dirt trails amongst rock outcroppings kept the beach more isolated back then. But given how tired he was now, he'd trade those days of solitude for this much easier walk any day. And the surf itself offered complete solitude once he was on his board anyway.

As Kaleho continued to hike up the path, he heard a rustle to the left of the path in the tall brown grass. Out of the grass popped a mongoose, one of Hawai'i's worst pests.

Years ago he helped his son with a school paper on the mongoose. They had looked it up and found that it was brought into Hawai'i in 1883, and had wreaked havoc on the delicate Hawaiian ecology. Wiping out many native birds due to its love of eggs and its contamination of natural ponds and streams with leptospirosis, the mongoose was one of a long line of ecological mistakes made in the islands. He kicked a pebble from the side of the path in the direction of the mongoose and it scurried into a hole in the dirt wall that was now only waist high.

The path curved to the right toward Diamond Head. The crater wall seemed perpetually brown. Water drained rapidly from the basaltic soil whenever it rained. The constant trade winds caused quick evaporation of any moisture that remained. Plants were nourished only during the rain itself, so the vegetation stayed brown for many months of the year.

A few people were sitting on the wall of lava rock and concrete that lined Diamond Head Road and its sidewalk. Several runners were passing the popular route – no doubt having started at Kapiolani Regional Park. A few more steps brought him to the upper end of the path, where a white message was painted into the path pavement itself. It read, PICKUP

23

AFTER YOURSELF AND YOUR DOGS. It was a shame this had to be posted in the shadows of such a magnificent natural landmark. It was just natural for Hawaiians to care for their land. Unfortunately, not so for many of the millions visiting Hawai'i's shores.

Since he had arrived late to the park, he had to walk farther uphill on the sidewalk to his car. This park was a popular surfing spot with locals, so parking was always an issue. And because he loved his car dearly, he sometimes parked it as far as possible away just to avoid accidental dinks from other surfers' boards. He placed his board in the back seat of his 1972 Chevrolet Chevelle SS convertible and reached in the passenger side for his towel. He dried off and slid into the driver's seat. Minutes later he was heading eastward toward home.

Spending time on his board had achieved its desired effect today. His current case was quite stressful, and was consuming much of his and his officers' time. The District Attorney and the Mayor had paid him a visit a few weeks ago and had demanded that he personally take over the case. Frequent calls and meetings with the ill-tempered DA to report the progress, or lack of progress, were adding to his ever increasing stress level.

As he passed by *Wahoo's* restaurant, he could smell the fresh fish cooking on the grills. His mouth watered and he noticed he was getting hungry. *A nice mahi-mahi sandwich would certainly hit the spot.* The thought of it made his mind drift back to his college days when he introduced Rick Bryant to spearfishing using a Hawaiian sling, and to surfing. Those were the good ole days. He remembered laughing as Rick tried in vain to catch a wave on the board that was too short for a beginner. He should have started in the small surf in Waikiki, but Rick wouldn't think of it. He wanted to start where the local surfers learned and on the boards the locals were using. Rick also thought he could analyze the techniques and solve the "equation" of surfing as he did many of his other undertakings. Kaleho chuckled. *At least he was good at spearfishing.*

Rick had convinced him to buy his Chevelle back when they were in college. It was 7 years old at the time and had been abused, but it still ran well. Rick had hardly a dime to pay for groceries, but he managed to scrape some money to donate to the car in return for getting rides to the beach to surf and fish. Rick would be surprised to see how nice the Chevelle was now. It took Kaleho 3 years of work in his garage, but it was worth it. The bright red finish with the classic dual white strips on the hood was envied by anyone who appreciated a nice car. It was the only extravagance Kaleho afforded himself. His wife sometimes joked that she was going to have to buy a red slinky dress with dual white stripes just to get him to look at her the way he looked at his car. She was, of course, exaggerating. Even more so than the bright red machine he was admiring right now, he couldn't imagine life without Leilani.

He was glad he had contacted Rick about the case. Rick had become even more successful than Kaleho could have ever imagined back when they went to school together. It had been a long while since they had last spoken, but the article he read about Rick and his family solving that case in Florida gave Kaleho reason enough to touch bases with him again. And Rick sounded excited to get started.

As he pulled into his driveway, Kaleho heard his phone ring. Caller ID showed it was the DA again. As he answered the phone, he wondered just how excited the DA was going to be when he finds out that the Bryants were asked to help.

# Chapter 5: *Malasadas and Taxes*

John O'Sullivan pulled up a chair to the desk in the small office with glassless, shuttered windows that sat on the edge of the wharf at the Port of Honolulu. The last glow of light on the western horizon had surrendered to darkness more than two hours earlier. Unlike most of the other harbor masters, he didn't mind the grave yard shift. The nights were cooler, so he could work in comfort most nights. There was hardly ever a ship arriving at night at the isolated port in the middle of Pacific. They usually waited 'til the morning to dock. He was especially looking forward to tonight because it was a quarter moon and even ship captains familiar with the port didn't like to chance running into a junkie or fishing boat at night. So he was practically guaranteed a relaxing night ahead.

John took a sip of his coffee he had just brewed on the coal stove, and opened up the paper wrapping of his malasada that he had bought at the Portuguese bakery. Although John wasn't particular happy about how the Portuguese were taking many of the best jobs since their arrival in the islands a few years ago, he overlooked it once he ate his first Portuguese malasada. The deep-fried, yeasty dough ball coated with the readily available island sugar had become his night-shift addiction. It was all he and his waistline could do just to buy one each night.

He bit down into his sinful delight and then reached for *The Daily Bulletin* to catch up on the news of the day. He checked the date to make sure he was reading today's paper. It read, "Honolulu, HI, Monday Evening, December 1, 1884" under the boldface type of the paper's name. He shook his head as the first thing he saw was another large ad for holiday goods at Sachs' store on Fort Street. It seemed like they were advertising for Christmas earlier every year.

Since the front page articles had been reprinted for days now, he turned to page two. There was an article titled "National Defences" that caught his eye. The newspaper was rebutting a previous article written by a correspondent that called for the creation of a militia and a navy to protect the people, plantations, and businesses from outside threats. As he read the paper, which always seemed to favor the royals' views, he grinded his teeth when he read how the newspaper thought it was a bad idea. The costs for such a force would be staggering and the likelihood of an attack was preposterous. The Kingdom of Hawaii was too far from anyone and had no real value worth an attack by a distant nation. The once powerful nation of hundreds of thousands of Hawaiian natives had been killed off to just a few thousand by western diseases. And the conglomeration of Chinese workers and other nationalities had no political desires or motivations. So the idea was just preposterous, according to the paper. John shook his head for the second time at the paper.

He heard the bell at the clock tower of Kawaiaha'o Church strike nine o'clock. The forty-plus-year-old clock donated by the King that sat prominently on the front of the tall gray steeple was still the most accurate timepiece in the islands. Glancing up the streets in the direction of the tolling bell, John noticed the streets were empty like they always were at this time on a weekday night. The only sign of life came from the grand, two-year-old Iolani palace. Word was that the King was entertaining many of his government cronies and military staff tonight. The only thing he could hear nearby was some Hawaiian fishermen that were laughing as they fished for squirrelfish snapper, or *Ehu* as they called them. Nighttime was about the only time they could catch them in numbers since they stayed well into the dark recesses of coral heads during the day. Their big eyes allowed them to see their prey in low light. He stared in the direction of the sounds to see if he could catch some kind of movement of the fishermen, but it was just too dark. He turned back to the paper and continued to read the article.

As he flipped to the next page of his paper, he lifted his head and did a quick visual survey of the port. A faint glow of distant lights caught his eye offshore near the port entrance.    John picked up his brass eyeglass to investigate the lights. He could make out the tall foremast of the ship, but not the sails. The occasional glint of light off the low bow wake showed it was moving slowly. It had to be a steamer, a combination sail and steam power ship – maybe preparing to anchor offshore until the morning. He put down the eyeglass and checked the port log.    There were only three ships scheduled for arrival today from the other islands, and they were already docked.    He quickly scanned the arrivals section on page three of *The Daily Bulletin* to see if there were ships that were not accounted for on the port schedule. None, it agreed with the port logs. He then checked the departure section to see if one of the departed ships had come about due to some sort of problem. No, the boat was too small to be the passenger ship *Alameda* and was definitely not the steamer *Likelike* nor the schooner *Haleakula* that had departed earlier in the day.

John picked up the glass again and stared at the ship. He now saw three tall masts with sails tightly stowed. *It was definitely a steam whaler,* thought John. *Must be one of those new whalers from Pacific Steam Whaling Company in San Fran, which had explosive-tipped, cannon-fired harpoons.* They were tough ships designed to handle the icy waters of Alaska. The crew would be between 30 to 60 men.

A few minutes passed and the ship dropped anchor and slowly drifted until it was parallel with the shore and with a westerly bearing. It made John wonder if the ship was just anchoring for safe harbor and then head out the next day, instead of coming into port. That was a rare event. If it was just an overnight stop, then there would undoubtedly be a tender coming in for supplies. In either case, the rule of the new collector of customs, Colonel Curtis Iaukea, was that any anchored ship was subject to collection of tax.    So John stepped out of his dockside office waved at one of the longshoremen that was preparing some cargo for loading in the morning to come over.

"Go to the customs house and let them know there's a steam whaler anchored off at the port channel entrance," said John.

"Aye, sir," said the longshoreman. He turned and hurried to the customs house at the next slip.

A few minutes later, he saw the longshoreman heading back. He looked in John's direction and waved in acknowledgement. The lights came up in the Customs' office and four men headed to their small boat. Two of the men had side arms and knives visible at their waist, and the port collector on duty carried a lantern. They stepped into their small boat tied to the docks and soon started paddling toward the mouth of the channel.

John returned to his office and fetched his signal lantern. He signaled the whaler that a boat was approaching to board, which he then repeated three times with a brief pause between each. He got no acknowledgement. Maybe his lantern was too weak to be seen.

He went back to his office and grabbed his eyeglass and extended its long tube. He peered toward the small boat and saw it easily moving on the calm waters toward the dimly lit whaler. He admired the courage of the Customs' staff. No one liked to be taxed and they were always grossly outnumbered when they approached a ship.

He saw a light appear at mid-deck, which was signaling the Customs' boat to move to the port side of the ship. *That's unusual.* It should have permitted the boat to tie to the calm side of the ship, which was on its starboard side in this case. The small boat disappeared from view as it moved from just off the bow of the ship to its port side.

26

More than forty minutes passed and he saw nothing of the Customs' boat. The deck of the whaler was still dimly lit, so it was too difficult to make out any movement onboard. He didn't know what his next steps should be. Soon he heard steps of several people approaching. He walked out of his office and saw Colonel Juakea himself in full uniform and several men marching directly to him.

The Colonel nodded and said, "Good evening, John." Without waiting for a reply, he continued. "Have you heard or seen anything from our men that went out to the port entrance?"

"No sir," said John. "I signaled the ship to let them know the custom's boat was approaching, but they didn't respond. After that, your boat was signaled to move to port side. Once the boat disappeared on the port side, I saw nothing else in my eyeglass."

"How long ago was that," asked Jaukea.

"Nearing an hour ago, sir."

"That is too long." Jaukea turned to one of his lieutenants. "Get another boat ready. You, and I will go this time. Bring a steamer pilot in case we need to bring the ship in to port. And send for several policemen to go with us as well."

The lieutenant acknowledged Jaukea and started barking orders quickly to the other men as they walked away.

"Sir, do you think it is wise for you to be going to a dark ship on a poorly lit night?" asked John.

"It is my job to collect revenue," he replied. "No ship is immune to taxes. If word gets out that taxes can be ignored, then everybody will challenge us. And if I do not show a strong hand, I will be seen as a powerless figurehead. Neither can be permitted."

"Yes, sir."

John could barely hear the Kawaiaha'o Church clock bells strike ten due to the ruckus on the wharf. Jaukea and seven other men, four of which were policemen, were pushing off from the Customs' dock. Jaukea had told John not to signal their approach to the whaler, but to signal their boat if he spied anything fishy on the mysterious ship. He also told John that as soon as he boarded he would make the ship's captain light up the deck. Jaukea brought several kerosene lanterns in case the ship couldn't manage the task on its own. John didn't understand how that could be possible, until Jaukea had left. After some thought, John reckoned that Jaukea was referring to a diseased ship with a disabled crew.

John eyed the second Customs' boat approach the whaler. Again, the ship signaled for the Customs' boat to move to the port side. The boat didn't move. Jaukea was probably challenging the signaler. But soon the boat moved as did the earlier Customs' boat to the bow and then to the hidden port side.

Ten minutes passed with no sign of Jaukea or any of his party. The steam whaler lay dark with the exception dim lights at its bow and stern. John was pacing back and forth on the dock. He stared so long at the ship with his eyeglass that he had to stop a while due to blurry vision. He jumped as he turned to see the longshoreman he had sent to the Customs house earlier standing still behind him.

"Sorry, sir. I didn't mean to startle you," said the longshoreman.

After he swallowed his heart, John said, "That's fine. But since you're here, do you mind. . . ." He stopped talking as he saw the longshoreman leaning and peering past him. John swiveled back around.

There was a flood of little lights now on the deck of the ship. They all seemed to be generally moving toward the center of the ship. It didn't take long before he realized that the number of lights were slowly decreasing. Shortly after, he also saw a glow toward the bow of the ship, which was then followed by a tender that seemed to be full of men with lanterns. Once it cleared the bow, it turned directly toward the port entrance. Then another boat followed. Soon a line of five boats were heading his way.

John's vision in his right eye had cleared, so he raised the eyeglass. He couldn't believe it. The men were heavily armed with guns, knives and cutlasses. "Damn, they're pirates!" he said aloud.

"Should I fetch your gun, sir" said the longshoreman behind him.

"No, it won't do us any good. I counted 15 in the first boat alone. They must have at least seventy men in those boats."

"Well should I run get help or something?"

John heard splashing and men yelling to his right. "I don't think you need to worry about that," said John. He and the longshoreman watched the fishermen running down the street toward Chinatown.

***

Paul Brown had locked up the Pacific Commercial Advertiser newspaper office just after ten o'clock and was heading toward Chinatown to catch a late dinner before retiring for the night. He was working on the final edits for his story to be printed in one of the upcoming editions. He knew he wouldn't be able to sleep if he didn't get it done.

Chinatown was the main social spot for Honolulu and Paul was eagerly awaiting decent food and a nightcap. There were always good stories to collect on such outings in Chinatown. Most stories were idle gossip, but sometimes he'd pick up some good tidbits. Like the arrest of a Chinese secret society on one of the other islands. Or the news that the mongoose brought over last year from Jamaica had done nothing to rid the rat infestation in the sugar cane fields.

As Paul was about to enter one of his favorite restaurants, he saw a group of Hawaiian men with fishing gear running quickly down the middle of the street from the direction of Honolulu harbor. The reporter in him took hold and he held out his hand and hailed one of the men.

"You there! What are you doing making such a ruckus down the streets? Don't you know what hour it is?

One of the men stopped and replied. "We're being invaded by pirates! There is an entire army of them landing at the docks." The man took off to catch the others.

*Pirates? There hasn't been a pirate ship heard of in the Pacific for a hundred or more years. I have got to see this.* Paul started walking briskly to the wharf.

He arrived to the harbor master's office just as he saw the first armed men stepping up onto the dock. He started to leave when he heard the first commands from the pirates.

"Not another step if you value your life," said the third pirate that was stepping up on the dock. The man was tall, had a red beard, wore a cutlass at his waist, and carried a pistol in his hand.

*That's not the voice of a pirate,* was the immediate thought of Paul. But given they were armed, he complied by standing motionless as did the harbor master and longshoreman near him.

"Very good. All English-speaking. I was worried I would encounter the Hawaiian language at the docks." The man speaking, who seemed to be in charge, addressed the other men as they continued to empty onto the dock. He used his pistol like a pointer when he began to direct the crew. "Remember what I told you. We have to move quickly and quietly. Boat number one crew. . .your task is to secure the docks and subdue anyone you encounter. Two of you should tie the boats up and then confiscate five more for our cargo. Sink all other boats. Boats two through five will follow me. Do you understand?"

28

"Aye, aye captain," replied the men quietly.

Paul's mind flooded with questions. *Where are they from? What do they want? What was going to happen to the three of them standing there?* The last question seemed the most pertinent at the moment to Paul.

"Uh, er, Captain. Excuse me. What are you going to do with us? With the city?" Paul was unaware of his movement to draw the captain's attention.

Immediately the largest of the pirates flanking the captain swung the butt of his Winchester rifle into Paul's chin. The impact put him off balance and he sprawled on the ground.

"Perhaps you did not hear me, but I said not to move," said the captain. "That is your last reminder. Tie these men up in the harbor master's office."

With that the captain stepped over Paul Brown and pushed forward up Fort Street in the direction of Iolani Palace. Two men picked up Paul, while another motioned for the harbor master and longshoreman to enter the office. There the three of them were told to take a chair in front of the desk where the leftover malasada and cold coffee sat. Each were tied in front by their hands and feet.

Paul was about to ask the filibusters what they were doing when a soiled cloth was stuffed into his mouth. The pressure of the man's finger on the back of his tongue combined with the filth he tasted made him retch. He watched as the harbor master and longshoreman were gagged as well. Then the men left the office and began securing the dock. Paul watched their actions through the wide windows of the office. He noted the absolute efficiency of their actions without a word spoken. It struck him that he was watching a precision machine. It was not like he imagined pirates to be; rather, they resembled the actions of a well-trained militia. Then he wondered, was "captain" the title bestowed by the crew to their pirate captain, or was this truly an earned military rank?

Paul's thoughts were interrupted by moaning from the harbor master. *Who is this man?* Paul tried to remember his name. *John? Yes John was his first name.*

He watched John point with an upward nod of his chin to the table. Paul looked back and forth between the table and John – trying to figure out John's pantomime. Then he noticed the newspaper that lay open on the desk next to the malasada. It was his competitor's paper, *The Daily Bulletin.* He looked back to John and tried to mouth through the gag, "Yes I am reporter for the paper." He tried a second time but couldn't even understand his own words.

John shook his head and then appeared to be trying to swipe his head to the left. It occurred to Paul that perhaps the man wanted him to read the paper. Paul leaned forward and focused on the paper, which was dated December 1, 1884. Then he turned back to John. John was still gesturing to the left. Paul read the title of the header on the left page, which read "National Defences." He had not read the paper's today since he was busy with his story most of the day. So he began to read.

Paul's eyes widened as he read the words written by the editor of the paper – a man he knew well. He stopped in disbelief when he read the words:

**A general rising for plunder alone, with no intent of usurping political control of the country, is a prospect that could only be an absurd dream.**

# Chapter 6: *Old Friend*

Kaleho had left the precinct earlier than normal today, and was driving in his Chevelle toward Waikiki. He was feeling tired. They were making progress on the case, but it was moving far too slowly. He would normally have been staying late, but Rick and his family had arrived and Kaleho was eager to see them.

He turned right off of Ala Moana Boulevard onto Kahanamoku Street. A bright red sign with Kona Mountain Coffee caught his eye, and he made a mental note to walk over for some before heading home. He rarely stopped for anything in Waikiki given the outrageous prices, but he could afford a good coffee. After showing his badge, the valet said that he could leave his car on the downhill ramp beyond the hotel front entrance. After a few more of the valets moved around to admire it, they told him they'd watch his car for him.

Rick had texted him that they were staying in the Ali'i Tower, which had a living room with a large table to one side that could be used for meetings. He added, that they were eating right now at the Tropics Bar & Grill. Kaleho walked from the lobby area by the koi pond and the man-made lagoon with penguins and turtles. "Ali'i" means "royal" in Hawaiian, which was certainly an appropriate name for the hotel. He moved around the left side of the pond and saw the restaurant. The restaurant had lava rock columns framing the soaring teak wood portico and ceiling. The right side of the restaurant opened to the beach and ocean. He saw the Bryants sitting at the outdoor tables as soon as he entered.

Rick was watching for him and got up before he could get to the table. Rick remembered the old days and shook hands bro-style and the followed it with a "shaka." He then introduced Shelli and Nikki, and the brother and sister who had come with them.

Upon seeing the family and friends, Kaleho became concerned after a few minutes of talking with them. Except for Rick and Ryan's casual appearance, they looked like a typical upscale family on an expensive vacation. Rick's girls were clicking on their phones and posting real time. Danielle was as beautiful as he remembered and immaculately dressed. And he didn't know anything about the two tag-alongs, but the girl Stephanie been talking incessantly since he arrived. He knew that Rick was wealthy, but somehow given what he read in the newspapers, he didn't picture the family as so...prim and perfect. He began to question his decision to call them. There is no way he could bring this family into police headquarters. The DA thought he was crazy for hiring them anyway. "Hiring" was probably too strong a word. Rick had asked for the sum of one dollar to help with the case. Still, Kaleho would be ridiculed for his decision. Rick was telling him something about the hotel, but all he could think about was how he was going to get out of this arrangement without hurting his long-standing friendship.

"So Kaleho, order yourself something on the menu. My treat. I still owe you for a lot of meals at your folks' house from our college days." Rick passed him the menu. "We know it's important to start going over the case right away, but we're hungry and need to adjust to the time change. So get you something to eat before we jump into work."

Kaleho squirmed while looking at the menu. Rick must have sensed his uneasiness. *How the heck am I going to tell them? Maybe I should just go ahead and be social. I can have a good time with them and let them know in the morning. Maybe blame to it on the DA.*

*It would be impolite to tell them they were off the case on their first night here.* Kaleho focused on the menu and selected the Aloha Lager Fish & Chips.

The food arriving at the table was the only interruption to the stories Kaleho and Rick traded about their college days in the islands. Danielle had obviously heard them all, but she good-naturedly sat through them again. The food was delicious and Rick asked for a Kona coffee as they cleared away the dishes.

"Make that two," said Kaleho.

After the plates were all gone, Rick changed the conversation. "Should we stop boring the kids here and discuss the case? I know you've had your hands full and that is why we're here. Do you mind going over the top-level details here in the restaurant, or would you like to move to some place less public?"

Kaleho rotated in his seat and saw that the restaurant was still quite busy. "Maybe it's best to go up to the room and go over it. We're trying to keep this out of the eyes of the press."

"I've got a better idea," said Rick. "We stayed at the Hilton because I like it, but also because it's closer to the boat marina, the police headquarters, and the Port. I need to check on our ship at the Port, so we can head there and discuss things."

Before the Kaleho could ask what Rick was talking about, the waitress arrived with two cups of steaming coffee. "I'm sorry, we need to go. Can you put those coffees in to-go cups?" asked Rick. "And bring the check, please."

"Are we all going?" asked Kaleho. "I've got my car out front, but it can't carry all of us."

Danielle saw that '*may-I?*' look on Rick's face, and volunteered, "We'll take a taxi to the Port. You can ride with Kaleho. I'm going up to the room first, so we'll be a few minutes behind."

"Cool," said Rick. Kaleho took the coffees as the waitress returned and Rick signed his name and room number on the check. As they headed to the lobby, Kaleho handed a coffee to Rick.

"You've got a great family there, Rick. And Danielle is still a gem. You're a lucky man."

"Believe me, I know. It won't be long before the girls will be gone. We're trying to make the most of these years. And I'm fortunate Nikki has shown interest enough in the company to want to stay around." He paused for a few seconds. "How's Kai doing? Is he out surfing you yet?"

"He's a good kid. He plays on the varsity baseball team and he absolutely loves surfing. He gives me a run for the money. It won't be much longer before he's showing me up. I'm happy he still tolerates me out there on the water with him."

They arrived at the lobby entrance and turned right to the ramp. Rick stopped when he saw the Chevelle. "When the heck did you get this?" he said. "This is beautiful."

Kaleho smiled. "You mean you don't recognize an old friend?"

Rick seemed puzzled for a moment, but then the light bulb went off. "No. It can't be. Is this the '72 you bought when we were in school?"

"We bought. Yes, I just finished it not too long before the case started."

"I can't believe it. I'm impressed with the makeover, but I am even more impressed by the fact you still have it."

"I just couldn't part with it. For years I couldn't afford anything else when I first entered the police force. And then there were kids."

"Holy cow, Kaleho. This is awesome. Let's get this on the road." He stopped and viewed at the inside of the convertible and then glanced at his coffee."

"What's wrong?"

"Coffee. I don't want to spill it on your car."

"Don't worry about that. I still take my surfboard around in this."

"Heck no. You know how much of a klutz I am. I don't trust myself." He took a long sip of the coffee and threw it away in the trashcan at the entrance. Then he jumped inside the passenger side with a large grin on his face. "Let's go, man!"

Kahelo started up the car and they were on their way down Ala Moana Boulevard. He watched Rick's eyes scan the car over and listened to his praise of the work. With all that money, he hadn't changed. He was the same down-to-earth person he knew in school.

"So where are we headed? Nimitz or Sand Island?"

"North Nimitz," answered Rick. "Left on Alakawa Street."

"Oh, yeah. Hawaiian Ice and Nico's are down that road."

"Yep, that's what the crew said. They said we should park in the back of that building."

"So what's with this boat you're talking about?" asked Kaleho. "I didn't know you had a boat here."

"It just got here. You'll see it soon."

The Port of Honolulu was quiet as always this time of night. Kaleho parked the car behind the large building that housed a number of businesses. They opened the car doors and Kaleho stopped at the rear of his Chevelle.

"One thing about owning a convertible," said Kaleho. "If you don't want to lose something important, put it in the trunk." He popped the trunk and pulled out a manila folder. It was about an inch thick and was labeled with a case number across the top. "It might come in handy as we discuss the case."

They walked slowly toward the center pier. Kaleho thought about the file contents and his newfound reservations about using the family on the case. He'd only show what was in the file if it appeared they could actually help on the case.

Lights had just come on from the light posts to one side of the pier. They walked a few hundred feet down when Rick announced, "This is it."

"What is 'this'? This big fishing boat?" asked Kaleho.

"It's a North Sea fishing trawler. The tall bow cuts through big waves and shields against high winds. It's reconditioned of course. Among the many upgrades, we modified the aft deck to accommodate a large helicopter landing pad. The ship was built back in the '60's, but you couldn't tell it now when you go onboard. Got it for a good deal. It came up at a government auction. It was confiscated by the DEA after a drug bust down our way in Florida. It can accommodate 12 people comfortably for long voyages. It's got a sixty-five hundred nautical mile range, which was just long enough for the trip from Florida."

"I thought you were going to show me some sleek yacht," said Kaleho. "I'm a bit surprised to see you on a fishing boat. Granted, it is well over a hundred feet long and it is in pristine shape.    But I should have known.    Leave it to millionaire Rick Bryant to buy a commercial fishing boat for pleasure."

"Although we've set it up to be pleasant onboard with all the amenities required for long voyages, it's actually more of a work vessel.  Come onboard and you'll see what I mean."

Being a police officer for many years, Kaleho had an eye for detail.  Other than some classical nautical décor, nothing on this boat shouted "fishing" vessel.  The boat was immaculate and Kaleho surmised that it was probably the cleanest it had ever been. According to Rick, the ship normally had a crew of six for long voyages.    There were two small yellow single-person, sport helicopters on the top deck.  Rick said that Danielle wouldn't ride on any helicopter that he or any other family member would pilot, so he bought these instead.  He said these were heavily modified and that they could now multitask by having two of them.

The bridge had a 270 degree view. Camera displays and the outer wings allowed for views for the remaining 90 degrees.  From the bridge, the captain could monitor all systems on the boat.  If the captain fell ill or worse, the boat had an autopilot that could be commanded from anywhere in the world remotely using the onboard satellite communication system. While docked, the ship was also protected by the dual DMT IDAR radars, which were all-weather security radars that worked over land and water.  They also automatically pointed thermal imaging cameras at whatever the radars detected.

While on the bridge, Kaleho watched the security displays warn of possible intruders approaching the ship from the direction of the parking lot, but then the facial recognition software recognized the girls and Ryan as "friendly" and stopped flashing.  Minutes later the whole gang was on the bridge.

Directly behind the bridge was what Rick called his command center.  The room was surrounded by circular portals.   A two-foot wide surface ringed the room with comfortable barstool-like seats.   A long conference room table with a computer console set in the middle of the room.  Rick motioned Kaleho to have a seat at the table.  He asked the steward to bring in some hot coffee.  Then Rick asked the girls to take their stations.

A push of a computer console screen button caused the portals to go dark, which made the room dim.  But the diminishing natural light from the portals was replaced by the glow from screens flipped up around the room.  Kaleho quickly established that each monitor, keyboard and mouse combination was a command station.   A big screen, the situation awareness display as Rick called it, popped up at the far side of the room.

"We have access to all ship systems, including the security and ship-protection system, the Internet, and a connection to criminal databases thanks to our friends in the law enforcement agencies," explained Rick.  "We can protect ourselves when we must.  We'll be using this as our center of operations.  Being that we're only five minutes away from the police station, we thought this was the most convenient place – with full access to water, land, air and our technology.  And the davit on the deck is now lowering the **Spearfish** into the water. It's a boat we developed for law enforcement.  Beside the 'toys' onboard this ship, we are going to keep the **Spearfish** docked down at the marina next to the Hilton."

"Well this is pretty cool," commented Kaleho.  "I'm not sure how this will be used in our case, but I can see its value nonetheless."

"Can you explain the case to us?" asked Rick.

Kaleho sat down at the conference table and placed the folder from the trunk of his car on the table. *What the heck*, he thought to himself. *It can't hurt to discuss this with them. I can still debrief them from the case if it turns out they can't help.* "I sure can," said Kaleho. He reached in the folder and opened the clasps of a manila envelope. From the envelop he pulled out a folded evidence bag. He opened it and without touching the item inside, he let it slide out on the table.

"It appears this item is key to the investigation," he continued. "We don't know why, but we believe a number of people have been murdered because of a couple of these that have been discovered."

Sitting on the conference table lay a large tarnished silver coin.

# Chapter 7: *Iolani Palace*

The Iolani Palace was the most impressive building in Hawai'i. At a cost of over $300,000, it should have been. No expense was spared for the building that began construction in 1882. It was a revival in Roman architecture with Hawaiian flavor. The rectangular structure was made of plastered brick and iron with concrete trimmings. It had two main floors and an elevated basement and attic. It had been built by mostly local contractors, but much of the materials for it were imported. It had redwood and cedar from western USA, the plate glass and etched glass in the doors and windows were from San Francisco, as were the many Corinthian-style cast iron columns that surrounded the deep veranda. The slate roof, which was not visible from the ground, was from stone quarried in Pennsylvania. The wash basins had marble from Italy, and there were door panels from England. The modern plumbing carried water from an artesian well in the back of the palace that was over 700 feet deep. And even though the telephone had been invented only six years earlier, the royals used them to communicate in the various rooms and other properties.

The four towers on the corners and the two majestic central towers in the front and back gave it the palace look. Wide carriage drives led up from King and Richard Streets, and encircled the Palace. A wide oval at the front steps allowed room for horse-drawn carriages to drop off their passengers, who were immediately attended to by the ample palace staff.

Wide steps led up to the main first floor, which opened to a grand hall with a beautiful wooden staircase in the center made of dark brown, Hawaiian *koa* wood. The throne room was to the right. The dining room was to the left. The families living quarters with an unheard of four bathrooms were upstairs. The entire place was elaborate and no surface was left undecorated, including the ceilings. Finished in November two years earlier, the royal family was now well established in the official residence.

The evening was going well for Mr. Walter Gibson. He was sitting at dinner as the Minister of Foreign Affairs with the King of Hawai'i, and a handful of other loyal members of the government and the King's Guard. Hawai'i had been good to him over the last few years given that he arrived in Honolulu after being first jailed in the East Indies and then excommunicated from the Mormon Church for embezzlement on the island of Lanai.

Gibson normally loved spending time with the King. King Kalākaua was an extremely intelligent man and he was one of the most widely traveled heads of state at that time. Although Hawaiian by birth, the King spoke English as well as any Englishman. The King had traveled the globe and was highly respected by monarchs around the world. Gibson loved to talk about these foreign travels with His Majesty. Earlier in the night he had been able to retell his story of the meeting with the Jamaicans, which had led to the import of their mongoose to the island of O'ahu. He lied when he said he had heard that the mongoose were indeed reducing the problematic rat population that plagued the sugarcane fields. He actually had no idea how it was progressing. But as for the rest of the night, he would have to share the King with other attendees from the government, the press, and the military. The conversation as a result, was a bit too boring for Gibson's tastes.

He sat listening to the King ramble on about the trade agreement that was going to be signed within the week in Washington. The agreement granted the US Navy unlimited access to Pearl Harbor, and included permission to construct ship repair facilities. In return, Hawai'i received full access to the

US sugar market. It was going to be great for Hawai'i's economy. It would also infuse more money and loans into the hands of the royal family, and in turn, to Gibson's pockets as well. Gibson, like the royal family, had an affinity for the finer things in life.

Of course, the night couldn't be complete without a rounding out of the standard topics at the table. The win by Grover Cleveland in November had caused a whirlwind in the political circles. There was excitement about the upcoming arrival of their newest work force, the Japanese. They were going to replace the long standing source of Chinese labor, and were expected to arrive in February. The newly minted Hawaiian silver coins, which featured the king's likeness, were discussed. The coins were not being used by the local merchants and residents as expected. For the most part, privately issued tokens and American coins were preferred. A million dollars of silver coins was too much money to sit uncirculated, so the King always queried his guests about their use. The census was brought up again, which had been conducted earlier in the year. The final report was still incomplete, but it was expected to show flat growth in the Hawaiian population, which troubled the king.

The clock at the nearby Kawaiaha'o Church rang ten. "Ah, the hour is growing late to be still sitting at the table. Should we retire to the sitting room or the music room? Speaking of music. . . Mr. Gibson, did you hear the band downtown today?"

The King's gesture to stand, along with the question pulled Gibson out of his thoughts. "Yes, Your Highness. They played a few wonderful melodies for the passengers arriving at the port, *God Save the Queen*, the *Star Spangled Banner* for the British and Americans, and *Hawai'i Pono'i*. And of course, your favorite, *Aloha 'Oe*."

"Splendid," said the King as he moved slowly into the Blue Room. "Did the passengers seem to enjoy it?"

The Blue Room was lined with chairs and couches of blue satin. The windows extended over ten feet from the floor and were framed by detailed, stained wood trim. Beautiful blue satin curtains hung to the floor and were tied with gold tassels. Most of the furniture had come over from the original Iolani palace that had to be torn down due to termite damage. This informal reception room was one of many elaborately decorated rooms in the largest and tallest building in all of the Pacific.

"Most certainly. Applause after each number."

"I was there too, Your Majesty," said Major Hayley. "I was most impressed with the efficiency at which the passengers were assisted off the ship."

*There goes the Major trying to steal away the King again*, thought Gibson. *It never fails. Let's see, I give it two minutes before the Major's long-term project is brought up before the King. The only thing more boring than reading a military manual is talking about one.*

"Speaking of efficiency, how is that manual you are writing for my guards, Major?" asked the King.

"Thank you for asking, Your Majesty. It's coming along very well. I have decided the name will be *Manual for the King's Guard*. No need to be fancy. I am on the last chapter now. It should be in print early in the upcoming year."

Gibson lowered his head and bit his lip when he heard the title. *Oh that's a clever title*, he said to himself sarcastically. *The King loves the fact that the Major was also a high-ranking officer in the British militia. The King was treated so well by England's Royal Family when he visited there, that he extended almost immediate friendship to anyone with even a remote link to the British Monarchy.*

The chamberlain, Colonel Charles Judd, and his staff entered the room with trays of fine china. It was time for a tea or coffee with a few desserts. Gibson moved toward one of the other Colonels for what he hoped would be some idle chatter.

As the conversation with Major Hayley continued on about how much the manual was going to help shape up the Royal Guard, Gibson noticed a flicker of lights out on the lawn in front of the palace. He picked up a tea cup and saucer and walked slowly back into the dining room for a better view. There seemed a large gathering of people carrying lanterns. They stopped in the large carriage oval, as if they were having a discussion, and then appeared to be moving up onto the portico of the palace.

Gibson wondered at first if it might be the Royal Guard. The palace was surrounded by a wall and had a large iron gate with sentries. Only the Guard should be moving around the grounds. But as he stared through the center window of the dining room, he caught a better view of several of the men. Those men carried rifles and were not in uniform. He sat down his cup on the dining room table, and walked briskly back to the Blue Room. He pulled Colonel Judd aside.

"There is something going on in the front of the palace. Is there some sort of drill going on with the Royal Guard or Honolulu Rifles?"

"Are they in uniform?" asked the Colonel.

"No," replied Gibson.

The Colonel walked toward the dining room as had Gibson moments before. But it was then that the large front doors of the palace with panes of imported etched glass opened. A flood of the sounds of shuffling feet and clanking metal poured into the room. Gibson was the first to step out into the Grand Hall.

Following Gibson was the Attorney General Neumann, Major Hayley, Mr. Ralph Smith of the *Saturday Press*, and the King himself. The men continued to pour into the hall with guns held in plain view. As soon as Gibson realized the armed men were not the Royal Guard, he stopped in his tracks. As he stopped, a tall man with a long red beard presented himself. From the reaction of the armed men, Gibson immediately pegged him as the leader. He raised his hand to address the bearded filibuster, but King Kalakaua pushed by him and spoke first.

"What is the meaning of this?" said the King in a commanding voice. Gibson was amazed that the King seemed to have no fear. "Do you know who I am?"

"What it means Your Highness, is that we've taken possession of this little kingdom of yours... and we mean to keep it, by God!" shouted the leader. He was pointing with his pistol as he emphasized his words.

Gibson drifted back as he watched the men fan out into the throne room, the Great Hall, and into the dining room. The men made clear their intensions as they started picking up the fine silver and stuffing it into sacks. Another three men stepped forward with large coils of rope on their shoulders. They pulled up the chairs that lined the walls and forced the King, Gibson, and the others dinner guests to sit. As their hands and feet were being tied, Gibson looked around and noticed someone was missing. *Major Hayley! The sly devil must not be just a bag of hot air. He's slipped out. He's off to get help from the Royal Guard, thank God.*

# Chapter 8: *Blue Hawai'i*

Stephanie, Shelli, Nikki, and Ryan simultaneously stood up and leaned in around the conference table in Rick Bryant's ship, the **Amphitrite**, in the Port of Honolulu to see the coin that Kaleho had just placed on the table. "Please don't touch it, its evidence," reminded Kaleho.

Rick and Danielle hovered over the shoulders of Nikki and Shelli to get a better view themselves. "It looks pretty old," said Rick.

"It's an 1883 Hawaiian Dollar," said Kaleho.

"Wow, that's cool," said Shelli. She took a picture of it with her smart phone. Using the corner of the manila envelope that had held the coin, Kaleho flipped it over and Shelli took another picture. Using her finger she swished both pictures in the direction of the 60-inch situation awareness display at the front of the room. The pictures then slid from the bottom edge up to the center of the large screen as if it were an actual piece of paper gliding over a flat surface.

Nikki went up to the large screen and dragged her fingers outward. The touchscreen display responded by enlarging the pictures of the front and back of the coin. "There we go," said Nikki. "Larger, but still too tarnished to read easily. Let's clean it up." She clicked on a few icons that she pulled in from the right. The front side of the coin appeared in a program. She clicked "Autolevel" and the "Edge Enhancement." The image of the coin became sharp and three dimensional. "Now let's clean it up and make it the color it should be." Nikki clicked on the "e" app and an Internet window popped up. She then searched for "silver dollar" and saw a picture of a shiny US silver dollar appear. She dragged the picture of the silver dollar into the program with the Hawaiian dollar. She clicked on the eyedropper tool and then on the silver dollar. A silver color appeared in the program's color palette. She then selected the paint function and clicked on the Hawaiian dollar. A few more finishing strokes and the Hawaiian dollar on the screen looked like it had just come fresh from the mint.

"What does a 130-year-old coin have to do with the case," asked Nikki when done.

Kaleho paused for a little while -- gathering the collection of facts in his mind so that he could relay them in a concise and informative manner. "The coins are a recent find. Two coins have appeared over the last three days. Each has been tied to murder victims."

As soon as she heard the first few sentences from Kaleho, Nikki moved over to one of the computer stations around to one side of the room. She motioned Shelli to come over. She spoke in a low voice to Shelli, and then the two of them sat down and started typing.

Kaleho saw the girls working and stopped talking, wondering whether he should continue. Nikki heard the silence, and glanced back at Kaleho. "I'm sorry, please continue with the story. We're listening."

"Oh, OK. We-"

"I'm sorry to interrupt Kaleho, but I wanted to let you know that everything you say and do is being recorded," said Rick. "I understand you might be concerned about this, but we do this for insurance and evidence. The data is stored on a secure server that sits in a blast-proof, waterproof safe with internal battery backup deep within the ship. If the ship sunk in the bottom of the Pacific, the safe would survive the crushing pressures at that depth. It is password protected and has three encryption algorithms that protect the data. A sheriff in Sarasota and I are the only ones that know how to access the files. I feel I should tell you since you're trusting us with the information."

"That's great," said Kaleho. "I actually feel better that such a record exists. Let's continue... from the beginning."

"It was more than a month ago now that I came into work and was told there had been five murders in one night. Although Honolulu is the 11th largest city in the USA in terms of size, we're one of the safest cities in the USA. Since the 1990's we have had only twenty murders or less a year. That may sound like a lot to you, but it was down to one-fourth of what it used to be in the years preceding 1990. And of the twenty murders a year, about a third of the murders these days are domestic in nature. So five in one night is extremely unusual."

"That first day of the investigation we found that all five victims had previous criminal records. We thought at first it must be gang related, but we quickly determined from our gang crimes unit that none of the victims had any past or current associations with gangs. It took us another few days before we found out that two of the five worked for the Blue Hawai'i Spring Water Company. The rest worked in various aspects of moving stolen merchandise."

"A water company? Was it a drinking water delivery company?" asked Rick.

"Yes," answered Kaleho. "When we found the connection, we put the water company under surveillance. I assigned a few men to watch the company and its deliveries. We also got a warrant for their phone records. It wasn't long before we found that the owner of the company was involved in a sophisticated gambling ring."

"A gambling ring?" asked Stephanie. "What does a water delivery company and a gambling ring have in common?"

Kaleho realized his story must be a good one since Stephanie hadn't spoken a word until then or touched her phone for minutes. He figured that was probably some kind of record. "Good question, Stephanie. We wondered the same thing."

"After two weeks of surveillance, we had pieced together that the water delivery company was a front for the gambling ring. Gambling is illegal in Hawai'i. The delivery trucks did in fact make some deliveries of water to bolster its appearance of being legitimate. But after half a day of deliveries, there were two trucks that would leave their routes early and appear at an empty warehouse or building somewhere in Honolulu. The side doors of the trucks would open and hinges on the water bottle racks would allow access to a hidden interior. Hidden inside were card tables, roulette wheels, and such. These would be rolled out and the clientele would start to arrive. Gaming ended after about four to five hours and the hardware was packed up. A veritable mobile casino."

"How did people know where to go to gamble?" asked Ryan. Except for the introduction, that was the first words he had heard from the young man.

"We don't yet know how they started the whole thing, but when we placed listening devices in some of the gambler's cars, we soon discovered that there's an app for that. Subscribers, which are verified in advance, are pushed notifications of the location and time. The recipient has 30 seconds to memorize it or write it down. Then the notification is trashed."

"That's quite the efficient organization," commented Rick.

"And that is not all of it," continued Kaleho. "The organization used their company phone service that took water orders to also take bets. A key word mentioned by the caller would result in transferring the call from the legitimate water delivery office to a back-room set of operators. Those operators would take bets on sporting events. They used an offshore, online betting service to facilitate the bets."

"One of the more clever parts of the operation was the payout and collection of debts" said Kaleho. "All bets were taken in cash only. The caller never passed money at Blue Hawai'i's office. Instead, the delivery men would pick up a bottle of water from their truck and walk to the door of the client. A bottle of water was always left and an empty always picked up. The client had to subscribe to the company's water delivery service if they wanted to place bets. If the client didn't pay the money owed for a lost bet, then the delivery man became the enforcer."

"It was an ingenious system. It appeared to be completely above-board. They were actually making money on the water they delivered too. But we had a problem. Although we had cracked a major illegal gambling operation that we had never known about before, we could find absolutely no connection between the murders and the operation. We needed more time to find the connection, but we couldn't let people continue to get hurt or killed by the company's enforcers. So we, as discreetly as we could, raided Blue Hawai'i's Spring Water office on the next day the owner was in the office. He is currently being held in a lockdown cell at the precinct. Half of all the enforcers were arrested as well and are all being held separately from the general population at the local prison. The other half were teamed with undercover officers from our precinct. They were given deals of lighter sentences if they agreed to cooperate with the investigation. All the men that remained in the operation were single, so they had no families to miss them. They wore tracking anklets in case they tried to escape and then came back to the holding cells at the precinct after their shift was over."

"Any progress on making a connection since the change in tactics?" asked Rick.

"No," answered Kaleho. "The owner spilled his guts on the whole gambling ring. He's been rigorously interrogated and he doesn't seem to know anything about the murders. He had made a significant effort to search for his two missing enforcers. Illegal gambling operations always worry that their own staff could be skimming or running off with collections. Running when you're on an island in the middle of the Pacific, whether you're an enforcer turned traitor or a client that owes money, can only be done by hopping on an airplane or a ship. We found the owner had people on his payroll at the airport that warned him if someone was trying to flee the islands. And he had paid for longshoreman eyes down at the docks."

"Had he find out anything about the murdered enforcers?" asked Stephanie.

"No. He had checked the police blotters to see if they were arrested or found dead, but we had not released the information yet. So he assumed they were in hiding. He had put out word that there was an award for information on their whereabouts."

"I heard you use the past tense in discussing the undercover operation. Is that over?" asked Nikki.

*Very perceptive*, thought Kaleho. "We had a...uh...wrinkle in the case that finally caused us to shut down the gambling operation completely. After two weeks of trying to find some connection without spooking the clientele, we still had nothing to link us to the murders.

But that wasn't our major problem. We had more murders over that time period – seven of them in fact."

"Twelve murders in less than a month?" asked Stephanie in awe.

"Yes, that's correct. The DA and the mayor agreed that we needed to send a strong message to whomever was responsible for the murders that we were now seriously on the case. The gambling ring was completely shut down and all the regular clientele were picked up and charged as well. That was four days ago. There hasn't been a murder since."

Kaleho stopped. That was all he was prepared to say. He needed to test the family. Although they had solved a murder case at the same time they had busted a drug ring in the article he had read on them, they were motivated because it was a family friend that was murdered. There was no emotional pull here. *Will they ask the right questions of me?*

"I don't understand," said Shelli finally breaking the silence. "You've said a key piece of evidence was sitting in front of us, but you still haven't said how it's connected or anything about it."

"And you didn't mention what the murder investigation did find," said Danielle. "Was there any kind of pattern to the murders? Were they all done by the same person or group of people?"

Kaleho noticed Rick nod and grin at this wife after she spoke. Then Rick looked at Kaleho and added, "Was there any kind of geographic pattern to the murder sites?"

He was relieved to see the family was capable of thinking like policemen. *Those were all the right questions.* He opened up his folder.

"All good questions. Let's start with Danielle's question first. Were there any patterns to the murder? The answer is yes. All victims were killed by stabbing. No evidence of guns was found at any of the crime sites. It resembles Chinese triad-type hits. Unless you need to see the pictures, I'll just summarize and say that there were no fingerprints or DNA evidence to link us to a murderer."

"We don't need to see any photos," assured Danielle. "And thanks for being sensitive."

"No problem, Danielle. Now as to geographic patterns, here is a map of Honolulu with all the murder locations."

Rick picked up the photo and moved over to the corner of the room. He lifted up the lid that Kaleho had not noticed earlier on the desktop that ringed the room. Rick then placed the map face down on the glass surface and then shut the lid. He pressed a button and a ray of light was barely visible seen moving across the edge lip of the lid. *A scanner,* thought Kaleho.

The pictured appeared up on the large screen at the front of the room next to the pictures of the coin. Rick walked to the front and clicked on a globe icon. Google Earth appeared. Rick entered 'Honolulu' in its search window and the map of Honolulu zoomed in on the screen. Rick then marked the location of each murder from Kaleho's map onto the Google Earth map, and then saved the Google map to file. He opened a new program that showed the map on a side window and a gridded table to its right. In the onscreen table, the program had automatically listed the latitude and longitude of each murder location in one column. Then he added another column to the table of the murder dates and times next to each murder site. Then he pressed a button on the bottom of the program window labeled "play."

On the Google map to the left of the program, the murders played in an accelerated fashion and in chronological order. Five of them the first night, followed by a string of seven

41

more. A yellow line connected each event. A new murder location was plotted every couple of days.

Rick stared at the screen. He hit the play button again and watched silently. "I don't see a geographic or chronologic pattern," said Rick still staring at the screen. He turned back to Kaleho. "Do you have any surveillance video of any of the victims over this period of time, like from traffic cameras or hotel cameras?"

*Impressive.* "You just repeated the exact steps I watched our crime lab take. And you asked the same question they did about video surveillance," replied Kaleho. "Oh, and there was no pattern discovered by our lab. I'll get to the video finds in a few moments."

"You said the first five that were murdered consisted of the two Blue Hawai'i employees and people involved in fencing of stolen goods. What about the other six people?" asked Nikki.

"One was a second-hand jewelry store owner, two were antiquities dealers, and three were pawn brokers," answered Kaleho. "One of the pawn brokers had a misdemeanor conviction and both antiquities dealers have been suspects in the sale of Hawaiian relics. Basically not fences, but all buyers of second-hand merchandise."

"It's not surprising the antiquities dealers have been suspects before," said Danielle seriously. "Hawaiian antiquities and remains are protected by federal law. The NAGPRA regulates human remains and there can be stiff penalties and even jail time in those cases. The law concerning the sale and trade of Native American and Hawaiian artifacts; however, is quite complicated. So antiquities dealers, good and bad, are often targeted in investigations. Depending on the value of the item, a questionable dealer might risk challenging the gray lines of the law. Most times, however, the rule is to avoid an artifact if the origin and owner history are vague or undocumented."

Kaleho seemed surprised at what he just heard. *How does she know this?* Rick recognized the look and chuckled.

"Remember Kaleho, Danielle works for the prestigious Ringling Museum of Art in Sarasota." Rick placed his hand on her shoulder. "She has degrees in art and art history. She started with Ringling as a part-time docent. But after they got to know her abilities, she was soon asked to take on a good deal more responsibility. She has to research a lot of the pieces of art the museum displays and buys."

"Well that might come in quite handy. It sounds like you know the law better than we do in this matter," said Kaleho.

"You've mentioned only eleven victims," said Shelli. "What about the twelfth victim? And I still don't see how the coins fit in?"

"I'm getting to the coins, but first let me tell you about the twelfth victim."

"Victim twelve was murdered just six days ago. It was a college kid – only 20 years old." Danielle let out an audible sigh and settled her eyes on her college-aged Nikki. "We haven't been able to locate the family to notify them, so we can't release the full name to you until you can come in and sign all the nondisclosure agreements. But I can tell you his first name was Paul. Paul was on the Dean's list for most semesters and was considered an upstanding, reserved young man. After the first couple of days, we could find nothing that connected Paul to Blue Hawai'i or to any of the other victims."

"What changed?" asked Rick.

"Three days ago we searched Paul's dorm room and found a coin like this one and a few other things hidden under a loose section of carpet. It didn't mean anything to us at first. But within a few hours of finding that coin, we made another discovery. The crime lab technicians had noticed days earlier in the videos from around town that the Blue Hawai'i employees carried a piece of paper into a number of places they were visiting. One of the technicians figured that the paper must have been a precaution. They were probably carrying the picture or print of the object instead of the object itself into those places. So he suggested that we search for something of value they may have had. We went back and raked over the two guys' homes, and as expected, we found nothing. But one of them had a safety deposit box. So we went there and found this coin and a lot of cash in it. As soon as we found the coin, we had a connection from the last murder victim to one of the first ones. The Blue Hawai'i employees had taken that coin from Paul. And the paper they were showing around was of the coin. And in fact, one of the antiquities dealers was a collectable coin dealer as well."

"Whoa, that's amazing," said Shelli. "How did they get Paul's coin?"

"We found out after questioning Paul's roommate that he had a good friend that lived a couple of doors down. He said that no one has seen Paul or his friend for a few days. We searched the friend's room and the first thing we saw was the Blue Hawai'i water dispenser sitting next to the door. Checking the records from Blue Hawai'i's office, we found that Paul's friend had placed a bet of $500 with Blue Hawai'i. So-"

"So Paul must have paid the debt of his friend with one of those coins," blurted out Stephanie excitedly. She was loud enough to startle the entire group.

"Well done, Stephanie," said Kaleho. "We believe that's what happened. We haven't been able to find the friend, but when we checked his bank balance we found it was overdrawn and had no more than sixty dollars at any given time over the last few months. How he expected to cover the bet is a mystery. Paul was barely making ends meet himself, so the coin must have been his last resort."

"The coins tie all the murder victims together, but that doesn't mean it was why they were murdered," said Rick.

"Exactly!" said Kaleho. "We don't know if coins were the cause, or if it was something the Blue Hawai'i employees dug up while they were trying to sell it. We need to find out the significance of these coins. Paul's family and his friend are still missing. They are presumably hiding or dead. But if we can find them, they may be able to shed some light on the coins."

"Well the coins are valuable," said Nikki. Kaleho had noticed that she and Shelli had continued to work on computers while listening to him.

"That's right," said Shelli. "That coin today is worth about $700 in fair condition. Paul must have known it covered the debt and then some. The coins were the last minted coins of the Hawaiian monarchy. In 1903, however, the US Government had all but 46,348 one-dollar coins melted down."

"That seems like a lot of coins to still be worth 700 times their face value," said Ryan.

"That's true," said Nikki. "But only a few hundred are owned by collectors. More than 45,000 are unaccounted for. What if the murderer is searching for the remainder? At $700 each, that puts the value at over 31.5 million dollars."

"I also found that half-dollars, quarters, and dimes were also minted at the same time as those dollars. There were 1,950,000 coins minted in all, and had a total value of one million US Dollars in 1883. After melting, the total remaining was 626,624 coins," said Shelli.

"And by my calculations," added Nikki, "those coins are conservatively worth 150 million dollars. Take out what is in already in the hands of collectors, and you still have more than 130 million dollars' worth of coins that are either lost or somewhere unknown to the general public."

Kaleho was stunned. They had considered that the coin might be valuable, but no one had conceived a notion of a possible treasure horde of coins. *I have my first possible motive.*

"That is so cool, Shelli," squealed Stephanie. "We've got another treasure hunt!"

"Well let's not jump to conclusions," said Rick. "That was good work girls, but we need a lot more facts before we can assume a treasure is the reason for the murders. I agree with Kaleho, the family and Paul's friend need to be questioned."

"That's just it, Rick," said Kaleho. "We haven't found a trace of them. Most of Paul's family lives on Maui, but he has a brother here in Honolulu. The brother, who is 25 years old, hasn't shown up for work for the last few days and has not been seen by neighbors lately. The parents are retired, but neighbors say they and his younger sister are on vacation somewhere. Paul's gambling friend has family in New Jersey, and when we contacted them they said he only calls home once or twice a month. They said he hasn't called lately, but they hadn't been concerned until we gave them the call."

"It's safe to say that Paul's brother and the friend did not leave the island. You would have some record of that, I'm sure," said Rick. Kaleho nodded. "And I also assume you would have and probably still are checking their phones."

Kaleho nodded. "Yes, we traced both phones. They both had left their GPS enabled on their phones for Facebook and Twitter, so it was easy to locate the phones. We found the friend's phone in a trash can on campus, and the brother had left his at his home."

"Both are young, so they won't be able to function without a phone or at least a computer," said Rick. "I have an idea."

Rick walked over to the far right of the room and knelt down. Kaleho could see a number of black metal shelves with cases of various sizes. He pulled one of the medium-size luggage cases out, and set it up on the conference room table. He flipped up the two latches and opened the lid. Kaleho walked over and saw a more than a dozen smart phones neatly arranged inside the foam-filled interior of the case.

"I always keep extra phones in case we lose or break one," explained Rick. "I want you to take this case with you back to the precinct."

"Why?"

"Each phone has a variety of apps that are quite useful, but there is one in particular that I would like your officers to use," said Rick. Rick powered up one of the phones. Then he swiped the screen until he saw the app he wanted. He tapped on it.

"What are we supposed to use this for?" asked Kaleho.

"Click here to add key words or phrases, such as 'Hawaiian coin,' or Paul's name or anything else you want searched. You said that your crime lab searched their Facebook and other social media accounts, so you could tell if they were using those accounts already. But since you can easily create a new account on any of those social media sites, you should add their friends to this search list. If the friend or Paul's brother buys a new pay-as-you-go phone, then it will likely be a smart phone with GPS enabled. So if those friends are friended by a new contact, then this app will tell you and will give you the coordinates of that new contact on the built-in map."

"But we can track this at the crime lab," admitted Kaleho. He felt a little uncomfortable about mentioning this because people would complain if this became public knowledge.

"I'm sure you can," said Rick. "But think how much computing power is required to search phrases, references, and patterns on the Internet. And by the time you can respond to hits found by the crime lab, that person will probably be long gone. If you distribute these to officers around the city, then you will have a much better chance of finding them."

"How is it any faster than my lab?"

"This app monitors all social media in a distance radius from your location. You can enter that distance here. The shorter the range, the more responsive the app is. That's how the phone can do what your crime lab can't do – immediate location of the persons mentioned. I have all these defaulted to 50 meters, but you can shorten or increase the range. Wherever you are, the phone can tell you who is on their phone within 50 meters of it. I've already plugged in a number of different search parameters." Rick clicked on a button. "This one shows you how many men and how many women are in that radius. So if you were walking down the sidewalk in Waikiki, you could tell just how many of each are in any given establishment."

"I guess that's nice if you're a bar-hopping single person, but how does that help me in this case?" asked Kaleho with a puzzled expression.

"You can 'and' or 'or' these search parameters. So we know that Paul's brother is a man. So 'man' is a search parameter. We have names like 'Paul,' and words and phrases like 'murder,' 'kill,' 'rare coin,' 'Hawaiian dollar,' and so on. If you tie all those searches together, you will narrow down possible candidates for Paul's friend and brother. If you tried to search the whole island for those phrases for all social media outlets, then you would need rooms of NSA super computers to be able to accomplish this near-real-time. And again you would not be able to respond fast enough even if you did find them. But by searching for any such data from phones with GPS locations within 50 meters of this phone, this phone can get responses as fast as one can walk down the street. Tie this phone system with experienced officers and it becomes even more powerful because those officers have their own hunches and ideas about where people hide. So if you have some of your patrol officers or even your plain clothes officers carry this as they walk or drive, then you will be able to cover a large area continuously. And more importantly, you will be right there when it detects the phone transmitting the message or post. This can all be done while the officers are doing their normal job, so you don't have to pull someone off duty. It will beep at them when a match is found."

Kaleho was momentarily stunned. *In the last hour of discussion, I have found a possible motive for the murders and have a way to more rapidly search for the last victim's brother and friend. And to think I was ready to let them go home to Florida at dinner.*

"I don't know what to say, Rick. This is great. Of course I'll use these."

Rick looked at his watch. "Although it's not late here, we're still on Eastern Standard Time. It is two-thirty in the morning for our body clocks, so can we call it a night?"

"Of course," answered Kaleho. "I'm so sorry to keep you up. Can you come in the morning to the office and sign those NDA forms Rick? That way I can give you the names of the victims and more details."

"By the way, what happened to those forms I signed and sent to you weeks ago, when you first asked me if I could help?" asked Rick.

"There are more victims now, so new forms needed to be drafted," answered Kaleho.

"Figures. Is 11 o'clock fine with you?" asked Rick. "I've got some things to check out here on the ship tomorrow morning first thing."

"That will be perfect," said Kaleho. "That will give me time to get the papers together. I'll also setup a conference room so you can meet the team."

"I'll check more on the coin's history," said Shelli. "Maybe there is more to the coins we haven't unearthed." She winked when she made the inference to treasure.

"I have a friend over at the Bishop Museum. I was planning on going over there tomorrow since we are going to have the Hawaiian art exhibit in May next year. I can discretely ask for information on the coins while I'm there," offered Danielle. Everyone nodded at the suggestion.

"I don't feel too tired yet, Dad," said Nikki. "So Ryan and I will take the **Spearfish** back to the marina tonight. That way we can use it for errands tomorrow. And Ryan and I can come back here with you tomorrow morning. I know you need my help unloading and fueling some of the toys."

"Toys?" asked Kaleho.

"Come below deck," said Rick with a grin.

They walked back into the boat's bridge and then to the port side to stairs that went down first to the quarters, and then down another level to an open expanse.

Two steps from the bottom, Kaleho halted abruptly. His jaw dropped as he saw the equipment before him. Rick laughed at his expression.

"Oh my gosh, what the heck is all this?" asked Kaleho.

"This is why it took us a while to get here," said Rick. "Take a quick look around. Then we've got to get back to the hotel. I'm exhausted. We'll show you how all this works when you can break free tomorrow afternoon or night."

Kaleho moved slowly into the room without saying anything. He could not imagine how much money was tied up in the 1500 or so square feet in front of him. It was overwhelming. Gadgets, underwater equipment, vehicles, and objects that he had never seen lay before him. He eventually realized he was the only one in the room. A few moments after this realization, his cloudy memory recalled someone had said to turn the lights out when he was ready to go.

Standing there by himself, he could hear all the hums and clicks of equipment being charged and onboard processors computing. He found the light switch next to the steps going back up. He flicked it off and started up. One last glance back to marvel at the constellation of power and computer lights in the darkness, and then up he climbed numbly to the main deck and then off toward his antiquated mode of transportation.

# Chapter 9: *The Royal Guard*

As Major Hayley sneaked away from one of the rear glass windows in the blue room, he could hear the red bearded leader of the gang of pirates continue his boisterous delivery. Red Beard told the King how he had fanned out from the docks and had taken the hotels, the streets, and the pitiful guards at the palace gates without a shot fired. As the pirates moved through each palace room, they held them at gunpoint and then tied up each person in the room. The last sentence he heard from the man before he got out of earshot was, "Stealing was as simple as picking food from one's own pantry."

As the Major cleared the last step at the rear staircase to the palace, he kept low and ran toward the Royal Guard's quarters on the east rear side of the palace grounds. He entered quietly into the unlocked center courtyard of their quarters and immediately gave orders in a loud whisper to the first soldier he encountered.

"Private, the palace is under attack," said the Major. We've got to respond quickly. They have already taken the whole city without a shot fired."

Clearly startled, the man saluted and answered, "Yes, sir! I'll get the men up immediately." He turned to run toward the sleeping quarters.

"Hold it!" The soldier stopped. "What is the status of the Krupp cannons?"

The soldier spun around with a worried look on his face. "Ah, they have never been fired, sir."

"What? They arrived almost a year ago," shouted the Major aloud.

"I know, sir. We haven't even put them on their mounts yet. We didn't have any powder to fire, so no one has bothered to assemble them."

The Major stared for a moment. *Those German-made cast steel cannons had sufficient fire power to reach the harbor. They could take have taken out the pirate ship without issue. Yet, another example of island life.* No one expended effort unless they had to. It was times like these that the Major missed the efficiencies of the British military.

"Well go ahead and wake the Guardsmen up," said the Major with a gesture of his hand. "And go fetch Captain Aldrich of the Honolulu Rifles. We can use all the help we can get."

"Yes, sir."

Although the Honolulu Rifles were a newly formed and untrained volunteer militia, the Major hoped the combination of their weapons and added numbers along with the Royal Guard would be enough to repel the pirates.

The small center courtyard of the barracks was open to the sky. The sounds of the night from around the palace and nearby Richards Street could be easily discerned from within the courtyard. *Unfortunately,* thought the Major, *the awakening guard might also be heard by the band of pirates. Why didn't the pirates attack the barracks first? The Royal Guard was the only armed response of any significance that protected the King. The police were formidable, but they didn't have the numbers to push back this force. And since that leader. . .that Red Beard. . . had said he had control of the town, the police must now be incapacitated. Attacking the barracks first would make the most sense to keep their own losses to a minimum. Unless. . .maybe they were new to the islands and didn't know about the Guard. Or maybe just the opposite. . .maybe they knew the cannons were not assembled and that the guard house was behind the palace. It was perhaps easier to take the palace first because it was closer to the docks, and once they had the royals, the soldiers could not respond without jeopardizing* them *Ah, impossible. How could they count on that scenario? They had to be new to the islands. And if they were new, they were about to get a big surprise.*

The thought of the Royal Guard being able to surprise the pirates made the Major excited. The rustle of the men gathering in the courtyard brought him out of his thoughts.

Just as he was about to discuss a strategy for attack, he heard the front and back doors burst open. Crowding around each of the doors was a hoard of pirates. They pushed through the stone portals with weapons drawn.

"Here is our sleeping Royal Guard," sneered the polished, red-bearded pirate he had seen earlier. "We were wondering if you'd be getting up. Nothing ever happens in Honolulu on a sleepy Monday night. All the ships that were expected to come today have done so. And the King was having a dinner party with the senior members of the government around him, and the loyal chamberlain at his side. So there was no need to keep a watch on the King, was there?"

The red-bearded man started giving orders to his men to take the weapons and tie up the men. The Major continued his thought. *So he did know of the Royal Guard. The pirates seemed to know the inner workings of the militia and the government much better than they should.*

A man with a large coil of rope walked up to Major Hayley and asked him to turn. As he was being tied with the rope, the Major thought. *Captain Aldrich and the Honolulu Rifles are now our only hope.*

# Chapter 10: *Honolulu Rifles*

Captain Aldrich walked to his bedroom after the clock bells of Kawaiahaʻo Church struck its last chime at 11 o'clock. The clock would remain silent until 6 am in the morning. Before he could disrobe, a loud knock came from his front door. *What kind of rude person would be up knocking on someone's door at this time of night?* He picked up his lit table candle and walked briskly to the door.

He opened the door to find a kanaka standing there. The native Hawaiian had obviously been running and gasping for breath. The man said that he had been stopped in the street and was told by a private in the Royal Guard to fetch Captain Aldrich and the Honolulu Rifles. The King and his dinner guests had been captured and the Royal Guard needed the Rifles help to drive out the pirates.

"My God," said the Captain. "Wait a moment. I want you to take me back to the palace. But I must get my pistol." The man nodded in acknowledgement. The Captain was back at his front door a short while later with his pistol and sword, but the man was gone.

Thinking that the man may have been drunk or that it might be a ploy to lure him from his house to then steal from him, the Captain stood in his door to weigh his options. Disbanded years ago, the Honolulu Rifles had just been reformed earlier in the year. They were an all-haole, or Caucasian, group of volunteers dedicated to a securing Hawaiʻi. If what the man had said was true, then this would be the first chance for the Honolulu Rifle Company to show itself.

He decided it was worth the risk, but he had to at least confirm the story before gathering the men. He headed toward Iolani Palace.

Staying as best as he could in the deep shadows, he made his way finally to the northeastern corner of the palace grounds wall. The wall structure was made of a stone footing and wrought-iron fencing. The fencing attached to large stone columns spaced at regular intervals. The Captain moved quickly from column to column until he could get a clear view of the palace and the barracks.

Straining at first in the low amount of light cast by the quarter moon and the outdoor lanterns, Captain Aldrich soon confirmed the story relayed by the man at his front door. The man had disappeared because he had most likely decided that he did not want to be put himself in danger.

It was time to get his men. He knew where a few of his lieutenants lived, so he would go to them first. They could then collect the rest of the company. By the time he arrived at the house of his most trusted lieutenant, it was a five minutes before midnight.

After minutes of nervous, loud knocking by the Captain, the lieutenant came bleary eyed to his front door. He opened it slightly and the Captain saw the barrel of a pistol emerge first.

"It's me, Captain Aldrich. We have a dire emergency on our hands. Let me get off this street and tell you most hastily."

The lieutenant swung opened his door and let the Captain in. "Yes sir, Captain. Please enter."

The Captain walked straight into the man's meager sitting room. He then proceeded to tell him what he knew.

"The fact that they have taken both the palace and the barracks means they have likely taken control of the city as well. I have heard no shots fired, so this has been a surprise attack. We need to rally the men and take back our city."

The lieutenant seemed anything but eager. "Sir, we are volunteer force with little training together. And we have just a few pistols and knives."

49

"What about the rifles? I am new here, but after all, we are the Honolulu Rifles."

"The King just approved our formation a few months ago, sir. We have brand new rifles, but unfortunately we have no ammunition. The guns have never been fired."

"No ammunition?" The Captain was visibly stunned. "Well send some men down to the stores in town to requisition some powder and ammo."

"Didn't you just say sir that the town was under the pirate's control?"

"Oh. . .yes I did. Well that's just my assumption. Go take a few men and see if you can make your way downtown. Maybe you can sneak into one of the supply stores and get what you need."

"I'm willing to try sir. But remember, we're a volunteer company. I can't be sure if anyone will rally considering the odds."

"Well on with it, man. We must at least try."

"Yes sir, Captain. I'll be on my way. I'll bring the group back here. You stay here and keep an eye out for our return."

The lieutenant gazed carefully up and down the street. He then headed eastward – staying in the shadows as best as he could.

"Good luck," said the Captain in a whisper as he shut the lieutenant's door.

***

An hour passed and the Captain had seen no sign of the lieutenant or anyone else on the street. He had pulled up a chair and had kept riveted to the window. Not being accustomed to being awake and out at this time of night, he had no idea if the lack of people was normal.

Finally he saw movement up the street in the shadows. He caught a glimpse of the men as they moved rapidly by a gas street lamp to the next shadow. Yes, it was the lieutenant. It certainly was not the entire company with him and he didn't appear to be carrying any extra weapons.

They hesitated momentarily in the darkness cast by the entrance of a building on the opposite side of the street. They were undoubtedly worried about being caught in the open if they crossed. Courageous hearts soon prevailed and they raced across the street toward the lieutenant's house. As they neared his door, the men stopped. Seconds later the Captain heard a man shouting at them from down the street.

The lieutenant looked back at the Captain peering through the window, and shook his head. Then he raised his hands. From the west came a group of about twenty-five armed men with weapons raised. They grabbed the meager weapons from the lieutenant and the other men.

The Captain, having seen his men's capture, bowed his head. *Honolulu is lost.*

***

It had been hours since Major Hayley and the Royal Guard had been surrounded and captured in the barracks at the palace. He had given up hope that Captain Aldrich would save them. The man sent for the Captain either never reached him, or worst yet, the Rifles were also captured. The Major's hands were almost numb from the tight ropes that bound his hands behind his back. His chance came when one of the Royal Guards leaned up behind his back and used his fingers to loosen the Major's ropes.

After minutes of effort, the ropes fell from the Major's hands. He kept his hands behind his back so as to not draw attention to himself. Once the feeling returned to Major's hands, he began to work to free the soldier who had freed him.

They whispered a scheme of attack. The Major had noted that there was now only one man guarding each of the two entrances to the barracks. Even with more than seventy men, the ranks of

50

the pirates would be getting thinned as they expanded their reign on the city. They used the force of many to capture and then left only two to secure.

The Major had decided that they should untie a few more men and then try to overpower the pirate at the southern entrance. The guard at the northern entrance would race in to help his fallen mate. At that moment, the Major would dart out the northern entrance and try to find help or Captain Aldrich if he wasn't already captured. While he was going for help, the Royal Guard would try to take the second pirate too, which would give them two loaded rifles with ammunition.

Three more of the men were untied, which the Major felt was enough. When he gave the word, the four guardsmen jumped up and charged the pirate at the southern entrance. Just as he hoped, the Major saw the second pirate guarding the northern entrance move swiftly to help his mate. As soon as the pirate passed by him, the Major leapt up and ran out through the north entrance of the barracks. As he headed to the west, he looked back one last time to confirm his escape was unnoticed. He stopped momentarily to observe the rifle butts come down on the four men that had assisted in his escape. *Brave men he would have to reward. . .if they made it out of this.*

The Major had run only a few steps from the barracks entrance when he tripped over the first of the Krupp cannons. As he fell, he reached out to catch himself. His left hand extended ahead of him and when he hit the ground he felt a severe pain in his left wrist. It had landed on a second canon. He rolled on the ground a few seconds holding his wrist with his right hand. It was all he could do to keep from screaming in agony. The left wrist began to swell immediately and he worried he had broken it. He wrapped it in strips that he had ripped from his shirt.

The pain eventually subsided enough for him to regain his composure. His eyes were now getting used to the darkness and he could see the line of cannons laying on the ground. Their mounts were unassembled and still leaning against wall of the barracks from the day they had arrived.

He could hear that the scuffle inside the barracks had been squelched, and then the pirates warning that the next such act would be resulting in death. It would be only a matter of minutes before they realized he was missing. He had to distance himself from the barracks.

The Major cradled his arm and managed to stand again. There were no lights on to the north, but he could see pirates on the lit streets to the south of, and all around the palace. Another gang was also moving through the stores to the west; they were stealing whatever silver or valuables they saw fit. His only choice was to use the darkness as cover and move to the north.

He managed to stay clear of the roaming pirate gangs around the residence the royals used while the palace was being built, and continued in the direction of Punchbowl Crater. The ancient volcanic crater loomed up over the northern edge of the city and at the foot of the Koolau Mountain Range. The Major had remembered that a couple of cannons sat at its rim. They were placed there by King Kamehameha to welcome the arrival of important visitors. He hadn't heard them fire in a while, but he hoped powder and shot still sat by the cannons. He knew he couldn't take the pirates on, but maybe he could bluff them into thinking there was an army battalion still around. Others might rally there too if they heard the cannons. Even if he couldn't use the cannons, he'd at least get a good view of the pirate activity and strategize in the morning.

He arrived near the base of the crater and noticed a series of dwellings amongst plowed fields. He hadn't visited the area in a long time and had forgotten that a settlement had started a few years earlier. Sugarcane and some vegetable gardens were the main crops. Fearing he might be mistaken for either a thief or one of the pirates, he stayed clear of the homes. He finally came upon a larger field of chest-high sugarcane.    Although he couldn't tell for sure in the darkness, it appeared to be growing part the way up the crater. He decided the sugarcane would give him cover and allow him to get to the top the fastest and undetected, so he headed up the nearest open path.

Major Hayley making good time, but he was stumbling often on the volcanic rocks that had been loosened during the tilling of the soil. He had to stop and rest for a few times. The lack of sleep and the constant exertion was taking its toll. At three in the morning, he found himself exhausted and near the end of the fields.    Just as he thought about stopping again, he tripped on a rock and fell to the ground. His heard a bone in his already injured wrist snap and he cried out loud. He sat up and rocked back and forth reeling from the pain.

He soon comprehended his predicament. He left wrist was severely injured. He was absolutely depleted of energy and was thirsty. Even if he made it up to the top, he'd have only one arm and no strength to fire the cannons. He was defeated.

He decided that he should just sit where he was and wait for morning. Tripping over more rocks in the darkness was not an option. The path here was a few feet wide and he had the cover of the sugarcane to hide his location. If he rested the remainder of the night, then he might be able to make his way up to the top of the crater in the morning.

As his breathing came under control, he could begin to hear the trade winds rustling the leaves of the sugarcane stalks, and the sounds of nature. Soon he heard the movement of animals – so much so that he began to worry. The start and stop of whatever was out there was disturbing and his imagination began to get to him. Try as he might, it was just too dark to see anything.

He's fears finally got the best of him. He reached in his vest pocket for a match and rested it in his lap. He searched in the darkness and pulled several stones near him. It was going to be difficult to light a match and throw a stone, but he'd have to be ready. He struck the match and light burst free into the darkness. The match flame flickered in the breeze, but stayed lit as he raised his arm. All around in the edges of the sugarcane he saw tiny reflecting orbs. Then just within the edge of the light he saw an almost foot long black body with long tail run across the path. *Rats. Wonderful.*

He checked to see if he was bloody at all, and he wasn't. The last thing he wanted was to fight off an army of rats thirsty for blood.    He transferred the match to his almost useless left hand, and picked up a small stone and threw it in the direction of the beady eyes. They scattered, but then slowly started to reappear just as the match burnt out. For the next two hours he sat throwing rocks in the directions of sounds and movements.

As the light of early morning appeared, the Major finally got a reprieve from the rats. Although he had not slept, he felt that he had regained some energy. Standing upright, he observed the Hawaiian flag up on the rim, where the cannons would be. So he began his walk upward on a footpath he found at the end of the sugarcane fields.

He had only walked a short distance on the path when he heard the twigs crackle in the vegetation growing along the path. A small brownish animal, a little larger than a squirrel, popped out on the path. Its sudden appearance alarmed the Major until he realized he was looking at one of Hawai'i's newest residents. It was a mongoose. He noticed another one rise up from a burrow close to the path.

The Major stopped for a moment and as his wits returned, he thought about what he had just seen. He gazed back at the field and saw no movements from any of the rats. *Gibson is an idiot. He brought a fast breeding animal to Hawai'i to kill the rat infestation. But rats are nocturnal and mongoose hunt by day. I can't wait to bring this up to the King; that is, if he is still alive.*

52

# Chapter 11: *The Mayor and the DA*

The morning came too early for the Bryant family. Rick was the first to appear in the hotel suite's large living room. He walked to the counter and started coffee brewing.

Soon Danielle, Shelli, Nikki and Stephanie sauntered into the room. They sat on the opposing couches and viewed the Pacific in the floor-to-ceiling windows that spanned one side of their room.

"After coffee, let's head down and get some breakfast," said Rick. "I've got to get over to the ship before going into police headquarters to sign the non-disclosure documents. Do you guys think you can get ready in about twenty minutes?"

"Dad, I look too ratchet to go down like I am. I need a shower," said Shelli with a frown on her face.

"What did you say?" ask Rick

Nikki giggled and then translated. "She's ratchet. That means she is too messy – unfit to be seen by others. Not sure, though, why this morning is different than any other time."

"Hey, I'm standing right here," said Shelli.

"Oh, thanks Nikki," chuckled Rick. "That will take a while for showers, even with two bathrooms. Why don't I shower up first and call room service. That way I can get going."

"Sounds good," said Danielle. "I'm kind of hungry this morning. Make it a big breakfast with some fruit – fresh pineapple and papaya." Rick nodded and reached for the phone.

"I'll text Ryan and let him know to come over in a few minutes," said Nikki.

"You better or he'll sleep through the morning," said his sister.

An hour later the family, Stephanie, and Ryan were eating breakfast together. A quick discussion confirming the day's activities and a tentative plan to meet up in the afternoon was agreed upon.

Rick was on his way to the ship with Ryan and Nikki at 9 AM.

***

It was a few minutes past 10 AM at Honolulu police headquarters and Kaleho's stomach churned at the information his front desk sergeant had just given him. The mayor and the DA were coming up to see him. He expected they were both anxious for a progress report and upset at the lack of results. He was debating whether or not he should mention the possible motive that the Bryant's had brought up last night.

A knock on his door a few minutes later signaled his guests had arrived. Both the mayor and the DA stepped in. Kaleho stood and came around his desk to shake hands with the men.

After a cordial greeting, the mayor initiated his tirade. "I came into the office a few minutes ago and it was a madhouse on my doorstep! The press were standing there demanding answers for the worst monthly murder record in Honolulu's history. And now they know a student at the university is dead. And it happened during my administration! How am I going to convince the voters that I'm strong on crime when we can't stop the killings?" The mayor sat down, clearly exhausted. Kaleho imagined the mayor was lacking sleep these days. "To top it off, I've got to go talk to the governor this afternoon. Please tell me you've made some kind of progress Kaleho."

Kaleho was the youngest chief of police in the long history of the Honolulu Police when he took the position. Even though he was much younger than the mayor, he was still the chief and would not cower at such attitude. "Mayor Dearborn, we've finally found a link between all the murders. It is this coin." Kaleho placed the Hawaiian coin on his desk. "Apparently the Blue Hawai'i Spring Water employees had taken it from the student, Paul Chang, for payment of his friend's gambling debt."

Kaleho continued to describe the paths taken by both Blue Hawai'i employees and how someone then retraced those steps and killed anyone that had seen the coin, up to and including Paul Chang.

"We are trying to figure out the link between the coin and the murders. And I've got my officers scouring the island for Paul's brother and his friend. We believe they are the key to the murders," concluded Kaleho. He decided it was best not to mention the possibility that a colossal sum of the coins may be the motive. There wasn't sufficient evidence to conclude this, and he knew the prosecuting attorney for Honolulu would remind him of it.

"I heard the Bryants are here now on the island," said District Attorney Kiyoshi. "You know I'm not happy about bringing in a family on this important case. We look bad enough now as it is. Of all the available expert criminal consultants and profilers, you bring in amateurs. I assume you've met them. Are you still planning to use them?"

"Yes sir, I did meet them. And I'm more convinced than ever it was the right thing to do," answered Kaleho. "And if you saw what they have at their disposal like I did last night, you would change your mind about them."

"Hardly. I'd rather see some good old fashion detective work. And I heard something about mobile phones they gave you. What is that all about?"

Kaleho had asked his men to keep it quiet in the morning briefing when he passed out the phones. *Loose lips sink ships.* He'd have to remind them again at tomorrow's meeting. He anticipated more ridicule headed his way for what he was about to say.

"I brought the phones in late yesterday for our lab guys to check out and then program with search phrases. The phones monitor social media and will notify us when the victim's brother and friend surface. The phones were handed out today at the morning briefing. We-"

"You have the Honolulu police surfing Facebook with taxpayer money? We're going to be the laughing stock of the Pacific when the newspapers get wind of this. I can see the headlines now." said the DA as he shook his head.

Kaleho was getting upset. These two elected officials had no actual experience doing police work and instead of asking how they could help, they kept pestering him. They were relentless with their emails and calls with ridiculous instructions on how to do his job. "That's uncalled for Sir. No one here is surfing the Internet or posting on Facebook. The officers don't have to do anything with the phones. They are automatically notified if the phones detect either Paul Chang's brother or friend."

"I can't believe you —." The DA was interrupted knock on the door, which then opened.

"Excuse me, Sir. You told me to let you know if anyone spotted Stephen Chang or his brother's friend, Stan Johnson. One of those Bryant phones signaled Joe Tyler and his partner Kinh Lee over near Keanu and 7th Avenue. And sure enough they saw him hiding at the school within about a 100 feet of the signal. They are bringing him in now."

"Thanks Bob, I'll be right out," said Kaleho. Bob closed the door.

The DA's back was still facing him. He dropped his head and was silent, probably trying to figure out how not to look embarrassed. Kaleho broke the brief silence. "Well gentlemen, it appears the Bryant technology found in two hours what we haven't been able to do for days now. Unless there is something else you need, I have get back to work." He didn't wait for an answer and started walking to the door. "I'll let you see yourself out." For the first time in weeks, Kaleho felt in command as he left the meeting.

# Chapter 12: *We are Weak*

Gibson was aroused awake by the rather obnoxious voice of the red-bearded leader of the pirate gang. He didn't believe it was possible to sleep sitting up in a chair with his feet and hands bound tight, but exhaustion had finally set in sometime during the night. He swiveled his head and observed that everyone else was awake in their chairs, looking tired and disheveled.

The pirate leader continued with his oration, "...as I said, we have been able to rob the treasury, the Royal Hawaiian Hotel, the homes and the businesses of many of your city's wealthy patrons, like Bishop, Irwin, Macfarlane, Dillingham, Wiseman, and Berger. And we have taken everything of value from your home. We were able to do this with one ship of men without a single shot being fired. Imagine if we had several ships? Imagine if we had a small navy? We could ransack the entire kingdom with such a navy. Think about this, when we leave."

The last sentence caught Gibson's attention. *They are leaving? This is unbelievable. But are they going to kill us before they leave?*

Almost on cue, the leader continued. "In a few moments, we're going to cut you free. But only those of you in the palace that are not militia. Your soldiers, the police, and all the other people we have tied up throughout the city will remain so. You will wait for one hour before you release your guard or anyone else. There will be no shouting or calling for help. No one will step foot out of this place. And if you think we will not see you, then you're mistaken. I have a crewman sitting in the crow's nest of our ship with a powerful eyeglass. If we see any movement from here, we'll fire our cannons on the city. If you send a ship for us after we leave, I will remind you that we are well armed, and we will fight. And even if you do miraculously defeat us, we'll sink your treasure to the bottom of the sea."

"You have my word that we will stay here until you leave," answered the King agonizingly.

"Your word means nothing to me," interrupted the leader before the King could continue. "I have warned you all."

"Are you coming back?" Gibson heard himself say.

"Should I?" replied the pirate leader. "Is there something of value that I left?"

The King strained his neck to give Gibson a look that could kill. "N...N...No," stuttered Gibson.

"Well then. If we're not followed and you can follow my instructions, you should never see me again," said the leader. "But I can almost promise you that others will follow in my steps...especially if word of this raid leaves the country."

With that, he walked out the front door. He nodded to one of the pirates guarding the door. The man pulled out a large knife and started walking toward the hostages with a smirk on his face. Fortunately for the King and his guests, the man cut the ropes on their wrists, leaving their legs still bound. As the last hostage's wrists were freed, the man left quickly through the front door. The King and his guests waited a few minutes and then untied their ankles. Then all stood slowly and stiffly walked to the front doors and windows. They watched as the entire pirate gang walked briskly with the last of their loot in sacks swung over their shoulders. Some even pushed wheel burrows filled with shiny silver, gold, picture frames, vases, and all sorts of personal possessions. As Gibson peered through the doors' glass windows, his eyes changed focus to the Roman goddesses etched in the glass. He was reminded of the sacking of Rome.

Mr. Neumann finally broke the silence. "Your Majesty, what are you going to do?"

"What do you mean?" asked the King. "You heard the man. I'm not going to jeopardize any lives. We'll stay put for an hour."

"No, I mean what about after they leave? We've got to let someone know. They've got money and national treasures. We've got to stop them."

"You listen here, Mr. Neumann. By royal decree there will be prison time for anyone who mentions this night's events in public speech or print. Make sure you tell all the other editors. There will be no story printed today, tomorrow, or ever," said the King in a commanding voice.

He walked away from the door and rubbed his eyes. "I was thinking about this during the night. These men had information about us. . .they knew exactly where and how to strike. Did you hear the names of the people they robbed? Some of our richest citizens. . .all with close ties to my family, the monarchy. They knew our weaknesses. . .they picked Monday night to attack. The weekend would have had too many people on the streets. But this is the first Monday after the New Moon. The least amount of light. And a lot of visitors left for San Francisco on the *Alameda* today. But because it's near Christmas, they knew that the wealthy would be home from travels. And they knew merchandise had been arriving for weeks for Christmas. The papers have been covering the fact that we are negotiating with America about the Treaty. The Treaty is going to be signed in less than a week, so they knew we would be having meetings. Meetings here in the palace."

The King was pacing now. "The Treaty is key to our prosperity. They know that if we were to let word get out, then America might think we're too weak. America wants to put their naval depot here, and we need to expand the sale of sugarcane there. It's unprecedented access to America's dinner tables. If word gets out of this, it could stop or at least stall the Treaty. And of course, you heard what the leader said. If it is printed in the papers we will be the target of more pirates. Or worse, we could be targeted by expansionists in other nations. You saw our militia's performance. We are weak."

"No gentlemen, we will say absolutely nothing about tonight. We will bear our losses and get on with our business. I will meet with the rest of the government and force funding for better defenses. Nothing will be printed or said about this. I will consider it an act of treason to mention this again."

The King absentmindedly reached for his watch, which had been taken earlier by the pirates. Instead of asking the time, shook his head and looked defeated. "I am going upstairs to rest. When one hour and fifteen minutes have passed, have my staff go out and start untying the Royal Guard. And I leave it to all of you to make sure you spread the word of my decree. No one will speak of this foul night again."

With that, the King started his ascent up the long wooden staircase to his quarters on the second floor. He never looked back as he ascended, even as the whispers and scuttle of staff and guests climbed to a dull roar within the Great Hall.

# Chapter 13: *Chang*

It was 10:30 AM and Rick was in the process of unloading equipment and Nikki's vehicle off the ship when he got a call. It was Kaleho. He answered, "Hi Kaleho. Let me guess, you need to change the time of the meeting."

"Hi Rick. No, but I'd like to change the place. Can we make it eleven o'clock at your boat?"

Rick was surprised, "Sure, but I thought I needed to sign some forms." His phone dinged and he took it away from his ear to see that he had just received an email from Kaleho.

"I just sent you an email," said Kaleho. "The forms are attached. Get them signed as soon as you can and send them back. And I don't want you to come to the precinct. The press is here, and I don't want anyone to know you and the family are on the case. You'll be safer and more effective without the publicity."

"Looks like I just got the email," said Rick. "I'll stop what I'm doing and get them signed and back to you immediately."

"Thanks, and I have more news. Your phones worked. We have Paul's brother."

"Wow, that's awesome," said Rick.

"Yes it is. But I want to bring him to your boat to be interviewed. I don't want anyone to see Paul's brother enter the precinct. If he knows the answer as to why all those victims were murdered, I don't want to put his life in jeopardy by plastering his face on the evening news being brought into police headquarters."

"That's fine. I'll let the crew take leave. It will be Nikki, Ryan, Shelli, Stephanie, and me here. Danielle is at the museum. I'll let her know what's going on."

"Sounds good. I'm heading there in the Chevelle now. A police car and two officers should be arriving about the same time as I do. Don't let anyone else onboard."

*\*\*\**

Around the conference room table sat Paul Chang's brother, Rick, Shelli, Nikki, Ryan, Stephanie and Kaleho. The two officers that had found the brother were told to keep his location quiet and to return to their normal patrol duties.

Kaleho made introductions of each of the Bryant team and then said, "...and this is Stephen Chang, older brother of the victim Paul Chang. I'm sorry for your loss, Stephen. I'm sure you don't know who to trust, but the reason you are here is for your own protection. The Bryant family has been hired as consultants on this case to help us solve these murders. This is their boat and it is one of their many tools they use in solving cases. Given the press is camping out at police headquarters, I thought this is the best place to talk to you."

"I don't know anything about my brother's death," said Stephen. "All I know is that I was visited by a member of the triad and was fortunate to walk away from the encounter. He asked about a coin and my brother, and I told him I had no idea what he was talking about. He obviously believed me, which is why I am still alive. After that visit, I kept trying to call Paul and couldn't reach him, so I headed to the campus to find out what was going on. When I got there, I found the police had cordoned off his room. I questioned a few students and finally one told me that a local student had been killed. Then I saw Paul's roommate, so it didn't take much for me to assume my brother was dead. That's why I went into hiding."

"Do you know Stan Johnson?" asked Kaleho.

"That's one of Paul's friends, why?"

"Stan is missing. Do you know if Paul or Stan were involved in anything questionable? Illegal?"

"I don't know Stan other than by appearance. But I can tell you my brother was a good kid. He would give you the shirt off his back if he thought you needed help. I refuse to believe he could do anything illegal." Stephen placed both hands on the table and looked squarely at Kaleho when he talked of his brother's innocence.

"I see. You mentioned there was a tong or triad member that contacted you. How did you know he was a member?"

"Tats. Then he told me not to go anywhere. I don't feel comfortable talking about them. It would be a certain death sentence if they find out I'm talking with you."

"We're going to protect you, Stephen," assured Kaleho. "Do you know which triad the man was with?"

"No," said Stephen curtly.

Sensing Stephen was ready to stop talking, Kaleho decided to ask the question everyone else at the table was wondering about. "You said the triad member asked about a coin. What coin do you think he meant?" asked Kaleho.

Stephen seemed a little anxious, but answered "I don't know. It's like I said, I don't know anything."

Kaleho pulled out one of the Hawaiian coins from an evidence bag and placed it on the table. "Your brother gave this to an enforcer to cover a gambling debt that Stan couldn't pay. Have you seen this coin before?"

Stephen looked like he'd seen a ghost. "He gave them one of these?" he asked.

"Yes, he did," answered Kaleho. "And we found others hidden in his room. Do you know anything about this?"

"I can't believe he did this. He should have never had this at school," said Stephen, not caring that he had just lied. "He knows better."

"What's the significance of this coin? We know they are worth at least $700 each, but that's not worth enough to kill someone over. What's the scoop?"

"These coins should have never been shown to anyone. I don't know their significance, but our grandfather showed us a handful of coins like this years ago. He mentioned an old Chinese legend that said a fortune in coins and other treasures were hidden by our ancestors here in Hawai'i. Grandfather said that the coins he had were kept as a reminder of the treasure. Something happened – I believe he said a massive fire – that wiped out our ancestor's neighborhood. No one knows what happened to the treasure after that fire. He said that these coins were the only remaining proof the treasure existed." He paused for few seconds thinking. "Damn it," he said to himself.

"What?" asked Kaleho. "Did you remember something else?"

"Well I just remembered the last time my grandfather talked about it. He said that if anyone discovered these coins, the family could be in serious danger. I don't know why Paul had the coins, or how he even got them. But grandfather was definitely right."

Rick had been quiet. He understood that Kaleho needed to connect with Stephen to pull the information. This was the first time Rick had been allowed to sit in an interrogation, so he sat in awe of the process. But, as a parent of a daughter almost the same age as Stephen, he couldn't hold back anymore. "Where is your family – your parents and sister, Stephen?" asked Rick.

"My parents, sister, and all my other relatives live on Maui. My family went into hiding."

"We thought they were on vacation," said Kaleho.

"No, that's what they told people. They own a small store. I don't remember my parents ever taking a vacation since I was old enough to remember. My mom would say, 'Why do we need a vacation? We live in paradise.' They're hiding with friends of the family."

"How did they find out about Paul? We didn't see any calls or emails from you to them."

"I Skyped my sister about his death and told them to hide. I told her to borrow a friend's phone and not to use her own. I've been talking to her using direct Tweets."

"What school did you send the message from?" asked Rick.

"The small school on 7th. My grandfather teaches Mandarin there. The school is closed most of the month of August, so I have been staying in the bed in their infirmary."

Kaleho turned to Rick. "He was near that location when we found him."

"Yeah, Grandfather gave me a cell phone from the school. It was a smart phone and had all standard apps...Facebook, Twitter. The Facebook account on the phone was public, and had no friends. So in addition to the direct Tweets, I told my sister to also watch for random posts from that Facebook account. I was walking south on 7th to get something to eat. I tried to stay clear of sidewalks and streets and was cutting through the elementary school when I made a post that said I had no word on Paul's murder. Before I knew it, two cops were right there."

"Where are your grandparents now?" asked Rick.

"My grandmother died a few years ago, but my grandfather lives near the school."

Rick swiveled in his chair toward Kaleho, who was already punching on his phone. "You need to pick him up, Kaleho."

"I know," said Kaleho. "I'm calling Joe and Kinh to tell them to pick him up. Hey Stephen, what's the address for your grandfather?"

# Chapter 14: *Daily Alta*

"Hi Mom," said Shelli on her phone.

Danielle was checking in and got the entire story about Stephen and the lost treasure. Shelli completed the story with, "Ryan took Stephen down to ship's galley. Stephen hadn't eaten much in the last few days, so Ryan was going to make him up a good lunch."

"Oh my goodness," said Danielle. "What an eventful morning."

"How's your visit at the museum going?"

"Thanks for asking, honey. It's going well," replied Danielle. "I'm about to wrap up the meeting on the art exhibit we're organizing. The curator I'm meeting with is taking me over to meet with the head of the library and research group within Bishop. I'm going to ask them about the coin."

"Why don't you use your tablet PC and use Go-To-Meeting. I'm sure Dad is going to want to ask more questions given all that has been going on. Plus I've been doing more research myself and have come up with some interesting finds."

"That's a good idea, Shelli. I've got a picture of the coin on my tablet, so I can describe it to her too. Let's plan to have the meeting in twenty minutes."

"OK, Mom. But remember, don't mention anything about the case yet. Kaleho didn't want us to talk to anyone about this without him present. Oh, and I'll send you a meeting notice to your email address. That way you can just click on it to log in to Go-To-Meeting."

"Thanks, honey. Bye."

***

At the conference room table onboard the **Amphitrite** sat Kaleho, Rick, and Stephanie. Shelli and Nikki sat at two of the many command stations that ringed the room. In the front of the room was a large display that was tiled with videos of people, photos of the coins, and a notepad for logging known facts.

Danielle's face appeared in a square tile in the upper left-hand side of the large display. Another person appeared in the lower left-hand side, and Shelli's face appeared in the middle left-hand side square.

"Hi guys, I'd like to introduce Barbara Stallings," said Danielle. "My tablet screen was a little too small, so she logged in from her computer. I'm sitting right next to her in her office. Barbara is head of the library research branch of the Bishop Museum." Barbara was warmly greeted by the group."

"I'm happy to meet all of you," said Barbara. "Danielle showed me a photograph of the coin. I'm not by any means a numismatist, but this appears to be an authentic Hawaiian coin you have. The fact that it tarnishes implies a high silver content. I suppose that if you weigh it, you could be certain it was the real thing. Or you could simply compare it to the one we have here at the museum."

"You have one of these?" asked Rick.

"Yes, we have one of each of the coins minted that year. Each coin is quite rare. This was called the Akahi Dala, which was equal in value to one US Dollar at the time. The US Mint coined this and the other three denominations in 1883. It has King Kalākaua's profile on the coin and his coat of arms on the reverse. It became available to the general population in Hawaii in 1884. But it was a failure as coins go."

"Why were they a failure?" asked Stephanie.

"By this time, the kingdom had formed its own monetary system. They used US coins, but they also used tokens. The tokens were basically like coins, but usually struck in less precious metals like pewter, and were commissioned by the railroad companies, ranches, and large plantations. Locals knew the value of those coins and all merchants accepted them. Even after the Akahi Dala and the other coins were minted, these tokens continued to be created and circulated."

"A large number of coins were not melted down in 1903," said Nikki. "And only a small amount of the coins seem to be held by collectors. Do you know what happened to the rest?"

Barbara paused a moment and looked perplexed. "I have never been asked that question before. No, I'm afraid I don't know."

"Where did the museum get its set of coins?" asked Rick.

"The Bernice Pauahi Bishop Museum was opened in 1889. These coins were only six years old at the time. The Museum acquired its set sometime in the 1890's. I need to look it up again. I didn't write down the date when the last gentleman called."

"When did this gentleman call, and do you know his name?" asked Kaleho.

"Oh it was about a month ago. He sounded to be a young man. I can't remember his name though. His last name was Asian, I think."

"Would it have been Paul Chang?" asked Kaleho.

"Yes, why I do believe that was it," replied Barbara. "May I ask why there so much interest in these coins? We get an occasional question about them and since we have a certified set, we get coin collectors interested in them. But I've never had the police question me about them."

"Ms. Stallings, I apologize, but I can't tell you why. We're in the middle of a confidential police investigation," answered Kaleho. "I hope you understand."

Sensing the teleconference was almost over, Shelli raised her hand, "Excuse me, but I think I have some information that might be important to the case. And I would like to ask Ms. Stallings about it while she is available."

"Shelli, can you share what you found with Kaleho and me first?" asked Rick. "Then we'll show it to the Ms. Stallings if appropriate."

"Sure," said Shelli.

"Ms. Stallings, we're going to mute your connection," said Rick.

In the silent digital feed coming from their computers, Danielle and Barbara could see Rick and Kaleho get up from their seats and walk around behind Shelli. She pointed at her screen several times and seemed to be stepping quickly through a hypothesis. A look of surprise came to Kaleho and he leaned in for a closer view of the computer screen. Shelli touched the screen with two fingers and flicked them outward, which made the content larger. The three continued to discuss some points and Kaleho nodded his head in approval of some comment by Rick. Then they sat back down and Rick enabled the sound again.

"I'm sorry for the delay Ms. Stallings," said Rick. "We decided to allow Shelli to share with you some interesting information. We would like your opinion on what she has to say."

"Ok, and please, call me Barbara."

Shelli ignored the last request, "Ms. Stallings, I was researching all the references I could find on these coins on the Internet. I found a reference to a pirate raid in 1884 in Honolulu. Supposedly millions were stolen from the treasury, including the 1883 coins. Are you familiar with that story?"

Barbara thought for a while, then said "No, I don't recall anything like this from that time period. Due to the fall of the monarchy in the 1893, the time leading up to that event is well studied. We have virtually all newspapers and documents from that time. I personally review those materials often. I can't recall any mention of a pirate raid. The law and its enforcement was well established in that time period. I find it unlikely that a record of the raid doesn't exist somewhere in our records. I can check if you like, but I doubt the credibility of an undocumented Internet source."

"I would agree with you, Ms. Stallings, about reliability of sources on the Internet. They teach us that in school these days. I found the description first on a treasure hunting website that seems to be respected."

"Shelli, I would not call a treasure hunting site a credible source. It would need to be a police report, newspaper account, or the like."

"I agree with you, Ms. Stallings, even though the source on the site was a historian. How about an account of the raid in a well-respected San Francisco newspaper?" Shelli slid her finger across her display toward the large display hosting the teleconference. There was a newspaper article from the Daily Alta California dated December 15, 1884.

"The newspaper printed this account of the event. It was told by a ship's crewman that had just returned from the islands. The paper deemed the man credible and printed the story."

Barbara furrowed her brow and squinted to read the article. "Hmmm. Yes, I am familiar with this paper and it is reputable. But still, just because it was a newspaper article in a respected paper doesn't mean it truly happened. Especially if it was a single, uncorroborated eyewitness account."

"Shelli, I'd like to make a suggestion," said Rick. "Why don't you take this offline and discuss the story with Barbara? We don't need to hear all the details, we just need to connect the dots between the events we discussed earlier and the coins."

"Actually Rick, Barbara is a valuable member of the staff here and she is quite busy," said Danielle. "She did me a big favor just to sit in on this call. I know this is an important case, but we need to be respectful of her time."

"That's all right, Danielle. I appreciate your concern. But I find this quite intriguing," said Barbara. She rubbed her chin as in thought. "Is it possible to have Shelli come over and help me research this? I would be willing to check out this story this afternoon, but I could use some help."

Shelli spun in her chair with a look of excitement. "Can I Dad? Stephanie too?"

Rick nodded, "Of course. Upload your findings to one of the tablet PC's and get ready. I'll drive you over." Rick turned back to the big screen. "Barbara, do you have time for some lunch first? It's the least I can do for all your help."

Daily Alta California.
VOL. XXXVII. SAN FRANCISCO: MONDAY, DECEMBER 15, 1884. NO. 12,664.
PIRACY.
Honolulu Captured and Sacked by an Armed Force.
The Most Audacious Piratical Raid on Record.
NO ATTEMPT AT RESISTANCE
The King, Public Treasury and Merchants Despoiled.
Over Three Millions in Coin and Plate Carried Off.
CAPTURE OF THE PALACE.
The Town in Possession of the Pirates for Nine Hours.
Not a Blow Was Struck Nor a Shot Fired.
BISHOP'S BANK PLUNDERED
The Piratical Band Supposed to Have Organized in This City.
KENNEDY'S FUNERAL.
His Widow Takes Another "Last Look."
AN OVERWHELMING CROWD.
METHODISM.
FATAL RESULTS.
THREE TOURISTS.
Special Notice
In Order to Reduce our large stock of fine WATCHES, DIAMONDS, JEWELRY, FRENCH CLOCKS, SILVER WARE, etc., we have concluded to deduct a liberal discount from every article we sell. The goods comprise all the latest novelties in our line and will remain marked as heretofore in plain figures, from which the discount will be allowed.
An examination of our prices and quality of goods will satisfy purchasers that we are selling lower than any house on the Pacific Coast.
This inducement is offered especially for Holiday Trade.
LOUIS BRAVERMAN & CO.
119 MONTGOMERY STREET.
WOLFF & RHEINHOLD,
506 BATTERY STREET,
CHAMPAGNE.
PIPER "SEC"
PIPER HEIDSICK
CHAMPAGNE,
Cachet blanc
CABINET
GREEN SEAL
CHARLES MEINECKE & CO.
GERMEA
FOR BREAKFAST.
JOHN T. CUTTING & CO.,
BURRFOLDING BED!
PIANOS
CHINESE
JAPANESE
UNION INSURANCE COMPANY
L. MEININGER,
NOTARY AND COMMISSIONER,
DR. ZEILE'S
AGE! YOUTH!
HOLIDAY PRESENTS
Muller's Optical Depot.

*Daily Alta December 15, 1884*[1]

---

[1] From California Digital Newspaper Collection: http://cdnc.ucr.edu/cgi-bin/cdnc?a=d&d=DAC18841215.2.1 &srpos=1&e=-------en--20--1--txt-txIN-Daily+Alta+December+15+1884-------1

"That would be lovely," said Barbara. "I'll have my staff pull some books and information from 1884 while we're at lunch. That should help speed up the process."

Rick thanked Barbara and told his wife they would be there soon. As they signed off, Ryan walked in to the room with Stephen.

"Thanks for lunch, Mr. Bryant," said Stephen. "Ryan also filled me in on you and your family. I appreciate all the help."

"No problem, Stephen. I'm just sorry we have to meet under these circumstances." Rick looked at Kaleho. "What's to happen now with Stephen?"

"Good question," said Kaleho. "Is it possible for Stephen to stay onboard the *Amphitrite* for the afternoon? At least until things cool down at the precinct."

"Sure," answered Rick. "We've got plenty of room onboard since we are staying at the hotel. We'll set him up with a room. And my crew will start rotating through in a few hours. They can keep an eye out for him."

"That would be a big load off my mind. Thanks. While you're meeting with Barbara Stallings, I'm going to the precinct to see if my men made any progress on finding Stephen's grandfather and Stan Johnson. And I'm going to place some discrete calls to check on triad activity."

"I'll stay here with Ryan and Stephen, Dad," said Nikki. "We need to get the rest of the equipment and the Audi SUV unloaded. Stephen can help, if he doesn't mind."

"I don't mind ... anything that will help catch my brother's murderers," said Stephen.

"I'll touch bases with you later today," said Kaleho as he started to leave.

"I'll walk you out," said Rick.

As they walked out through the bridge and down to the main deck, Rick and Kaleho talked. "I am impressed that Danielle was able to get such access to the museum and its staff. It has always been helpful when the police needed them on crimes related to artifacts, but this level of access is quite amazing."

"Danielle is way too modest to ever mention it, but she makes a donation each year to several museums. The Bishop was just added this year. That was part of her reason for personally going over there. She said she was going there to make arrangements for an exhibit, but she can make arrangements by phone and email. Once they found she was going to be here in the islands, the chairman insisted on personally thanking her. She had already been a premier member for a couple years, but it was a sizeable donation and I suspect that there's not a department head there that doesn't know her name."

Kaleho remained quiet. *What can one say to a comment like that?* If Rick considered the contribution to be sizeable, Kaleho expected the donation must be many times his pitiful annual salary. Although he was dying to ask, he resisted. "I'll say it again, Rick. You are one lucky man. Snagging her was one of your all-time greatest accomplishments."

"You got that right. We've had those tough times that all couples face, but she's always stuck with me. She's why I'm where I am today."

They walked quietly down the gangplank to the pier.

"I haven't given you enough time to offload your vehicles Rick," said Kaleho. "Do you want me to give you guys a ride to the museum?"

"No, I've got to take Barbara, Danielle, and the girls to lunch. That's too many to fit in a taxi once I get there. It will only take a few minutes for us to offload the SUV."

"I'll stop by after you all get back to the boat later today. I know you guys are probably still jet-lagged, so we'll call it an early day for you." Kaleho started walking toward his car, but then spun around and walked backwards a few steps. "And besides, Leilani wants you guys to come over to dinner tomorrow night. It's been years and the last time you saw Kai he was in elementary school. Stephanie and Ryan are welcome, of course."

"Sure, we'd love to come," said Rick. "See you later."

As Kaleho headed toward his car, Rick walked back up to the ship's main deck. As he stepped onboard, he saw Nikki swinging the large davit with the family's SUV toward the pier. Ryan said "hi, and excuse me" as he ran down the gangplank to be the spotter on the pier. A few minutes later Stephanie and Shelli surfaced. Shelli had a backpack with her, which Rick knew had her tablet PC.

"The car will be ready shortly, Shelli. You and Stephanie wait for me by it. I've got to get something from below deck. I'll be back in a few minutes."

***

Five hundred yards away on the other side of the port sat Peng Li. He was looking through his large binoculars he kept in the control booth of the tall container crane he worked in five days a week. He watched a man walk from the large fishing vessel that had arrived at the port a couple of days before to his wonderfully restored, bright red Chevelle. Although the man wore street clothes, he was pretty sure the man was a Honolulu police officer. He had seen the man carrying a sidearm holstered to his belt with a shiny gold badge attached. The gold color meant he was a Sergeant or higher rank.

Peng had worked at the port for more than five years and he loved it. Steady work, good hours, and the great benefits were wonderful for a man with practically no education. Although Hawai'i has a relatively low employment rate compared to the national average, many of its citizens worked multiple part-time jobs and struggled to make ends meet in the high cost of living that comes with a popular island paradise. He enjoyed weekends with his family and only occasionally was asked to perform some minor task for his benefactor. He had no problems helping that benefactor any time he was asked. He was never paid for that help. His job and cozy way of life more than compensated for whatever was needed of him. After all, it was his benefactor that got him the job, made sure he was properly trained, and guaranteed he would never be fired.

Today was one of those days where he had to use his unique job to gather information. As had been the case in the past, the guard at the front gate gave him a new phone whenever there was a favor needed by his benefactor. The phone explained the job in the phone's notes app. The information would be relayed by text messages to his benefactor from that same phone. When the task was done, the benefactor would tell him to destroy the phone.

For the last week, his instructions were to use his high post on the crane to monitor any new vessels coming into port. And once he had reported the **Amphitrite** had arrived, his instructions were to give continual updates on anyone coming and going from that vessel. This morning he had also been given a camera with a telephoto lens. The resulting pictures from it were much better than his smartphone camera. He was told to snap pictures of anyone new. The camera came with a dozen SDHC cards for storing the pictures. He removed the

66

day's card and left it with the guard at the end of the day.  He had quite a few pictures of the young Asian man that had been escorted to the boat by two police men.  He had reported this via text message.

As Peng reached for his lunch pail, he noticed a large SUV being lowered from the fishing boat.  He picked up his camera and furiously clicked away.  He had suspected there was something strange about the boat from the fact that he had seen no real fishing gear on the deck since it had arrived.  But to see a car being lifted from a fishing boat was something he had never seen before.

Two young haole girls walked off the boat and waited at the car.  Then a man came down and met them.  He was the same man he had seen earlier talking with the police officer.  He was maybe in his late-forties or early fifties; he was fit and wearing shorts and colored short-sleeve shirt.  The man didn't look like a fisherman, pilot or captain.  And why were the girls onboard?  He kept taking pictures until they drove off in the Audi SUV.

He picked up the phone and typed in short sentences describing what he had just seen and hit the send button.   He never received any response back to his text messages and he never met anyone in person other than the guard at the gate.   But he didn't care if he ever spoke or met anyone from his benefactor's organization.  He didn't need to care, he had the perfect job.  He was fine with being a Chai for the rest of his life – a lowly 49.

# Chapter 15: *Numbers Don't Add*

After a pleasant lunch, Rick dropped off Barbara Stallings, Danielle, Shelli and Stephanie back at Bishop Museum. As they stepped out of the vehicle, Rick told Barbara that he had to talk to the girls briefly and that they would be in shortly. She thanked him again for the lovely lunch and headed toward the museum entrance. Rick then raised the back door of the Audi Q7 and flipped open the lid of the black case he had retrieved earlier from the boat. He gave Stephanie, Shelli and Danielle a watch. He instructed them on its use. It had the newest version of the Bluetooth interface to their phones, which had a substantially longer range. The watch also transmitted its own tracking signal via satellite. Rick said that between the Bluetooth connection and the satellite connectivity, he could keep tabs on their position at all times. It also had a built-in mobile phone service to 20 people, which in this case was only programmed for the family, Ryan and Stephanie. It also had an emergency button that signaled all the same programmed numbers and 9-1-1. And the real bonus was the replacement, rechargeable batteries Rick had purchased to replace the original Lithium-Ion batteries allowed them to last almost a full month between charges. After having seen *Back to the Future* for the first time recently, Shelli teasingly asked if they ran on plutonium.

Fortunately Rick had consulted Nikki on the style of the watches, so the Stephanie and Shelli gave no arguments on the design or lack thereof. After the watch orientation, Shelli and Danielle gave him a kiss on the cheek and left with Stephanie for the museum entrance. It was agreed they'd text him when they were finished and he would pick them up.

He turned right out of the Bishop Museum entrance onto Bernice Street, and the right again on Houghtailing Street. As he crossed Dillingham Road, Houghtailing became Waiakamilo Road, which then emptied into the port. However, the port is large with more than one entrance. For their berth, he had to turn left on Nimitz and then the first right at the light. From doorstep to parking to gangplank the drive from Bishop was 1.7 miles.

When he pulled in to park, he noticed a black GMC Yukon pull in a few spaces away from him. He got out and walked toward **Amphitrite**, but looked back to the Yukon and saw that no one had exited. As he walked back up the gangplank, he checked one more time. The driver and any occupants remained in the vehicle.

When he boarded the boat, he went straight to one of the command stations, and then pulled up a map of Honolulu on the Situation Awareness Display. He saw the three signals coming from Shelli, Danielle, and Stephanie's watches. He also noted that Nikki's watch was showing up from the aft section of the boat. He pulled up the video feeds from the thermal and daylight cameras mounted above the bridge and swung one in the direction of the two ultralight helicopters on the flight deck. There was Ryan, Nikki and Stephen checking the tie-down straps after adding the floats for water landings. Shelli had started calling the aircraft "mini-copters," and the rest of the family soon adopted the term.

Then Rick pointed the camera over the bridge toward the black Yukon he had seen pull in earlier. The car was still there. He flipped to thermal and could see the bright signature of the motor and the exhaust system. They were still hot from the drive. The driver and rear left passenger windows were down, which allowed for the thermal imaging camera to make out that there were three people inside.

Rick snapped a picture of the license plate and sent it to his mobile phone. Then he placed a motion detection square around the vehicle itself. He instructed the program to send him pictures via email if there was significant movement, like that of the vehicle moving or someone getting in or out.

Unsure what he should be doing next, Rick pulled up the Daily Alta newspaper article on his command station screen. He read it again and began to wonder what significance this had to a Chinese triad. If it was true event, how would an elderly Chinese man end up with coins from it? Maybe the triad thinks the story is true and greed is their motivation. That would explain a lot. But to kill twelve people and bring down the wrath of the Honolulu Police Department and the FBI, there must be some element of truth to take on this risk.

He thought about what Barbara Stallings, Shelli, and Danielle were doing now. They were checking the validity of the story. They were undoubtedly looking up each person listed, the ship names and schedules, the newspaper accounts of the day and examining the list of valuables. But for the sake of argument, what if the story was true? A pirate ship sailed away with millions in coins, silver and other valuable treasure. *Sailed away .... The story said the ship might have sailed away for the Gilbert group or perhaps Tahiti. But the beginning of the story said it was rigged like a steam whaler. What's a steam whaler?*

Rick entered "steam whaler picture" and "1884" into the search window of the browser. A picture from the archives at the University of Alaska, Fairbanks popped up. Three tall masts with sails dominated the picture. But there toward the stern of ship was a smoke stack. It was steam powered and had a typical crew of thirty to sixty people.

He read the story again. That number seemed to be plausible for the description of the number of filibusters. And a whaler carries a lot of oil-saturated blubber, which had to be heavy. So that makes for a good vessel to bring away all the heavy silver and coinage mentioned. Plus the ship may have carried more than the typical crew for the raid.

He read that these new steam whalers came about after the invention of a rocket powered harpoon in Europe. The new harpoon allowed a brief resurgence of whaling, which had suffered earlier in the century from the hunting impact on the slower species. The faster and more skittish whale species in colder regions like Alaska could be approached at a distance with the new harpoon. The whaler he was looking at was used in the cold waters of Alaska and the northern Pacific in large numbers.

*So if they used a steam whaler, they had both wind power and steam power. It did not mention that they took any new fuel, like coal. So maybe they relied mostly on wind power to get there.*

Rick did a quick search on the Internet and came up with a map of ocean surface winds. Pinks, blues, yellows and greens filled a globe with a black background. The false color was accented with white lines and arrows plotted over the surface of the globe. The arrows indicated the direction of the average wind patterns for the month of December. Long parallel lines ran from the US West Coast through Hawaii and on to the Philippines. Another set of lines ran from South America to a similar latitude as Hawai'i, but in the Southern Hemisphere.

About four hundred miles to the north of the island of O'ahu, there was a curvature in the wind pattern. It looped around and traveled straight to western Canada, Alaska, and northwestern USA.

Rick pulled up Google Earth and began using the ruler tool to measure voyage distances from Honolulu. Tahiti was to the south at over 2,700 miles and perpendicular to the wind patterns. Guam was due west in the direction of the winds at about 3700 miles and the Philippines at about 5,200 miles. Then he measured 400 hundred miles to the north of O'ahu and on to the closet point of land to the east along the wind vectors shown on the surface wind chart. That closet point was Vancouver, and the distance was just under 2,700 miles.

Then something triggered when he saw the trajectory of the vectors. It was a term he remembered from his college days and again during the winter of 2014. "The Pineapple Express" was a wind pattern that brought moisture laden air to the west coast of the USA and Canada. It resulted in heavy downpours of rain on the coast and heavy snowfall during the winter in the mountain regions in the northwest.

The distance to the west coast was the shortest route for the ship, but just barely. It was likely a well-traveled route. It would make sense from a logistics point-of-view to travel back to Vancouver or northwestern USA.

Rick studied the map and thought some more about the story. The pirates spoke in English. Tahiti was just a few miles farther than to Vancouver, but due to the winds would have taken longer to reach. Rick did a quick Internet review of the history of Tahiti. In 1880, it ceded to France. That language spoken was Tahitian, which was similar in many ways to the Hawaiian language. It was another 2500 miles to New Zealand and 3700 miles to Australia, which were the nearest English speaking countries.

Rick turned his attention to the Philippines and China. Another search of events in 1884 and Rick found that the Sino-French War occurred between August 1884 and April 1885. The waters around China to the Philippines were filled with the French Navy, so it was not a great place to go if you're a pirate ship.

So the best bet was to go to back to Vancouver or northwestern USA. Ports kept records, so maybe there is reference of a ship from Hawai'i coming in around Christmas 1884 or the New Year 1885.

He decided to open a new browser window to search for ship records for Vancouver and Seattle. He started to slide Nikki's spreadsheet she had used to calculate the current value of the Hawaiian coins. A passage he remembered in the story made him stop.

Rick pulled the story up again of the pirate rate. He scrolled down to the section labeled "Sacking The Treasury." The second sentence stated "$700,000 in Hawaiian currency – silver dollars and half-dollars – and $200,000 in American gold and silver."

*$700,000 in silver dollars and half-dollars...how is that possible?* Rick examined the numbers again on Nikki's spreadsheet. The bottom of the sheet said that after melting there was $175,867.60 in coins left. *There was one million dollars in coins minted and less than a fifth of that remained after melting. The numbers don't add up.*

| Coin Denomination | Number Minted 1883 | Number Melted 1903 | Number Remaining Coins | Value (US Dollars) | Total Value Remaining |
|---|---|---|---|---|---|
| Dollar | 500,000 | 453,652 | 46,348 | 1 | $ 46,348.00 |
| Half-Dollar | 700,000 | 612,245 | 87,755 | 0.5 | $ 43,877.50 |
| Quarter | 500,000 | 257,400 | 242,600 | 0.25 | $ 60,650.00 |
| Dime | 250,000 | 79 | 249,921 | 0.1 | $ 24,992.10 |
| Total = | 1,950,000 | 1,323,376 | 626,624 | | $175,867.60 |

The only place to spend Hawaiian currency was in Hawai'i. Converting money from one currency to another would have been done only at a bank back then, and that amount would have been pretty suspicious.  If the story was real, then half a million dollars of the pirate loot had been spent in the islands after it was stolen! Either that or they melted it down themselves and sold it at silver market prices. Obviously that hadn't been done since the US Government had melted most of it years later.

Rick's thought pattern continued. How could the coins have been spent in the islands if the pirates sailed away? Maybe they didn't leave. Maybe they pretended to sail south, changed course once out of sight, then offloaded and hid the treasure somewhere in the islands. That would explain why the Chinese triad would be interested in it.

So why would the pirates steal the money, pretend to be sailing away, but stay on the island instead? What happened to the ship and the crew afterwards? Surely someone would have recognized them and the police force or perhaps even the some of the stationed US Navy sailors would have arrested them.

Rick zoomed out the Google Earth map he had opened on the Situation Awareness Display so that it framed the Hawaiian Islands --from the island of Hawai'i to the southeast to Ni'ihau to the northwest.  He knew that Honolulu on O'ahu, and Lahaina on Maui were the two main ports in 1884.  Even after the Pacific whaling boom had passed in 1850, the ports stayed active with the introduction of sugar cane. They obviously would not have anchored into either of those.

They would moor the ship somewhere they would be sheltered by the waves and weather, but close enough to transfer treasure to shore.  And since it was being spent in great quantities, it most likely would have been on one the more populated islands.

He zoomed in on the map to frame O'ahu and Maui.  Molaka'i and Lana'i sat between the two.  They didn't have much in the way of natural harbors, and Moloka'i had a well-known leper colony on it.  Rick opened up another instance of Google Earth and zoomed one to O'ahu and the other to Maui.   Both islands had natural harbors on their north shores.

Rick thought a little more. The weight of treasure would have been in the thousands of pounds. He searched for old maps of O'ahu and Maui online.  He searched online and found an archived census report from the time, which included maps.  O'ahu did have a road system established by that time, albeit rough.  Maui not so much.  It would have been difficult to move that much treasure on Maui at that time.

He pulled up another Internet browser and found a visual horizon calculator.  The horizon calculator determines the distance an object can travel before the limb of the earth obscures it.   The distance varies based on the height of the observer and the highest point of the object -- something even Columbus had to contend with on his travels.  Rick used the height of the Punchbowl crater rim, which he knew was easily climbable, and the height of a common ship's mast.  According to the calculator, the ship would need to sail about 35 miles offshore to ensure it was not visible from Punchbowl.

Rick used the tools with Google Earth to draw a possible circular route the ship could have made to reach back to the north shores of O'ahu.   The path was about 200 miles.  Rick assumed about a 5 miles-per-hour sailing speed, which resulted in about one and two-third days.  Given the pirates left in the morning of December 2, that would have put them mooring at sunset on December 3, 1884.

*That's perfect timing,* thought Rick. *They could move the treasure back off onto the island and leave the next morning. If they were stopped by authorities or the US Navy on their way back to America, they would have no evidence of the robbery on their ship. Their only incrimination might have been the US currency they may have kept for themselves.*

But Rick was still troubled with his hypothesis. Why would pirates offload the treasure? $200,000 in US currency was an extremely handsome bounty for a crew, so it is conceivable they were commissioned to do this.

He thought of Barbara and Shelli and decided he should go and discuss his findings. He checked the security display and saw the Yukon was still parked there. The fact that there had been no alarm meant that no one had exited or entered the vehicle. He saw on the other camera display that Nikki was no longer on the flight deck with Ryan and Stephen.

Just then the door opened and Nikki walked with Ryan and Stephen tagging along behind her. She saw Rick's computer screen and asked what he was doing. He explained his entire thought process to the group.

"That is incredible, Dad. I can't believe we didn't catch that difference in monies when Shelli first brought up the story. I agree, you should go back over to Bishop. Can we come?"

"I'd say yes, but we promised to watch Stephen. And I'm beginning to wonder if we're being watched," said Rick. He showed Nikki the Yukon video feed. "I think that SUV was following me. Maybe I'm just being paranoid, but I don't want to lead them back to Bishop. I was going to take a surreptitious route to get there. I'll drive to Ala Moana Shopping Center, park, and then take a taxi to Bishop."

Nikki appeared concerned. "Do you think Mom and the girls are alright?"

Rick pulled up another screen, which showed their position at the museum. "I gave them the tracking watches, similar to, but less sophisticated than the one you're wearing."

Nikki looked down at her watch. She knew her dad had given her a pre-production model of the next generation watch that he had given rest of the family had. It was fairly big for a woman's sport watch, but it had a lot of features that were more in line with what a spy might need. She hoped she would never have to use all of its feature set, but she felt pretty special that her dad had thought enough of her abilities to ask her to test it for his company.

"They are still at the museum, and haven't called. So I think they are fine," said Rick.

Nikki looked relieved, but then frowned. "Should we be worried Dad? I mean do you think they'll come for us?"

"I think they would come for Stephen, not for us. But it's better to be safe than sorry, and I know you will be secure here on the boat. There are enough safeguards to protect you and the guys. I'm also going to send a text message to Kaleho and ask him to check on the license plate number of the Yukon. He could tell us if it belongs to any known triad member. It could be just someone waiting for a boat, but I'd feel better if we knew for sure."

"I have an idea, Dad," said Nikki. "What if I follow you with the mini-copter? I can start it up now and lift off. I can track you at a standoff distance and keep an eye on the Yukon. If it follows you, then it confirms your suspicions. Once you've parked the car, call me when you're in the taxi. I'll be able to tell you if the Yukon follows you to Bishop Museum."

"That's a great idea Nikki," answered Rick. "Ryan, you stay here with Stephen. If anyone tries to board, you know what to do."

"Roger that, Mr. B." said Ryan. "We'll be just fine. I'll keep a line opened to Nikki so that we can help her land safely on her return."

"Perfect," said Rick. Rick sent the text message of the license plate to Kaleho, and then followed up with a call to tell him to meet him at Bishop Museum in an hour. Kaleho asked what was going on, but Rick told him to meet him there to find out.

Rick left the boat with a tablet PC in hand. All his new analysis was safely encrypted on the tablet's solid-state hard drive. He got in his Audi SUV and drove southward to the Ala Moana drive. His tablet beeped and glanced down at the first light. The motion detection software from his command station on the ship had detected the Yukon had pulled away. While on route, he received a call on his phone from Nikki. She confirmed the Yukon had left the port and was about five car lengths behind him now. Nikki was airborne and flying over the water and parallel to Ala Moana Boulevard.

When Rick arrived at Ala Moana Shopping Center, he parked at the first spot he could find near the southern entrance to the food court. He made sure to park above ground and in the open so that Nikki could easily spot him. He walked briskly on the second level toward the Sears store. Then he took the down escalator on the opposite side of the shopping center. He arrived just in time at the curb at street level to see a taxi dropping off a passenger. He flagged it and hopped in quickly. In less than ten minutes after parking at the mall, he was now heading up Kapiolani Boulevard in a taxi. Kapiolani merged into South King Street. The taxi turned right on Punchbowl and then entered the freeway, H1, toward the museum.

Nikki confirmed that she saw only one person leave the Yukon in the direction he had gone into the mall. She had followed his taxi to King Street and saw no one else following. She doubled back to the shopping center where she saw the Yukon still sitting. By the time Rick had arrived at the museum and had paid the taxi, Nikki called and reported the Yukon appeared to have given up on him and was moving out.

Forty minutes had passed since Nikki had taken off. She would need about five minutes to get back to the ship and land. Since the mini-copter had a one-hour fuel supply, Rick told her to head back to the ship where she could refuel the copter.

Just has he neared the main entrance to the museum, he heard someone call out his name. He looked back at the parking lot and saw Kaleho waving to him. He waited for Kaleho to catch up and then entered the museum together.

"So what have you found, and what's with the license plate number you sent me?" asked Kaleho.

"In good time, my friend. Let's find the girls. I'd rather explain what I've discovered just once. And let me know what you find out about the vehicle plate as soon as you know."

Shelli found them and walked with them to the Great Lawn and the Hawai'i Hall. The three-story Hawai'i Hall has an expansive open lobby. The second and third floors have large wooden arches that open inward to the lobby. Moments later they entered Pāki Hall, which is where the Library and Archives resided. Neither Shelli, Rick nor Kaleho noticed the man standing on the second floor of the Hawai'i Hall. He was holding his mobile phone and pretending to text. But he wasn't texting, or at least not then. He was taking a rapid sequence of pictures as they walked through the hall.

The man then walked down to the bottom level and in the direction he had seen them walk. There was a building straight away, and his map told him it was the Library and Archives. Probably limited access and he'd be certainly noticed if he entered.

The man then returned to his car. He never saw his benefactor, and he didn't need to now or ever. He loved his job at the nearby auto repair shop, which he got thanks to his benefactor. He scheduled all appointments for the shop. A man dropped in for an oil change that morning, and after paying his bill he left him a mobile phone with instructions in the notes app. It was always the same man that came by. When he finished whatever assignment that had been given to him, his instructions were always to stop at the coffee shop nearby his work at the end of the day. The same man that gave him the phone would be waiting to take the phone back. Not a word was spoken. Today would be no different.

# Chapter 16: *Committee of Safety*

Rick and Kaleho followed Shelli in the large office of Barbara Stallings. The sizeable office was lined with real oak paneling and wide heavily shellacked trim. The ceiling was high and an old, dull brass fan with large blades spun slowly in spite of the obvious cooling from the air conditioning ducts. One could easily feel like they were in an Ivy League school in upstate New York or Massachusetts if it weren't for the tropical view out of the two sizable paned windows on one wall.

Dr. Barbara Stalling's desk sat towards the back and adjacent to one of the two windows. Rick noted there were books sprawled all over her desk. On the wall behind Barbara sat two diplomas from east coast schools. A wooden conference table sat in the center of the room, and was lined with six padded leather chairs with brass tacks. On it sat an LCD projector and it was shining light dimly on a white screen on the wall at the far right of the room. Although washed out by the light filling the room from the windows, it was still easily readable. Shelli's tablet PC was attached to the projector using one of the many dongles she carried in her backpack. Stephanie was sitting next to the chair that was obviously Shelli's. She looked up from her phone and waived.

The room had another doorway to the back left that lead off to bookshelves. *The archives*, thought Rick. Out of the doorway walked Danielle with her head down reading a book with a bright red cover. She looked up and smiled.

"Hi honey…, Kaleho. Just reading this incredibly detailed volume on Hawaiian history."

Rick twisted to see the cover, but Danielle helped him by closing it and showing him the front cover. A large gold "3" was on the cover. The white text was easily readable on the red cover jacket. The Hawaiian Kingdom 1874-1893. "R. S. Kuykendall was the author of all but the last chapter, which was added after his death. It took about forty years for the University of Hawai'i to complete and was published in 1967. I think we'll rely heavily on this, since it is painstakingly accurate," added Danielle. "And you know, it's sort of interesting just how much happened in the late 1800's around the world. If you recall, Rick, I've been doing some background studies on the historical connections of some of the artwork we have at Ringling and collectors from around the Sarasota area. The connections between events around the world at that time are quite fascinating."

Rick reached for the book and started leafing through the pages. He started to ask some questions, but when he glanced back at Kaleho he could see he was rapidly losing interest. Rick decided it was time to introduce his hypothesis while he still had Kaleho's attention.

"Speaking of the late 1800's, I have made some progress myself on the pirate story. Can we sit down and go over what I found? It might help short-circuit all this research."

As they sat down, Kaleho apologized and gave a quick speech to tell the group about the importance of what they were doing and that "loose lips sink ships." He had apparently decided that Barbara was knee-deep in their investigation and asked her to keep all that he was about to tell her confidential. He then preceded to summarize the entire case. Barbara gasped several times when he described the twelve murders, with the last being Paul Chang. The same Paul that she had talked to a month earlier.

As Kaleho talked, Rick pulled out his tablet and his mini-projector. He attached them with a black cable and shined the mini-projector's white light up on a blank section of the wall to the right of the main projector screen.

Rick then started by nodding to Shelli, Danielle and Barbara as they moved to seats across from him at the conference table. "I know you three are investigating the characters and events in the story for the purpose of checking the authenticity of it. But I decided to take a different approach. I decided to regard it as being a true story…authentic. I mean, coins have been found and people are dying because of it. If the pirate raid story is not true in its entirety, maybe it has some elements that are sufficiently plausible and worth risking murder. If there was a stolen treasure, what happened to it? And where would the pirates have gone?"

With the use of visual aids, Rick took the team through his hypothesis in a step-by-step approach. The maps, the ships, and even the wind directions were discussed. In conclusion he said, "Spending these coins outside of Hawai'i would have been like shining a beacon at night, drawing attention on those who stole them. So the smart thing would be to melt them down if they were taken elsewhere. We know, however, that they were not melted because most of the Hawaiian coins were in circulation until 1903. So if this story is true, I believe the coins stayed on the island of O'ahu. And since the pirates didn't stay, someone else was spending the money."

"So you're inferring that someone may have orchestrated the raid," stated Danielle. "It makes sense, I guess. If the pirates were hired, their identities could be passed on to the authorities if they didn't stick to the plan. Without some sort of leverage, all the money would have ended up with the pirates. Do you know who would want to hire a band of pirates to do such a thing?"

"No, I don't," said Rick. "Possibly someone that has a grudge against the monarchy."

"I believe I might know," said Barbara. "Shelli, can you please pull up the OneNote project file we created."

"Sure," said Shelli. A stern look from her mother resulted in, "I mean yes ma'am." The software OneNote appeared on the screen. Across the top of page were colorful tabs, like those one would find in an efficient filing cabinet. The digital labels on the tabs were "Pirate Article," "Interesting Facts," "Pictures," "Characters," and "Newspapers."

"Thank you Shelli. I started using OneNote a few years ago to help organize my research into historical events or artifacts. So far, with the help of your wife and daughter, we have compiled information into categories you see across the page."

"Click on Characters please Shelli." Shelli complied. Barbara continued. "Here are brief biographies we made from Internet and library resources of each of the characters. It turns out it was completely plausible that all people mentioned were indeed there and most had the posts or jobs mentioned in the newspaper article. There were a few discrepancies, but we wrote those off as being either errors in the person transcribing the story or errors in the telling. For instance, the story mentions that Colonel Curtis Iaukea went out to collect the tax and didn't come back. He was the port collector of taxes, beginning sometime in September 1884. But unlike the story implies, he did not die. He went on to hold many other government positions, including Sheriff of Honolulu, Secretary of State, and even Governor, until the day of his death in 1940. And General A.B. Hayley was actually a Major. But most of these errors were not sufficient to cause us to question authenticity."

"Scroll down lower Shelli." Shelli clicked on the scroll button again. "The majority of the facts were amazingly accurate. For instance, there is a reference to a Mr. Bishop. It is the Mr. Charles Reed Bishop that founded this museum, and he did lose his wife as the story relays. His wife died on November 2, 1884. Letters he wrote during the next few months show that he had gone to the Meyer family home on Molaka'i before the end of the year. We know he was the executor of her will, so he could have been here for another month before heading to Molaka'i."

"Barbara, you mentioned that you might know who commissioned the pirates. Is this somehow related?" asked Kaleho. It was obvious he wanted to get to the point.

"Oh, I'm sorry. I got side tracked there. What I mean to say is that the newspaper article cannot be rebuffed due to facts."

"Speaking of the newspaper articles, I tried to find out if there was any other reports of it anywhere else on the web," said Shelli. She clicked on the OneNote tab labeled "Newspapers" and three newspaper names were listed. "From the article, we know the raid happened on the night of December 1, 1884. The first thing I did was to check all local papers you told me about Ms. Stallings -- the Daily Bulletin, the Hawaiian Gazette and the Pacific Commercial Advertiser -- for the next few weeks and there was nothing mentioned. And I went all the way to November 1st on all those papers just in case the date of the raid was earlier than what the paper stated. Again nothing."

"The fact that no other paper printed the story still makes me suspect of its validity," said Barbara. "But research requires one to be unbiased, so I cannot completely rule out the story given that freedom of speech was not guaranteed at that time in the kingdom of Hawai'i. Given the severity of the raid, the King had the power to restrict any mention of it."

"Since I couldn't find any other articles, I started checking out some of the other places mentioned in the Daily Alta article. I was surprised to find many of the places and people did exist back then. But I also found some facts that didn't seem right. Like there was a mention of the Royal Hawaiian Hotel. And based on my research, that wasn't built until 1927."

"I'm impressed, Shelli. You make an excellent researcher. The Royal Hawaii Hotel that we know today on Waikiki beach was built in 1927. But there was a Royal Hawaiian Hotel that existed before then. It was in downtown Honolulu, not Waikiki. And it wasn't nearly as elegant as the hotel you are familiar with now. We have a copy of an 1884 Christmas menu from the Royal Hawaii Hotel in one of our displays."

"Wow, that's so cool," said Shelli.

"The entire story is plausible," said Barbara. "But in investigating the people in the story I found an interesting pattern."

Barbara asked Shelli to click back on the "Characters" tab and to scroll farther down the page. "Shelli put this table together for me. The first column has the names. All the names of people mentioned in the story are listed. In additions to those names, I've added the names of prominent members of society not found in the story. The second column has a place for an "x" to signify if persons in the first column were friends of the monarchy. Similarly, an "x" in the third column indicates that the person is a member of the Committee of Safety. And the final column is for marking whether or not the person was robbed during the raid."

"What's the Committee of Safety?" asked Rick.

"They were a group of leading members of the Mission Party in the government," answered Barbara. The Mission Party was pro-American and pro-business. In 1884, they won 9 seats in the government in 1886 they won 13 seats. Sometimes referred to as the Committee of Thirteen, and the Annexation Club, the Committee of Safety was the predecessor to the Hawaiian League. The Hawaiian League was a secret group whose goals were to overthrow the monarchy and annex Hawai'i to the USA. They succeeded in the overthrow in 1893. And the annexation came in 1898, which is when the US Congress approved the creation of the US Territory of Hawai'i."

"Wow, so in 1884 the Committee of Safety had a grudge against the King," said Shelli with wide eyes.

"Most certainly," said Barbara. "And look at the table now. Notice that all those on the list that were loyal to the king were robbed. And of all the people that were on the Committee of Safety, only one was robbed. The Committee members were incredibly wealthy and it is suspicious that only one was robbed. That one person was Dillingham. Dillingham was a member of the Committee, but he did not believe in the overthrow of the monarchy. "

"So it sounds like the Committee of Safety could have been behind the pirate raid," said Rick. "They would have known the King's meeting schedule and they had motive. And maybe the Committee decided to add Dillingham to the list for the pirates to hit in order to teach him a lesson."

"Perhaps," answered Barbara.

"But why would they have planned such a raid? They were all wealthy," said Danielle.

"The monarchy continually spent large sums of money," said Barbara. "They were always searching for new revenue sources. For instance, Honolulu had a strong opium trade. There were opium dens that were sanctioned by the monarchy. Even the King himself accepted large sums of money, tens of thousands of dollars, for licenses for opium den operators. Perhaps they figured that by cleaning out the Treasury, it would weaken the monarchy. But there could be another reason."

"Move down to the section on the Honolulu Rifles," said Barbara. "This was an independent militia group. It was around for many years, but then was disbanded by the King in 1874. But in 1884, it formed again and consisted of all white Americans and Europeans."

"According to the story, the Honolulu Rifles did nothing to stop the raid," said Shelli.

"It appears so. But the Honolulu Rifles continued to grow stronger from that year on. They started with no gear and soon were well armed. They also associated themselves with the Hawaiian League, and were indeed involved in the overthrow of the monarchy in 1893."

Rick's mind was racing. Then he and Danielle started to talk at the same time. Rick signaled Danielle to go ahead first. By the look on her face, he would bet money that she was thinking the same thing as he was.

"So in essence, the Committee of Safety could have used the stolen money and other treasures to fund their campaigns, fund the Honolulu Rifles and gain their support, and weaken the monarchy. It could have been the unknown key to the success of the overthrow."

*Bingo*, thought Rick. His thoughts exactly. "And they spent a good deal of it, but not all of it. There are still a lot of coins and other valuables unrecovered. And the leftovers are worth over one-hundred-million dollars, which is enough to get the triad interested. And when they saw two coins appear, they assumed Paul and his family knew where the rest were."

"So how then, would Paul Chang's ancestors get hold of it?" asked Kaleho.

"There was a considerable population of Chinese in Honolulu at that time," replied Barbara. "There was a Chinatown back then as it is now, and a good deal of the businesses and restaurants were located there. If the money was being spent for arms and supplies, then the Chinese business men would have seen the influx of these coins. Rumors of the raid would have been hard to squelch, so it wouldn't take them long to figure out that the coins they were seeing were the ones stolen."

"So maybe they somehow found out where it was hidden and took it all," said Shelli.

"In 1886 and in 1900 there were two major fires in Chinatown," added Barbara. "They resulted in the destruction of many businesses and residences. The fires were so bad, that many of the Chinese inhabitants left. A large number went to Maui, for instance. Many of them opened up businesses there."

"When we talked to Stephen earlier, he said their family owned a store on Maui. And he also mentioned stories told by his grandfather of a great fire. Maybe their ancestors were some of the Chinese businessmen from Chinatown that fled to Maui. And just maybe they brought the pirate treasure with them," said Kaleho.

"And I looked up some of the history about triads in Hawai'i," said Shelli proudly. She glanced down at her notes and was half-paraphrasing and half-reading them. "It appears secret societies, which were the early starts of the triads, were well established in 1884. The triads are also known as 'tongs,' and 'Tiandihui.' I don't know if I pronounced that last word right. I read in one of the archived newspaper articles that 23 members of a secret society were arrested one year later, December 2, 1885. The sheriff that arrested them didn't know what they were planning, but they knew the group had knives. Maybe the tong somehow learned of the treasure."

"You are so smart, Shelli," said Rick proudly. Shelli almost blushed. He thought a minute. "Maybe they have known it existed but lost track of it after the fires."

"They have many traditions, Dad. So they may have passed the story of the treasure just like Stephen's grandfather told him and Paul," said Shelli.

Everyone sat in silence for a while, rethinking all that had been said. Kaleho then spoke, "I have motive. I have a story now that ties all the murders, the coins, and the Chinese triads. It would be good if we could find Stephen's grandfather. If he knows where the treasure is, we could confiscate it and end the reign of terror by the triads."

Kaleho's phone sang. He had received a text message. He opened it and then let Rick know, "That license plate you sent me is from a car of a known triad member. You want to tell me why you have this?

Rick frowned with the news. "We may be in trouble then. The triad knows where Stephen is hiding now. And Ryan and Nikki are there too."

# Chapter 17: *TCM*

"Dad, we're fine," confided Nikki. She knew her dad had his speaker phone on and that her mom was probably listening. So she explained more than she knew she had to for her dad's sake. "No one new has pulled up in the parking lot here at the Port. I've put the ship's defenses to high alert. The bow and stern radar systems are scanning 360 degrees for any movement within 500 meters of the ship. The cameras are automatically slewing to any movement detected by the radars. The dazzlers are ready and the acoustic hailing systems are ready to blast sound at literally eardrum-piercing levels. Water cannon intakes have been enabled too, so we'll peel the paint off that triad car if it comes near us."

"Super, Nikki," said Rick. "I know you've got the drill down pat. Do me the favor and retract the gangway." Rick thought for a moment about ship access and remembered that the boat's gangway could be extended using his mobile phone app. "And shut off the remote access feature – we'll contact you when we're back there." In case they were attacked, he didn't want someone to hack his phone to gain access to the ship.

"We're heading there in a few minutes," said Rick. "Remember you can track us on the situation awareness display."

"Ok, Dad. Will do. See you in a little while," said Nikki as she signed off.

"Water cannons, acoustic hailing systems?" asked Kaleho. "I'd rather have good ole fashion fire power." He touched his holstered pistol as he said it.

"You have only so many bullets in a gun, but as long as the ship has power they can hold off anyone approaching the ship indefinitely – or at least until we get there," said Rick. "Now let's get moving."

Rick, Danielle, Shelli, Stephanie, and Kaleho walked through the museum quickly. Kaleho noticed Rick looking at his phone several times as they walked and talked. He assumed he must be checking on Nikki.

"I can fit three in my car," said Kaleho to Rick as they walked toward the Bishop Museum main entrance. Danielle, Shelli and Stephanie were beside them.

"I can't take any chances on my family or Stephanie. My car will be safer," said Rick.

"Where is it? I saw you arrive here in a taxi."

"I had to abandon it temporarily at the Ala Moana Shopping Center when I found I was being followed. I grabbed a taxi from there."

"It's farther to the shopping center than it is to the Port, so why take a chance with another taxi?"

"It's not at Ala Moana anymore, it's here," said Rick.

"Who drove it here? And aren't they leading them right to you?" asked Kaleho as they left the main entrance and walked toward the parking lot.

As they stepped on to the parking lot, a high-pitched mechanical hum drew the attention of the group. They saw a small helicopter-like object flying about fifty feet above the parking lot, and it was heading in their direction. The squeal of the Audi SUV tires pulled their gaze back to street level.

"The car is driving itself," said Rick. "The small helicopter drone was launched from the low-profile, aerodynamic pod on the top of the SUV once it began to move. It's a short-range quadcopter, only a few miles at best, but I knew it could make it to here. Once I saw no one was following from my screen, I directed the SUV to come here." Rick showed the screen of his phone so that Kaleho could see the view of the parking lot and their group from the small camera underneath the drone.

The girls jumped into the back seats of the car, and Rick and Kaleho into the front. The dashboard was lit up from the displays and dials littered over much of its surface.

"It appears that we just sat down in a star fighter," said Kaleho.

"Not quite, but we are safe in here for the time being. It's bulletproof up to thirty-caliber rounds. Fifty-caliber would penetrate if shot from a short distance, but I think we'd see that kind of gun before it got close to us. And it can drive itself defensively at speeds of up to 75 mph if I were to get hurt in the driver's seat. It's able to do so because of the long-range radar coupled with motion compensation algorithms, GPS and accelerometers." Rick began to explain the science of the vehicle.

Kaleho shook his head. "This is awesome, *Han Solo*. But you know I'm a political science major and a cop. I don't need to know how it works, just that it does."

Rick grinned at the comment. Then he asked, "Do you think Barbara will be safe here? Should we be doing something for her?"

Kaleho reached for his phone as they pulled out of the parking lot. "I'll call in for a couple of officers to come by and keep her company for the next few days. I'll stay with you guys and will get one of them to drive my car back to my place when Barbara is ready to head home."

They moved quickly through the streets toward the Port. The quadcopter drone stayed a half-mile ahead of the SUV and the feeds were on the integrated map and video display in the dash. The video feed was split – color on the left and black and white thermal image on the right. The heat from motors and exhaust pipes glowed bright white.

As they entered the Port, Kahelo got another text. He sighed as he read it to himself. "They found Paul Chang's friend, Stan Johnson. He was found dead in a sugarcane field near Waialua. He looks to have been tortured to death."

Danielle gasped, "That poor kid. Why on Earth would they do such a thing?" No one answered and sat quietly for a few moments. "His parents will be devastated. And still nothing about Paul's grandfather?"

"Nothing. We are going door to door now in the Chinese neighborhoods," replied Kaleho.

"Rick we have got to find that grandfather. That family has had enough loss," said Danielle sympathetically.

"We'll keep trying, honey," said Rick. "He's apparently not a technology user, or we would have detected him by now like we did his grandson, Stephen. But perhaps we could question Stephen more about his grandfather's habits and associations. Maybe it would help narrow the search."

Rick called Nikki to let her know he was there and to extend the gangway when they walked to the boat from their parking spot. Of course he realized that she had already knew they were there because she was tracking them from their watches. She also saw the feeds from the quadcopter. The radar systems would have detected their arrival and trained the high resolution cameras on them. He could see the cameras pointing at them now. And finally he knew Nikki would have already confirmed from both facial recognition software and voice analysis on the call that it was indeed him.

The warm humid air of O'ahu was offset by the mild trade winds of the Pacific as they walked briskly to the boat. The skies were clear with only a few puffy clouds dotting the horizon. Rick could see on his phone's display the color and thermal images on the drone above them. There was no suspicious movements around them, so he clicked the "Return Home" button on the lower right of the display. He watched the drone immediately descend to the Audi SUV they had just left. The aerodynamic pod opened and the drone safely landed inside. The tone and volume of the props steadily dropped as its props wound down. Shortly thereafter a beep from his phone indicated the drone had docked and was being recharged.

As the Bryants, Stephanie, and Kaleho approached the ship, the gangway lowered. Rick waved at the nearest camera to thank Nikki. They walked single file up, with Kaleho at the rear. With his hand on his holstered pistol, he scanned the area as he walked up.

Although there was no indication that their lives were in immediate danger, the tension of the group was eased when they were all onboard the **Amphitrite**. The entire group came together at the conference room table in the command center. The large situation awareness display illuminated the room with data and pictures from Rick and Nikki's earlier research, while video and radar feeds from around the ship continually updated on the smaller screens around the perimeter of the room.

Stephen Chang and Ryan arrived to the room with trays of chilled water, a carafe of coffee, and light *pupus*. Stephen was grinning as if he had been joking around with Ryan before they entered. It was apparent that his attitude had changed significantly since he came in earlier. Nikki and Shelli took their seats at two of the command stations.

After they settled, Rick brought Nikki, Ryan and Stephen up to speed on the coins and the possibility that the pirate raid, if it truly happened, may have been sponsored by Committee of Safety in 1884. And Kaleho broke the news of Paul's friend, Stan. With this news, Stephen lowered his head and clearly struggled to keep his emotions in check.

"Stephen, I know it's difficult for you to talk about it, but we need to figure out where your grandfather is," said Kaleho. "He has to be hiding somewhere, or we would have found him by now. We think his life is in danger because of what he might know about the pirate treasure, so anything you tell us of his habits or friends might help us find him."

Stephen shook his head and stared at the floor quietly for a few moments. "Grandfather is a quiet person and since grandmother died he became even more withdrawn. He has few modern conveniences – no cell phone, PC, or anything like it. He led a simple life." He saw a room full of eyes directed at him. He blew out a big breath and continued. "My parents visit from Maui every couple of months, and that's when Paul and I would drop in as well. He was more interested in hearing about what we were all up to and didn't talk much about work or his friends. He taught for the school for many years, so I know he had good friends there."

"We're tracking down his school associations, but so far they have not been able to direct us to his whereabouts," said Kaleho. "Can you tell me if he took any medicines or had regular appointments with doctors?"

"Grandfather was old-school. He relied on traditional Chinese medicines, acupressure and acupuncture. I've never known him to go to a western hospital or doctor. The only complaint about his health I can ever remember him mentioning was arthritis."

"That's good information," said Kaleho. "We'll check what the traditional Chinese treatment for arthritis is. Knowing that might help narrow our search for him."

"It looks like acupuncture two times a week helps," said Shelli. She had started searching the web as soon as she heard the word arthritis.

"What about any herbal treatments?" asked Danielle. "I know the Chinese herbal medicine dates back more than a millennia. I've seen ginger, teas, and many types of powders depicted in their artwork."

Stephen spoke up again. "Chinese medicine often consists of blending a number of ingredients. These are often mixed based on the description of whatever ails you. I don't know specifically what he was taking … if anything. As Mrs. Bryant said, the medicines are often teas, leaves, and powders. I made my parents and him some tea on our last visit, and I recall seeing some packets in the kitchen cabinet to the left of the stove. Sorry, but I don't recall any store labels on anything,"

"That's a good lead. Do you know where your grandfather shopped for groceries? Maybe places he liked to eat out?"

"Grandfather kept to himself most times. I don't think I can ever remember him eating out. My parents always brought him bags of groceries and made him meals when they visited. Besides the local supermarket, I know he sometimes went into Chinatown. He had plastic bags from Chinatown that he kept under the sink with Chinese characters … you know *Hanzi*."

"There are a few grocers and traditional medicine stores in Chinatown," said Kaleho. "I have officers on regular beats in Chinatown, so I'll call them as well."

"I found twenty-three TCM practitioners in the downtown Honolulu, so you may want to check some of these out," said Nikki. She slid a map onto the situation awareness display. It had a cluster of twenty-three numbers on that map and underneath a list of names, addresses and contact information. "I limited my search from Waialae to the east and the airport to the west."

"What's T-C-M mean?" asked Ryan.

"Traditional Chinese Medicine," answered Nikki.

"Based on what Stephen has told us, I doubt his grandfather would have traveled as far as the airport or Waialae. Can you narrow down the search down to places to Chinatown, the area on 7th near the school and his home?" asked Kaleho.

"Sure," responded Nikki. A few more clicks of her mouse and the list dropped to eight listings. Four of the listings were in Chinatown.

"That's more like it," said Danielle. "Kaleho, could you ask some of your officers to check for Stephen's grandfather in those four places in Chinatown?"

"I doubt that will help," said Stephen. "It might even hurt our chances of finding him."

"Why?" asked Danielle. "If the police said he was in danger, they would certainly help."

Kaleho shook his head. "No, I think Stephen is probably right. Those shop keepers will be suspicious of any policemen searching for an elderly Asian man. For centuries the people of Chinatown have been out-of-sight and out-of-mind, and have had no one but their own to watch out for them. They would not trust us enough to give us any useful information. And they'd probably be too scared that the triad would find out they were helping the police."

"So what do we do?" asked Danielle. "We can't let him wander on his own. If the triad finds him first…" She paused and looked at Stephen. "…well we need to find him and keep him safe."

"Maybe I could get some of our Asian officers that can speak Chinese to go in plain clothes?" said Kaleho.

"No offense," said Stephen. "But you can tell an officer a mile away. I think I should check it out. It makes since that I am looking for my grandfather. Heck, I think I might even get some sympathy help."

"That's dangerous," said Kaleho. "You'd be potentially exposing yourself to triad spies. I've got a missing person and a trail of death now. I don't want to lose anyone else."

"I don't think you've got much choice. I'm not going to sit around while my grandfather is in trouble. Besides, I don't think you can stop me," said Stephen.

"I could have you locked up for hindering a police investigation," said Kaleho in a stern voice. But after a few seconds, the tension dropped from his face. "But that's not going to get us anywhere. How about taking someone with you?"

"It can't be another officer," said Stephen. "That will be just as bad as sending two officers. It's got to be someone that won't draw suspicion."

"I can go with you," said Ryan.

"I don't know. I like you, brah, but you're...a *haole.* No offense, but you'll stick out."

"I'll go with you Stephen," said Nikki. "I can pretend to be...your girlfriend."

"Hey, no way," said Ryan.

"I said pretend to be his girlfriend," said Nikki.

"I'm with Ryan," said Danielle. "All this talk about the triad, I don't think it's a good idea."

"Mom, I'll be perfectly fine," said Nikki. "I'll keep an open line going so you guys can hear what we hear. And besides, we can use a quadcopter to watch from above."

"What good will that do if no one is around to help in time?" asked Ryan. "The three of us can go. Like we're all friends."

"You heard Stephen," said Nikki. "We'll just scare everybody away."

"I can put a couple of cars out there on the streets. We'll keep them hidden out of sight," said Kaleho.

"And I can give those officers a tablet to listen and view the audio feeds and the UAV video feeds," said Rick.

"Rick Bryant!" said Danielle. "That's your daughter we're talking about."

"Which is why he's taking the precautions, Mom," interrupted Nikki. "Stop worrying. I'll be fine. Tourists, and shoppers are always down there walking the streets. We'll have police officers nearby geared with our latest surveillance equipment. And I want to help."

No one spoke. Eyes in the room went between Danielle and Nikki. Only the slight the hum of the air conditioning was heard.

"OK," said Danielle. She looked at Stephen, Kaleho, and Rick. She pointed her finger at them as she talked. "You three better take care of her."

The group starting talking at the same time as Danielle sat with her arms crossed. As they began to plan, she got up from the table and walked away. Rick noticed it and started to follow her. Nikki spotted him getting up and said "Dad." He stopped and saw Nikki shaking her head. He slowly sat back down and after a few moments of silence, rejoined the conversation.

# Chapter 18: *Jade*

Stephen and Nikki got off the bus near the corner of N. King Street and Maunakua Street. It was decided it would be best if they looked like college students taking TheBus from the university.

The older part of Chinatown consisted of mostly two-story brick buildings with covered sidewalks. If you ignored the Chinese signs, you could have imagined you were in an old western town. They headed down King and turned right on Kekaulike Street. Although awnings from the buildings and palm trees fully shaded the sidewalk, it was hot. The tropical breezes didn't seem to be penetrating into these streets. A food market sat at the corner and had large shelves and bins of pineapple, mango, papaya, bananas, and other tropical fruits. An elderly Asian woman had a basket on her arm and appeared to be squeezing one mango after another. A small group of mainland tourist were listening to a walking tour guide's speech while profusely sweating. One kid had wondered from the group and was busy touching each piece of fruit in the low-lying bins of the food market.

Nikki and Stephen held hands as they walked. Nikki wore a small purse on a long strap over the opposite shoulder. She held her phone in that hand. They talked as if they were the only ones that were listening to each other, although they both knew everything said was being heard by the nearby police cruisers and the rest of the family on the **Amphitrite**. They came upon the first herbal medicine store. Nikki glanced up as they entered the store at one of the larger palm trees and thought she saw a movement in the shadows under the fronds. *Probably the new camo painted version of the quadcopter that Dad or Shelli is piloting*, she thought.

Stephen didn't loiter and went straight to the middle-aged Asian woman behind the counter. Nikki stood right next to him with her arm in his as he explained that he was trying to find his grandfather. At least that was what she thought he was saying. Except for a few English words, most everything else spoken was not. After a few minutes of conversation, Stephen nodded and he and Nikki walked back onto Kekaulike Street. As they continued in the same direction Stephen said that the woman knew of his grandfather by name, but that he didn't shop there. She said that her shop catered more to visiting Asian tourists and that his grandfather likely shopped in one of the older TCM shops.

Stephen was carrying a picture of his grandfather that was taken with him sitting between Stephen and Paul. He showed this, as he did at the first shop, to the young woman behind the counter at the second shop. She had not seen or know of Stephen's grandfather.

The third TCM shop they went in was run by an older Asian man and woman. Nikki assumed they were married. They were both busily sorting and moving boxes of a new shipment of herbs that had arrived. Both of them nodded as they talked to Stephen. The woman retrieved several small packet of herbs and showed them to Stephen. He nodded as she spoke to him about each packet. The woman then pointed to a back hallway and continued to talk as if she were explaining something that went on down the hallway. The conversation ended and Stephen walked up to the cash register. He paid for the items with cash and nodded to the woman and the older man.

Nikki and Stephen walked out of the store and paused a few steps away. "She said my grandfather had been here two days ago. He had bought some herbs for his arthritis and had asked for some 'moxa stick' treatment."

"Some what?" asked Nikki.

"Oh, sorry. That's why I was talking so long with her. I only wanted to know if she'd seen my grandfather. But she felt it was important that I understood why he came and what he took. And she also felt it was important that I know what the herbs and treatments did. Apparently arthritis is considered to be 'blood stuckness.' The treatments all work to relieve the pain and get the blood flowing. Moxa sticks are herbs rolled in a tube. They are lit on one end – sort of resembles a cigarette. It's held over the skin in the areas that ache. The lit moxa stick causes the skin to turn red. The procedure can be painful itself, but does relieve the pain of arthritis for a while. There are treatment rooms down the hallway and my grandfather had gone down there."

"Well that's good news," said Nikki with a smile. "Did she say when he came by?"

"It was late in the day near closing. He was hoping to sleep better without discomfort."

"So we know then he was...alive less than 48 hours ago," said Nikki.

"Yeah, but I wonder where he went?" said Stephen. "He didn't go home and he's not staying with anyone we know. The lady back there said Grandfather never talked much and she didn't know where he lived."

"I don't know Stephen. Seems so weird that no one has any idea where he is. Maybe they know but just don't want to say."

"Perhaps. The shop owners we've talked with so far seem to be acting normal. Nothing strange in their behavior."

"Do you want to hit the last shop?" asked Nikki.

"Guess so. Maybe he goes to more than one TCM shop."

They walked around the next corner and passed two young men leaning up against the brick wall of a shop. Nikki was holding Stephen's hand as before, and she squeezed it as they passed the two men. One was smoking and she held her breath as they passed. She heard a grinding motion as they passed and saw the man that was smoking had put out the cigarette with his flip-flop. She strained to hear footsteps. The street traffic made it difficult, but it wasn't long before she heard the foot drag followed by the characteristic foot slap that gave the footwear its name.

Stephen heard the men too and started to look back, when Nikki leaned against him and pointed across the street at a store selling Buddha statues of all colors and sizes. "Hey check out all those Buddha's. I've never seen so many," she said. As she was leaning she also whispered, "Don't look at them."

Stephen pretended to acknowledge the first comment and continued looking ahead. They saw a police car up to the left about a block away. Nikki said, "It's a beautiful day, isn't it sweetie." That was one of four preplanned codes, which meant "we think we are in possible danger." Nikki felt Stephen tense.

They were coming to the final TCM shop. Just before they got to the door, Nikki swung Stephen suddenly into a shop selling bright Chinese lanterns, jade statues, and trinkets. Nikki pulled him to one of the jade counters and said quickly. "You know I love jade, sweetie. There's no reason for us to go anywhere else. This place has an awesome selection."

She looked him right in his eyes when she asked the question, "What's my budget?"

Stephen seemed puzzled by the question, like he didn't know how to answer. "Uh, well...."

Nikki interrupted and said, "You know how much I loved that statue your grandparents have. They have such a great selection here. There's no reason to go to any other shops." She hoped Stephen understood her hidden message -- no more TCM shops.

The woman at the counter was smiling and started reaching inside the glass counter to pull out samples to show. She remained smiling until the front door closed. Stephan and Nikki looked to the door to see the smoker had followed them. He flipped the closed sign on the glass door and locked it. The sounds from the street immediately muted. Only the louder, but still dampened sounds from passing vehicles sounds made it through the louver window that was tilted open above the door. Nikki looked back at the woman behind the counter. Her face looked concerned and she said, "I'm sorry, excuse me." She walked back through a doorway behind the counter. Then came the muffled sound of a back door squeaking open and then clicking closed.

Stephen stepped away from the counter and beside Nikki. "Hey brah, what's up? Why'd you lock the door?"

"What are you doing in Chinatown?" said the smoker.

"We're shopping," said Stephen. "We don't mean any trouble. We're just about to leave."

"We don't want you to leave yet," said the smoker. "We don't think you're shopping. We think you searching for someone."

"What are you talking about, brah? We're students at the university. Nik-, uh, my girlfriend and I are just shopping. Really, brah. Just let us go."

Stephen took a side step as if he was going around the smoker. The smoker took one step and swung a roundhouse punch to Stephen's face. Stephen staggered back a step. He then shook his head as if he was clearing out the cobwebs.

"I'm not finished with you. I'm not letting you out of here until I get answers," said the smoker. The other man was larger, and didn't say a word. He seemed calm but menacing. His stood straight with his arms folded.

Stephen's head must have cleared. His expression went from surprise to serious, and he began to step forward. Nikki reached out and blocked Stephen with her arm. "I got this." Stephen looked at her as if she said she was an idiot.

"We are going out of that door," said Nikki. "If you try to stop us, I'll scream. The police are just a short way down the street." Nikki heard a faint whining sound and saw the quadcopter hovering just outside the louver window. It was seeing everything; hearing everything.

"And if they don't get here soon enough," said Nikki. "They'll be peeling you off the floor instead of just arresting you." A slight foot shuffle from her feet and her sandals were off.

The smoker looked at his friend and laughed. When he turned his face back toward Nikki, he saw her bare foot for about a second before he felt his nose crack and his vision blur. Nikki swung a solid left then at the large man, but he swatted it away with one arm and pushed her with his other hand.

Nikki stumbled back and spun to catch herself on the counter. Stephen tucked his head and charged the large man, who quickly stepped to the side and clotheslined Stephen with his left arm.    Stephen's feet flew upward in front of him and the large man then punched downward with his right.  Stephen landed flat on his back with a gasp followed by a moan.

Nikki was still facing the counter but watching over her shoulder as the large man moved toward her.    She feigned left and then spun right to deliver a backhanded fist to the large man's face.    The large man blocked her with his right arm and pushed her arm downward. It was a good block, but was exactly what Nikki expected.  It left the man open in the center. Without stopping her body's rotation from the original swing, Nikki took a step and continued with a left punch to the large man's face.    But this time it wasn't her fist that was connecting with his face.  In her left hand was a jade statue of Buddha on a marble stone base.    The large man perceived the object and his eyes went wide.    But he was too late.  He took the blow full force and spun around against the side wall of the store and collapsed to the floor.

She looked at the statue in her hand.  A blood smear on the base showed the contact was as deadly as she hoped.

The smoker sat up as he came too.  Nikki heard the movement and reacted instinctively. She threw the jade statue with the precision of a major league pitcher.  The smoker's vision cleared just in time to see Buddha's faint smile rotate toward his forehead.    The thud resonated in the room and the smoker's head flew back to the floor.

Nikki whipped into a ready stance and watched for movement from both of her assailants.  She saw none.    She stood straight to admire her handwork, before hearing a moan from Stephen.

Nikki was kneeling over Stephen when the police kicked in the door.    The glass fractured in response to the splintering door jamb.    Two police officers stepped in with their guns drawn.

"Jeez," said one of the officers when he saw the two men sprawled out on the floor.  He lowered his gun and asked.  "You OK?"

"Yeah, I'm fine.  I think Stephen is too.  He just got the wind knocked out of him trying to protect me."    Nikki was sure that he felt a lot worse than that, but she figured she needed to bolster his pride at this point.

The officer put his gun away and helped Nikki get Stephen to his feet.    The other officer knelt to the floor and checked the men's pulses.  "They're both still alive, although I think just barely."    He radioed for an ambulance.

As they walked out the door, Nikki glanced right toward the last TCM shop. The door was closed and a sign on it also said such. It would be no use to talk to them now. They knew the police were involved.

By the time they got to the cruiser, Stephen was walking on his own. They got into the back seat and the officer took them back to them back to the *Amphitrite*.

As they neared the ship, Stephen asked. "You didn't want us to go into the last TCM shop because you didn't want the triad to know we were looking for Grandfather in them. Right?"

"Yeah. Let's hope it worked," said Nikki as she saw her Mom walking to meet them.

# Chapter 19: *Leilani*

Kaleho was driving home after a day of revelations and frustrations. He had the top down on the Chevelle and felt the wind blow his straight black hair in the evening air. H1 was in gridlock from an accident, so he had taken Alohea Avenue. Others had decided to make the same decision to bail on H1, so traffic was dense and slow. But at least it was moving.

He thought of the day's events. They had discovered there was a pirate raid in 1884 and that the murders were most likely linked to finding the lost treasure from that raid. But he had lost another person today, Paul Chang's friend. He knew that a triad was involved, but exactly how was not clear. And he still had a missing person, Chang's grandfather. He was alive two days before, but missing now. A long day with twists and turns. But in the few short days of their visit, the Bryants were making tremendous progress. And he chuckled to himself when he thought of Nikki's assailants. Their embarrassment would keep them quiet. They would say nothing to the triad.

Diamond Head loomed dark ahead of him. It was too dark to tell, but he knew the rocky outer walls of the volcano was still covered in dry brown vegetation. Kaleho enjoyed looking up at it each time he passed. Show a picture of it to almost anyone in the world and they would know where it was taken. Of course, from this backside view it might be more of a challenge to some to identify.

He merged onto Diamond Head Road, which hugged close the base of the volcano to the north, east and south. Traffic had become lighter here as car after car peeled off. He'd be home in another ten to fifteen minutes at this rate. As he passed the entrance road to go inside Diamond Head, he knew the Pacific Ocean lay directly ahead of him. Unfortunately, homes and the various palms, Hitachi, Rainbow Eucalyptus and other trees blocks the view both day and night. After a day of historical discoveries, he drifted into thought. *Wonder what the view was like in the days of the Kamehameha?*

As he turned left onto Kahala Avenue, his mobile phone rang. It was Leilani. She was probably wondering where he was. He answered, "Hi honey. I'm on my way home."

"Kaleho, please hurry. Someone just kicked in the door. I'm locked in...." The line went dead.

Kaleho reached into his glove compartment and pulled out his strobe light and lit it up. He threw the toggle switch hidden just below the dashboard radio, and his siren started to blare. He jammed his foot to the floor and the throaty engine roared as the wheels screamed.

He weaved through traffic, barely missing cars left and right that were trying to move to the side of the road. He blew through a red light, narrowly missing the rear end of a stopping city bus. But beyond the red light was open road.

He reached for his phone to call the dispatcher directly, but it rang instead. He couldn't take his eyes off the road to look at the display, so he hit the green phone icon to answer.

"Is this the Chief of Police?" said the voice.

"Yes, it is. If this is not urgent, please hang up. I'm responding to an emergency."

"I would bet you are. You're trying to get home and save your wife," said the voice.

"Who is this? How did you know that?" asked Kaleho.

"Because we are going to take her," said the voice.

"Leave her alone! I'm on my way to the house right now. You can take me instead," he shouted over the roar of the engine.

"We don't want you. We want Chang, the old man. You will turn him over to us and we'll give you back your wife," said the voice.

Kaleho almost burst out the truth, that he didn't have the Chang, but caught himself. "You better leave now while you can. And if you touch one hair on my wife's head I will hunt you down. I will make you regret it."

"Another Liam Neeson wannabe. You won't find us. And if you love your wife you will not tell your police force or any other law enforcement agency to look for us. If we find out you have, we'll kill her. If you cooperate with us, we will let her live."

In the last few words, Kaleho heard the squeal of tires in the background of the caller. They were his own.

"You don't have to do this. Let her go now and I'll not press charges. It's not too late," said Kaleho.

"We'll be in touch. We will... ah, you're here. Better timing than I expected," said the voice.

The Chevelle's tires were locked and leaving black rubber marks as the car came to a halt. There was a van out front of the house and three men with guns at the front door and in the yard. When they saw him leaping up from the seat with his pistol in his hand, gunfire erupted. Kaleho rolled when he landed and came up in a kneeling position with both hands on his guns. Two of the men scrambled, one to the front of the van and the third man ducked behind their clump of three palms. Kaleho fired two shots directly at the person still standing at the door and then two more at the person shooting at him from in front of the van. Both dropped immediately. Another shot at the palm trees kept the man there hunkered down.

Kaleho took that moment and sprinted to the front door. As he neared the door, the ground and house's wooden siding virtually exploded in response to the sweep of the automatic weapon discharged by the man behind the palms. Kaleho didn't stop and dove into the front door. He knocked over the plant near the door as he hit the floor and rolled into his darkened living room. A burst of gunfire behind the couch hit the wall above his head. In the prone position, he fired directly at the dark outline of the person that was firing. Three down.

Kaleho got up onto his knees beside the front door jamb. The door was still open. He leaned quickly out of the door with his pistol aiming straight away. The man in the clump of palms had stepped out from behind the trees to follow. He was startled by Kaleho's sudden appearance at that door. It was the last emotion the man ever had. Kaleho put two rounds in him. Four down.

He stayed low and moved toward the hallway. He knelt at the corner wall to the hallway and did a mental check of rounds. *Eight used, nine left*. He heard a subdued scream from their bedroom. *Leilani*.

He poked his head around the corner of the wall and the fire from an automatic at the end of the dark hallway sent plaster flying. He ducked back behind the corner just in time to feel the spray of splinters from the bullet exploding through the two-by-four framing in the wall.

Knowing time was essential, he visualized where he saw the shots come from and reached around and blindly shot at the ceiling above where the man was standing. There was a risk of killing Leilani by shooting blindly down the hall, so shooting at the ceiling would reduce the risk. And he guessed it would cause the shooter to stoop or drop. Kaleho then quickly laid flat on his belly and rolled into the hallway entrance. As he rolled he held his weapon with both hand and fired three rounds. The man, who was on one knee, collapsed backwards and his gun bounced down the hallway.

Kaleho got to his knees and ran toward the bedroom door, which was opened. There could be an ambush waiting for him, so he fired a shot at the bedroom door frame to get a reaction. There were no shots.

When Kaleho reached the doorway he saw a man dressed in black with a backpack crawling out of one of two opened bedroom windows. He fired at the man in an attempt to wound him. The man fell forward out of sight. He saw no sign of his wife.

Kaleho sprinted to the window and saw the wounded man on the ground reaching for his assault weapon. Another quick shot ended the man, and Kaleho dashed to the front of his house.

The van accelerated from the curb as its side door was sliding closed. Kaleho raised his weapon to fire, but then lowered it. He couldn't take a chance at killing Leilani.

He ran to the side of his car and jumped over the passenger door and landed on the driver's seat. A quick hop allowed him to fall cleanly on his seat with his butt. He turned the switch and the engine came alive. He jerked the car into gear and looked over his shoulder as he pressed the pedal to accelerate backwards out of his drive. The front end shook violently and the screeching of metal on concrete echoed down the neighborhood street.

He stopped and stuck his head out the window to check the front driver's-side tire. It was flat. He jumped out and looked at the other front tire. It too was flat. He spun around in the direction of the van and saw it disappear at the intersection a block away. They were gone. Leilani was gone.

# Chapter 20: *Holes*

Rick was sitting next to Kaleho on the front lanai of Kaleho's house. Bullet holes lined both sides of the door. Kaleho set with his knees up and his head resting in his palms. Rick watched as the last of the six dead men were wheeled away down the driveway by the coroner. CSI team members were all over the place.

"I thought you said that the man on the phone said no police," as he watched the crews at work.

"Can't have a shooting, especially one that results in death, in a neighborhood and have it ignored by the police," said Kaleho. "This was well planned, so they'll know there will be an investigation. What they meant was that they didn't want me to cooperate in the search or send my policemen to search for Leilani."

"Oh," said Rick. "I know you're the Chief of Police, but can you stop an investigation?"

"No," answered Kaleho. "The FBI will be on this in a heartbeat. And the media will be broadcasting it on the eleven o'clock news. Best I can do is to relieve myself from this investigation and to take some time off."

"It certainly was well planned," said Rick after a few moments of silence. "Officer Lee told me that someone had purposely plowed into a pylon and then lit the car on fire to cause H1 to be closed. They needed to make sure you didn't get here in time. You probably surprised them that you got here as fast as you did."

"I know I did. I don't think they expected to have a gun battle, although they were certainly prepared for it."

"You were lucky you didn't get killed. You took out six people with automatic weapons with a single pistol. And you still had rounds in it." Rick paused for a couple of seconds. "And you didn't even get a scrape. Just a few splinters in the side of your face and holes in your shirt."

"Holes in my shirt?"

"Yeah." Rick tugged at the side of his shirt. Two holes with jagged edges were plainly visible.

Kaleho glanced down at the holes and then grimaced like he was trying to think of the event that created the holes. "I guess it came from the guy firing at me from the palm trees. I dove through the door as he was shooting."

"Like I said, you were lucky," said Rick.

"Uh huh," said Kaleho as he looked back at the ground in front of him.

"So what are you going to do?" asked Rick. "You know of course, that I'm willing to help in any way."

"I can't risk any more lives. I'll find her, and it will be on my own terms."

"Let me rephrase this. I'm going to help, so tell me what you want us to do. We're not the police and we can be discreet."

"We? There is no we. I'm not bringing your family into this. I can't...I won't."

"Don't argue with me on this Kaleho. Once my family finds out, there'll be no stopping them anyway. We are family. Let us help you find Leilani."

Kaleho sat awhile, then nodded and spoke. "Alright."

# Chapter 21: *Melting Point*

It was early morning on the **Amphitrite**. Shelli, Nikki, Stephen Chang, Stephanie, and Kaleho sat at the conference room table. Rick and Danielle walked in with trays of breakfast foods, pineapple juice, guava juice, and coffee. Eyes were sunken and the room was mostly quiet. No one had gotten much sleep.

Everyone ate in relative silence, unsure what to say given what had happened the night before. The portals were open, which let the morning sun and the distance sounds of a couple of *manu-o-Kū* seabirds. The situation awareness display at the front of the conference room had a view of the harbor from one of the cameras on the top deck.

Rick broke the silence. "I can assume you haven't heard from the kidnappers yet, Kaleho."

"No. They called me on my unlisted mobile phone when they took her, so I can assume that's what they will call on again."

"And they said they wanted Grandfather?" said Stephen.

"Yes," said Kaleho.

"Since we don't have him, what are your going to say to them?" asked Stephen.

"Well first of all, I'm not trading your grandfather even if we did have him."

"Grandfather has led a long life. He would think it would be dishonorable to allow your wife to die to let an old man live," said Stephen.

"That's not the point, Stephen. Even if we were to deliver your grandfather, they will likely get what they want out of him and kill both him and Leilani. We need leverage. We need to get ahead of them on this.

"How do you propose we do this?" said Rick.

"We need to find Leilani first. If we find her, we might be able to develop a plan to get her out of wherever they have her. Maybe we use S.W.A.T. or maybe hostage rescue. But whatever we might do cannot happen until we find her. And since they told me they'd kill her if I searched for her, it makes finding her difficult."

"We have ways of performing an extensive, covert search by air, land and sea. In fact, we were preparing this while you were sleeping."

"I don't think I slept a wink. Tried, but I just tossed and turned. But to the point, how would you undertake this search? They may interpret you searching as the same as me searching."

Ryan came in the room and nodded to Rick. Then sat down to eat and listen. Nikki smiled at him as he hoovered his food.

"No boots on the ground, so to speak. We'll use electronic surveillance only. As I said, it is covert. But covert doesn't mean undetectable. There is no such thing as a zero percent chance of being detected, which is why we would not dare to begin without your approval."

"So we search for her. Say we find her. Got any ideas as to what to do at that point? They obviously think we have Stephen's grandfather. If they find out we don't have him, they will likely kill Leilani and renew their search for him."

"What if we got someone to dress up and put on a disguise to look like Chang's grandfather? We could give him some secret gadgets to help him escape while we attack them," said Stephanie.

"Hey yeah, sort of like a Trojan horse," said Shelli.

"Who would do that? No disrespect, Stephen, but none of us could fool anybody to think we're Mr. Chang. We'd have to use an older person and we'd be back in the same boat, so to speak," said Nikki.

"I think we're forgetting the big picture here," said Danielle. "Why does the triad want Stephen's grandfather?"

It was quiet for a moment, and then Shelli said, "They want the treasure and they think he knows where it is."

"Precisely," said Danielle.

"So if we had the treasure, we could trade that for Leilani instead of my grandfather?" said Stephen.

"Of course," said Danielle.

"We haven't been able to find Stephen's grandfather. If we can't find him, I doubt the triad can. So maybe we should spend our time searching for the treasure," said Shelli.

"Wait a minute," interrupted Kaleho. "We have no idea where the treasure is. We don't even know if Stephen's grandfather knows or if it is even real. I could get the call from the kidnappers any minute, and I don't feel it's the best use of time searching for a treasure."

Again, quiet in the room.

"I'm afraid Kaleho is right, we don't know where the treasure is," said Danielle. "Unless Stephen's grandfather knows exactly where it is, we might as well try converting lead into gold. It's just not possible."

"Lead to gold? Sure it is," said Rick.

"What? Come on, Rick. That's alchemy," said Danielle.

"No, it isn't. Lead has 2 more protons than gold. Shed the protons and you get gold."

"That's not possible, Rick. If it was, gold would be worthless now," said Danielle.

"Actually it is possible. It's called transmutation. It's not done through chemistry, but physicists have been able to do it. It is believed the Russians did it accidently with one of their reactors back in the early seventies. Other heavier elements were turned to gold in small quantities back in the early eighties. But it's not cost effective...the cost to transmute is greater than the worth of the end result."

"And besides, the coins were silver – not gold," said Shelli.

"What difference does it make, we can't make lead into gold, lead into silver, or the lack of clues into the treasure for that matter?" said Danielle.

"Trojan horse," whispered Rick to himself. He walked around to Shelli. "You're brilliant, Shelli. Sweetie, pull up the silver Hawaiian Dollar picture on the screen."

Shelli looked at her dad and smiled for a moment as she absorbed the compliment. Then she spun around in her seat and pulled herself up to the command station. Seconds later, the video view of the port outside gave way to the large digitally enhanced photo of the silver Hawaiian coin on the situation awareness display.

"Now do a search on the Internet for metal weight comparisons," said Rick.

94

Shelli clicked away again. "How's this?" She slid a numeric table with the metal weights per cubic foot next to the photo of the coin on the situation awareness display.

"Perfect," answered Rick. Rick paced the room as he talked. "What if we build our own Trojan horse? Well not an actual wooden horse, but what if we built a fake treasure?"

"Fake treasure?" asked Stephanie. "Like those chocolate pirate coins?"

"Well, sort of," said Rick. "We could construct a hollow coin and fill it with something to make it weigh the same as a real coin."

Everyone started to talk at the same time, but Rick motioned for them to be quiet, and continued. "Bear with me while I explain. If we made hollow coins, we could fill them with a heavier substance and paint them to match the real coins. Notice on the table that there are only three metals that weigh more than gold. Iridium, Osmium, and Platinum. If the coins were made of gold, then we'd be in real trouble because those three metals cost more per ounce than gold. But our coins are made of silver, like Shelli said. Silver weighs 654.91 pounds per cubic foot according to the chart. Check out the weight for lead -- it's 707.96 pounds per cubic foot. So we can build a hollow coin and fill it with lead."

"Shelli, open two more browser windows," said Rick. "Type 'melting point for lead' in one browser window and 'melting point for aluminum' in the other window." Shelli completed the task quickly and placed the two answers below the table and coin on the situation awareness display.

"Notice that lead melts at 621.5 degrees Fahrenheit, and aluminum melts at 1,221 degrees Fahrenheit. So we could pour liquid lead into aluminum coins and match the weight of silver."

"Rick, this sounds border line crazy," said Kaleho. "How are you going to make thousands of coins? And even if you could build the perfect coin replicas in that quantity, don't you think they would have an expert verify them before the trade?"

"That's two good points," said Rick. "As to the first point, I think we can indeed do this. I suspect there are plenty of machine shops or companies with CNC machines here on O'ahu that could machine the quantities quickly. And if there aren't, I know there are in California. I'll have one of my mechanical engineers create the computer drawings necessary for the machinists, and they will email them to the various machine shops. Although we could melt the lead ourselves using kilns, I think it would be unhealthy for us to do this for thousands of coins. I think we'll need to hire a lead weight manufacturing company to fill them."

Kaleho looked at him expressionless for what seemed to be a minute. "You're serious, aren't you?"

"Yes I am. What do we have to lose? My engineers can do this while we search for Stephen's grandfather and Leilani. If we don't get it done, we'll have to go with plan B."

"What is plan B?" asked Kaleho.

"I don't know," said Rick.

"If we did make the coins, what about the expert? How we going to get around that?" asked Kaleho.

"I don't know," said Rick again. "We need to know how the experts test them."

"I know," said Shelli. "We already know that not all the coins were melted down. And we have good pictures of the coins because there are coins collectors around the world that own them.   What if we go buy whatever real ones are available and put them on top of the fake ones?"

"Brilliant," said Rick. "We'll let you be the one to track down the coins.  Check the island coin stores first and then online collectors.   Buy not only the dollar coins, but any of the half-dollars, quarters, and dimes. "

"What if the expert picks up one of the fake dollars we make?" said Kaleho.

"Shelli, do a search on silver coin testing," said Rick.

After a few quick strokes on the keyboard, a Shelli slid a website up on how to test for fake silver coins.

"Just as I figured," said Rick when he glanced through the list. "Weight and an inspection of dimensions and lettering.   We'll pass those easily.   And aluminum and lead aren't magnetic, just like silver.   So we'll pass that test.   What concerns me is the bleach test.   Our coins will not pass that test – they won't tarnish like silver.   We'll need to do silver plating."

"That sounds like a lengthy process," said Danielle.   "And how will you know if you get the right purity?   Just how pure do you think the silver content in those coins were?   And the patina, how are you going to get that right?

"All good questions," said Rick.   "First, the silver plating is sometimes used when fast heat transfer is needed in the electronics world.   So there are a lot of electroplating companies around.   I've used those shops before when building some of our specialty hardware and printed circuit boards.   I can get a 24 to 48 hour turnaround with an expedite fee.   The question on the patina can be addressed with baths of acid and bleach.  Acid will do minor damage and pitting, and like the article says, bleach will tarnish.  We'll just have to be careful not to take off too much of the silver.  Purity is a tough one.   How are we going to address that one?"

"Dad I don't know if this makes any sense or is even legal, but what about just buying other coins from that time period and melt them down?   It shouldn't take a lot of them if it's just for silver plating."

"I like that idea a lot, Nikki," said Rick. "That would get us as close as we're going to come to creating the perfect counterfeit. But I don't know the laws on destroying collectables." With that statement, they all turned to the only policemen in their group – Kaleho.

"We do have a lot of laws here in the state on artifacts, but coin collecting probably isn't included under those laws.   But frankly speaking, I don't know every law there is."

"Since we're all conspiring to create counterfeit currency, let's not get into any more trouble by destroying artifacts," said Rick. "Since you're in charge of coin acquisition, Shelli, find out the percentages of other metals present in coins from that day.  If significant, we'll add those to the plating mixture."

"Will do, Dad," said Shelli.

"I don't know what to say," said Kaleho. "This still sounds crazy to me – and crazy expensive."

"Don't worry about cost," said Rick. "Leilani is worth more than any amount of money."

"You got that right," said Kaleho.   "Tell you what, if you're willing to do this, go for it.  I'll work up a backup plan – a raid in case this fails. But remember, we must find her as soon as possible."

"We're ready to start searching right now," said Nikki.

"Can you explain how?" said Kaleho.

"Of course," said Nikki with a smile. "I'll be happy to go over all of it with you. Dad put me in charge of getting the equipment ready. Ryan and I worked on this most of the night. That's why Ryan was late to breakfast this morning. He was getting the last piece ready to deploy in case you said go."

"You mean you spent all that effort in case I *might* say yes?" asked a surprised Kaleho.

"It takes a while to get this amount of equipment properly staged. Better to have to put it away if you say 'no' than to have to start preparing now if you said 'yes.' And as you said before, we need to get ahead of this."

"Alright then, explain it to me," said Kaleho

Nikki walked up to a free command station. She waved to Kaleho. "Come, have a seat."

# Chapter 22: *Approval*

A map of O'ahu was on the display. With a click of the mouse, dotted lines of various colors showed up all around it. The lines were labeled with all sorts of sensors and gadgets. Kaleho felt as if he was being briefed by the Secretary of Defense before going to war. Nikki was concise and didn't try to explain how the technology worked, just what it did.

"The two ultralight helicopters, or mini-copters as we call them, will fly in continuous rotations along the shore and mountain ridges. The forest of the mountains is dense, so we'll be using thermal cameras to detect heat signatures under the tree canopy. When we see something of interest, we can also launch small drones from the mini-copter, from the ship, from the **Spearfish**, or the Audi SUV if we need to do so covertly."

"I saw the one from the SUV... it was impressive," said Kaleho.

Nikki clicked on an icon on her screen and up came a video wall. Tiny thumbnails of video covering the entire screen. "We've also tapped into every video feed we could find on the island. This includes those feeds at the airport and port terminals too. A facial recognition system searches all these feeds continuously for Leilani and known triad members. And we will deploy the same social media search tool that we used to locate Stephen, except this time we'll be searching for references to 'hostage,' 'chief's wife,' 'Leilani,' and the like. Two of the men you took down were young, so we're looking for trends in social media from those two over the last few days as well. We can also tap into wireless networks, like those used in coffee shops and book stores. But that would require a warrant. If anyone is on the inside of the judicial system and has connections to the triad, then they'd know you violated their demands. So we're avoiding that for now."

"That is amazing," said Kaleho.   He thought for a minute. "That seems to cover land, but what about the water?"

"When you went down below to see our suite of technology, you probably saw a bunch of surfboards.  They are actually solar powered surfboard sensors.  The surfboards will relay panoramic digital snapshots several times a minute.   Besides cameras, they have sensors that enable them to monitor water motion, such as tides and currents.  We have added programming so they will also monitor the Kelvin, or V-wakes, coming off of ships as well as the turbulent wakes that trail directly behind.  The Kelvin wakes travel for substantial distances from a ship, and the sensors can detect them even if the human eye can no longer see them.  The boards can monitor these wakes and pinpoint ship positions that are miles away.   Ryan sent a truckload of these up to the U-of-H facility on the north shore known as HIMB, the Hawai'i Institute of Marine Biology.   We trained a few MOP students on how to use them.  The rest of the boards will be released from here."

"What are MOP students?" asked Kaleho.

"Oh, sorry," said Nikki.  "MOP stands for Marine Option Program.   It's like a minor's program in marine science offered at the university.  And they often work out at HIMB.   Dad was a MOP student."

"Hey, I remember that.   He asked me for a ride out there a few times," said Kaleho.

Nikki slid a mechanical drawing of the **Amphitrite.**   The drawing showed each deck of the ship, and at the bottom was the launch portal for the mini-submarine.   "We'll also launch our new mini-submarine, the **Stingray**, from below the ship."

"From below the ship?" asked Kaleho. "How does it do that?"

"The hull has what you might think of as a trap door.   The cradle for the **Stingray** is welded to that door.   So the cradle and the **Stingray** itself are lowered into the water when the door is lowered.   No one will know it is out there.   The **Stingray** can stay out for up to a week at a time, although I think you might go crazy if you had to stay underwater that long in such a relatively small space."

She then referred back to the broader map view of O'ahu. "The surfboards will be always moving with the currents. For persistent surveillance, we're also deploying surveillance buoys. Because they are pretty big, we only have four onboard. They have radar, daylight and thermal cameras, and communication systems onboard. They are solar powered as well. We're going to put them at points around the island that we think could use long-term surveillance.   We loaded two buoys on the **Stingray** for Mom to bring out."

Next, Nikki showed a mechanical drawing of the mini-copter on the screen.  It was labeled with all of its features, sensors, and equipment. "We also have sonar buoys, also known as sonobuoys that can be dropped by the mini-copters to track underwater movement if we need them."

"We're going after the triad," said Kaleho.   "They don't normally buy into fancy technology. They typically do business at the personal level…beatings, extortion, and killings. They won't be expecting this."

"I think we'll find her if she's still on or near O'ahu," said Nikki.

"They can't do a trade if she's not here," said Kaleho.

"True.   So you feel satisfied with what we're going to do?" asked Nikki.

"I approve," said Kaleho.

"Good, we'll start in few minutes.  You're welcome to watch," said Nikki.

# Chapter 23: *Deployment*

Kaleho stepped into the bridge of the **Amphitrite**. It was clear that the bridge had been completely modified with state-of-the-art navigation technology. The bridge windows had waist-high-to-ceiling glass. The bright Hawaiian sun was subdued and the sky seemed a deeper blue in the glass, which appeared to be over an inch thick. *Was it bulletproof? Likely.* Kaleho marveled at the suite of built-in monitors in the consoles that surrounded the perimeter walls of the bridge. Additional displays in an island next to the captain's chair had 360-degree views around the boat. One large display sat on the back wall of the bridge, next to the door going to the conference room. It was similar to the one in the conference room. It had digital maps of the harbor and of O'ahu on it.

Nikki was standing in the middle of the bridge with her tablet in her hand. She had a headset on, and was talking to her dad, Ryan, and to someone at the HIMB facility on Coconut Island in Kāne'ohe Bay. Rick was on the **Spearfish**, which was tied up at the dock in the Port of Honolulu. A video camera mounted on the underside of the **Spearfish** console roof was aimed at him. It followed his movements as he was securing the solar surfboards behind and in front of the console. Ryan was on the helicopter pad, preparing to take the first shift on the search. Shelli and Stephanie were in the conference room monitoring the facial recognition software on recorded and new video feeds. They were also booting up the social media search software.

Stephen Chang and Kaleho stood behind Nikki. Two outer windows on the bridge were slid open and the slight breeze from the trade winds caused strands of her long hair to dance on Nikki's shoulders and her back. She had on tight fitting shorts that, like the style of the day dictated, covered little of her leg. She also had on gray Nike Free sneakers, and a Hawaiian floral print top with cropped short sleeves over a tank top. Her skin was tanned, she was exceptionally fit, and she was one hundred percent focused on the job at hand.

"Weather looks good over the mountains, Ryan. Since there is frequently cloud cover along the Pali ridge, I would suggest you check there first. I've uploaded a schedule of search routes to your phone and to the onboard *nav* computer. Keep an eye on your fuel gauge. I've set up fueling accounts at Honolulu Airport and Dillingham Airfield. In case of an emergency, you can land at the old Bellows Base in Waimānalo. But if you do land there, try to make it to the old concrete pad near the Hughes Road entrance. I've marked that spot in the map database as well. You can also land at the Wheeler Army Airfield, just off H2 and near Schofield Barracks. But you must radio them first before landing. Same goes for the Marine Corp Base in Kailua. Both Wheeler and the Marine Corp Base have significant helicopter facilities. And I think I'd choose the airport for emergency fueling over Hickam Air Force Base if you can help it."

"Roger that," said Ryan's voice over speakers in the bridge console. "I'm lifting off now."

"Remember to keep checking both the nav radio and your cell phone for communication," reminded Nikki. "And the installed GoPro cameras on the chopper are streaming through the cellular network. You'll get better frame rates and better quality images on the cameras when you're hovering."

Even though the rotor blades were at spinning blindingly fast, his voice from the speaker was crystal clear. "I know, I know," said Ryan. And he slowly lifted off deck.

"See you in one hour," said Nikki.

"Can't wait," said Ryan.

"Dad, you ready?" asked Nikki.

"Casting off now," said Rick.

Rick pulled away slowly from the dock. Video from the onboard camera showed Rick in the foreground and the dock and the **Amphitrite** receding in the background. Another camera from **Amphitrite** followed the **Spearfish** as it headed north around Sand Island. Kaleho noticed the boat sat considerably lower in the water than when he saw it before. Undoubtedly due to the weight of all the solar surfboards onboard.

"I've mirrored my email and voicemail to your phone and your sister's phone, Nikki," said Rick. "I'm going to be preoccupied with the surfboard deployment, and the motors are too loud for me to hear a ring. I'm expecting to hear progress on the contracts we sent out for the coins sometime in the next hour or so."

"Ok, Dad. I've tied the nav console on the **Spearfish** to your phone via Bluetooth. So messages will pop up on that if you're still in cell range out there," said Nikki. "I did check and it appears you should have cell coverage for at least 20 miles from shore for your planned deployment route along southern O'ahu."

"I've got such a smart daughter," said Rick.

"Hey, I heard that," came Shelli's voice over the speakers. "What am I, chump change?"

Before Rick could answer, Nikki spoke, "Yes."

"Dad, did you hear that?" said Shelli.

"You're just as smart, Shelli," said Rick. "Remember what I said to you when you thought of the Trojan horse idea?"

Nikki swiped her tablet and studied it for a few seconds. Kahelo felt a slight tremor in the floor, but didn't hear or see anything that might have caused it. He looked back at the big display in the back of the bridge and saw an animated side view of the **Amphitrite** with the hull trap door completely extended. The cradle below the **Stingray** was flashing.

"Mom, the mooring locks have been released. You can launch when ready."

"Ok, Nikki," said Danielle. "Lifting ... five percent throttle now."

Kaleho saw the animated submarine move slowed from the cradles. It proceeded to head south of the stern. The dark shadow could be seen from the stern mounted camera for a few seconds until it blended into the deeper blues in the center of the harbor.

"I'm taking Honolulu Channel south by the cruise ship terminal," said Danielle over the radio. "That's deeper than going north. Let me know if there are any large ships coming in."

"Will do, Mom," said Nikki. "AIS shows a container ship heading this way. At its present speed, it will take it twenty minutes before it gets to the channel. Radar shows only the **Spearfish** and a couple of other fishing boats in the area. Nothing to worry about."

"Thanks," said Danielle. "I'll do a coms check at twenty-minute intervals."

"OK, be safe," said Nikki.

"AIS?" asked Kaleho.

"Automatic Identification System," answered Nikki. "Commercial ships are required to have AIS transponders. It allows the vessels to be tracked miles away. It allows harbor masters to manage ship traffic at ports."

"Oh. Why doesn't Danielle have camera feeds or AIS feeds?" asked Kaleho.

"Radio signals don't travel far underwater," said Nikki. "Mom will have to surface or get close to the surface and release a floatable antenna in order to communicate."

"So that means she is all alone when submerged," said Kaleho. "No wonder you said that you might get a little crazy being in that for a week."

"Yeah. If you're not busy or focused, it's like being in solitary confinement. We have a pretty powerful computer onboard with several Petabytes of stored scientific, geographical, and historical data stored online. The *Stingray* can basically pilot itself, and the acoustic sensors and cameras onboard search automatically. So until there is something to look at, she'll be reading. Mom contacted Barbara Stallings this morning and I know she downloaded a lot of additional historical data on the last quarter century of the 1800's and the early 1900's. I think she's trying to figure out where those pirates might have gone after the raid."

"Is Rick OK with your mom being on the sub by herself?" asked Kaleho.

"That's probably the safest place any of us could be. She's just going to release two of the sensor buoys today—west and north of the island. Then she'll cruise between them in case they spot something offshore. She'll come in is she starts to get tired. Mom wanted more hours on the *Stingray,* so she's good. She knows how to pilot it, but she wants to stay sharp."

Nikki looked at Stephen. "You ready?"

"Yes, I'll be starting in Chinatown and then cruise all the places Grandfather might be."

"You feel like you can operate the SUV equipment and drone well enough?" asked Nikki.

"Yes. It's not that difficult. I'm outta here."

Stephen left the bridge, and a couple minutes later appeared on the gangway. He jogged to the Audi SUV and got in. He disappeared a few minutes later.

"He's searching for his Grandfather?" asked Kaleho.

"Yep. We all thought that it was worthwhile to try to find him. He may know where the treasure is. As you know, the Audi is mostly bulletproof and can drive itself, so it can get both Stephen and his grandfather back here safely."

Kaleho lowered and shook his head. When he lifted his head, Nikki was looking at him. "You know, I appreciate what you and the family are doing for me... for Leilani."

Nikki smiled. "Don't thank us. Dad considers you family, and there is nothing we Bryants wouldn't do for family. Besides, we're going to need your help. Ryan and I didn't get much sleep last night, so we're going to need some help with flight rotations. Dad would like us to train you on the mini-copters. That is, once you've figured out your strategy for Plan B."

"Ultralight helicopters...awesome," said Kaleho. "Kai will be jealous."

Kaleho's mobile phone rang. His heart raced as he reached for it. He sighed. "Speaking of which, it's Kai."

Kaleho took the call and talked with his son for a while. He didn't like what he heard, so he ended the call with "and stay put until I get there. Bye."

When he hung up, he said, "I need to pick up Kai. He's staying with one of his friends and they headed down to the Diamond Head to surf. If the triad wanted to pick him up, it would be one of the first places they would look for him."

"Does he know about Leilani?" asked Nikki.

"He knows. I spared him the drama that took place at our house, but he knows she was taken. He desperately wanted to help, but I told him it would be better to stay with his friends. They'd keep him preoccupied. And I've got a unit parked out front of the friend's house 24/7 for protection. They live within a healthy hike from Diamond Head Beach Park. Surfing lets you forget the world, so I can't really blame him for going. Kai said they left out the back door, and forgot to tell the security detail out front. So I need call the detail, and go pick him up."

Kaleho called his unit. "They are on the way to the park. It'll take me at least a half-hour to get there with no traffic. So I feel relieved they will be there in a couple of minutes."

"Mom thinks you and Kai should both stay onboard until we find Leilani. Dad checked us out of the hotel, and with Stephen now staying here too, we're getting a little tight on space. But if you don't mind close quarters, we would be happy for you guys to stay with us."

"That's a good idea. And I think I would feel better with Kai here."

"Before you go, let me check with Shelli."

"Shelli, are you all set on the command station? Are all the feeds coming in?"

"Yes," answered Shelli over the radio speaker. "We'll be right there."

The door opened at the rear of the bridge, and Stephanie and Shelli entered.

"There are literally over a thousand live feeds coming in," said Shelli. "Based on what Dad and I discussed, I selected all the likely places they might go. We've reached the limit of our bandwidth on the satellite and cellular networks. And Officer Lee got me access to the airport feeds and all the archived feeds from the airport since the Leilani was kidnapped. He also got me the recorded feeds from traffic cameras too. If the triad appears with Leilani in the open, we'll likely see her. The social media software is running too. Everything is automated at this point. I have it sending results to Stephanie's and my phones if it needs our inputs. Otherwise it will signal you if it finds Leilani or anything related to her is found."

"Please let me know if you guys get anything at all that could be a lead," said Kaleho. "You've got my number. I've got to go pick up Kai."

"Stephanie and I can't drive, and I'm in charge of finding coins. I found some coins in town, and I'm going to try to buy them. Dad didn't want us to go out on our own. Could you take us to those coin dealers after you pick up Kai?"

"Sure," said Kaleho. "Are any of them in Waikiki?"

"Yes, in fact there is one," answered Shelli.

"Well then, I've got just enough room for you two and Kai in the Chevelle. Kai will have to leave his board with his friend, but I expect this will be one time he won't mind it."

Shelli and Stephanie looked at each other and giggled. "Great," she said.

Kaleho examined all the displays one last time. Little icons were spreading along the southern shore from the port, and the northern shore from the HIMB facility. They were the solar surfboards. He saw video feeds coming in from the helicopter. He grinned and walked off the bridge with Shelli and Stephanie. Still in earshot of the bridge, he heard Danielle performing her first radio check from somewhere west of Pearl Harbor.

# Chapter 24: *Youth*

Kaleho drove slowly down Kalakaua Drive in his bright red convertible. He often felt pride in his ride as he saw heads turn as he passed the beach crowds to his right and the last hotels to his left. Shelli and Stephanie's long flowing hair in the back seat probably added to the tourists' prolonged stares. He'd be amused by it all if he could stop thinking about Leilani.

As was typically the case, the beachgoers thinned as he approached the Waikiki Aquarium and the large Banyan trees of Kapiolani Park to this left. As he slowed in front of the circular fountain, he heard a flurry of fake digital camera snapshot sounds from his backset. The girls were snapping pictures with their smartphones of the fountain with the backdrop of Diamond Head.

He turned right onto Diamond Head Road, and slowed to a crawl in traffic that formed at Makelai Beach Park from tourists taking selfies with offshore breakers, and again at the lighthouse just before Diamond Head Beach Park. Minutes later he arrived at the beach park. He thought he was going to have to park his car in the striped no-parking area in front of the trail down to the beach, when he saw a spot open up along the road just beyond.

Kaleho hopped out his car and scanned the area at the top of the trail head. He saw the police car of his son's security detail parked farther up the road. No one was in the car, but then he saw one of his officers standing near the edge of bluffs looking out over the water with his binoculars. He must have sensed someone was watching him, and glanced around his shoulder. He saw Kaleho and gave a nod, which without saying implied the police brotherhood had his back. Kaleho nodded back, affirming the untold appreciation. Knowing at least the entrance was secure, Kaleho walked briskly down the trail.

The girls, young and seemingly oblivious to his angst, drifted behind him down the trail. They were consumed in their zeal to get the best selfie all the way down to the beach. He was constantly reminded of his youth whenever he saw his son. The feeling of invincibility when young made death an unreal concept. *Oh to be young again.* He reached the beach well ahead of the girls. He stopped and said hello to the second officer on the security detail. He was watching the beach for potential problems.

He took a deep breath and let out a sigh of relief when he saw is son crouching on his board for stability inside the mouth of a curling wall of water. After seeing his son safe, Kaleho felt the tension in his shoulders subside for the first time since his wife was taken.

Kaleho long ago gave up on trying to get his son to meet him up at the road. He knew that a stern look from the shore was about the only thing that would pull his son from the waves. He pointed out Kai to the girls and they shouted and waved in unison when he caught his last of nature's watery rides into shore.

Leilani often told him over the years that Kai was his father's son for sure. Kaleho agreed that he might have contributed a little to his son's skill on the water. But when it came to his appearance, Kai could thank his mother. He had an athletic build, and was handsome. His Hawaiian heritage gave him his smooth caramel skin and dark hair, but his classic good looks were all Leilani. Kai's phone never stopped buzzing from high school girl's texting or snap chatting, and he had to warn Kai numerous times of the perils of teenage flirtations. But when it came time for surfing, the phone stayed in the car or buried in his towel on the beach. Surf first and everything else second – including girls.

Kaleho shook himself free of his thoughts and worries. He didn't want to upset Kai. He thought about smiling, but decided that might give a false sense of progress...of hope. Despite the tremendous turmoil inside, he tried to squelch his emotions.

His son emerged from the blue Pacific with his surfboard in hand. The cloudless Hawaiian sky of pale blue silhouetted his tan body. He ducked his head and then swung his head back to clear the hair from his face.

Realizing that all he could hear was the sound of the breeze in the trees above him and the surf in front of him, Kaleho looked at the girls. Both were spellbound and speechless. No photos, texting, talking or even giggling. Stephanie was closest to Kaleho and she stood with her mouth agape. Shelli had no expression and stood motionless with her phone in her hand. Kaleho could see she was recording video, but seemed to have forgotten that now.

"Kaihekoa, meet Stephanie and Shelli," said Kaleho. His voice snapped them out of their trance. "You probably don't remember, but you met Shelli Bryant when you were much younger."

"Hello again, I guess," said Kai as he stepped forward and shook Stephanie's and then Shelli's hand.

"Kaihekoa, what a marvelous name. The brave spear," said Shelli. "It's nice to meet you ... again."

Kai was surprised that the beautiful girl in front of him knew what his Hawaiian named meant. He stared for a few seconds until he realized he was still holding her hand. Then he let go and took a step back. "Wow. Uh...my friends call me Kai."

Kaleho watched the brief, shy interaction. Now he wished he had been recording all this on his phone. *Leilani would have loved to have seen…. Leilani.*

"Son, girls, we need to get going," said Kaleho.

Kai asked about his mom as he quickly rinsed off the saltwater from the outdoor shower. Kaleho gave him an abbreviated status as they began their walk up the steep trail. The same trail Kaleho had come up days ago, before Leilani had been taken. At the first bend he saw a mongoose peek its head over the uncut brown grasses and then duck and scurry out of sight. Probably the same one he had seen before. Pests...time to do some pest control himself, thought Kaleho.

# Chapter 25: *Update from Home*

Rick was focused on his task of deploying solar surfboards along the southern coast of O'ahu. He had discussed the deployment locations with Nikki and she had programmed the drop positions into the nav console. Rick loved going out on the boat to fish with the girls. He also enjoyed the occasional SCUBA dive, or snorkeling and spearfishing. But he was never out on the water enough to be able to judge his distance and bearings like a true seaman. So he was grateful for the nav console – especially since he had never been this far out on a boat in Hawai'i.

He was deploying from West to East. He was now more than 2 miles south of Waikiki Beach. He was in blue water and well beyond the surf. The console showed the water depth at over 1400 feet. He gazed back in the direction of the beach as he rubbed his sore back. He couldn't make out people, but he could still see the skyline of the massive hotels that lined the shore. Diamond Head was also clearly visible with its brown summertime color contrasting strongly from the greener mountains in the background and the city in the foreground.

The surfboards were substantially heavier with the gear on them. He was using the portable hand-cranked davit to lower them in the water, but he was still having to maneuver them to the davit first. He was old enough to see that his body was not nearly what it was in his youth, despite his workout regimen.

The console beeped, and he noticed a call was coming in with a Florida area code. He remembered that Nikki had tied in his phone by Bluetooth to the console. Only a few people had his unlisted number, so he killed the motor and clicked *Answer.*

"Hello, this is Rick."

"Hi Rick. Mike Steele here."

"Hi Mike. How are you doing?"

"Fine. I hope you're enjoying Hawai'i."

"We've been busy, but it's beautiful, of course. We're hoping to get some good fishing in too once the case is solved." Rick knew Mike liked to fish on his time off too.

"Well let me not hold you up. I'm calling to give you an update into the investigation on William Hawthorne. First off, we located the helicopter that was used in his murder. It landed at the airstrip in Arcadia. It's a municipal airport used primarily by the public. You know, small aircraft like Cessna and Piper planes. The helicopter was abandoned and forensics said it was wiped clean."

"Did you find out any information about the people that rented it?"

"No," answered Mike. "The pilot used falsified licenses. Looks like they planned this out well in advance. They gave us a description of the pilot at the rental center, but it's pretty vague. We reviewed the surveillance camera feeds at the rental center. The pilot wore a cap and sunglasses, so that was not very helpful. No one boarded the helicopter when he took off, so he must have picked up the shooter after arriving in Sarasota."

"What about pictures or video from Arcadia? Did they get any details at all, like the number of people on the helicopter? Anything at all we could use to search for them?"

"Arcadia is a small town and the airport has very few flights. No one would check on or question a helicopter landing there. There are several cameras mounted around the hangar, but they didn't have a view of the helicopter's landing. The airport is fenced, but it would be easy to cross it with one of those multipurpose ladders. But I expect they could have just as easily walked out to parking area and driven out unnoticed. The local police force is assisting us. They are canvasing the neighborhood, but admitted upfront that they expect to find nothing that will help us."

"Well that's disappointing," said Rick. "What about Bill? Did you find out more about him?"

"It seems like he was spending a lot of time following your family. In fact, he seemed to spend more time on them than on watching you. That seemed a bit odd to me. Given all the work you do, I had assumed he was focused on you."

"That does seems odd. How were you tracking his movements?" asked Rick.

"My lab guys studied all the data from your home and office surveillance system that you sent us. It took them a while to figure out how to use your program to look for abnormalities, but once they did they added more refinements. I don't understand it how it works, but we were all glad we didn't have to screen weeks of video to get to the important stuff. We also pulled the GPS system data out of his rental cars. He had several burner smartphones, but he didn't shut off the GPS on them. So we had that data too. We checked airport feeds and found he flew in to SRQ from Chicago. The FBI is also working on this case now, and they have tracked his movements from Chicago to other cities. "

"Does he have a home base?"

"We haven't been able to determine where home is exactly for him, but he spends a lot of time in California, Vegas, the Chicago area, and the Northeast. Never more than two weeks in any place, well except for here."

"Anything else?" asked Rick.

"Bill didn't use any aliases when he traveled. He had no criminal record – not even a parking ticket that we can find. He was in the military. The FBI has asked for those records and is getting a court order to obtain his financials and tax records. That may tell us more. We don't know what he did for a living or why he was following your family. The ease at which he killed the woman in the parking lot implies he had killed before, but we have nothing that proves he had."

"This is troubling. I'm going to have to call my office to see what they came up with regarding that voice recording of his last moments."

"I called your office to find out their progress myself," said Sheriff Steele. "They were not making much headway on it. They said their software algorithms were more focused on removing noise from underwater acoustic sensors. They were going to do some reprogramming. I sent the files you emailed me straight to the FBI lab. They analyze that kind of stuff all the time."

"Great idea, Mike. I know you guys are always swamped with work, so am I extremely grateful for what you're doing to help us."

"We're here to serve. I'll keep you informed. It's probably good you're working with the police out there on the case. You should be safe. No one will likely mess with you or the family while you're involved in something that important."

They said their goodbyes. *"I hope he's right,"* thought Rick.

# Chapter 26: *Follow the Red Dots*

About three hours and thirty minutes after leaving the **Amphitrite** to pick up Kai and to buy coins, Kaleho, Shelli, Stephanie, and Kai arrived back at the ship. Shelli and Stephanie had been relaying their coin buying progress during the morning. Not only had they bought a bunch of coins, one of the shops agreed to acquire other coins that were on the market from around the world for them. The girls each walked into the command center carrying a large box that clinked with the sounds of coins. They found Nikki busy at one of the stations. On the situation awareness display lay a host of images of vans, cars, boats and a large ship.

"Nikki, this is my youngest son, Kaihekoa," said Kaleho.

Walking up to Nikki with his hand outstretched, "My friends call me Kai."

"Nice to meet you, Kai." Nikki glanced over to her sister and grinned. Sisters communicate volumes without ever saying a word.

"And Kai, you'll be happy to know that we've found your mother while you guys were buying coins."

Kai and Kaleho looked stunned at the news. Kaleho was the first to speak with a weak "What?" That initiated a flood of simultaneous questions from the whole gang.

Nikki held up her hands to signal a stop to the inquiries, and said, "It's complicated, but take a seat and I'll tell you where she is and how we found her."

Nikki swung around on her chair and pulled up a satellite view of O'ahu. Yellow dots appeared in five places

"From your description of the van, we had searched all video feeds that we could find from private web cams to public traffic cams. As you recall, we have been monitoring these for some time in the search for Stephen's grandfather and then after Leilani's abduction. We found the van passing by these five locations."

Next to each of the five dots popped up a snapshot of the van. "Yes, that's it. That's definitely the van," said Kaleho.

"The van was last seen at the Honolulu Zoo parking lot that night. A hotel camera across the street with views of the zoo and Kapiolani Park provided the feed," said Nikki.

She clicked on the image and a video clip played of the van entering.

"The van never left and it was confirmed to be abandoned by Officer Lee, who I called to covertly check on it. But a few minutes later an SUV turned right out of the zoo on Kapahulu Avenue."

She clicked on a second image next to the zoo and a short video clip of an SUV played. When the license plate became visible, the video stopped. Nikki clicked on the license plate and it popped up as a blurry image. She clicked again and the image sharpened from the video enhancement algorithm being employed.

"I asked Officer Lee about this plate, and he said it was from an SUV reported stolen from the North Shore this morning. It was probably stolen last night, but the owners didn't realize it until they walked out to see it missing this morning."

She clicked on the display again, and blue dots appeared in three locations.

"The SUV was seen on three separate cameras before disappearing last night. Its last known location was on Kapahulu Avenue just past Date Street. It never exited that area or crossed the H1. The area has a large number of residences. Most of those residences have car ports, street parking, or just driveways. But there are over one hundred residences with garages. We could assume they might have even stopped at a house with two garages – one for the SUV and one for the next vehicle they use. And if they switched to another vehicle, there were just too many possibilities to check."

Nikki dragged an Apple iPhone display up on the command station. In the center of it was a highlighted app.

"We found all of this about thirty minutes after you left the ship this morning. We didn't want to upset you with false leads, so we preceded to our next step in the search. We looked at the social media search tool we used before and checked for all people with active accounts on Twitter, Facebook, Instagram, and so on in that area. Trying to find anything from local residences or from people who would have known the two young men you shot. We didn't find out anything unusual, so we posted an ad out on all iPhone and Android phones. We offered $25 to anyone who would test our new apps. They were all types of games. But each one accessed the phone's GPS and reported the position of each phone."

"At the risk of sounding ungrateful for all the work to get to this point, do you know for sure where Leilani is Nikki?" said Kaleho.

"Sorry, I was just being thorough. Anyway, there were a lot of takers on the game app. And we cross-referenced the GPS history of their phones and found only one phone that was near your house the night before, at the zoo, and in the neighborhood we last saw the SUV."

"So you have their address? If so, I'll just call our S.W.A.T. team," said Kaleho excitedly.

"Actually we know the address, but they are not there now," answered Nikki. "The programs were executing the rules we gave them faster than we could go through the results. So they were about twenty-five minutes ahead of us before we discovered their new location. Since the game app was installed on their phone, it kept accessing their GPS sending position updates to us."

More mouse movements and a set of red dots now appeared on the map. These were much more frequent. Hundreds of them created a line on the screen all through Honolulu. The red dot trail went by the State Capital, Iolani Palace, and through Chinatown. On North Nimitz, it went west until Sand Island Access Road. It ended at the last set of slips at the marina just before the bridge to Sand Island.

Kaleho stood up when he saw the position. "That's about a mile from here. Let's get moving."

"Excuse me, Kaleho, but they are not at that location anymore. And we didn't know for sure if Leilani was with them until we got this video about an hour and twenty minutes ago," said Nikki.

She popped up a video of four people getting out of a sedan at the marina. "We got this from the marina's security cameras," continued Nikki. She stopped frame when the long-haired woman walking with the three men looked around and then toward the camera."

"It's Mom," said Kai anxiously.

"Yes, and she gets on that boat where there are already two other men," said Nikki. The video confirmed what Nikki said. "The first three men that transported her left, so we could not track with GPS anymore. And there were no camera feeds nearby to confirm her whereabouts as she left the marina. But we used the surfboard sensors to track wakes.

Using the timestamp from that video camera as the start, we tracked one wake to the west about seven miles offshore from Makaha."

Nikki clicked on a location on the deep blue area of the map. "That fishing boat then returned back to the marina. Two people got off, and Leilani was not with them."

Kaleho's head dropped. "Oh my God."

"But before you get worried, we tracked another larger boat from that offshore location. It headed north, coming within five miles of the first buoy that Mom had deposited two hours earlier."

Another symbol of the buoy location showed on the map off the most western point of O'ahu, Ka'ena Point. "The buoy has a 6 nautical mile radar onboard and a long-range daytime and thermal camera onboard. The radar detected the boat and automatically pointed the camera toward the boat. We got this video." As the video began to play, she described what was being shown. "It's a sizeable tender. You commonly see them on mega yachts. It was too far away to pick up the registration number. The boat made a slight adjustment in course to the northeast before it exceeded the radar's detection range."

Nikki then clicked on a point on the map of O'ahu that was a good distance offshore from an airstrip. "Mom was working her way around to the north of the island when we got up to the point of seeing the tender from the buoy. She was ten miles offshore directly north of Dillingham Airfield. She surfaced for her twenty-minute check-in with us, and I filled her in on the tender. She launched the small helium-filled aerostat we have onboard. It goes up to about 1,000 feet and carries a long-range camera. It took her a few minutes, but she found the tender paralleling the shoreline near Hale'iwa. We estimated it was three miles offshore. The tender went out of range to the northeast not long after she found it."

Nikki checked to make sure she hadn't lost her audience. "I redirected Ryan from his run of the mountain ridge to head to the northernmost point of O'ahu, and then move southwest offshore about two miles out. He had just refueled in Kailua, and was over the mountain ridge near Punalu'u when I contacted him. It took him only ten minutes before he was moving southwest along the shoreline.

Nikki slid another video to the situation awareness screen. "Ryan spotted the tender turning toward shore. He didn't want to draw attention, so he stayed back about a mile behind it. The tender pulled up to a mega yacht anchored at Waimea Bay."

A video from an elevated position showed the tender pulling up to the mega yacht. "He was too far from the boat to make out the people onboard, so he kept southwest and then turned inland about a mile from their position. He turned again to northeast and followed the mountain ridge to Waimea Valley. That valley ends at the beaches of Waimea Bay. Ryan hovered briefly at the entrance to the valley and launched the onboard drones, then turned back to the southwest."

The four recorded video feeds played simultaneously on the situation awareness screen. "Ryan headed slowly toward Hale'iwa and acted as a relay for the drones' video. The drones surrounded the ship at a good distance. They stayed far enough away to be difficult to spot them from the ship. Watch the video from the drone at the stern."

No one spoke, but as soon a woman appeared from below deck of the tender, "Leilani" said the group in unison.

Nikki resumed, "We did not see her again after she went onboard the yacht. We tried to move two of the drones in for a closer look, but when each came close to the yacht we lost the video and control of the drone. Dad suspects an onboard jammer is blocking signals."

"How long ago was that last view?" asked Kaleho.

"Not more than thirty minutes ago. Dad put the *Spearfish* in at the marina in Hale'iwa. Stephen Chang met him there with the other mini-copter. Dad lifted off on that mini-copter to get a better look at the yacht. Stephen is hanging out with *Spearfish*, but we don't like him by himself out on the water right now. Dad's worried about the triad getting to him."

"I can send officers up there to be with him," said Kaleho. "And I want to get up there and see the situation for myself."

"Dad knew you would say that," said Nikki. "He said we should pack up my vehicle. It will be tight, but all five of us can fit. I've started gathering the equipment Dad wanted. Just a few more items and I'll be ready to go."

"Kai, help Nikki load up the equipment. I'll call my officers to meet up with Stephen Chang," said Kaleho.

"Sure thing, Dad," said Kai.

"Stephanie and I can help too," volunteered Shelli.

# Chapter 27: *Quadcopters*

As Nikki left the H2 freeway and passed by Schofield Barracks, she checked her watch's screen. The built-in map display showed Ryan had touched down not too far away at the Wheeler Army Airfield to refuel his copter. Her father was nearing Waimea Bay. Stephen was still with the **Spearfish** at the marina in Hale'iwa, and her mom was about halfway between Hale'iwa and Waimea and more than five miles offshore.

Kaleho was sitting beside Nikki in the front seat. Kai, Shelli, and Stephanie were squeezed together in the back. She heard Shelli's phone chirp in the back seat.

"Just got word that the coins will be delivered to the **Amphitrite** tomorrow morning from the coin collector in Waikiki."

"Good job, Sis," said Nikki.

"You know I've never seen anything like it," said Kaleho. "The man at the store was pretty skeptical about a teenager buying coins. But when he rang up the coins she acquired from his store and the credit card cleared, he almost fell over himself to offer to help her find more coins. But let me ask you, what kid can charge over a hundred thousand dollars on their credit card and it clears?"

"I'm sure Dad bumped up her credit limit," said Nikki.

"Bumped it up? Geez," said Kaleho shaking his head.

A few moments later Nikki looked at her watch again. She was nearing Hale'iwa. "Dad's hovering low above the water at more than a mile from the yacht. I've connected the car here to the command center on the ship via satellite. Kaleho, if you pull down your visor you can watch the video stream from his copter on the visor display. Shelli and Stephanie, turn on the head rest displays to watch what's going on."

Kaleho pulled down the visor and saw the monitor power up. He could see video from the mini-copter. He watched as the four small quadcopters launched toward the mega yacht that lay ahead. Then the screen split into quadrants and four video feeds were visible. The car phone started ringing, and Nikki clicked an answer button on the steering wheel.

"Hi Dad, its Nikki. I've got Kaleho, Kai, Shelli and Stephanie with me. We're headed your way."

"I can see that," said Rick. "That's why I'm calling. I wanted to make sure you guys are seeing these feeds while you're making your way here. You should be seeing my mini-copter's view and three views from the quadcopters. One of the quads does not have video."

"Yes, we can see them, Rick," said Kahelo.

"I can see it as well," said Danielle. "I just surfaced in the sub about four miles north of you. I just dropped off another buoy off the northern point of O'ahu."

"Glad you could join us, sweetheart," said Rick.

"Yes, I can see them too," said Ryan joining in on the conversation. "By the way, I've refueled and I'm heading back your way Mr. Bryant."

"Great Ryan," said Rick. "It would be good if you fly north over the mountains at... hold a sec to let me check... at 3-5-7 degrees from Wheeler. When you have flown about 10 miles, you'll change course to 3-1-0. That will put you into Waimea Valley, which ends at the beach at Waimea Bay. Keep low and quiet. You'll have the opposite view of the boat as I do. Do you copy?"

"Copy that," said Ryan. "3-5-7 degrees and then 3-1-0 at 10 miles. See you in about 10 minutes, sir."

"Now back to the video. I'm going to send the quadcopters in line at a distance of 100 meters apart. The third quadcopter has a portable spectrum analyzer attached, which will allow me to measure electromagnetic interference across all frequencies up to forty gigahertz. All forms of marine radar, security systems, TV, and communication are below forty gigahertz. I had to strip off all non-essential equipment off that quadcopter to give me sufficient payload for the analyzer, so both cameras came off as did one of the four power cells. The fourth quadcopter's cameras will watch the third drone so I can maneuver it."

"Are you going to try to look in the ship windows for Mom?" asked Kai.

"I doubt I will be able to get that close, but I do have another idea for checking on her," answered Rick.

"I think there is a spherical boundary of the interference caused by an onboard jammer. So I'm going to try to get a sense of the range of that interference by slowly moving in the first quadcopter closer to the yacht."

The video switched from a quadrant view to a half-screen view from the first quadcopter. The other half of the screen showed a map of Waimea Bay. In the center of the map was a boat symbol, which represented the mega yacht. One hundred meter concentric circles surrounded the boat. Four dots moved toward the ship, and a blinking dot representing Rick's copter stayed motionless on the screen at eighteen rings, or a mile out. When the first quadcopter crossed the 500-meter ring, the video feed froze and the dot came to a quick stop. Seconds later it disappeared altogether from the map display."

"I lost control of the first drone. It will hover at that spot until it runs out of battery power," said Rick. "It takes a good deal of power for that kind of interference range. I'm going to move in the second quadcopter toward the stern of the ship."

They watched as the second quadcopter moved slower than the first one did toward the yacht. At about 525 meters, the second quadcopter's video began to get distorted, with digital error patterns and skipped frames increasing with closing position.

"I dare not push that any closer to the ship. I'll keep it right there. Next is the quadcopter with the spectrum analyzer. Now that I know the interference boundaries for control and video, I can attempt actual interference measurements."

The fourth quadcopter's video now filled half of the screen. The third drone moved forward and was followed by the fourth by about one hundred meters.

On the bottom quarter of the screen, a graph popped up. It had frequency on the x-axis and power in watts on the y-axis. A line was being plotted on the graph in real time showed signal strength was weak. As the quadcopter approached 600 meters away from the ship, the signal strength being plotted had reached the top of the graph.

"That's about as close as I can come. That's an impressive response. They are effectively jamming most of the RF spectrum – certainly all the spectrum of any equipment I use would be effected by this interference. I'm going to bring back the third quadcopter before it falls in the ocean. Probably should pull back the other two as well. They're small and not likely to be detected, but we shouldn't take a chance. Once I have recovered them, I'll use *Dolphina*."

Kaleho turned to Nikki. "What's *Dolphina*?"

"*Dolphina* is a diving scooter that holds one person," answered Nikki. "At a distance, it looks like just like a dolphin. It even surfaces and moves like a dolphin in the water."

Being somewhat unfazed now by the introduction of a steady stream of technology, Kaleho leaned in to the car speaker. "Rick, this is Kaleho. Aren't you worried you'll be spotted by the crew?"

"The quadcopters were too small to be seen by their shipboard radar. I kept my mini-copter approach speed equal to a sport fishing boat's speed on the way here. I'm hovering ten feet off the water, so I now resemble an anchored boat to their radar. There's another fishing boat north of me about three quarters of a mile and they don't seem to even know I'm here. So as long as I keep this distance and remain low, they won't recognize me. And *Dolphina*, well it just looks like any other dolphin at a hundred meters out."

Rick retrieved the quadcopters. "The mini-copter can remain in a hover state on autopilot. It has a winch on it to lower people or equipment to the ground or water surface. It has a remote control keypad for the winch so that you can get back up to the helicopter later. I think Dad is going to unstrap and then lower *Dolphina* into the water first. Then he'll lower himself. He'll try to get closer to the vessel for a discrete inspection," said Nikki.

"I'm in position," said Ryan over the comms. The video feeds on the vehicle displays split and the camera from the front of Ryan's copter viewed the ship and Waimea beach in the foreground. The other half display still showed the view of the ship from Rick's copter.

As they watched their respective displays, they saw Rick's copter symbol blink as before to the left side of the map. The ship symbol was still in the middle of the map and Ryan's copter symbol blinked to the far right side of the map. A fourth, light blue, symbol appeared on the screen next to Rick's copter.

"If you click on that symbol and drag two fingers outward like you do with pictures on your phone, you will zoom in on that map," said Nikki.

Kaleho and the girls in the back seat each did as Nikki instructed. "Cool, that must be the *Dolphina*," said Stephanie. "The icon is in the shape of a fish."

Rick came back into the conversation. "I'm now in *Dolphina*. Dolphins don't normally swim on the surface. They swim underwater and pop up for a look and air. So I'll be mimicking that pattern. When I'm underwater, I can't communicate and you won't see any video from the nose or side cameras. So hang tight until I can make my pass. I've powered up my position transponder, which is low enough in frequency to work while I'm at depths less than ten feet. You can watch my progress on the map display."

"Please be careful, Rick," said Danielle. "We are too far from you if something happens."

"I'll be fine. I'm going to just do a quick check of the hull of the ship underwater and make one slow pass around it like a curious dolphin. I'll then resurface back at the mini-copter and reconnect with you all."

"Dad, we've made it to the marina at Hale'iwa," said Nikki. "We'll park and wait here."

"Good, I'll be seeing you soon," said Rick.

Nikki turned off the motor and pulled up her tablet PC so that she could watch as well. They all watched intently as the fish symbol moved closer to the ship. They caught the

114

*Dolphina* surfacing once in Rick's mini-copter video when it was a few hundred meters out. But it was too small to see after that one instance.

It continued to move in a meandering fashion across the map display, as a dolphin that was hunting might. When the *Dolphina* came within 500 meters of the ship the symbol flickered and then dropped from the screen.

"He's inside the 500-meter interference barrier," said Nikki. "Now we wait."

"I wish we would have told him a safety time, so that if he's not out by then we go in after him," said Danielle over the speaker.

"He'll be fine, Mom," said Shelli. "You know Dad, he loses track of time when he's focused on something."

Ten minutes later *Dolphina's* symbol reappeared on the screen near the point where it had originally disappeared. The car erupted in cheers.

"Thank heavens," said Danielle in relief.

"He'll take his time to be sure the *Dolphina* doesn't draw attention. It will probably be another five minutes before he reaches the copter."

They heard a beep sound coming over the speaker. "I just got a warning on my intrusion radar," said Danielle. "Let me see what it is." After a few seconds, she spoke. "I'm uploading the feeds to our data network. You should be able to see it on your screen now. There's something about six miles due west moving fast. At first I thought it might be a plane, but it is not appearing on my long-range camera. But that's just too fast to be a boat. The radar is registering a speed of … one hundred and five miles per hour."

Nikki expanded the scale on her map. Seeing her do it, Kaleho and the girls did the same to their displays. A red symbol appeared at the edge of the screen.

"Mom, that object is heading directly to Dad's mini-copter, and it will be there in four minutes. It's got to be a helicopter or plane of some kind flying low. It's trying to stay off the national defense radar screens. We use a more sophisticated, pulsed-Doppler radar technology, so that's why you picked it up on the *Stingray* radar."

"I'm going to hop over the ridge here and come out over the water at Three Tables," said Ryan. "That yacht won't be able to see me. And if I put my camera at maximum zoom, I might be able to see what is heading toward Mr. Bryant."

"Ok," said Nikki. "But be discrete. We don't want to draw any more attention to ourselves."

"Nikki, your father will be back to the mini-copter in about three minutes. That's about the same time as that plane, or whatever it is, will arrive at the mini-copter."

Nikki's gut flinched. Her mom was right. "He'll pop up and communicate first, Mom. But we do need to warn him. I'll send a text message, which he'll receive as soon as he surfaces." Nikki quickly typed the message. *Airborne threat approaching, stay submerged.* She hit the send button and said a quick, "Please God," to herself.

Each person watched from their own location as the two symbols moved toward the hovering copter. Moments later the video from Ryan's copter zoomed in at the horizon. A dark smudge was visible and moving extremely fast. Ryan was manually controlling the camera, so the video was jerky and kept coming in and out of focus as the camera struggled to acquire the image.

115

"I don't like this a bit," said Danielle. "The timing is awfully tight."

As if Rick was reading her mind, the *Dolphina* slowed its approach. The mini-copter was on autopilot, and the controls were locked by passcode and biometric encoding. There was no way to move it remotely from their position. The image of the ship from the hovering mini-copter remained on everyone's screen, as the dark object approached at a speed that was now near 200 mph. The object was still blurry on Ryan's video feed. *Dolphina's* symbol brightened as it came within a few screen pixels of the mini-copter's position – the increased brightness being a sign of it beginning to surface.

At more than 500 meters from the mini-copter, bright streaks blazed from the dark object toward the helicopter. Rick's mini-copter video glowed to the left edge, then suddenly jerked. The video then flickered and the image tilted wildly and began to rotate with the mini-copter. The image dropped to the ocean's surface, where bubbles of air were easily visible.

"Oh my God," said Danielle. "Rick!"

The video from the mini-copter rolled skyward as more streaks zoomed by. The video jerked again and continued to roll back toward the ocean horizon. For a few seconds before plunging into the ocean, the mini-copter's video showed the wide wingspan and narrow fuselage of an aircraft receding into the distance.

"Rick!" yelled Danielle again.

The symbol for the chopper flickered and went out. The symbol for the *Dolphina* was gone. The symbol for the mystery aircraft made a wide arc.

Nikki couldn't believe what she was seeing, and when she twisted around in her car seat and quickly realized everybody else appeared as shocked as she was. She looked back at the screen and studied the symbols again. The black aircraft turned sharply and headed back at the site of the copter. She saw her mom's symbol to the north, and Ryan's symbol to the northeast.

"Ryan, you're in possible danger. Set your mini-copter down quickly and go for cover," shouted Nikki at her tablet.

"Roger that," responded Ryan. His symbol moved away from shore and quickly touched down a clearing behind the local Foodland supermarket.

"Mom, you need to dive. You're wide open and that aircraft could come for you next."

"Your father, he could be hurt. We can't leave him," said Danielle.

"Just dive, Mom. Head out to the west of the mini-copter's last position. Dad will go away from the ship and farther out to sea if he got my message in time. We're at the marina, so we will hop into the *Spearfish* and head that way too."

"Don't you dare go out there," yelled Danielle emotionally. "You'll be a sitting duck."

Nikki began to respond, but Kaleho put his hand on her shoulder and shook his head. "Danielle, please just dive. I have two officers that just arrived in the *Spearfish* with Stephen Chang. I'm going to run out to the dock and pull Chang off the boat with one of my officers. They'll stay here with the girls. I'll take the other officer with me on the *Spearfish*, and I'll meet you out there to search for Rick. I'm told the *Spearfish* console is bulletproof, so we'll be safe. Ok?"

There was silence on the speaker. Finally the more controlled voice of Danielle Bryant said, "Diving now."

# Chapter 28: *Ko'a Aloha*

Not long after the **Spearfish** left the marina, the sound of Rick's voice came over the cellular network that linked them all together. Danielle had launched her communication torpedo, which was a bullet-shaped buoy that was towed on the surface behind her sub. The buoy had an antenna and allowed Danielle to hear the news. Cheers boomed from the Bryant gang for the second time that day at the sound of his voice.

Rick had moved another three miles out from the shoreline before surfacing and contacting everyone. He had received Nikki's warning text just before surfacing at his mini-copter and quickly pushed the **Dolphina** deep enough to avoid the falling remains.

The first to arrive was Kaleho on the **Spearfish** and he gave Rick a hand in getting out of the **Dolphina**. The sub surfaced and Rick jumped from the boat to the sub and hugged the waiting arms of Danielle.

The radar on the sub continued to search the skies for the return of the dark aircraft. The large drone had revisited the downed mini-copter, probably allowing the operator to admire his work, and then left as fast as it had arrived. The group decided it was too dangerous to go back for the remains of the mini-copter, so the **Spearfish** lead the way back to the Hale'iwa marina.

Nikki contacted the **Amphitrite** captain first, and instructed them to bring the vessel up to the Hale'iwa marina as fast as they could.

The boat arrived a full five hours later, which was pretty remarkable given the crew had to get to the dock from their hotel, prepare the ship for its move, and then sail the 80 miles to anchor beyond the breakers at Hale'iwa marina entrance. The **Amphitrite** was too big to go into the marina, whose largest boat was generally under sixty feet in length.

The sun was setting on to the west when the Bryant team settled down at the conference table in the command center on the **Amphitrite**. The sub was docked back in its cradle and the **Spearfish** was tied off the stern.

Rick pulled up three photos on the situation awareness display. One was Leilani looking out one of the portholes on the ship. Rick had managed to take a photo of her during one of his passes near the mega yacht. The second photo was an enhanced shot of a side view of the aircraft that attacked Rick's mini-copter. The third shot was the rear view of the aircraft from the mini-copter's camera before it short circuited. Rick recognized it as a Chinese made unmanned air vehicle, or UAV.

Rick got off the phone call he had received and announced, "That was my lead mechanical engineer. He said that the six local machine shops will be ready with their first batch of coins at 10 am tomorrow. And the twenty-four California and eleven Florida shops we hired will fly out their batches of coins, which will arrive at Honolulu airport around noon."

"How many coins have they made?" asked Stephanie.

"Each shop is pumping out 15 to 22 coins an hour, and they are working through the night. So my engineer estimates we'll have near 20,000 coins. Most of them will be the dollar coins. We had three of the shops do half-dollars. No time to do any quarters or dimes."

"That's a lot of coins, Rick. But that's far less than we know the quantity should be. Do you think it will be enough to be credible?"

"That's going to be about eleven hundred pounds of coins. To make it manageable to move, it's going to take six chests to hold them all. They would be worth over fourteen million dollars if they were real. It should be enough to bargain."

"We bought about five hundred coins from around the state and online. That included all denominations. More than two hundred were dollar coins, and about a hundred each of the half-dollar, quarters and dimes," said Shelli.

"That's good, sweetheart," said Rick. "We could put all the real half-dollars, quarters and dimes in the same chest with the fake half-dollars. The odds of a failed test of any kind would be quite low for that chest. We'll have to spread the two hundred real Hawaiian dollars equally in the other five chests."

"Forty real dollar coins with about three thousand fake dollar coins in each chest doesn't sound like good odds in the rest of the chests," said Danielle.

Rick saw Kaleho register the comment and look down. He was sure he was worried. And he had good reason to be.

"We'll buy deep chests so that the first inches of coins are real," said Rick. "And remember, the fake coins will pass all the tests with the exception of the sensor tests. I think we have good odds."

"I hear what you saying, Rick. And I agree with you," said Kaleho. "But we're talking about Leilani's life. And if you told me the plan was absolutely full proof, I'd still be worried."

"Understood," said Rick. "And to be honest, we don't know whether they will even agree to such a bargain. We need to plan for all contingencies."

"I have the power to pull in S.W.A.T., the FBI, or even the military if I need to," added Kaleho. "But an attack on them could get...." Kaleho stopped and suddenly remember his son was in the room with him. Kai was looking straight at him. "It would not be good for Leilani if we conducted a raid."

"But we have a few things going for us," said Rick. "First of all, we know where Leilani is. Secondly we know a bit about her captors. According to the vessel name and number, Shelli and Nikki found out that it is owned by a Taiwanese company."

"And that company is believed to be a front for a triad," said Kaleho.

"Correct," continued Rick. "Shelli found out the approximate size of the typical crew for that ship class, and I'm sure your sources could find out exactly the crew count when they had their passports stamped at their last docking."

Kaleho nodded his head in agreement, and took the opportunity to text a message into the office to check on the ship's last port of call and their crew count.

"And we know at least some of their defenses. They have a UAV at their disposal and an onboard electromagnetic jammer," said Rick.

"And we know they have sensors onboard that could detect and determine our mini-copter was a threat," said Nikki.

"Right," said Rick. "To be able to communicate to the UAV out to that distance means there might be a weakness in their electronic curtain. So we have a lot of information that we didn't have this morning."

"And they think we have Stephen's grandfather," said Danielle. "As soon as we tell them we have the treasure, they will lose interest in Stephen's grandfather."

"But we should be vigilant in our search for him just in case he comes out of hiding," said Rick.

"Absolutely," said Danielle.

"So when they call me about Leilani, what am I going to say?" asked Kaleho. "If they agree to a swap, we need to decide how, where and when. We can't just hand over the fake treasure." Kaleho paused and took a deep breath, then continued in a more calm voice. "Their demands will be to give them the treasure first, and then they will hand over Leilani. But you know just how wrong that could go."

Everybody knew what Kaleho wasn't saying. That once they had the money, they could just kill Leilani and whomever brought it over.

"There are too many variables here to consider," said Rick. "Let's agree how we would want to do the trade. We will yield to your guidance and decisions, Kaleho, but we also would like to help as much as possible. And since they said to keep the police out of this, you don't have many options anyway."

Kaleho nodded. "I appreciate all the help I can get. But I will not risk any other lives. And Leilani certainly wouldn't want anyone hurt either."

Just as they began to make their plans and equipment lists, Kaleho's phone rang. The room went quiet. Kaleho answered and put it on speaker phone.

"Hello, this is the Chief of the Honolulu Police Department. Who is this?"

"I am the man who has your wife," said the voice. "Are you alone?"

"For your sake, Leilani better still be alive," said Kaleho. He held his hand over the phone speaker. "It's the same man that called me before."

"I am not worried about your threats. Answer my question, are you alone," said the voice with a clearly Asian accent.

"No, I am not," answered Kaleho.

"I warned you of the consequences of bringing in help," said the voice.

"You told me not to bring in any police or other law enforcement agencies. You didn't say I couldn't get help from others."

"Hmmm. Ah, you're talking about Mr. Bryant and his family."

Everyone looked startled. Kaleho didn't answer.

"You twisted my words," said the voice. "Why should I not kill your wife right now?"

"Because we have what you want," interrupted Rick.

"Mr. Bryant, it is a pleasure to hear your voice. But you have put you and your family in great danger."

"I'm not worried about your threats. You have what we want and we have what you want. Let's cut to the deal."

Clicking on the phone could be heard and mumbles in the background. There was some sort of conversation.

"Did you hear me?" asked Rick.

"Yes I did. You have Mr. Chang, the old man with you?"

"Before we say anything else, we need to hear Leilani's voice," said Kaleho sternly.

"Do you have Mr. Chang?" said the voice.

"If I you don't put Leilani on the phone right now, I'm hanging up," demanded Kaleho. He was now standing and breathing deeply. "And after that I'll bring in every law enforcement agency there is to nail you. All my law enforcement brethren and I will be gunning for you. You think you have a tight knit community…you haven't seen anything until you mess with the police brotherhood. You have ten seconds to put her on…starting now."

Seconds later, the voice said. "Hold on."

Then in a few more seconds, Leilani came on the phone. "Kaleho?"

Kaleho sat down quickly so that his mouth was closer to the phone. Relief washed over his face. "Leilani, are you OK? Did they hurt you?"

"Oh Kaleho, Ko'a Aloha," said Leilani. *It's her, alright* thought Kaleho. She always said that to him … Kaleho, my love.

"I'm fine," she said. "They have not beaten me. They have kept me –"

"That's enough," said the voice. "Now you have heard her voice. Answer my question. Do you have Chang? Do not lie to me. We have been watching you."

Rick motioned to Kaleho to let him talk. Kaleho nods. "Yes we have Chang," he said. Kaleho looked surprised, as did the rest of the room.

"Mr. Bryant, do not lie to me. We have not seen him with you or your family or on your boat. And we know that you were asking about him in Chinatown."

"We have him," said Rick.

"Then, as you said, we have what each other wants. You give us Mr. Chang and we will give you Leilani."

"You've got to be kidding," said Rick. "Forgive us if we don't trust you."

"That is the only deal," said the voice. "Take it or we feed Leilani to the sharks. Then we will come after Chang with contempt."

Kaleho stood up quickly again, ready for a verbal assault. But Rick held up both hands to motion him to be calm.

"No deal," said Rick. "We will not give you Mr. Chang. But we are willing to trade you the treasure you seek for the return of Leilani. And that's our only deal."

It sounded as if the phone was dropped. There was a lot of muffled conversation. Then the voice came back on the phone. "What treasure are you referring to Mr. Bryant?"

"The treasure taken from the great pirate raid of 1884 here in Honolulu. That's what you want Mr. Chang for, isn't it? You think he has something to do with it, don't you? Well let me save you some effort. He didn't know anything about it, but we have managed to find the treasure ourselves. That's why we were in Chinatown. That's what we've been researching. And if you know us, you know we are quite experienced at finding treasure."

The phone was silent for a few seconds. "You surprised us, Mr. Bryant. That is not easy to do. But how do we know you have this treasure that you speak of? How do we know that you aren't planning something else?"

"You don't, but we're not handing over Mr. Chang," said Rick. "The treasure for Leilani. We know where she is, where you are. We meet half way between the shore and your ship. You bring Leilani and we bring the treasure."

"Haha," laughed the voice on the phone. "You think we are foolhardy? We give you Leilani and then Kaleho and his men and maybe even the Coast Guard visits us."

"Well then, we have a stalemate," said Rick. "Giving you the treasure first gives us zero leverage. You will leave..." Rick stopped, looked at Kai, then turned away. "...no witnesses and then you escape. That's just not going to happen."

There was a short pause. "Mr. Bryant, we agree with your terms. We will come out on our tender with Leilani. You meet us with the treasure. Kaleho can even come out on the boat if he wishes to fetch his lovely bride. But ... you must come with the treasure until we verify it is real. We will test it and Mr. Bryant will be blindfolded and released somewhere in Hawai'i unharmed."

"No, Rick," pleaded Danielle. But before Danielle could say anything else, Rick spoke.

"Agreed. But we are going to have the place surrounded. If you kill Leilani, Kaleho or me, then you'll quickly regret it. Take that as a fact."

"Understood," said the man. "It is getting late. We will meet tomorrow at 2 PM. You will bring the treasure to us on a boat and meet us about 500 yards away from the ocean side of our ship – not the beach side. We will contact you on this phone number."

"Agreed," said Rick again. "But we will meet at these coordinates." Rick gave them the latitude and longitude, which would put the meeting a full 200 yards beyond the jammer range of the ship.

"That is satisfactory. But I will remind all of you that if we see anything out of the ordinary, it will not end well for Leilani or any of you. We have a big organization. We will not stop until we are avenged," said the voice.

"I echo your comments," said Kaleho in defiance. He ended the call and threw the phone down on the table.

"Rick, what the heck are you doing? They'll kill you as soon as they verify the treasure. And it will likely be right after it passes or fails their tests."

"I'm buying us time," answered Rick calmly. He looked at Danielle, who by this point and time had her head in her hands. He then turned back to Kaleho. "Look, if the treasure passes the test they will need me as a hostage so that they can escape to international waters. They probably won't try to get rid of me until they are in Taiwan, or Hong Kong, Macau, or some other such place. They can't risk the retaliation."

"But how does that help? I don't have any jurisdiction after they leave our waters," shouted Kaleho.

"We'll act before then. They have to test the coins. They'll bring someone in to do that. If they pass, they'll then contact you with the location to find me. They will feel in charge because they have me, the treasure, the backing of the triad, and a dreadfully lethal drone. We need to create a plan that allows me to escape and then you attack with your men."

"Rick, you're scaring me," said Danielle. "I want to get Leilani back as much as anyone else, but you're committing suicide."

"There is no alternative, honey," said Rick. "They could just as easily decide to come after us if we do nothing. They could come for Stephen's grandfather or the treasure or both. We could probably hold them off, but I don't want us to be looking over our shoulder forever. And I don't want to see Leilani killed. Let's stop arguing about this and strategize."

Kaleho stared at Rick for a while, then said, "Well I agree with you that we need a plan. Let's see what we can do."

"Dad," said Nikki. "The only way we can rescue you is by taking out their security systems. They have a jammer to interrupt communications near their ship. So we can't eaves drop on them. And they have men onboard with guns, and they have a drone with guns. We have to overcome those before we can get you."

"That's good," said Rick. "You're identifying their strengths. So the only way you can help me when I get onboard is to first counter those strengths. But you have to wait until I am onboard; otherwise, they will react with a vengeance."

"We can't even get close to the ship as long as the drone is flying," said Nikki. "How do we stop the drone? Our one remaining mini-copter isn't fast enough. And we can't shoot it down."

"The drone may fly autonomously, but its mission tasking has to be communicated. If we find out how to communicate with it, we can take control of it. I'm sure they have some sort of onboard antenna to communicate to it for short to medium ranges. But we know from our first encounter that their communication range is considerable. Long-range, over-the-horizon communication dictates low-frequency transmissions, which would require a big antenna. I didn't see a big antenna on the ship, so it must be on land. And my bet is that it is on this side of the island somewhere. That's why they are not anchored in Honolulu Harbor or somewhere off the calmer waters of the southern shore of O'ahu. The cost to own and operate the antenna and the UAV would be sizeable, so maybe they were planning to make Hawai'i one of their main centers of operation," said Rick.

"I don't understand," said Stephen. "If the communication to the drone is onshore, how do they communicate to it from the ship?"

"The ship can communicate either by short bursts over cellular networks or direct radio link to the long-range onshore facility if it is on this side of the island. That facility, in turn, passes it on to the drone. Just think of it as a classic radio relay."

"But how do they transmit anything from their ship? Won't that be effected by the jammer?" asked Stephen.

"Not if they encrypt the transmission and ride it on the jammer's frequency," answered Rick. "They decrypt it at the radio relay station, which is where the antenna would be installed. And if we can kill the long-range radio station, we could put up our own transmitter and take control. We would have to be close to control it, like somewhere on the beach and in line of sight of the ship."

"Why wouldn't they just use satellite communication directly to the drone?" said Nikki.

"Good question," said Rick. "Satellite communication is frequently used by the military for control of drones. But that's for satellites they have full control of. The triad would not have access to those satellites. They'd have to go through commercial satellites in this part of the world. And the U.S. Government would undoubtedly be able to monitor all those transmissions. And without control of satellite bandwidth, poor weather conditions could hamper its use. No, I'm sure they have an onshore radio relay station."

Rick stood up and began to pace, thinking of what to do. "If we first put a transmitter near the ship, like on the shore nearby, we can monitor the signals controlling the drone. We feed those into our computer system to decrypt. Those types of drones have onboard computers with volumes of data storage for storing complex missions. Communication is likely just a simple set of encrypted ASCII text or binary commands, and there can't be that many commands for control.  Once we decrypt it, we'll hack the software, and then take down the radio link.    Then we use our own radio link to control the drone.   Even if we don't figure out the control commands, at least they won't be able to use the drone against us."

"How do we defeat the jammer?" asked Shelli.

"I measured the interference it causes with the quadcopter spectrum analyzer.  I don't think there is anything I can do to stop that transmitter.   That is, unless we figure out the encryption code used to transmit outwardly to the radio relay station.   I'm going to be on the ship.  Maybe I can convince them to take me up to their bridge or command center.  If I see the code, which should be like a digital key -- a set of numbers and letters -- I can send it to you guys and then we can command the plane."

"That's a lot of 'ifs' Rick," said Kaleho. "I don't like the uncertainty."

"How about this?" said Rick.  "I agree that getting out a message will be difficult.  So let's set a time.  If I haven't communicated the codes to either the jammer or the drone by a certain amount of time after they take me, you bring down the radio link and the plane.   If I can get them to let me out on the deck about that time, then I could dive off the ship and you run the plane into the water or even into the ship itself.  If I can manage to create a diversion before the allotted time, then that will be your cue that it's time to attack.  And if it all fails to happen, then come in after me full force."

"How do you propose we do that?" asked Danielle skeptically.

"We could put officers Lee and Tyler offshore in the *Spearfish*," said Rick. "And Kaleho could call the Coast Guard.  They would respond to the Honolulu Chief of Police pretty quickly.  And the Marine Naval Station could take out the plane.  But that's our Plan B – our last resort."

"I don't like it Rick," said Kaleho.

"It's not ideal, but we have all night to revise the plan.   We'll do the best we can to prepare.  I am the logical choice to go onboard, and they want me anyway."

"OK," said Kaleho reluctantly.   "But I am going to reserve the right to veto this."

Hours later and after substantial activity in the conference room of the *Amphitrite,* the plan had taken shape. The coins were arriving in time to move it to the chests that they had purchased. The *Spearfish's* bullet-proof console and unsinkable hull made it the best choice for the boat to use for the delivery of the coins and the transport of Leilani to safety.   Kaleho and Rick would take the *Spearfish* from Hale'iwa Harbor to Waimea Bay for the trade.  Kaleho would pilot the boat back to the *Amphitrite*, while Rick went along with the treasure as their new captive.

Once the *Spearfish* arrived back at the *Amphitrite*, Officers Lee and Tyler would take it back out to deep water past Waimea Bay and wait for orders just off shore at Three Tables. Stephen Chang insisted on going with them and no one argued the point.

Nikki had searched for building permits on the north shore and found there was a new antenna site near a satellite communication company at Sunset Beach.  The new antenna site was too recent to appear on online digital maps, so they didn't know exactly what to expect.   Shelli and Stephanie had volunteered to investigate it.  Danielle had argued their involvement, so Kaleho had committed Kai to go with them.  They were only to scout it out.  If the site was unmanned, they would attempt to disable it.   If it was manned, then they would contact Officers Lee and Tyler, who would call in local backup to shut the place down.

Nikki would be in charge of the whole operation. Her training on all the equipment over the last month and her level head made her the right choice. She would set up communication for all their team, as well as assemble the link that would command the drone on the beach at Waimea Bay. Ryan would be her muscle. He'd help carry the equipment as needed. A full-blown PC with substantial processing power would be required to decrypt the transmissions. It was agreed that Nikki and Ryan would take one of the many rackmounted PC's that ran in the command center on the **Amphitrite**. It would be mounted inside one of the shock absorbing mobile racks they kept stored onboard. The mobile rack just barely fit inside Nikki's small SUV, which was parked in the lot at the marina.

The only thing that remained was to figure out how Rick could communicate from the ship. When he got onboard, Rick hoped they would not drug him. He was sure they would check him for wires and weapons. He'd bring his phone, but he was pretty sure they would take it. He'd have his watch too, which they may allow him to keep as long as it didn't draw too much attention.

He finally set his tablet PC down on the table. He needed a break from the stress. Maybe some sleep would help. Across from him sat the only other person in the conference room -- Kaleho. The rest of their team was getting prepared or eating in the galley. Kaleho with a pad of paper and pencil. He was making notes on the plan, but he also looked stymied. He had the pencil between two fingers and was slowly rocking it back and forth, which created a steady rhythm of "clicks." The sound was almost mesmerizing.

After a few minutes, Rick felt his head snap. Had he fallen asleep to the rhythm of the clicks? He shook his head to clear away the drowsiness, and then glanced at his watch for the time. It was a fine watch. It was one of the most sophisticated gadgets he owned. The only thing it didn't do was tick. He jerked his head up quickly. *Tick,* Rick thought. Then he looked back at Kaleho's pencil that was now resting beside the table. *Click.*

Kaleho noticed the jerk of Rick's head and asked, "What is it Rick?'

*Tick. Click.*

"Rick?"

*Tick. Click. Rick.*

Rick smiled. "I know how to communicate the code if I see it." He called Nikki to come up to the room and he raced through the explanation with both her and Kaleho. It method seemed the best option, and Nikki spread the word to the rest of the team.

Rick swiped through the web browser on his tablet and quickly located the address of the place he needed to visit. After a quick collection of gear from his lab below deck, he was off on his errand.

It was well past mid-night when they all met again at the conference room table. Rick had completed his errand and everyone had prepared as best as they could. The group went over the plan one last time. Rick then asked the group to try to get some sleep. They'd need clear heads in the morning.

# Chapter 29: *Preparation*

From above, Waimea Bay is an open-ended square in shape. It has a wide sandy beach, named the Waimea Beach Park, which sits between the two-lane highway and the turquoise sea with its rock and coral formations. The sand on the beach is deep and porous, and retains little moisture. In August the beach is complete with no interruptions, but in the winter season the rains in the nearby mountains causes the Waimea River to flow swiftly and it cuts the beach in half on its way to the ocean. The sea floor drops off rapidly beyond the mouth of the bay and the ocean's deep blue color bounds the horizon to the west. The Waimea Valley and the northwestern end of the Ko'olau Range offer a lush green backdrop to the beaches and bay.

Kamehameha Highway is the road that brings locals and tourist to the bay. Upon arriving at the bay, the road leaves the shoreline and sweeps inland to form a rounded "V." As a result of wintertime flow of the river, a low bridge and a pedestrian walking bridge are at the "V." The beach parking lot exits the highway on the bay side of the road before the bridge, and Waimea Valley Road exits toward the mountains after the bridge. Most people go to the easier accessible southern part of the beach, closest to the parking lot.

Nikki and Ryan were sitting on beach at Waimea Beach Park. They were set up on the northernmost section of the beach. The easiest way to get to this part of the beach is to hope for a parking spot along Kamehameha Highway, which they got, and then traverse down one of several rocky sloped paths. They had a good view of the triad mega-yacht directly in front of them at a distance of more than a thousand feet from the beachfront.

Nikki was sitting on her knees and was working on a circular antenna of about two feet in diameter that was attached to a two-axis gimbal. The gimbal set level on tripod legs that extended soundly into the sand. A white metal box, the transceiver, attached behind the antenna. Nikki's tablet PC linked to the gimbal reflector via Bluetooth. Her tablet was also linked to her cell-enabled watch, and all of it was connected via the cell network back to the larger PC in her vehicle. The large PC was the processing muscle of the entire system.

Ryan was trying to help her, but nice as he was, he was in the way. He didn't know what they were trying to do with the equipment. He hadn't had the hours of training that she had, and she didn't have time to explain. There was many simultaneous activities going on, and she had to stay focused on managing the incoming data and communications. Dad was counting on her to be the information hub – to be team leader, as he put it.

No one thought the plan was ideal, but it was the only plan they could drum up. Step one: Dad gets on ship after a successful trade for Leilani. That was the only absolute of the plan. The rest of the steps were probabilistic. Step two: Dad figures out the encryption key for either the jammer or the black UAV, and would send it to her. How he was to do that was an unknown. He did, however, know how he would transmit the key. Step three: We take out the UAV or drone as everyone else was calling it. Crashing it into the water was the best choice. The only way to crash the drone required power to be disabled to the large transmitter on shore. Disabling the transmitter was Shelli, Stephanie, and Kai's job. If that failed, the U.S. Marine Naval station would be called by Kaleho, and they would scramble jets to take out the drone. Step four: Get Dad off the ship. There were several ways that could happen, but all of them worked best with some sort of a diversion from her dad prior to any attack or raid on the ship. Everyone agreed the probability of a successful diversion was a low. Kaleho was ready to swoop in with last remaining mini-copter from their ship if need be. He had been practicing take-offs and landings all morning. Mom was on standby offshore in the **Stingray**. Officers Lee and Tyler and Stephen were on the **Spearfish** a short distance north of Waimea near Three Tables Park. Plenty of options on the rescue, but in reality no one knew how it would actually go. Step five: Once Dad was safely off the ship, arrest anyone else still on it.

They were less than two hours from the allotted time of the trade. She had noticed there was an increase in activity on the ship, but they hadn't seen any sign of Leilani. They were not likely to see her until minutes before she boarded the tender that would meet the **Spearfish**. Nikki was nervous for her dad, and also worried she would disappoint. She was just about done with her preparations, and then it would be time to test it all.

Because of the wind, Nikki had an earpiece in so that she could hear the entire team more clearly. She asked Ryan to take a break and make them some lunch. Minutes later she saw that he had made her a sandwich and had pulled out some diced pineapple that the ship's crew had picked up at the Dole plantation. A cold bottle of water sat beside it. The hot sun shining down on it glittered, and condensation was forming droplets on the outside. Ryan pulled out a low-height beach chair. He was shirtless and wore only his smile, his six-pack abs, and his swim trunks. He had his water bottle in one hand and his sandwich in the other. He had his ear buds in and was listening to music on his smartphone. He winked when he saw her glance at him. He was nodding his head to the music as he chewed his food.

Nikki smiled as she looked back at her tablet and clicked on the last of the control buttons to test operation. Ryan was a great friend and seemed to be genuinely in love with her. He flirted constantly, but was nothing but a … a gentlemen as her mom would say. Shelli, and most of Nikki's friends said he was hot. She glanced at him again and he was still smiling at her.

*What is he listening to?* Nikki's watch had many features, and one allowed it to pick up various electronic transmissions. It had a limited range, but he was close enough. She pressed the bottom right button twice and then slowly turned the dial on the watch. She could listen through her Bluetooth linked earpiece, but at first only static could be heard. Soon she found the transmission.

*A boy band? He's listening to One Direction. Whatever.* Nikki heard the lyrics clearly.

*You're insecure,*
*Don't know what for,*
*You're turning heads when you walk through the door,*

He was loyal to her and she wished she could let her feelings for him mature, but she still pained from the hurt of her last boyfriend. Her friends told her that she was afraid to get attached again. Perhaps she was.

*Don't need make-up,*
*To cover up,*
*Being the way that you are is enough,*

Ryan never pried or pressured her. She did enjoy being with him and couldn't think of anyone else she'd rather be dating. And she did get regular offers, but she turned them all down.  She knew he was looking, rather staring at her now, and she had to admit it made her feel good.  A thought came to her as the song played on.

*Wait for it…*

*Everyone else in the room can see it,*
*Everyone else but you,*

*Wait for it…*

*Baby you light up my world like nobody else,*

*Ready… set….*  Nikki dipped her head.

*The way that you flip your hair gets me overwhelmed,*

Nikki swept her head in an exaggerated twist, which caused her hair to flip in the air and drape over her shoulder.  She had never practiced it, but she tried to imagine a sexy look and gave it her best.  She looked straight at him as the song continued.

*But when you smile at the ground it ain't hard to tell,*
*You don't know,*
*Oh, oh,*
*You don't know you're beautiful….*

Ryan sat motionless with his mouth open.  He dropped his water bottle and it fell over on the sand and started to drain out.  The grip on his sandwich in the other hand loosened, and the lettuce also fell out on the beach.  He finally said, "Oh, my God."

Innocently Nikki asked, "Could you pass me my water bottle please?"

It took it him a moment to process what she had asked, but he then scrambled quickly for her bottle and handed it to her.

"Thanks."  She twisted off the top and drank a little.  It was cold and felt good.

"You think you can give me a hand now?"

"Sure," burst out Ryan.

Nikki leaned in to him with the tablet in her hand and she asked him if he understood how the controls worked on the gimbaled reflector.  He shook his head.  She was finished with everything she could do now until she heard from Shelli or her dad.  She could enjoy a little quality time with Ryan on this breathtakingly beautiful beach.  Anything to relieve the tension she had felt all morning.

"Well let me explain how it works.  It would be good for you to know in case things get busy."  Nikki and Ryan sat close, shoulder-to-shoulder, as she explained the controls.  She was sure she could talk about thermodynamics and get the same enthusiasm from him.

*\*\*\**

With an hour to go, Rick contacted Nikki. He was talking through the cell link that Nikki had setup on the **Spearfish**'s center console. It was always enabled and keyed with the talk button to reduce ambient noise. "The treasure is loaded.  Kaleho and I are pushing off now."

"Roger, Dad," said Nikki. "Ryan and I are ready here on the beach at Waimea. No word yet from Shelli, but I don't expect to hear from her for at least another thirty minutes.  The triad yacht has their tender in the water.  There are people standing out on the aft launch platform of the ship, but still no sign of Leilani."

127

"Contact me the minute that you see her," said Rick. "We will not get close to the ship until we know she's in the tender."

"Understood," said Nikki. She shivered involuntarily even as the hot sun and sand cooked her skin. Apprehensiveness rose in her. She thought about her dad. He was knowingly going into the belly of the beast, possibly to never return.

"Dad, good luck out there," said Nikki.

The roar of the **Spearfish** engines could be heard when Rick responded. "Thanks, sweetie. Don't worry about me. I'll be fine."

"Dad, I love you," said Nikki.

After a few moments, "Love you more," said Rick. It brought a slight grin to Nikki's face.

# Chapter 30: *Captive*

Rick sat calmly in the state room of his captor. The morning had gone as expected. Men with guns had come in the tender from the mega yacht with Leilani. She had obviously been crying, but other than that she seemed to be unharmed. She and Kaleho embraced one another as soon as they were close, but ended the reunion quickly at Kaleho's urging. Then they departed safely at full throttle on the **Spearfish**. Rick had boarded the tender along with the treasure chests. Four people and the treasure chests made the tender ride much lower in the water than it did on its trip to the rendezvous point, so they made their way slowly back to the yacht.

Rick hadn't seen anyone that he could pinpoint as the leader, and not a word was spoken between his captors. As soon as he stepped on the yacht, a man came up and scanned Rick with a handheld sensor of some sort, most likely a spectrum analyzer similar the one he had used on the quadcopter. Rick thought his watch and phone were going to be confiscated because they both beeped when scanned. The man finally ignored the watch after a second scan, but he took his phone from him after making Rick enter the unlock pass code. The man slid his finger across the phone's screen to check out the installed apps. A few seconds of inactivity caused a picture of Rick's family pop up as a screensaver. The man grunted at the sight of it, and threw the phone back to him. They were apparently not worried about either device given the sophisticated jammer they had onboard.

The room they put him in had deep-red, cherry wood paneling with a high sheen. The bed sat against one of the paneled walls, which also acted to separate the bedroom from the private bath. The wall behind the bed curved slightly for bathroom privacy when the door of the bedroom was opened. He walked around into the bathroom, which had a black lacquered wood vanity with a black onyx stone top and a stone-like bowl sink. The vanity sat in the center of the rear wall and was filled with all sorts of rolled towels and toiletries. A tall silver spigot sat to the right of the bowl and had the shape of a bamboo spout. A sizeable glass-walled shower, which was rare for a ship, was off to the left. The thick glass was green tinted, and was semi-transparent. You could make out shapes if you stepped inside, but not detail. The toilet and bidet were in a walled alcove to the right of the vanity with white slatted door for privacy. Rick walked to the sink and splashed water on his face and then wiped it dry with the thick monogrammed white towels that sat beside the sink.

He walked back into the bedroom area. Two rather large portholes with perfectly buffed brass trim were on one wall. The portholes added natural light, but there was a light switch on the wall that made them fog over if desired. Designer wall sconces placed tastefully around the room and recessed lighting provided all the light at night. A large red chaise lounge sat below the portholes. A black lacquered oriental-design dresser and ornate framed mirror were against the wall opposite of the bed. A large piece of traditional Chinese artwork hung centrally on the wall with the door, and was lit by a small brass light above it. Rick had seen such artwork before at a special exhibit that Danielle had organized at Ringling Museum. He remembered that Danielle had called it ink and something, maybe ink-and-wash? He looked closely. It was of mountains, waterfalls and trees. It appeared to be quite old and could be authentic. Under the painting sat a small black table with burnt-red chairs that matched the Asian theme of the room. There was a small dish of strawberries, cheese and wafers. A wire cheese slicer, a small serving fork, and a napkin sat to one side. On the other side of the dish were two small bottles of water and an acrylic, square-shaped drinking glass. The strawberries were cool to the touch, so they must have been placed there just before he was brought to the room. Rick started to eat one, but then wondered if they were poisoned and wiped his hand on his pants instead.

He looked back toward the bed. He saw two side tables. One table had an alarm clock with big red numbers for the time, and other had a phone. It was the kind of phone with the keypad on the phone handset and resembled something from the nineteen seventies. It was most likely for talking to people on the ship itself -- maybe for ordering food or reaching the steward.

At the foot of the bed was a black lacquered cabinet about forty inches tall. It had a three-inch slot running down that top of the cabinet that was about four feet long. He pushed down on the slot and a widescreen LED TV slowly raised up from inside the cabinet. Another push caused it to retract back into the cabinet. In front of the black cabinet was a rug as wide as the bed and imitated some of the Chinese tapestries he had also seen in the Ringling exhibit. He drifted to the center of the bedroom and rotated once more to take in the space. The entire room had the aura of wealth. As best as he could figure, there were no outward connectivity to the rest of the world. Its guest could enjoy the ship's comforts, and the owner had complete control of their stay.

He completed the tour of the immaculately clean room and sat on the corner of the bed and sighed. Although the room was more than adequate for any guest, Rick couldn't enjoy it. How could he? He was held captive by a Chinese triad.

He knew the guard outside his door would cut him down without hesitation. His family would be worried about him, and they probably had good reason to be. He was glad Leilani was free and that his family was unharmed, but how long would that last?

Rick felt his mobile phone pressing his thigh in his pocket. He pulled it out and looked at the signal indicator. No Service. The onboard jammer was good. The phone was designed with higher gain antennas for better quality service, Wi-Fi, Bluetooth, and quad-band cellular. The only thing he saw that seemed to have any signal on the phone was the Bluetooth sync he had with his watch. That had a beefed-up, frequency-hopping transmission, which seemed to be holding synchronization solidly. But at what distance? He sat his phone down on the bedroom dresser and started walking backward to the bathroom. He checked the digital signal indicator on his watch as he walked. The indicator had five dots that signified signal strength. Standing next to the phone, he had five dots. By the time he reached the bed he still had five dots solidly lit. At the bathroom entrance the fifth dot began to blink, which meant ninety percent signal strength. By his calculation, he could get no more than 120 feet separation in the devices while on the yacht. He had chosen these particular devices so that wherever he sat his phone down in his office or home, the watch would still be synchronized with it. He had been able to get over 600 feet without effort at his house. The jammer onboard was amazingly powerful and agile. It must have cost millions.

He thought about the Bluetooth radio transmitter and receivers in his phone and watch. Because of its short range, which was due to low transmitter power, the jammer manufacturer had obviously not worried as much about that frequency band. The maximum output power of a Bluetooth device is twenty times less than the power of a cell phone. Fortunately, Rick knew his integration algorithm in his model of phone helped compensate for the power difference considerably. Without it, the maximum range between the watch and the phone would be lucky to reach five feet in this environment.

It occurred to him that maybe the Bluetooth transmission frequency might be the Achilles heel of the jammer. What if he could boost his signal? If so, he might be able to reach someone on the beach. Maybe even his family.

He sat back at the small table with the dish of strawberries. The Bryant phones had a waterproof case and they often used them for underwater pictures when swimming and diving. He used the flat end of the handle of the cheese slicer to help pop open the phone case to see the electronics and battery. He located the Bluetooth integrated circuit, but it was too well integrated for him to access. Increasing its signal strength increases the range. He could increase the signal strength by increasing the gain on the antenna. The antenna was a microstrip affair – a row of rectangular patches "printed" on the printed circuit board. Rick concluded quickly that it would be impossible to amplify the signal by modifying the phone itself.

He wasn't willing to give up yet. Rick looked around the room for items that could be used to build a higher gain antenna. He ran through a mental checklist of antennas he could make...monopole, dipole, yagi-uda, helical...a helical antenna! A helical antenna would increase the signal strength by at least a factor of ten. This type of antenna resembled a wide corkscrew. He would need rigid wire to construct this. He opened to the closet, which cleverly fit in the curved wall opposite of the vanity. He saw wooden hangers with silver colored hooks. He was disappointed until he saw the white bathrobe, which had been laundered and hung on a wire hanger. The wire hanger was covered in white paper advertising the laundry service company's name. He dropped the bathrobe to the bottom of the closet and brought out the hanger.

Rick walked into the bedroom and inventoried items he could use. His mobile phone was apart on the table and the hanger was in his hand. He could strip the alarm clock electrical cord and use the wire to attach the antenna to his phone. Before he began, he had to think of how it should be constructed. He needed the right coil diameter and coil spacing, or the antenna would do nothing with the Bluetooth frequency. He calculated the parameters and then searched for something that might help him to create the perfect coil. The bed had no posts, just boxy legs. He spied the side table legs. They were tubular in shape, but not wide enough.

He looked up again and caught movement in his porthole. He walked over to the porthole and gazed out. His jaw dropped. The yacht was moored quite a distance from the shore – more than a thousand feet. The movement he had seen was the glint of sunlight from a passing car at the beach parking lot. He stepped back and sat down on the bed. He dropped his head. It was no use. There was no way the helical antenna would have enough gain to reach the beach. A few more calculations and he shook his head in disgust at himself. A factor of ten in gain results in only a three time increase in range. If he could only get 120 feet without a high-gain antenna, then he would only get to maybe 360 to 400 feet. He was upset that he had wasted his time. Plus, he still didn't have anything to tell his family yet, except that he was alive.

He laid back on the bed with his feet still on the floor.  He felt weary all of a sudden and closed his eyes.  He didn't like feeling helpless, but doubt started to come over him.  He had always been able to depend on his wit and technology to get him out of predicaments in his life.  At 50-plus, was he starting to finally slip?

Then he thought again about what was around the room.  He thought of each item and how it could be used.  It made him think of the old TV show MacGyver.  MacGyver could get out of any dangerous situation.  He avoided firearms; he didn't need them.  He could use ordinary household items and jerry-rig them into amazing devices. *Toothpaste, a paperclip and a few household cleaners and he'd have a bomb strong enough to destroy the house they were being held in.*  Rick chuckled at the thought.  *A bomb from toothpaste…a bomb.*

He set up quickly with his eyes open wide.  "A bomb from toothpaste … no.  But a bomb from superheated lithium ion…yes," he said out loud.

He got up and walked over to his phone.  It was still dissembled on the table.  He saw the cheese cutter next to the phone.  He then went back to the bathroom and started looking through the toiletries.  He found what he was searching for—tweezers.  He took them back to the desk.   He was about to start, but remembered he hadn't charged the phone since yesterday.  His watch lasted for weeks on a charge, but the featured packed phone was lucky to make it a full twenty-four hours.

He looked back over to the clock.   As he expected, it was modern and had a charger cradle on top for multiple types of phones.   Rick reassembled his phone, but left the waterproof cover off.  He sat it on the charger.  It probably needed at least thirty minutes for a decent charge.

He began stepping through the tasks ahead of him.

# Chapter 31: *Lithium-Ion*

Rick knew the bomb he was thinking of constructing wasn't actually what one would consider a bomb per se. It might explode, but it wouldn't be punching a hole in the side of the mega yacht. Given the battery size, the worst it would do is to pop, throw shards of metal, chemical electrolyte, and plastic. What it would most likely do is flare up with an intense flame that would burn at extreme temperatures. Any debris would be molten too. It would serve well as an electronic fuse. *What would blow up with an ignition? Fuel and fuel fumes.*

While the mobile phone charged he strategized. Rick noticed the old phone next to the bed on the side table. He picked it up and held it to his ear. Almost immediately a thick Asian accented steward came on. "May I help you Mr. Bryant," said the steward. Rick looked at the headset and then hung it up. He waited a moment to make sure the steward did not call back. Then he unplugged the phone from the wall. He forced the bowed tweezers he had taken from the bathroom into the tiny slot at the base of the plastic handset. The plastic shell of the phone clicked open into two halves, with one side being the front with twelve square holes in the center, a few longer holes for the paging buttons, and then many small circular holes for the ear and mouth piece. In the opposite side sat all the internal electronics. The keypad was in the center and a speaker sat on each end. He pulled free one of two wires to the ear speaker, which disabled it. He then snapped the two halves of the phone back together, and plugged it back in the wall.

He stared at the fruit dish. He had to do something with it – the strawberries were still fresh. He suspected it came from the mainland quite green, ripened in the store, and were most likely tasteless. Better to have pineapple, mango, starfruit, kiwi, and papaya in Hawai'i. He first ran them under hot water in the sink. It didn't seem to have much of an effect. He searched for a hair dryer, but didn't see one. Then Rick noticed the wall sconces. He dried the berries with a towel. Using the tweezers, he held them near the bulb in one of the sconces. Its heat took a while, but eventually yielded the result he hoped. The strawberries started to haze and slowly contract. He didn't want to burn the berry so he watched it intently. After a few more moments, he examined it. "Just right," he said. He repeated this procedure for all the strawberries on the plate.

Next was the door. He examined the door handle and the door strike plate. It appeared they had reversed the knob so that the locking mechanism was on the outside. The door still swung inwardly and the strike plate curved inwardly. He picked up the cheese slicer and fit its flat handle between the door and strike plate. He gently pushed the handle to see if the door or the door jamb moved. It did. He couldn't risk much pressure in fear the door might creak, which would cause the guard to open it. While keeping the pressure constant, Rick got on his knees and could now see the cylindrical door latch. Rick guessed it stuck out of the door about a half inch into the square hole of the strike plate.

Rick stood and reached in his pocket and found some change. He found nickels, pennies, and a couple of quarters. The nickels were about the right size of the latch, but he only had two of them. He took the cheese slicer and two nickels and two pennies to the bathroom. He used the cheese slicer to shave off thin slices of the hand soap. He held them in his hands and then stuck them under hot water. The water was quite hot, but he kept his hand under it. Soon the soap became soft and began to dissolve. He picked up two nickels, which were already rather warm from being in his pocket. He placed some of the melting soap between them and pressed. Then he set them on the vanity top to cool. He repeated the process with two pennies. After they cooled, he checked to see how well they were stuck to each other. Not a strong hold, but sufficient for the job. He then repeated the process one more time by joining the two nickels to the two pennies. He rested the set of coins on their edges to cool. Some of the soap oozed out and allowed the group of coins to sit up on their edge without falling over. He was happy with the result, and brought it over to the table.

He checked on the mobile phone battery and it was fully charged. He pulled it off the charger cradle on the clock radio and brought it over the table. He disassembled the phone once more and pulled the battery out easily. The battery would be the electronic fuse.

The battery was black and was about the size of a credit card but several times thicker. The name brand and 3.7V was in big letters, while 1000mAh and a model number was printed smaller below it. The battery had a cap on one end, which appeared to be glued in place. The cap had four copper pads, which made contact with the spring contacts on the phone itself.

Using the small fork on the table, Rick tapped the tines down around the edge of the cap's lip. He continued to move the fork around the entire edge and tap, tap, tap. He had to be careful not to damage the battery since he had to reinstall it in the phone and have it work. It was tedious, but he eventually felt the glue give and the battery cap popped off. He held the battery upright, so the cap was up. He gently lifted the cap off the battery housing and found wires leading to the cap's four copper pads. Inside the battery were layers of lithium foil, graphite, and a plastic separator. A goopy electrolyte was the magic sauce that made it work.

Using the tweezers, Rick squeezed down on the plastic separator with the tweezers and pulled a little chunk out in two places along the top. He could feel the tingle of the current passing through the tweezers whenever they touched both the graphite layer and the lithium foil layer. After he cleaned off the tweezers, he then opened them wider so that lithium foil and the graphite layers at the point where he had ripped off the plastic separator was between the pointed teeth. Then he squeezed as hard as he could, feeling a sustained tingle from the current rush. He held it for a few seconds and then released. The tweezers' teeth had perforated the lithium foil and the graphite and they adhered to each other. He repeated the step at the other notch he ripped out of the separator.

He flipped the cap over gently and saw a small bulbous wire hanging from it. The wire was most likely the thermistor...a heat sensor. It was used to help regulate temperature in the battery. Rick used the tweezers to pull the tiny sensor off. Temperature monitoring had just ceased forevermore on that battery. He closed the cap on top and pressed down. It clicked into place. He held the battery upside down. No electrolyte was leaking out, so it was probably OK. He put the battery back into the phone and powered it up.

Rick had a thermal camera embedded in the edge of his watch. It had originally been a daylight color camera, but Rick asked his technicians to replace it with a small focal plane array. A focal plane array is like the electronic film for a thermal camera. Rick thought the quality of the original daylight camera was useless, whereas the focal plane array could at least be able to see someone hiding in the darkness of an unlit room.

The thermal camera actually sees heat, so Rick enabled the thermal camera. He aimed his wrist so that he could see the battery in the one-inch display on the watch face. He started the stopwatch function and watched the battery glow on his screen. The watch display had 256 false color levels representing 256 temperature readings. It took 34 seconds to change levels. That meant the battery would have little over two hours before it reached the hottest level monitored by the watch, which was 105 degrees Celsius or 221 degrees Fahrenheit.

Lithium-Ion batteries can explode due to a phenomenon known as thermal runaway. The battery temperature climbs exponentially, which leads to an explosion. Although rare, it can happen in phones and laptops when their battery is damaged. In videos Rick had seen, thermal runaway had caused batteries to explode well before they reached 100 degrees Centigrade.

Rick knew he had done enough damage to the battery for it to heat up quickly, but he didn't know if he had done enough to cause an explosion – it was just a guess. Even if it didn't blow up, he hoped that it would at least catch fire. And that's all he needed it to do, but his time window was somewhere between 90 to 120 minutes for it to do its damage.

He reassembled the mobile phone, placed it in the waterproof case, and rested it on the table. He sat for a moment to go over the plan one more time, and then nodded to himself and put it into action.

# Chapter 32: *"A" Team*

Ryan watched the mega yacht from the shore with high powered binoculars. Nikki was constantly looking up at the yacht and then back at her tablet PC, hoping to pick up some signal from her dad. It had been about an hour since her dad had gone aboard the yacht. Nikki unconsciously shifted her weight from one foot to the next, swaying as she did it.

Perhaps sensing her anxiety, Ryan held her arm and spun her around to him. He gave her a big hug and said, "He'll be fine. He's got the A Team backing him up."

Nikki squeezed him tight, then relaxed and rested her head on Ryan's chest. She needed this.

"This waiting is killing me," she said without looking up. "I can't imagine what it must be like for Mom."

As if on cue, Danielle came in over the cellular network. "Nikki, anything to report?"

Ryan lowered his arms to her waist and she looked up to him and gave him a kiss. "Thanks."

She stepped back and held up her tablet. She swiped it with her finger, enabling her Bluetooth mike. "Hi Mom. Not really. Ryan is watching the yacht and thinks he got a glimpse of Dad at one of the portholes. But that's it. There's no change on the jammer."

"What about your sister?"

"We saw her, Stephanie and Kai just pass by a few minutes ago on the highway. It will be a while before they get to the antenna site. I've patched their position feeds to the *Stingray*, so you should be able to see them on your display."

"Yes, I see them," said Danielle. "Any word from Kaleho?"

"Leilani is on board. She's already taken a shower and is eating something. She refused to eat with them when she was onboard. Kaleho has officers and S.W.A.T on standby in Hale'iwa, and he's already notified the Coast Guard of the situation and that he may need their help."

"Good," said Danielle. She was quiet for several seconds. "I know I'm supposed to be monitoring the sonar and the feeds from our robotic sharks swimming a few hundred meters from the yacht, but I was thinking. Maybe I should send in the sharks to get a closer look. They could do a loop around the yacht ... perhaps check out the launch platform at the stern. Once they clear the jammer barrier, I could review their recorded video."

"That's a great idea, Mom," said Nikki. "But make sure they pass by close to the ship. They have short-range camera systems, so they'll need to be within fifty yards."

"Acknowledged. I'll send you the feeds once they come back. Be sure to let me know if you hear anything. I'm going to stay submerged with my communication buoy deployed. So I'll be able to react to anything."

"Roger that, Mom. You'll be the first to know," said Nikki.

Nikki thought of the hug she had just had from Ryan. "And Mom?"

"What, honey?" asked Danielle.

"He'll be fine. He's got the A team backing him up."

The line was quiet for several moments. Nikki imagined the tears in her mom's eyes. Then she heard her mom say, "No...he has the A plus team."

# Chapter 33: *It's Time*

*What am I missing?* Rick' eyes were closed as he began to imagine the scenario that would begin in a few moments. Timing was crucial. He had used up six minutes of the minimum of the ninety he had before a possible explosion of the battery in his phone. It could take much more time than that, but he couldn't count on it. The best case scenario was that he caused enough damage to distract people long enough to escape, or for Nikki to possibly take control of the UAV and crash it. The worst case was that he would be killed.

He checked the room one last time. The room's phone was on edge of the side table – angled toward the bed as if it had been used. The strawberries in the small dish looked like they were spoiling. The cheese slicer was clean and was sitting next to the cheese. He had a dab of moist, pliable cheese rolled up as a bead, and it was sticking nicely to the stack of waxed nickels in his hand. He felt the mobile phone in his front pants pocket and could feel the warmth of it through the material and on his leg. *It's time.*

He knocked softly on the door. Nothing happened. He knocked a little harder and heard the floor creak some as the guard swiveled to open the door. He heard the click of the lock and saw the door knob turn. The door opened slowly and Rick could see the hulk of a guard holding the door knob in one hand and a pistol in the other.

"What?" said the guard in a deep baritone voice. Rick was a tall man of moderate build. The guard was slightly taller, but he had massive arms and shoulders.

"I'm hungry. I need something to eat," said Rick.

"Tough," said the guard and began closing the door.

"No, wait. I'm dreadfully hungry. We have been working nonstop to find the treasure. I haven't had time to eat for almost a day now. Can't you get me something from the galley?"

"Fruit and cheese on the table," said the guard.

"I'm lactose intolerant and the fruit is rotten."

The guard paused for a few seconds. "Stand back from the door."

"Sure," responded Rick. He took a step to the left of the door.

The guard swung the door open to Rick's right. He stuck his head in and checked out the fruit in the dish. Then he looked back at Rick.

"Call for the steward on the phone." He used his gun as a pointer.

"Can't. It's broken," said Rick.

The guard waved Rick out of his way with his gun hand and walked beside the bed. He picked up the phone. It was at that time that Rick thought about a mistake in his plan. He could have wired the phone so that it shocked the guard…maybe knock him out. Then he could have had more time to accomplish his task. *Oh well*, he thought. *Too late for that now.*

The guard spoke into the phone and listened. He spoke a second time and listened. There was no dial tone. Then he checked the phone cord. It was still plugged into the wall.

"It's broken," he said.

"I know, I told you that a few seconds ago," added Rick.

"I can't leave my post," said the guard. "You'll just have to wait."

"Would your boss like to see me pass out before he gets to talk with me? What would he do to you if he knew I had passed out after asking you for food? Would you be in trouble?"

Rick could tell the guard was conflicted. He could see the guard weighing the possibilities. He couldn't call on the room phone – it was broken. And the jammer prevented the guard from using his own mobile phone.

"Come on. Just ask the cook to make me a sandwich. You can lock the door. I'm on a boat full of armed people happy to shoot me. What do you need to worry about?" said Rick.

The guard just grunted and headed for the door. He turned back around after passing through the doorway. "You better not move. I'll be back."

The guard started closing the door when Rick grabbed the door knob with his right hand and stepped right up to the door frame. The guard kept his left hand on the door knob and pushed the pistol in his right hand forward into Rick's ribs.

"Just one other thing," Rick said in an apologetic tone. "Could I get a cup of coffee? It would probably help with the light-headedness I'm feeling right now."

The guard hesitated for a moment, and then nodded. He pushed harder with the pistol in Rick's ribs, which was the sign for Rick to move back from the door.

The guard pulled the door shut. Rick grabbed the doorknob again and held it tight in his hands and wedged his right foot to the bottom of the door. The door lock clicked and there was a momentary push by the guard to verify the door was indeed locked. With Rick's foot holding steadfast, the door did not budge. Seconds later Rick heard the guard's footsteps down the hallway to the left and then on metal stairs. *The galley must be on the deck below.*

Rick released the door handle and stepped away from the door. The door popped open easily with a slight pull. Rick checked the door latch hole in the door frame. When he had stopped the guard to ask for the coffee, he had used the distraction to push the waxed coin stack with cheese into the hole with this left hand. It prevented the door from actually locking, and Rick's hand and foot was the only thing that prevented the door from easily popping out. Rick's slight-of-hand had been so smooth that he was even impressed himself.

He eased his head out of the door and glanced the direction the guard had gone. All clear. Only the utility cart of the cleaning crew was parked near the end of the hall. Then he looked down the hall in the opposite direction. He listened carefully, but could not make out any sounds other than the background noises of the ship itself.

He stepped out into the hall and walked right – opposite to the guard's direction. He tip-toed past two other doors. He heard nothing and kept moving. At the end of the hall was another staircase. It was a spiral one that led both up and down. On the hall across from the stairs was a placard. Rick stepped up and examined the placard.

The placard was a plan drawing of each deck on the ship. He saw the red star indicating the location he was standing now. Two decks below him was where he needed to go. That would be a challenge to get there unnoticed. He had asked for a sandwich, which would take all of five minutes to make. But coffee would give him a few more minutes. He knew tea was the preferred drink in the Asian culture and would be poured in seconds. But they'd have to brew coffee, and that would take a little more time to make. At least that's what he hoped.

He went back to the utility cart, which was basically a large canvas bag snapped over a metal frame. Inside the bag were smaller cloth bags stacked haphazardly. From the smell of it, this must be dirty laundry collection.

Rick picked through the first two bags and saw bed sheets and towels only. He found clothes in the third bag. He saw a deckhand uniform shirt amongst the clothes. He pulled it out. It was smelly from sweat, but there were no noticeable stains and was wrinkle free.

Rick's shirt was made of lightweight cotton and was a button-down. It was blue and white and had raised prints of outlines of mahi-mahi and marlin on it. He had thick cotton khaki shorts with lots of pockets, white ankle height socks and gray Nike's with white soles.

The crew uniform shirt was a loose-fitting red polo with navy blue short sleeves and collar. The crew's name was sewn over a left breast pocket. In nice blue print was the name Huang. *Great*, thought Rick. *At least it's an XL size.* His khaki's didn't compliment those of the other crewman, but they didn't look bad with the polo. The crew all wore dark canvas deck shoes. Rick didn't even bother to search for those – he wore size thirteen, which he knew would be hard to locate on the boat. He unbuttoned his shirt and threw it back into his room on the bed. Then he slid the dirty uniform shirt over his head.

He walked silently down the spiral steps across from the placard. Rick leaned over the rails as he walked – trying to spot others before they spotted him. He just hoped the smell from the uniform wouldn't be detected by the crew first.

He arrived at the landing on the next lower deck and stopped to the right of the door. He was afraid if he was seen, someone would call him to help or do some chore on the ship. He listened for a few moments. He could hear clicking sounds to the left of the door, which was in the direction of the bow of the ship. It was where the galley was located. His guard would be waiting impatiently for the cook to complete his meal. Rick heard no other sounds.

He crossed the door and headed down the steps to the next lower deck. He made it to the landing and paused again at the doorway. He heard talking toward the bow end of the hallway. Those were the quarters for the crew. A boat this big would have crews working in shifts to keep things running smoothly day and night. He needed to go toward the stern.

He looked down at his watch. Three minutes and thirty-eight seconds had passed since the guard had left his room. He had to hurry. He lowered his head stepped into the hall and turned right. The door at the end of the hall had a circular plastic window, which allowed him to see out into the large room ahead. Below the window was the sign with the words "Equipment Bay." He peeked in and saw crewmen. He glanced back and saw the closed crew quarters' door behind him. There was no window on that door, but he could clearly hear people talking beyond it.

He turned back to the circular window in front of him and watched the crew. There were three of them. They were mostly quiet and were doing maintenance to the tenders, Jet Skis, and other equipment. They were a mixed crew of Caucasian and Asian workers. English seemed to be the language of choice for these guys. The aft wall had two large doors that were closed, but he assumed they led to a launch platform at the stern of the ship. He saw what he was searching for against the starboard wall of the vessel. It was a white polypropylene-plastic fuel tank with a built-in pump. You could see the slightly darker fuel through the tank's skin. It was quite large, and Rick guessed it held at least a hundred gallons. They used it to fuel the tenders and Jet Skis.

Rick watched the men moving around on the various chores. He knew if he opened the door, they would all glance up. They would immediately recognize he wasn't Huang.

139

He stood there a full minute and he was about to give up when he heard a muffled "Stand back, I'm going to start it up" from a crewman in front of him.

The other two opened up the two large doors and pushed down large bolts on the base of each to lock them open.    The third crewman attached the hanging chains from the overhead hoist to the cradle on which the Jet Ski sat.    Then he reached to the ship bulkhead and picked up a control box with two buttons – up and down.    The man pressed on one of the buttons and the Jet Ski and cradle lifted off the floor.    He easily pushed the rig through the open doors and out to the launch platform.    He came back in and picked up the control and pulled its long cable with him to the platform.    He then lowered it into the water.    The Jet Ski was an open loop cooled model, which intakes water to cool the motor.

Rick also knew the sound would have been deafening inside, which is why the crew wanted to start it out in the open.    The crewmen inspected the Jet Ski one more time.    The crewman that had been working on it was pointing to the motor; he was probably describing the work he had done.    Rick looked at his watch.    Five minutes and fifty-two seconds had passed since the guard had left for his sandwich.

*Come on…. Start it up.*

Twenty seconds later he saw two of the crewmen step away as the crewman that had completed the repairs reached up to the starter on the steering handles and cranked up the Jet Ski.    The sound was incredibly loud and could be heard easily through his door.    He could no longer hear the voices in the crewman's quarters.    He watched the third crewman step away from the Jet Ski and all that was visible was the Jet Ski and water it was churning.

Rick pushed through the door and headed straight for the tank.    It had warning labels on every surface.    The tank had a twist cap at the top for filling it.    The tank was filled almost to the top.    After a few moments of force with both hands, the cap gave and Rick spun it off quickly.    Although the smell of gasoline was strong from the tank, it was easily masked by the exhaust fumes of the Jet Ski.    He pulled his phone out of his pocket and was about to drop it inside the tank when he stopped at the sight of the sloshing fluid.    Even though the fuel would ignite easily, it would also act to cool the phone down in the absence of spark or flame.

He swiped the display and started scrolling through his software apps.    He found the app he wanted and started it.    The oscilloscope app computed Fast Fourier Transforms, or FFT's, which are used to calculate frequencies in digitized data.    In the 1960's, an FFT required a room-size computer hours to compute.    His smartphone could compute thousands of FFT operations in a second, but at the price of high processor loading. Higher processing loads resulted in greater heat.    Rick set the app to run continuously.    He just hoped the app wouldn't drain the battery before it could catch on fire or explode.

He dropped the phone into the tank and heard a "bloop" sound as it sunk and then rose back to float inside the tank.    He reached for the cap, but was then stunned by the sudden silence of Jet Ski motor.    He stopped motionless -- bent over the tank with the cap in his hands.

The crewmen started laughing, so Rick pushed the top back on and twisted it three full turns.    He heard steps on the platform and the hoist's motor lift the Jet Ski.    He bolted for the door with the circular window, and heard someone shuffle into the double doors behind him.

"Hey Huang, what are you doing up?    You're supposed to be off duty."

The shout startled him, but Rick didn't look back.    He must have been about the same build as Huang, which is why the called him by name.    Rick just waved and sped through the door.   With the door swung wide, he noticed the door to the crews' quarters was opening. He heard two other crewmen talking to each other on the other side of the door.

"Huang.  Did you hear me?  Come back brah."

Rick took two giant steps and turned left into the stairwell.   The door with the circular window banged back closed, but he could still hear the Jet Ski guys calling for Huang.

He was bounding up steps when the two crewmen from the crew quarters passed by the spiral stair landing.  A few steps later, he heard the bay door open and one of the crewmen shout, "What to do you want? You know the boss doesn't like us shouting."

By the time he had reached the next floor landing, he thought he heard one of the crewman say something about a shark.  Rick didn't stay to hear anymore.  Up he went.

He leapt out of the stair landing on his deck and ran toward the door to his room.  He heard the pounding steps of the guard heading back up the staircase from the other end of the hallway with his meal.

He knelt quickly to the floor and tried to fish out the coins from the door frame, but heard the change of pitch of the steps.  The guard was at the stair landing.   Rick rolled inside his room and came up on his knees.  He pushed the door closed as fast as he dared without slamming it.  He then stood up and forced his foot against the bottom of the door.  He would need to time this just right so that the guard would think the door was locked.

The guard paused to unlock the door.  Rick held his hands tight to the door when he remembered too late that he still had Huang's uniform shirt on.  The guard checked the door knob and Rick tightened his grip on the knob to keep it from turning.   Then he released it and took his foot from the bottom of the door.  He quickly pulled the uniform polo over his head, slid the chair out from the table, balled the shirt up and sat on it and the chair.

The door itself blocked the guard's view of him as he swung it open.   As he stepped into the room Rick saw the platter of food in one hand and the gun in the other.   The guard looked at the shirt on the bed and then around at Rick.

"What are you doing?  Why is your shirt off?" asked the guard.

"It was taking a longer than I thought it would for you to get back, so I was about to take a shower to get my mind off food. But then I heard your footsteps, so I sat down.  I'm starving."

The guard shook his head, and then walked to the table with his food platter.   The coffee was in a carafe and there was a large white mug.   The sandwich was on a plate.   The coffee smelled strong and the sandwich did look good.

"Where's the mustard?" Rick asked.

The guard just said "Humph," and walked back to the door.   As he opened the door, he turned back to Rick and said, "You stink."  Without looking back, he walked through the doorway and pulled the door closed.  Rick jumped back up and held the door firm with his hands and foot.  The guard checked the lock and then became quiet.  Rick imaged the guard had resumed his stance next to the door – hands crossed and feet splayed in a wide stance.

If the phone blew up, he would need to get out of the room quickly.  So he was glad he didn't get to take out the coins in the door.  He would just have to make sure he repeated the hand grip and planted foot trick whenever he heard a sound outside the door.

Rick smelled himself and agreed with the guard's assessment.  He left the food and walked back to the bathroom.   He might die within the hour, so he might as well enjoy a shower. It might be his last.

# Chapter 34: *Sunset Beach*

The north shore of O'ahu felt like another world to Shelli as she moved north along Highway 83, Kamehameha Highway, on a moped. Shelli smiled at Kai riding next to her on her left and turned to check on Stephanie following behind. Stephanie's golden hair was whipping around behind the helmet she wore. Mopeds were the only thing they were legally able to drive at their age in Hawai'i. The top speed of these were only 45 mph, but that didn't matter since the road from Hale'iwa was curvy and slow going anyway.

They were north of Waimea Bay in the small town of Pupukea. The beach was to their left. They passed a lava promontory that extended out into the water on the south side of a wide beach lined with tropical trees and shrubs. Kai signaled for them to pull over at the first beach entrance, which had room for a few cars to park. A couple of spaces were free, and the threesome pulled into one of them facing the beach and water. The greens of the vegetation gave way to the light tan sand. A slight surf churned at the edges of the emerald water inside the reef that was several hundred feet out. Beyond the reef, the water went from azure to dark blue. All three of them had sunglasses on, which made the colors even deeper.

"This is Sunset Beach," said Kai. "Home to many of those pipeline surfing contests you have probably seen on TV."

"It's beautiful," said Stephanie. "But if it is such a hot spot for surfing, how come there are small waves out there?"

"The surfing season is November to February," answered Kai. "Big waves, taller than houses, come rolling in at that time. It's an awesome site. Not much action though in the summer. That's why you don't see any surfers out there now."

"Have you surfed here?" asked Shelli.

"I've been out here when the waves were not their best. Like in late April and May. But you can't be out there unless you're world class during the peak of the season."

"I'm hoping they get to have the Eddie this year," said Kai.

"The Eddie?" asked Stephanie.

"That's a surfing championship," said Kai. "They have it whenever the waves are over 40 feet high."

"40 feet? Wow. But why do they call it The Eddie. Is it something to do with water eddies?" asked Stephanie as she whirled her finger.

"Ha, ha. No, it refers to the surfing legend Eddie Aikau. He was a lifeguard and surfer. He saved over a hundred lives. When someone was in seriously trouble in the water, he would go out and save them. There used to be a famous saying, 'Eddie would go,' because of his courage. They named the surfing contest in his honor."

"Is he still alive?" asked Shelli.

"Naw. He died back when my dad was in college. Dad did get to meet him once. It meant a lot to him that Eddie knew him by name."

"Cool. Would you like to be a professional surfer?" asked Stephanie.

"Are you kidding?" replied Kai. "What surfer wouldn't want to be able to do that? But it takes a lot of practice. And you got to show them you can handle the big waves before they let you compete. You got to be respected first."

"You been surfing your whole life?" asked Shelli.

"Yep," said Kai. "Dad started pulling me around on a board as soon as I could hold on."

"Was he a good surfer, your dad I mean?" asked Shelli.

"Heck yeah. He was awesome. He's still pretty good. Mom told me once that he went pro one year. Dad doesn't talk about it much, but I think he felt that it wasn't the best career path."

"What would he think about you going pro one day?" said Shelli. Shelli didn't know why she was asking all these questions – she just hoped to make a connection. He was drop-dead gorgeous and he was certainly athletic. His hair was black and longish. His skin was almost brown from the considerable time he spent outdoors. She could see a lighter line of skin around bottom of his shorts, which had ridden up some during the ride on the mopeds. Shelli had boyfriends in the past, but they were often more of a nuisance than fun. But Kai was different. Kind of exotic and mysterious. He didn't talk a lot, but that was OK. He had the kind of look that said he was smart, but she didn't know for sure if he was. Only way to know was to talk.

"Dad says I can be whatever I wanna be. He said if I stick with it, I could go pro one day."

"Must be tough to be a cop's son," said Shelli.

"Dad's pretty cool. You know it's not that easy making friends when your father is chief of police. But when he doesn't have the uniform on, you'd never know he was a cop. Weed is pretty common here – more so than booze. Sort of part of the surfer scene. Dad doesn't put up with that while he's at the beach or anywhere else for that matter. But he used to be a surfer, so everybody respects him."

"You ever smoke any weed?" asked Stephanie.

"Heck no," answered Kai without question. "I don't have a good enough imagination to figure out what Dad would do to me if I ever did drugs. I just know that it would be harsh."

"God, I don't know what my dad would do if he ever caught me," said Shelli.

"You ever do any drugs?" asked Kai.

"Oh no. My parents' constantly drilled it in us growing up. Plus, I'm so busy with dance and such that I don't have time to get in trouble."

"What about you, Stephanie?" asked Kai.

"Ditto with what Shelli said. Plus my big brother was in sports and he kind of looked out for me. If my parents didn't kill me for doing drugs, he would've. And I pity what he would do to any person that would give me any."

Kai laughed. Shelli liked to see him laugh.

"I know what you mean. My big brother is in college in California now, but when he was here he'd do the same."

"Isn't it kind of the surfer culture to do drugs?" asked Shelli.

"It used to be, but drugs are pretty common around the island whether you're a surfer or not. People don't need much excuse to do drugs these days, and well, it got to be more of a pride thing to say that I was clean."

Shelli and Stephanie both nodded. They were all quiet for a moment. It was easy just to sit and look.

"This is nice, you know. I'd love to stay here longer, but we've got something we're supposed to do," said Shelli. "She unsnapped her phone from its cradle next to the speedometer. According to this, we're about two miles from the turnoff to the antenna site."

"Yeah, it's called Girl Scout Camp Road," said Kai. It cuts behind the houses on the mauka side of the road."

"The what side of the road?" asked Stephanie. "I swear he doesn't speak English," she said looking at Shelli.

"Mauka – it means toward the mountains," said Kai. "Makai means toward the sea."

"Mauka mountains, makai sea," said Stephanie. She pointed her hands in those directions as she spoke. "Got it."

"And when you're in Honolulu, they use Diamond Head and Ewa," said Kai."

"Oh, I know," said Stephanie. "Diamond Head is east and Ewa is west."

"You got it," said Kai with a smile.

*The smile*, thought Shelli. She was starting to realize that she pretty much liked everything about him.

"We will go up about another mile and pull off to meet a friend of mine that lives in town here. He knows the area better than I do. He'll go with us."

"Did you say 'he' knows?" asked Stephanie.

"What?" said Kai. He looked puzzled at first. Stephanie was beaming. "Oh, yes he – Tim."

"How old is Tim?" asked Stephanie.

"Same as me."

"Does he surf?" asked Stephanie.

"Yes – maybe even better than me," answered Kai.

"Well what are we waiting for?" said Stephanie. "We got to go meet Tim."

"Let me call him first. He wanted me to call him when we got here," said Kai.

Kai pulled his phone out of his pocket asked it to call Tim. Kai put the phone to his ear. "Hey brah," he said. He listened for a few seconds. "See ya there."

"He wants us to meet him up at Sunset Beach Park, which is about a mile up ahead on the mauka…

"Mountain," Stephanie said excitedly.

"…side of the road," continued Kai. He's saving us a parking spot."

They headed off to meet Tim. The trees and rich homes thinned on the makai side of the road, and the beach came into view again. The beach came almost to the road. Only a narrow space for cars to park separated the road from the beach. Kai motioned to pull into the beach park on the right. He pulled into the park first, and Stephanie and Shelli followed.

Tim did the shaka sign and Kai countered. Tim was tall, tan like Kai, had a head full of sun bleached hair, and was handsome. Stephanie signaled Shelli with her hand and mouthed "mine."

They parked their mopeds. Stephanie made sure to stop closest to Tim. Shelli knew this would be fun to watch. Stephanie swung her leg over the moped, and then unbuckled her helmet. One a fluid motion, she removed the helmet and flung her hair like a fashion model. It fell perfectly over her sleeveless top and toned arms. She popped her hip and rested the helmet on it. She reached out her hand and said, "Hi Tim. I'm Stephanie. Glad to meet you."

Shelli parked to the side and slightly behind Stephanie. She pulled her helmet off in not so a dramatic way, then snapped the strap and hung it over the handle bars. She stuck her hand up and waved, "Hello Tim. I'm Shelli. Shelli Bryant."

Tim turned to Kai, "You didn't tell me they were hot, brah."

"Wanted to surprise you," said Kai with a smile.

Stephanie looked at the beach across the road. "It's breathtakingly beautiful here."

"Yeah, just like you," said Tim with a smile.

Shelli enjoyed seeing the blush on Stephanie's face.

"Thanks, Tim. That's so sweet. Have you lived here long?" asked Stephanie.

"I've lived here practically all my life. My parents were professors at the University. They moved here when I was two. My dad does research now with Dole Pineapple."

"That's wonderful," said Stephanie. "Maybe we ...."

"Sorry to interrupt," said Shelli. "But Dad is depending on me. You guys can socialize when we finish."

Stephanie rolled her eyes, but then remembered the mission. "Sorry," she said.

"Tim, so what's up there?" asked Kai.

"There is a Girl Scout camp, which is how road got its name, and a satellite communication company. If you look up along the ridge there, you can see the main road that takes you up to both places. The camp is way up in the mountains, and the satellite place is just beyond the switchback up there." Tim pointed to the ridgeline as he spoke. "It's flat once you get over the ridge and then it slopes kinda gently until you get to the mountains."

"Like a plateau. From the satellite views, we can see that the satellite site is big," said Shelli. "But the views are pretty dated, and I couldn't find any up-to-date aerial photos of it online. Has there been any new construction over the last year or so?"

"Wow, dude. Where did you get her?" said Tim.

"I told you she was smart," said Kai.

Shelli smiled when she heard it. But not because of the compliment. *Kai was talking to Tim about me before we started out today. He's told Tim I was hot and smart. Oh my God, he's into me. OK, calm down. Focus.*

"Yeah, about a year ago there was a lot of heavy moving equipment that came in. Then about six months ago, they had to close down Kamehameha for a while to let this seriously large antenna be moved up there. The truck could barely make it up the road. They hired a bunch of carpenters, electricians and other kinds of construction people. About three months ago it was done."

"What does the new antenna do?" asked Shelli.

"Beats me," answered Tim. All the locals up here knew about the construction, but there hasn't been a word about what they do there. None of the people that work there were originally from the area. I think most people assume it's another satellite company."

"It's got to be the one, Shelli" said Kai. "Your dad said it's the only logical site."

"Tim, did you ever see the people that work up there in town?" asked Shelli.

145

"Most of the people that work for the next door satellite company live here in town or down in Hale'iwa. Some of the kids at my high school have parents that work there. But the people that go to the new site don't live, shop, or eat in town. There are not a lot of people that work there. I'm often up real early to catch some waves before the tourist get here to the beach. I've seen a car go up in the morning and one come down right after it. So I would guess they work shifts."

"You ride the pipeline?" asked Stephanie. "Wow, I'm impressed."

"Heck no ... I catch waves in the fall and spring. Surf's pretty good then, but not as gnarly as during the winter."

"Stephanie please," said Shelli.

"Sorry."

"Tim, how do you know that cars you see going up and coming down are going to the new facility? They could work in any of the buildings up there," said Shelli

"The new site was built as close to the edge of the ridgeline as was possible. According to my dad, the reason why they allow them to be up there is because you can't see them from the shoreline. If you look to the left of the switchback, there is a cell tower that barely peaks into view. That was a big deal for that tower to be seen, but people gotta have their phones. The new place is right next to that cell tower. It's still pretty dark when I first get out there on my board in the morning, so I can see the headlights light up that tower when they pull up."

"He's incredibly observant," Stephanie said as she nodded her head.

"Do you know a way that we could get close to that without being seen?" asked Shelli.

Tim thought for a moment. "Yes, but it's sorta hard to describe it to you. They got a lot of cameras up there, but if you go in from the farm off to the left over there you can work yourself into the trees along the ridge and pop out real close to the building they constructed next to the antenna."

"I can pull up the satellite view on my smartphone. Do you think you could show me on that?" said Shelli.

"Sure." And he did. He pointed out the route that would conceal them the entire way.

Shelli glanced at her watch. Her dad would have been taken by now if all was going as planned. They had at best and hour and a half to get their job done. "We can't afford to get lost up there. Too many people are counting on us. Tim, could you take us up there?"

Tim looked over at Stephanie. Shelli could tell Stephanie was about to burst with excitement. "I'd love to," he said.

About an hour later, they were peering through the trees at the small building sitting just twenty or so feet away from them. The new white antenna was on the other side of the building. It was different from the other antennas of the satellite company. It was more of flat disc instead of a bowl shape. It wasn't as big either. It moved in small, fluid increments as they watched.

"It doesn't look like the other antennas," said Stephanie.

"And it's pointing to the horizon instead of up like the other antennas," said Tim.

"This is got to be the right antenna," said Shelli. "Dad said it communicates to the UAV drone when it is at a long distance away from the ship. He said that if it had a flat face, that it would be a phased array antenna."

"What's a phased whosits antenna?" asked Stephanie.

"I don't know," answered Shelli. "Dad said it allows it to rapidly point a radio beam over an angle of about 60 degrees from where it's physically pointing."

Stephanie thought a moment. "So based on where it's pointing now, it could be talking…" Stephanie made air quote signs with her fingers on both hands. "…quote unquote, to the UAV anywhere from due south to out that way…makai," she said with smile to Kai as she pointed due west.

"Yeah, that's right," said Shelli. "We got to shut it down."

"Shelli, your dad said to get help if it's too dangerous. There's a car parked here, so there has to be someone inside." We need to call the police officers."

"There's no time Kai. My dad's life depends on that antenna being shut down. We got to do it."

Kai looked directly at her. *Those eyes of his could melt* thought Shelli. But Kai nodded in agreement. "We'll do it," he said.

"And how are we supposed to do that?" asked Tim.

"Right there," pointed Kai. "See where the power comes into the building, just below that window? There's a meter and then a small box with a handle on it. It should cut power to the whole building."

"How do you know that will cut power to the antenna?" asked Tim.

"Dad said that the transmitter in the antenna is powerful," said Shelli. "It's not safe for you to stand close to it. He said they would definitely want to be able to shut down power from the building for maintenance or emergencies. So Kai's right. If we cut the power to the building, it will cut power to the antenna."

"And not be seen when we do it," said Stephanie.

"But what if they come out and see the switch is thrown. Won't they just turn it back on again?" said Tim.

"Good point," said Shelli. "Hadn't thought of that. Dad said that it would probably take a few minutes for the system to come online again if it was powered back on. But Dad's going to need more than a few minutes."

"We could cut that big back line coming up from the ground to the switch," said Stephanie.

"With what?" said Kai.

"Doesn't matter. Cable like that has a thick plastic coating and has big braided-like copper wire inside. I saw them put it into our house during the remodel. They had special cutters for it. Maybe we could break the handle," said Shelli.

"Yeah, but if they have a big pipe wrench or a set of pliers, they could throw it back on again," said Tim.

They stared at the building and said nothing for what seemed to be a few minutes to Shelli.

"Hey guys. What's all that stuff on the side of the building? It looks like something spilled on it?" asked Stephanie.

"I don't know, Stephanie. Maybe birds land on the eave and make … deposits," said Shelli.

"Yuck! That's disgusting," said Stephanie. She quivered when she thought about it.

They sat quietly for a few moments. Shelli was getting frustrated. She knew everyone was counting on her. Why did she come all the way up here with no tools?

Just then the window opened above the meter. It was a tilt-out kind of window instead of the up and down kind of sash windows. A hand came out of the window with a skillet in it. The hand flipped the pan and shook it. Grease dropped and splattered down the siding of the building. After a few shakes, the person's other hand came out with a metal spatula and scraped the pan. A gelatinous square disk bounced on the switch, then the meter, and onto the ground. It landed on the black power cable that came out of the ground.

"That is disgusting," said Stephanie. "What on earth was it?"

Tim and Kai looked at each other. "Spam," they said in unison.

"What's Spam?"

"Ground up pig parts, salt and preservatives. Comes in a square can."

"Ugh," said Stephanie. "Who would eat that?

"Its great fried up in the morning with eggs," said Tim. "In fact, what he threw out will still probably be good tomorrow morning."

"Oh gross," said Stephanie.

A rustle in the bushes to their left drew their attention. Then a small brown head popped out of the bush. Then the rest of the mongoose. It skittered to the site of the mystery meat. It had obviously discovered the regularity at which leftover food was dumped out the window.

"Now what do we do? They have a pet mongoose guarding the power line," said Tim.

Shelli noticed that Kai was still and was concentrating on the mongoose. She looked at the mongoose and then back at him. "What is it Kai?"

"Watch the mongoose eating," said Kai. "See how it's gnawing on the power cable. The grease and the Spam are coating the cable. It thinks the cable is part of the food. Watch it as it scratches at the cable."

"See that...it lifted up the plastic coating on the cable," said Stephanie.

"What are you thinking, Kai?" asked Shelli.

"If the mongoose has chewed away the coating, we might be able to get to the individual pairs of braided wire inside," said Kai.

Shelli got excited. "And if the two lines touched, they would arc. Maybe catch fire, or at least blow some fuses."

"But how do we do that without getting shocked ourselves?" asked Stephanie.

"We have got to be careful. We don't have to make the wires touch, we just need to get them stripped. Then we can drop a piece of metal across it."

After a few minutes of discussion, the scheme was set. Since they might be seen or be heard cutting the cable sheathing, Tim was going to move through the trees to the cell tower where he could see the side door and anyone coming from the front of the building. If necessary, he would cause a distraction to give them time to cut power and get away. Stephanie would stand at the corner of the building so that she could watch for someone coming out of the side door or for a warning from Tim. Kai and Shelli would tear away as much of the cable housing as possible. They found an old piece of rebar that had been discarded in a mound of block, dirt and other debris near the edge of the trees where the

148

mongoose had come from. Kai and Shelli would short the wires with the rebar and they would all then take off running for the trees. They would all meet back at Sunset Beach Park if they got separated.

Their scheme was going great. Tim was in position. He had a small pile of rocks at his feet. Shelli and Kai were prying off the cable sheathing with their fingers. They were being careful not to touch both of the copper lines with their hands. Stephanie was in place and waiting to report anything.

And then they heard, "Stop what you're doing and put your hands up." A chubby Asian man stood facing them on the opposite corner of the building with a pistol aimed right at them. They hadn't checked for a second door.

Kai looked at Shelli, and shook his head. They stood. Shelli glanced back at Stephanie. She was waiving her arm.

"You there, what are you doing?" said the man with the gun.

"Nothing, just waving off a bug or something," said Stephanie.

"Well stop it," said the man. "All of you, move around to the parking lot."

As they walked to the parking lot, the man beat his fist on the wall. Another man came out of the side door. He was lean and about Shelli's height. He too was of Asian descent. He had pock marked face – remnants of a bad acne problem when he was younger. He had a gold chain on his neck and a big watch on this wrist. His tanned skin made both chain and watch stand out. "What's dis?" he said. *Probably not direct from Asia*, thought Shelli. *He's a local guy.*

"I saw them on the security camera we have out on the cell tower. They were digging in the back of the house outside the kitchen," said Gun Man.

"Bring them inside," said Gold Chain. "We'll find out what they're doing."

As they walked inside, Shelli felt her watch vibrate. She glanced at her watch and saw the text from her sister. It read, "How's it going? They have Dad and we need that transmitter shut down soon."

*Oh no, I've failed Dad.*

# Chapter 35: *Fu Shan Chu*

Twenty-two minutes after the guard had left his sandwich and thirty-six minutes after the phone had been rigged to blow, Rick had finished his shower, returned to his own clothes, and sat on the edge of the bed. He had stuffed the crewman's polo shirt deep between the two mattresses on his bed. The food and coffee sat untouched on the table.

He assumed that at any minute he would be summoned by the guard to talk with the guard's boss. Rick had taken the time to absorb the briefing by Kaleho at the typical triad hierarchy. There were four levels, and each of the levels had a name and a code number. Who was his guard's boss? It would likely be either the gang leader, Hung Kwan. Hung Kwan was sometimes called Red Poles and its code number was 426. Or maybe his boss was the deputy leader, Fu Shan Chu. The Fu Shan Chu was sometimes known as the Deputy Mountain Master or Deputy Dragon Head, and had a code of 438. The highest ranking member of the triad, the Shan Chu might be on board. The Shan Chu was sometimes called the Mountain Master, or the Dragon Head, and had a code number of 489. Was this treasure important enough to pull him out of the shadows?

Rick was also wondering about his phone. Would it blow sooner than the ninety minutes he originally calculated due to the heavy number crunching app he had launched? Or would it blow later due to the cooler temperatures inside the fuel tank? Or would the battery die first before the thermal runaway and subsequent explosion could occur? Or would the fuel in the tank deteriorate the waterproof case and cause a short circuit in the phone, which could also cause an explosion or massive fire? Rick shook his head in silence. *Too many variables.*

The door lock clicked and the knob twisted. Rick jerked in surprise. His guard stuck first the gun and then his head in the door. "Come," was all he said. Rick was surprised the guard wasn't suspicious of the lock. The guard stepped back to the left and waited for Rick to leave the room. Rick dug his index finger into the door in one last attempt to pull the coins out. One coin popped out and dropped into Rick's cupped hand. *Enough for the lock to catch again.*

He walked down the hall to the right. The guard used his gun to point Rick toward the staircase he had gone down earlier. Rick halted at the landing and the guard flicked his gun upward. Rick began climbing. He reached the next highest deck landing. A placard, just like the one that was one on his bedroom level, showed this was the main deck. Lots of large entertaining space here. The guard flicked his wrist again, signaling to move up the steps. Rick climbed to the next level.

He looked back at the guard and he motioned for him to enter this deck level. According to the placard on this level, he had reached the upper deck. And one level above him was labeled Flybridge.

The walls of the forward deck were enclosed, but the entire back half was all glass windows. The windows ran from the ceiling to about three feet from the floor. It was an impressive view of the North Shore of O'ahu through the windows. The room interior had an unmistakable Asian motif – and more cherry wood accents.

Beyond the glass surround was the open-air deck. Rattan patio furniture with big blue cushions sat on the deck. A table with what appeared to be a fire pit in its center sat in front of a grouping of furniture. A portable bar sat to one side and big comfortable chairs grouped in pairs with small glass tables between them lined the perimeter of the deck. He knew from the deck diagrams on the placard that if he stood at the far end of this deck, he would be able to see the rear section of each deck below him. The ship's stern was sort of like a pyramid from deck to deck to the waterline.

Rick's attention came back inside to an odd arrangement directly in the center of the rear glass wall. There were two glass door exits from the room to the outer deck. The span between them was about ten feet. Plenty enough room for a fine couch to watch the beautiful Hawaiian sunsets. But instead of furniture, there was a modern and probably expensive desk about eight feet in width. The lower structure of the desk was made of Koa wood. But the desk had two unusual features. First, the desktop was a dark smoked glass that was immaculately clean. And secondly, the desk was not the standard rectangle box; it was shaped like a trapezoid with rounded edges. And the shortest side, which faced inward to the room, was concave. A cut-out at the center of the concave side allowed for a black chair, the kind with a finely meshed backing for ergonomic comfort, to be parked so that its back touched the edge of the desktop. Although the Koa wood made the desk less industrial-like, the piece still appeared strangely out of place.

Rick turned around to take in the rest of the room and his captors. They were standing behind a set of chairs and a coffee table. There was one man that appeared to be about Rick's age. The other four were younger, maybe in their thirties. All were in expensive suites of varying neutral colors, which contrasted with the tropical view out of the window.

Beyond the five men was an expansive round dining room table. Rick did a quick count and saw it had a setting for eighteen people. Fine engraved chopsticks, rolled cloth napkins tied with a gold ribbon with black characters on them, a tea cup and saucer, a glass goblet, plate and other tiny dishes sat at each spot. A huge bouquet of fresh flowers set in the center, just below an ornate chandelier. Serving carts with wheels sat off to the sides of the dinner table. There was a man standing by one of the serving carts. He stared in Rick's direction, but did not move. There were china tea cups and a tea pot with steam rising from it. The superstructure of the ship blocked the port and starboard outdoor views from the table. Replacing the view on the walls were exquisite Asian paintings of mountains, trees and streams. Beyond the dinner table, the walls came inward and had doors on each side. *Most likely restrooms*, thought Rick. Forward of that were more glass windows, with the bar and bar stools in front of it.

Rick marveled at the details in the room. He thought of his own ship, which paled to this when it came to such refinements. Although Rick expected a technology comparison would leave this vessel lacking.

The oldest man gave a slight nod to him, almost a bow, and the others followed suit.

"Mr. Bryant, please have a seat," said the oldest man. He held out his hand with open palm the direction of a chair directly in front of him. His accent was thick, but he was easily understandable.

Rick complied. Following him was the older man who sat as well. The other four remained standing. The men standing were mostly likely were of the lowest rank -- Rank 4. Rank 4 was known as the Chai in the triad, code 49, but these men might be the best of that rank and had the potential to rise.

Rick didn't know the culture. He had traveled much of the world prior to selling his sensor manufacturing business and moving to Florida, but he had not been to the Orient. Danielle had been a number of times for the art museum and was well versed on traditions. She would know what to do and say, but not Rick. He began to feel a little uncomfortable, feeling as though he might embarrass himself from the lack of decorum. Then he remembered that these were killers, extortionists, criminals. He didn't need to be friendly or polite.

Rick was sitting on the edge of his chair with his hands on his kneecaps. He felt tense and he didn't care if they knew it. He decided it was time to get some answers before his surprise event happened. He glanced at his watch and then off to the far left intently. A slight twist of his hips in that direction added to the misdirection he was attempting. In his peripheral vision, he saw head movement from the others in the same direction and he casually moved his right hand over his watch and pressed one of the many buttons on the watch.

Rick turned back to older man and waited for man's eyes to return to him.

"Why am I here? What do you want of me?" asked Rick. Rick knew the answer. They needed to confirm the treasure was real and they needed a hostage to escape. But he wanted to get them talking.

"Mr. Bryant, please, introductions first," he said. "My name is Qiang Suo. These are my men." He continued to name each member in a specific order, which probably indicated their rank or position within their rank. Each man did a slight bow with his head when he was introduced.

Rick couldn't remember a single person's name beyond Qiang. The language was too unfamiliar to him and he couldn't visually create the English spelling of the names in his mind. So he didn't bother remembering them. And he didn't bow to any of them.

By the posture and respect in the presence of the man named Qiang, Rick wondered if he might be the leader of the triad. But then he thought better of it. With this many men standing with him, he is probably the Hung Kwan, a.k.a Red Poles. That would make him a Rank 3.

"Let me guess. You're Hung Kwan," said Rick. He didn't know if he pronounced the Chinese names correctly, so he added. "Red Poles."

Qiang nodded slowly.

"I wish I could say it is a pleasure to meet you, but that would be a lie. You have the treasure. Let me go."

"All in good time, Mr. Bryant. Let us have some tea." He raised his hand and the man next to the serving cart moved instantly. He went to the rear of the cart and pushed it carefully to a stop near Rick. He served Rick first, then Qiang, and the rest of the men in the order in which they had been introduced.

*All in good time.* Rick looked at his watch. Twelve more minutes had ticked by. He was at forty-eight minutes from the time he had modified the battery in his phone. He was perhaps no more than forty-five minutes from detonation.

When the tea was poured, the man pushed the serving table back and stood motionless, awaiting his next orders. Qiang sat with a slight smile on his lips. He glanced down at his tea, then at Rick's tea, and then at Rick. Rick assumed he was supposed to drink first, but he remained stoic. Qiang repeated the gesture with his eyes again. Rick remained still.

Qiang finally broke the silence. "Please, Mr. Bryant. Enjoy."

152

Rick shook his head, "No thank you. I'm not thirsty. I had coffee earlier, but please feel free to enjoy your tea."

"But you didn't drink your coffee, Mr. Bryant. Nor did you eat your sandwich."

*Oops. Mistake. I didn't trust them enough to eat or drink anything, but I should have flushed part of the sandwich and some of the coffee. How did he know? They must have examined his room as he walked up. Or did they have a hidden camera? That would be bad if they did.*

Rick didn't answer.

"Perhaps you don't trust us. Maybe you are worried about being poisoned. Really Mr. Bryant, we don't need to be so covert in eliminating you. We are above reproach. You would have been killed instantly if we wanted you dead."

Rick didn't respond and he didn't reach for his tea. Qiang sat quiet for a few moments. His eyes stayed focused on Rick.

"Or maybe you needed a distraction? Which was it?"

Rick sat motionless. "Just drink your tea. I have no interest in being social. And you still haven't answered my question. Why am I here?"

A whine with an increasing pitch interrupted the conversation. The sound came from the far corner of the room near the bar. Qiang heard the sound and turned his head slightly. The men standing shuffled slightly and stood straighter as the pitch dropped.

A door opened at the far right – near the bar in the front. A tall slender Asian woman stepped out of the ship elevator. She was quite attractive and had long black hair that glistened as she walked. A Plumeria flower somehow sat to the front of her right ear, which in Hawai'i meant she was unattached or single. She had a silk blue patterned dress that fell just above her knees. The brilliant blue color of the dress contrasted the red tones of the room, which when coupled with her poise as she walked, made it hard not to stare. Rick thought she looked familiar – like an actress he'd seen fighting Wolverine in one of the X-Men movies. *Kelly something*, he couldn't recall her name.

Qiang stood as she approached, so Rick figured she was important, maybe the wife of one of the leaders. But then he noticed the placement of the flower in her hair again and checked for a ring on the finger. No ring, so probably not someone's wife. Maybe she is the triad messenger, *Straw Sandal*, or the administrator, *White Paper Fan*. Both of equal status to Qiang. Rick stood as well.

She was wearing elegant black high heels, which shortened her stride. She worked her way around the circular dining table to the left side of Qiang, who bowed slightly to her. She held her hand out to shake Rick's hand.

"Good afternoon, Mr. Bryant. It is a pleasure to meet you."

Perfect English. Although Qiang spoke English, his accent betrayed him. English was his second language. But this woman spoke with no noticeable accent. He couldn't make out her age. Maybe she was in her forties. She could have passed for thirty-something easily. He looked at her hand and debated whether he should shake it. Qiang seemed a little tense and the other triad members were as well. She was certainly of higher rank.

"And your name is?" Rick reached out and shook her hand.

"You're not interested in my name, are you Mr. Bryant? You are wondering who I am within this organization. Have you guessed?"

153

"I thought you must be of Rank 3, but by the sweat I see running down Qiang's temples, I believe that guess would to be too low. But I don't believe you're old enough to be the Shan Chu, Dragon Head. And I don't recall any women triad leaders. I would say you are of Rank 2. Maybe the Vanguard or the Incense Master."

Qiang shuffled again. *He was uncomfortable with this exchange. She must be something higher.*

"Come Mr. Bryant. You underestimate me. You are correct about my rank. But there are three Rank 2 positions. The one you didn't mention is the Deputy."

"Deputy?" asked Rick with a puzzled look.

"Yes it is rare for a woman to be Deputy, and especially rare to be a Rank 1, the Dragon Head. But communism and commerce with the West has had an impact. A few years ago there was a bold woman in our homeland that changed the triads in an almost revolutionary way. I doubt you saw her trials in the West. The trials were riveting, however, in the East. Have you heard the name of Xie Caiping?"

"No."

"She was all over the news a few years back."

"Not in America," injected Qiang almost reverently with his head slightly bowed. "It's not news here unless it is has a puppy or kitten in the story." Rick didn't know if Qiang meant to be funny with that comment, or if he was showing disdain for American journalism. There was a brief pause in the conversation as people pondered what he said. No one laughed.

"Please, be seated," she said. Rick lowered himself back into his seat and was followed by the woman and Qiang. All the other men stood.

"Xie was part of the 2009 to 2011 Chongqing gang trials. She was 46 and the leader. She had power and influenced many within the government. It was said that she had a twenty-man harem."

"Everybody has someone they aspire to be. I'm not surprised at your choice."

The woman had a fleeting expression – it appeared and then left her face in no more than a couple of seconds. But Rick saw it. A nerve might have been plucked.

"Come, come Mr. Bryant. I expected more of you. Ill behavior is not tolerated in the presence of the triad leadership. Strict discipline and swift action are our mantra. We take oaths that are considered binding without exception. Unconditional loyalty to the triad, and respect of the rank are cornerstones of all triads. Disrespect within and to the triad results in severe punishment. Sometimes torturous."

"That's a far cry from heaven, earth and man," said Rick dryly.

"Ah, you're referring to the ancient roots of the triad. Sanhehui...the Three Harmonies Society. Some of the old founding principles are still present. We do take care of our own and of our families. But we're now more like a business. A business that prides itself on efficiency and profitability. And like most business executives, I seek power and wealth. I seek to be Rank 1 one day. "

Rick was growing impatient. He knew time was ticking away on his homemade bomb. The talk of family made him think of his own. He glanced at his watch. 55 minutes had passed, and maybe 35 to 40 minutes before detonation.

"For the sake of efficiency and for my sanity, I ask for the third time. Why am I here? Am I disrupting your operations? Your bottom line? Why am I being granted an audience with the Deputy Dragon Head?"

154

"I must admit you and your family have been bothersome. But I know more treasure is to be had Mr. Bryant, and you will help me get it. The treasure you provided us is now on its way to my master. He and the rest of the organization will surely be impressed. It will be proof that I was right to come here and search for it. The legend of the 1884 pirate raid talks of far more coins than those you brought us in those chests. And the legend says there was more than just the rare Hawaiian coins. American money, artifacts, and other valuables were stolen by the pirates. We believe we now have a small token of the entire treasure. We want all of it, and now the Dragon Head will give me full authority to do whatever it takes to get it."

"You have it all. In 1903 the US Mint melted down the majority of Hawaiian coins. The only way that many Hawaiian coins could be melted was if a good deal of the 1884 Hawaiian coin treasure was recirculated before 1903. And we are pretty sure the American pirates headed back to Seattle or San Francisco to spend their prize of the USA currency. Who would stop them? And we don't believe all those artifacts were stolen. We think it's an exaggeration – nothing more than gossip. The result of too much retelling, just like a great fishing story. Maybe some of the items like silverware were stolen, but most would have been melted down for the silver and dispersed around the world. There's simply nothing left to find."

The room went quiet. The Deputy and Qiang looked at each other like something he said had connected with them. *Maybe they have come to the same conclusion,* thought Rick. *Or maybe they have suspicions, but needed some confirmation.*

"Lying will get you nowhere," said the woman. "We counted that coinage. There were about 20,000 coins in all. Given today's value of the coin, that's about 14 million US dollars' worth. Good enough for a deposit and the life of your friend's wife. But we know there are more coins Mr. Bryant. We know about the US Mint melting and came to a similar conclusion. But we know there is enough coinage still unaccounted for to fill between 15 and 20 more chests. Those remaining chests are worth well over 80 million dollars in today's market. And until we see all the chests, we are not prepared to give up on the remaining treasure described in the newspaper account."

Rick did the best he could to keep the look of surprise off his face. *They had followed much of the same logic as Rick and his family. The triad could have been searching for the treasure for years, and may even know more facts about it than anyone else.*

"You have had enough time to check me out. If you know me at all, you know I'm not driven by money. I wouldn't risk the life of someone I care about for any amount of money. That's all we found. If there's anymore, it is hidden somewhere else."

"We indeed checked you out, as you called it. You are quite wealthy yourself, Mr. Bryant. You are not from old money, you earned it. Very admirable. We also know that you value your family more than any amount of money and even more than life itself. And we admire that even more. But let me ask you a question, Mr. Bryant. What is the well-being of your family worth to you?"

Rick looked down and placed his hands on his hips. He took a deep breath and tried to calm his anger.

"That's all the treasure we have or will have. If you want anything from me, you need to leave my family out of this. I can guarantee you that you'll regret any action against my family. And I don't understand why you are willing to risk retaliation from Honolulu Police Department

155

and likely the FBI and every other three letter agency for 80 million dollars?   This ship and the rest of your equipment and personnel are worth more than 80 million.    And even if the coins do exist, if you try to sell them all at once, their value would plummet and you may not even get half the value."

"Mr. Bryant, you are smart but it is clear you are not a criminal mind," said the woman. "What would happen if the story got out that the treasure was from the last known pirate raid in history and the only one to take place in Hawai'i.    Right now the story is just an unsubstantiated footnote in some old forgotten newspaper. Without corroboration, it was likely deemed a hoax. But what if the public found out it is true?   Not only will the coins be worth 80 million, they may rise to 300 or maybe even 500 million dollars if they are properly authenticated as part of the treasure. And there is still the matter of the rest of the items – the US currency, the artifacts and other valuables. Some would be considered almost priceless."

"But you're talking like this is a legitimate find.  You've left a trail of murders.   It will be confiscated from you as soon as you're arrested," said Rick.  He looked at his watch.

"Who says there will be anyone to dispute us?   Death or the threat of death of loved ones goes a long way to legitimacy.  We believe you know where the rest of the treasure is Mr. Bryant."  The woman's voice had become stern.  She stood up.  "And for the health and well-being of your family, you are going to tell us where it is."

She turned and said, "Qiang, let us show him what we mean."

Qiang nodded and then said something to one of the Rank 4 men.  The man walked back to the steps that Rick had climbed to arrive on this deck.  Qiang walked around Rick to the desk that sat between the two glass doors.  He slid his hand under the lip of the desk top and heard a series of clicks, like muted throws of solenoids.

After a few moments, the smoked glass flickered alive with backlight color images. Directly in front of the chair were two keyboard shapes with fluorescent green keys at 45-degree angles from each other.  One in English, and the other had a large number of Chinese characters.   Rick was impressed that the keyboards and other backlit illuminated screens and feeds were easily visible in the bright natural light that filled the room through the glass windows.   All sorts of displays appeared in random fashion. Dial, gauges, sensor readouts, and computer screens filled the desktop.   It was a custom-built "holoscreen," or holographic projection screen.   In this case, the holoscreen was called a "holodesktop," since it served both as a screen and as a desk.  And given it was a holodesktop, Rick guessed that the entire surface was likely sensitive to touch control by fingers and perhaps even other objects.

Rick heard footsteps at the stairs and saw a short, thin Asian man pop out at the landing followed by the Rank 4 member that had been sent to retrieve him.  The man said not a word and walked straight to the command station and took a seat.  His phone was in his hand, and he rested it on the holodesktop.  A glowing green disk appeared on the holodesktop around the phone. It began an animated rotation, which Rick assumed was the synching process of the phone and the command station.

The man began to work his fingers quickly over the luminous keyboards.   A new rectangular square lit up on the holodesktop; it was one of the computer displays that were being driven by massive computer power that resided in a computer server inside the desk. The man reached with his right arm and touched a backlit display area with his index finger and dragged the display to the center of the holodesktop and directly in front of him.  He tapped a small tile on the screen with this finger and then he swiped forward in an exaggerated fashion as if it was a Vegas dealer sending the final winning card to a professional poker player. As he lifted his finger off the glass, the rectangular display continued to move toward large green characters spelling "3-D." The computer display made a game-like animated twist and spin and dissolved away. "3-D" then went from green to red.

A large piece of thick glass lowered from a slot in the ceiling. Rick wondered for a brief second what it might be until he saw a ring of light appear around the entire edge of the glass. It was a transparent monitor, sometimes called an electronic window. The monitor came to life with a giant map of the coastline of the northern shore of O'ahu. It also had several video feeds, cellular phone monitoring, and various other sensor inputs. *A situation awareness display*, thought Rick. One of the video feeds showed something moving swiftly on the water. Rick didn't see any symbol moving that fast on the map display, so he wondered where the feed was coming from.

After a few moments, the 2-dimensional, north-oriented map tilted and began to slowly spin into a 3-dimensional map with the steep green mountains rising above the narrow coastline. The map movement stopped when its orientation lined up with their current view out over the stern of the ship. Being transparent, one could watch the digital view overlaid on the real world view.

Sitting in the center of the 3-D map is Waimea Bay. The ship itself in precise miniature was listed with the word "anchored" next to it. Other moored sailboats were also visible in 3-D form on the map. There were small white dots along the beach, and small blue dots moving on the rounded "V" of Kamehameha Highway. A key off on the right of the map showed that white dots represented people and blue dots represented vehicles. Two green dots seemed to be moving in figure eights or in large circular patterns that intersected the ship. The label "Tiger shark" stayed next to the dots as they moved. Rick remembered the crewman saying something about a shark when he had been bounding up the spiral stairway back to his room.

The command station operator tapped a few keys on the Chinese keyboard and the bright green English holographic keyboard became a combination mouse pad and 3-D joystick. Four computer displays were visible over various locations on the holodesktop. One of the four of the desk displays was a duplicate image of the overhead situation awareness screen. The operator used his fingers and in a dramatic gesture, swiped inward over the map section. The map scale enlarged so that the whole of O'ahu was visible, like the view from a camera being zoomed outward from a space craft.

A bright red dot glowed on the far edge of the map. It appeared to be something moving rapidly on the surface of the water toward Waimea Bay. But after a few moments watching it, Rick realized that it was just *over* the surface of the water. *The drone.*

As if reading his mind, the red dot had a pop-up label appear above it with the words "drone aircraft." Then the labeled changed to read "Wing Loong." The command station operator pushed the holographic joystick with his index finger, and the red dot jogged to the left, but remained on course. Then he repeated but to the right and the red jogged to the right and stayed on course.

"One of our many superior technologies, Mr. Bryant. I know you are impressed, yes? We call it the Wing Loong Unmanned Aerial Vehicle. The West knows it as the Pterodactyl UAV."

"The Pterodactyl, largely a copy of the US Predator, has a top speed of about 175 miles per hour. Used mostly for surveillance, but in examining the video recorded from our mini-copter, you seem to have figured out a way to attach a Gatling gun to it."

"Bravo, Mr. Bryant," said the woman. "I am told, however, that this is Type II of the Pterodactyl. It has a higher top speed and greater payload."

"So that's how you managed to get both the gun and the ammo installed within the limits of the available payload. I had heard rumors that this UAV was in test, but couldn't find confirmation."

Rick watched the progress of the drone and asked, "How do you communicate with it?"

The man at the command station turn and looked at the woman. She nodded her approval for him to speak. "We control it through an encrypted radio link from this ship."

"But how do you talk through this cone of silence you've established by the jammer?" asked Rick. "Even with encryption you couldn't integrate enough signal to get through to that aircraft at that distance."

"We open a momentary slot in the jammer's frequency range to emit our signals. That slot hops from frequency to frequency. And even if someone can figure out the pattern, there is a 2048-bit encryption key to overcome. Not even the NSA has enough processing power to defeat the system within a few years."

The man proceeded to explain how the plane, as well as other triad member's off the ship, would synchronize with the transmission. Rick felt his stomach tighten as the man spoke. There were two reasons they would tell him this information. One, because they knew he would appreciate just how impressive this arrangement was technologically speaking, and two, he would not be allowed to live to tell anyone about it.

Rick checked his watch and the UAV's progress on the screen. A quick calculation later and he realized the UAV would make it to Waimea Bay before his earliest estimate of his phone exploding. If the phone and fuel tank exploded, it might be powerful enough to punch a hole in the superstructure, but it would not likely stop communication to the UAV.

"I understand how you transmit and the encryption process, but you haven't said how those listening would know which frequency to listen to at any given time? I mean, it's like knowing the winning lotto number but not knowing when or where the drawing is. They need a starting frequency and a time and date to enter it."

This time Qiang spoke up. "That is easy Mr. Bryant. The frequency range of our transmission is 2.4 Gigahertz to 5.8 Gigahertz. Our starting frequency is the minimum frequency plus the date number, times the current hour, times a four-digit number provided by us to each of our operatives that use the encrypted link."

Rick thought a minute. Being a part-time programmer himself, he knew that date numbers in most software development packages is a number representing the number of days since January 1, 1900. He recalled the date number for the first day of the current year was 42370. Today's number; therefore, is about... 42600. The hour could be 0 to 24. And by using the hour number, it meant that the transmission slot changed frequency once each hour of the day. It was about 4:30pm, so the hour number would be 16. He thought of a random four-digit number, 2000. He used round numbers ... 43000 times 16 times 2000 equaled about... $1.38 \times 10^9$. One Gigahertz equaled to $1 \times 10^9$, or 1 with 9 zeroes. So the transmitted frequency at that time should be 2.4 Gigahertz + 1.38 Gigahertz, which was equal to 3.78 GHz. Rick studied the transparent monitor and then the holodesktop for a number similar to his calculation.   In the lower left of the desk appeared two rows of numbers.   One was a lengthy series of letters, and the second was 3.684104. *That is the frequency slot right now – 3.684104 Gigahertz*, thought Rick. *And the string of characters above it is the key.*

Rick's calculation of the number had assumed 2000 as the four-digit number.  He had been close – just a little higher than the actual number.   It then dawned on him.

"1884 is the four-digit number," said Rick.  "And for the next few minutes, the frequency is 3.684104 Gigahertz."

"Excellent, Mr. Bryant," said Qiang.  "And did you figure out what the key is?"

Rick stared at the long series of characters.  They were letters of the Greek alphabet.

τηερεωασαϖασττρεασυρεηιδδενβψρεδβεαρδτηε

A 2048-bit encryption key would be over 600 numbers.  That would difficult for anyone to remember, let alone enter.   But if letters or characters are used instead, then only 256 characters are needed.   The Greek alphabet is used by physicists and mathematicians to represent variables and angles in equations, so Rick knew the English alphabet equivalent.

He began to read them out, "T...H...E...R...E...W...A...S...A."   He paused as he recalled that a catch phrase is often used to remember the key. "There...was...a...vast...treasure...hidden by red beard the...."   The command station operator hit a key on this keyboard and the next set of letters scrolled into place.

λεαδερροφτηεγρεατπιρατεραιδοφηονολυλυιν1884

It dawned on Rick that the catch phrase was all about the pirate raid of 1884 when he saw the numbers.   He continued, "...leader of the great pirate raid of Honolulu in 1884."

The process continued in forty-character chunks until the last set of 16 appeared to create a 256 character key.   Rick now knew everything.  He could easily join the network if he had a computer to do so.

"Why are you showing me all of this," said Rick to the woman.  "I told you there is no more treasure.  We gave you all we found."

"You know the armament on that UAV and you know that your daughter and her boyfriend are on the beach," answered the women.  "Either tell me the location of the rest of the treasure or she will be the first to perish."

Rick's blood began to boil, but he had to stay calm and get the information to Nikki and he wanted a better view of the aircraft.   He walked toward the deck beyond the glass doors.  He glanced over his shoulder and saw that Qiang, the woman, and the Rank 4's were following.

So Rick moved toward the starboard side of the ship, which faced west.  As he walked toward the bulwark, he kept is eyes fixed to the western horizon while he rotated his watch on his wrist.  A thick white rail ran around all sides of the upper deck on the bulwark.  Upon reaching the rail, Rick placed his arms over the rail as if he was relaxing while looking out.  His wristwatch face resting against the outer skin of the vessel.  It was the first time he had an opportunity to touch it since being onboard.  With his right hand, he touched another button on his watch.   He stared in the direction he thought the UAV would be coming from, but it was still too far to see.  He turned and saw the woman and the Qiang and the others standing well behind him.  And beyond him he could see the shore and the small figure he knew to be

Nikki. His wrist remained against the hull of the ship. He felt small vibrations along his wrist and his fingertips that rested on the hull.

After about a minute, he felt a long pause. Then the vibrations repeated. His mind drifted back to their planning session on the **Amphitrite**. The clicking of Kaleho's pen had reminded him of the age old method of communication – Morse code. And Morse code could be communicated by sound. The ship he was currently on had the latest technology, including an active wideband jammer. Using sound pings, like the old subs, one could communicate with using Morse code. He just had to figure out how to communicate this effectively. He thought of his watch. That had a built-in cell phone and speaker. By changing out the speaker in his watch to send out ultrasonic sounds, he could transmit Morse code in the form of pings that could not be heard by the human ear. His only indication that they were working would be to vibrations against his skin. And the jammer had no effect on them. Kaleho didn't quite follow the explanation when they were briefing him. So Nikki pulled up a font on the situation awareness display to illustrate.

Kaleho grasped the concept immediately upon seeing the example. They all decided it was a good option for communicating information, so Rick found a watch repair shop on the outskirts of Honolulu, and then dashed there with the equipment he needed to change out on the watch. It took over an hour for the watch change to be made.

The mega yacht was well insulated and that required him to be in contact with the outer hull of the vessel for the acoustic signal to transmit the message effectively. It was like he was ringing a bell with a jack hammer in the electronic world. He just hoped that the **Stingray's** hydrophone was sensitive enough to pick it up the transmission at its current distance. The transmissions consisted of the entire conversation he had been recording since he pressed the record button on the watch when he first sat down with the triad leadership.

He wondered how long they would watch him standing at the rail of the ship before saying something to him. It was then he saw a faint disturbance far off on the horizon. He recalled the horizon calculator formula that he had used in determining how far south the 1884 pirate ship could go before disappearing from view from Punchbowl. Using the same formula, he estimated the UAV was about 15 to 18 miles out. At 200 miles per hour, the UAV would be at the ship in about five minutes. He had five minutes to save his daughter's life.

"Mr. Bryant, stop stalling. We need you to tell us where the treasure is, or your daughter will become a memory," said Qiang.

Rick glanced back at him and then stared forward again. "If I tell you anything, how do I know you won't still kill her? You could just kill us all after you get what you want. You admitted already that killing is a way of keeping your treasure find legitimate."

"I said death or the threat of death," said the woman. "We will allow your family to live under a cloud of death if they ever speak of this."

Rick heard her words "your family" and understood its implication. His family would be left alive under the threat of death, but he would have to be killed. He knew too much.

# Chapter 36: *The Crane*

Entering the building, Shelli immediately noticed the air was chilly. She didn't know any of her captors' names, so she had given them some of her own. Gold Chain stood by the door they had entered, and Gun Man stood by the door to the kitchen. There was another man seated at a command station on the right side of the room. That man wore silver rim glasses and appeared older than the other two. He had on a long sleeve T-shirt tucked into faded jeans. Although he was wearing glasses and at the command station, he was not nerdy. He was amply able to protect himself. Shelli decided to name him Silver Rims.

The command station consisted of a phone, a single LED monitor, a keyboard, a mouse, and stub nose pistol on its wall-mounted desk. On one side of Silver Rims was a six-foot tall rack of black PC's. Each PC had a row of small green and red indicator lights. Some blinked, while others just stayed solidly lit. To the other side of him was a signal row of equipment. They looked like the test equipment Shelli had seen in her dad's labs. One of them had a sizable display built-in that had multiple graphs that were labeled with acronyms. The command station itself was centered under a window that had a view of the antenna outside.

To the left of the room, opposite of the command station, was a table with four chairs. The table was positioned in front of a tinted window facing the back of the property. A dirty dinner plate sat with a fork on it on the far side of the table. Between the dinner table and the kitchen door was a small desk with a laptop PC, which displayed two video feeds. The feeds were of the antenna, and of an overall view of the grounds from high on the cell tower.

"Empty your pockets on the table," said Gold Chain. "And do it slowly. Yung will cut you down if you try anything."

*Yung is Gun Man. One down, two to go,* thought Shelli. Shelli reached slowly in her pocket and pulled out her phone. Stephanie and Kai did the same.

"What are your names and what are you doing here?" asked Gold Chain. No one answered. He walked over to Shelli's phone and picked it up. The screen had a picture of Shelli and Stephanie at the beach. The screen was locked and needed a four-digit pin or thumb print to unlock. "What's your password?" Shelli refused to speak.

"I can shoot one of them and then maybe they will talk," said Yung.

"Not just yet," said Gold Chain. "We'd have to clean it up. Let's call the ship and see what the boss wants to do with them. If he says kill them, then we'll take them outside. You three, sit down at the table while we find out."

Stephanie and Kai sat on the kitchen-side of the table, and Shelli sat on the side closest to the side door through which they had entered.

As Silver Rims reached for the phone, a crash and a bounce of something landed in the kitchen. Yung spun around. "Somebody threw a rock in the window," said Yung.

"There must be another kid out there," said Gold Chain. "Search for that kid and bring him or her back here."

"OK Chuck," said Yung as he headed through the door in the kitchen.

*Chuck is Gold Chain and Yung is Gun Man,* thought Shelli. *One to go.*

Gold Chain, a.k.a. Chuck, moved to the door they had entered through, looked out at the parking lot, and then back at Silver Rim.

"Jack, get over there and watch the kitchen door for Yung."

*Silver Rim equals Jack,* thought Shelli. *Yung, Chuck, and Jack.*

Silver Rims Jack got up from his chair, forgetting his gun at his command station. Kai, stuck out his foot as Jack passed. Jack tripped over the foot, and as he fell did the best that he could to block the roundhouse punch from Kai to his face. Although he was successful in blocking the punch to his face, the force of the blow caused him to roll to the right as he fell. And as he fell, Kai was diving toward him with his next punch.

Stephanie stood up and squealed, and ran into the kitchen.

It was as this moment that Shelli knew she was in for a fight. Just like the two times she had to fight for real in her life, she played out what would happen in her mind. The gun was left at the command station and Silver Rim Jack was falling to the ground with cutie Kai punching him. Yung was not currently a threat, but would be if he came back into the room. So in case he came in, she needed to have the gun in her hand. Gold Chain Chuck seemed to be the leader and the most dangerous. *Mental check list: Stop Gold Chain Chuck, grab gun, get ready for Gun Man Yung.* That's as far as she got before the first movement was required.

Gold Chain Chuck saw the pistol was left and moved toward it. But one step into his move he experienced the painful jolt of a sneaker in his face. The blow knocked him back.

Shelli stood calm in her self-defense stance. It was the Cat Stance – weight on the back foot light touch of her forward foot. One hand raised above her head and the other curled in front. Gold Chain Chuck rubbed his face and also stood in a martial art stance. Shelli recognized it at once – the Horse Stance. Wide separation of bent knees, one arm at twelve o'clock above his head and the other at three o'clock pointing at her. This should be interesting. Shelli smiled, and for moment she perceived a puzzled look on his face. Or maybe it was concern.

He struck with a two-kick combination. Shelli stepped back two steps, and as she did so pushed off the kicks. She didn't need to do that – it was wasted energy, but her teacher said that fighting was a mental game more than a physical one.

The man was clearly stronger than Shelli, but she saw from the fluidity of his moves that he might be a little rusty. She had ended in a forward facing crouching stance with one hand forward. She could feel the edge of the table against her butt, so she countered with a forward punch from the fist at her side and went into Crane Stance. Then she punched again with an opposite fist punch and returned to the Crane Stance with the opposite leg up. Without hesitation she came down in a crouching stance and delivered two punches to the center of Gold Chain Chuck. It was the classic punch drill from kung fu 101 delivered perfectly, and all were blocked effectively. But just barely. And she was now only one step forward of the table.

Gold Chain Chuck came in with a forward punch followed by crossover knee-kick. Shelli blocked them both and delivered a punch-toe kick and moved into White Stork Stance. He blocked Shelli's punch, but she got his shin good. He took a step back.

Shelli heard the door in the kitchen close. It was the same one Yung had gone through. Through the window on the door, Shelli glanced back to see Stephanie looking cautiously around. She had something in her hand, but the door jamb blocked Shelli's view.

Gold Chain Chuck took advantage and delivered a punch to Shelli's face. Shelli felt that a block was almost impossible and barely moved her face in time. Gold Chain Chuck thought he was going to connect and overextended. This left her with the ability to deliver a forward kick in the stomach, and a forward punch to the face.

Shelli flashed back to the hours and hours of exercise that her teacher had made her undergo. After her technique was perfected, she worked hours at exercises against the wall to develop her triceps for forward speed and strength. Many hours were also spent with her teacher doing leg exercises like the Hindu squat, which developed the hamstring, calves and quadriceps. Like the triceps exercises, these resulted in speed, strength and endurance. And dance kept her flexible and added strength to muscles not used in kung fu.

Gold Chain Chuck staggered from the punch. Shelli smiled. It had the desired affect – he was definitely angry. He came at her with a side kick followed by a step and then a spinning hook kick. The spinning hook kick is powerful. The foot is hooked as the person spins. As the body comes around, the hooked foot is extended. The momentum of the body spinning and the force of the foot forward can actually be lethal to the unexpected. Shelli decided to duck instead of block it and remained in a low crouching stance.

He took a step back and breathed deeply and came in with another side kick to what would have been Shelli's face. But she anticipated another kick and leapt with all her leg strength and landed on the dinner table in a fully crouched Twist Stance. The stance gets its name from the appearance of the feet, which were twisted. The front foot is twisted outward and both arms are extended outward, which gives balance.

Gold Chain Chuck punched forward and Shelli simply twisted her legs and blocked it. The Twist Stance has a hidden chin-na kick. Chin-na means cease control. And that's exactly what Shelli did to her opponent.

He knew the kick was coming, but there was nothing he could do. It landed solidly in his face. She came back into the stance and he tried a modified crescent kick. It was a different technique – maybe taekwondo. Her ballet and dance training was the first thing that came to Shelli's mind. She leapt and the swinging kick came under her. Then she spread her legs and came down in a full split on the table, with both of her hands behind her.

Gold Chain Chuck didn't quite know what to think of it. Neither the split nor the hand position was a kung fu stance or move. His nose was bleeding and his eyes were glazed, and he punched only half-speed.

Shelli twisted her body and dodged the strike. With her left hand she came up rapidly and impaled the soft fleshy part of the edge of his hand with the fork that had sat on the table behind her.

He yelled as he withdrew his hand. Then as if he had completely forgotten all his training, lunged at her as if to strangle her. Shelli swung her opposite hand out behind her and connected the porcelain plate with the side of his face. The plate shattered, and caused Gold Chain Chuck to stumble back into the wall.

Shelli twisted her body into a forward split and then hopped back up into the Twist Stance. Gold Chain Chuck stood motionless for a second and then fell forward face down on the floor.

It was not quiet behind her. The fist fight was still going on behind her with Kai and Silver Rims Jack. Shelli decided to not waste time looking, and did a cartwheel off the table. She landed on both feet and came up with the gun in her hand as Yung stepped in the doorway next to Gold Chain Chuck. Yung's gun was pointed straight at Kai.

163

He yelled "Stop, or I'll shoot."

"Put your gun down or I'll shoot you," said Shelli. "And don't think that I won't do it. I know how to use this."

"If you shoot me, I'll shoot the kid," said Yung, as he nodded toward Kai.

Shelli could see Kai hovering over Silver Rims Jack – his fist clenched. He had gained the upper hand, so to speak. But she couldn't allow him to be shot. Her watch vibrated. She knew it was another text – probably pleading with her to hurry.

"Put the gun down," said Yung. The room was quiet except for breathing. The sun from the opened kitchen door was pouring into the room. Yung's shadow filled the floor in front of him. Languid dust motes danced in the sun beams.

Shelli thought she saw shadow pass next to his on the floor and a loud metal clang echoed in the quiet space.

Gun Man Yung's head drooped forward, and he fell head first on the floor. He stayed motionless on the floor as did his partner, Gold Chain Chuck.

Stephanie stepped into the doorway with a skillet in her hand. It had a small dent in it. "Oops. I hope I didn't kill him," she said.

Shelli laughed, but then remembered Silver Rims Jack. She pointed the gun at him. He looked dizzy. Kai decided to finish his punch and Silver Rims Jack was down for the count.

Tim burst through the outer kitchen door and charged past Stephanie into the control room, but stopped when he saw the three men laying completely out on the floor.

"Whoa. Remind me to never cross you guys," he said.

Shelli's watch vibrated again. She read its display. "We've got seconds to shut down power to the antenna," she said panicked.

"Shoot the computers," said Kai.

Shelli swung around and started firing at the PC's and the test equipment. But the antenna was still seen spinning through the window.

"We've got cut power like we started to do before we were caught," said Shelli. She threw the emptied gun down and bent over and pulled the fork out of the Gold Chain Chuck's hand. "Come on," she said as she pushed by Stephanie and out the outer kitchen door.

They burst around the corner and came to a dead halt. A mongoose, was standing on its hind legs and was eating a small piece of Spam in its two front paws. It was standing inches from the power cable that they had been working on earlier.

"Shoo," said Shelli as she flicked her wrists at the animal. It just stood and stared at them like they didn't exist.

"I'll get Yung's gun. We can scare the mongoose or shoot the cable," said Kai. He started to turn to get it.

Shelli felt the timer in her head counting down. '5...4...3...' They were going to be too late. Then the unthinkable happened.

The mongoose had finished chewing what was in its two front paws, and set its two front feet down to get more. Each paw landed squarely on the two exposed copper wire.

The kids held their arms up to block the bright fireball that lit up in front of them. In the place where the mongoose had been was a smoldering, cooked carcass. On the far side of the property, they heard the whining down of the big antenna as it went lifeless.

164

# Chapter 37: *Kill Mission*

The smudge in the distance became more defined. At 200 miles per hour, the UAV would be kicking up water if it was flying less than 30 feet off the water. Small vortices of spray would trail just behind the craft. It was flying low from the west so that it wasn't picked up by the U.S. radar systems on the northeast shore at the Marine Corps Base at Kaneohe Bay. Rick remembered hearing the roar of jet aircraft leaving that base, which sat nearby the small islet research facility he had worked on, HIMB, when he attended college at University of Hawai'i. That base had several combat helicopter squadrons, which were more than capable of taking out this UAV.

His watch stopped vibrating again, so he pressed the same button on his watch to disable the transmission from repeating. As he lifted his arms back over the rail, he twisted his watch on his wrist to its normal position. At that moment he heard voices from the stern and he walked toward it.

He glanced over the rail and saw a tender being readied. Two of the crewmen he had seen before were fueling the tender. Fueling it from the same tank that he had dropped his phone in. The thought of the possible explosion entered his mind, so he stepped back and checked the time on his watch. In about five minutes the UAV would be there. And anytime now the phone could explode.

"Mr. Bryant, time is running out for your daughter. We know where your ship is anchored, so your wife will be next. Are you going to cooperate?" said the woman.

Before Rick could answer, the man at the command station came out and said, "Jie and Song are in position. I am pulling up the camera on them now."

"Back inside, Mr. Bryant," said Qiang in a stern voice.

Rick led the way back inside and stood behind the command station operator. Qiang stood next to him and the Rank 4 gathered behind the two of them. The woman stayed framed within the glass doorframe to the deck.

"Mr. Bryant, our patience is wearing thin. We have two men now on the road parked next to your daughter's car. One of them has a gun trained on your daughter in case she tries to run. The Pterodactyl will be here soon. Her life is in the balance."

"Upload the mission," stated Qiang. The command station operator began tapping on the keyboard. "We're uploading the kill mission to the Pterodactyl. First your daughter, and then it heads to your ship in Hale'iwa to sink it."

The command station operator made one final dramatic click and a pop-up window appeared on the transparent situation awareness display. It was labeled *uploading* and had a progress bar below. Another screen popped up and he saw the video feed of two men in a small sedan. One had binoculars and the man in the passenger side was sighting through a rifle scope that protruded through their car window. Presumably that was Jie and Song. The image panned out and he could see Nikki's car behind them. It then rotated to the right until Nikki and Ryan were in the center of the screen. Nikki was on her knees and was feverishly controlling the dish antenna using the handheld tablet PC in her hands. Ryan was standing behind her, but he was looking in the direction of the man with the rifle.

Rick did not know where the treasure was located, or even if it was real. He had crafted a chest that had fooled them, which managed to get Leilani released and got him on board as he hoped. But now he had run out of decoys and misdirection. They believed he knew where the treasure was. Any guess would have to be backed by facts. And anything he said might be considered a bluff. And a bluff wouldn't be tolerated. He looked at his watch. Three minutes to go – before either the UAV arrived or the phone exploded. The only thing he could come up with was to reiterate the truth.

"I do not-", he said, but was interrupted.

A pop-up window appeared on the holodesktop. First a voice came over with heavy static. "Dad, do you hear me?" Then the static reduced and the voice came in clearly. A single squiggly line moved as the voice spoke. "Dad, come in. This is Nikki. Are you there?"

The room became a mad-house. Qiang exploded in his native tongue to the Rank 4's. The woman literally leapt in front of the screen to see what was going on and to yell commands at the operator, who had broken out in a sweat and was frantically pressing controls.

The squiggly line went to a static-filled screen, then black, then in vivid color with Nikki's beautiful face filling the center of the screen. Rick could see that she was quite concerned.

"Dad, are you OK? I can't pick up your video yet."

"I'm fine honey," answered Rick. "You should get video in a few seconds." Rick thought of the time sequence and knew he had to say the most important facts first.

"You've got a sniper aiming right at you, and the Pterodactyl is heading your way locked and loaded," he said as saw Qiang spin around and glared at him.

Qiang's strike to Rick's face was so fast as to be virtually invisible. Rick stumbled from the blow and felt the back of his legs bang up against the table. The tea service rattled from the vibration. The sharp pain on his cheek and chin was minor compared to the nausea overwhelming him from his dizzying eyesight. Another swift movement from Qiang and Rick felt a sharp blow to the chest. It was as if his chest had imploded. The momentum from the kick Qiang had delivered and the table at his legs caused him to fly backwards. His legs landed on the table and the tea set shot out in all directions. The bone china broke into thousands of pieces on the floor. His back landed flat on the floor, which knocked the wind out of him. He gasped for breath for a split second before his head bounced on the floor between the legs of the two chairs that had been previously occupied by Qiang and the woman. His vision went black and he lost consciousness.

His eyes opened and his vision was blurry, but Rick sat up and rubbed the back of his head. He had a lump that was tender to the touch, the side of his face hurt, and his chest ached. His vision cleared to a room of chaos.

On the display he was watching Nikki, who was yelling for him at the same time as she was clicking on her tablet. She must be able to see him now.

The command station operator had the woman yelling at him and pointing at all the screens. He was trying to close the window with Nikki's face, but it was ignoring the requests. Nikki was rapidly taking control of the command station.

On the large transparent situation awareness display, Rick noticed a small purple dot blinking just outside the bay. Its label was "UV," which he guessed meant either unidentified vessel or underwater vessel.

Qiang had his phone out and was barking orders at the video feeds of Jie and Song as if they could see his commands.

On either side of Rick were two of the Rank 4 men. They were standing ready to deliver more deadly blows if he moved the wrong way. Rick slowly stood up and felt the stiffness in his back from the fall. He saw movement out on the deck beyond the glass doors. The other two Rank 4 men were shouting and making big arm gestures. They were probably telling the crew to hurry up with the tender.

The woman turned to Rick and gave him a menacing glare. She pointed as she talked. "Mr. Bryant, I don't know how you were able to get into our computer system, but you can say goodbye to your beloved daughter."

Still groggy, Rick felt he was moving in slow motion. He started to say "No," and he might have as far as he could tell, but no one listened to him. Qiang yelled again. The only word he could understand was "fire!"

The camera was still pointing at Jie and Song, when he saw whichever one was holding the rifle slide the bolt action into place. But just the man's finger rested into the trigger guard, the windows of the vehicle shattered to pieces and the two men leaned over and held their hands over their ears. They seemed to be in real pain. The rifle fell barrel first to the ground, and then toppled over.

The camera zoomed back out and it became apparent why the men were in pain. Nikki's vehicle was equipped with a directional loud hailer, the LRAD, and it was aimed directly at the men at point-blank range.

The woman screamed in rage and clenched her fists. She turned back to Rick and said in a deeper, irritate voice, "Your daughter has just delayed the inevitable. Our Pterodactyl will slice her in half."

"Dad, you're OK. Thank gosh. I heard what that lady said. I'm working on the UAV control, but it's taking longer than we thought. I think their signal on the ship or the mainland is still stronger and keeps stepping on my transmission."

The woman glared back at him and said, "You could have saved her Rick. If you want to save the rest of you family, you need to tell me where the treasure is...now!"

Rick scanned the ocean and saw the UAV was no more the 30 seconds out. When it cleared the ship it would start firing at the shore. He checked his watch.

*Its past time for the explo-*

Before he could finish his thought, he saw a bright flash from the stern. A shock wave raced through the superstructure of the boat and Rick felt the floor roll by his feet. He closed his eyes and raised his arms to protect his face just before he heard the crash of glass and felt shards pepper his forearms, and legs. The woman and the men screamed in unison.

He opened his eyes to see the front half of the tender flying upward in the air followed by a fireball and massive heat. He now had a clear view of the ship's stern, since all the superstructure, glass wall, and transparent monitor had been destroyed by the explosion. Scanning the damage he noticed that the deck floor was partially gone. The two Rank 4's that had been out on that deck moments earlier were gone too.

The fireball was still rising when the UAV skimmed over the ship and began firing its machine guns at the front edge of the beach. Rick ran port side of the room and looked over the remains of the glass wall in horror. He saw Ryan run in front of Nikki, ready to protect her from the bullets. The bullets came within yards of Nikki and Ryan, when the front half of the tender landed on the deck above Rick. It crushed the antenna used to communicate with the UAV, and at that instant the UAV stopped firing and banked sharply to the south.

Rick craned his neck to see the UAV turning to the west. He smelled smoke intensely and noticed that heavy smoke and flames were billowing above the deck floor at the stern. Additional smoke also drifted toward the shoreline from the deck above him where the tender had undoubtedly started another fire. He looked out at the beach and saw beachgoers running for their cars. He was too distant to hear their screams, but he could only imagine their fears.

Nikki had come back out from behind Ryan and was working on her tablet again furiously.

When he first met the woman 30 minutes ago, she was beautiful, poised and not a hair out of place. Now her clothes were shredded and somewhat revealing. Her hair was a mess. She had blood trickling from her earlobe that appeared have been sliced by shards of glass, and blood coming down her calf. She was completely exasperated at the situation, and virtually screamed to Rick.

"Mr. Bryant, you and your family are dead to me. We are but a local control of the Pterodactyl. The UAV is instructed to halt its mission if communication with us fails, but in a few seconds the main radio control station in the mountains of O'ahu takes control. And they will finish the job. And you will die knowing that your family will perish too. Qiang, kill him."

Rick glimpsed the UAV off in the distance to the west, but lost it in the sun. He picked it up again to the southwest. It was lining itself up for another pass. Slower than the first, but just as deadly.

Rick held his hand up to Qiang, who was also bloodied by the glass. "Stop. Before you do anything to me, you should first consider your predicament. You should check your holodesktop one last time. The underwater vessel you seem to be ignoring is my submarine, which is going to finish this ship for me. My daughter has disabled your men on the shore, and the police are on their way here now." Rick walked toward the center of the room, leaving the two Rank 4's behind him.

"You think the treasure will still help you, but there is no hiding what you have done here. You'll go to prison at the very least. But that will probably not help you, because I did not give you any treasure. It was a fake. I don't know where any of the treasure is. For all I know, the whole story is just a legend."

The woman looked perplexed. "We tested the coins. They are genuine. Their weight was consistent with the number of coins," she said.

As she spoke, Rick felt his watch vibrate from an incoming call. *The jammer! The explosion and fires must have taken out the jammer. I can get reception.* Rick clicked the answer button without looking down and continued his dialog with the woman.

"With the exception of some coins we bought from local collectors, the rest were silver coated, lead filled aluminum coins. And unlike the coins you seek, many of those were finely machined here in the great state of Hawai'i," said Rick. "When your Dragon Head finds out what you've let happen, you'll be grade 'A' shark bait."

Rick watched as the woman's fists clinched. He also heard the roar of the UAV. He spoke into his watch.

168

"Do you have control?"

"Ye...Yes. I just got it. Shelli was successful. It took a few seconds to override their backup protocols," answered Nikki.

"Bring it home...now," said Rick.

"But Dad, you'll be killed," said Nikki.

"I said now!" shouted Rick.

"Kill him!" screeched the woman.

Qiang and the remaining two Rank 4 men charged him. But Rick was already bolting toward the half-wall on the starboard side. The glass on the top part of the wall was gone – shattered during the tender explosion.

As he dove over the wall he saw the UAV directly ahead of him. It was veering toward the ship and approaching at over one hundred miles per hour. He tucked his head for what would have been a perfect dive. But the impact of the UAV above him into the side of the ship and into the wide-eyed Qiang and Rank 4 men created a fiery blast that slammed him downward into the water on his back. The percussion of the blast and the slap on the water was too much. He couldn't move, and started to sink underwater as metal debris and burning fuel rained down on the water's surface. He knew he was hurt, but felt nothing. His vision began to tunnel and he was faintly aware that he was sinking. He knew that as he sank, the increasing pressure on his lungs would cause him to exhale. He watched his air escape his partially opened mouth as bubbles, which were expanding as they rose to the surface. He thought of Danielle, Nikki and Shelli. He hoped they were safe now. Yes, they should be. The threat was gone. He sensed a peacefulness unlike anything he had known before. A glow, no a shimmering of light, emanated in the water below him. As he drifted downward, the waters around him became brighter and the colors of the fish swimming near him, his clothes, and even his skin became more vivid. He couldn't move; he could only observe. This was it ... he was passing on from this life. His mind shut down before his body came to rest.

# Chapter 38: *Lost Connection*

Nikki stared at the tablet screen in her hand. The screen showed a picture of her father with the words, "Connection Terminated" centered in front of it. She let the tablet drop on to the sandy beach on which she stood.

"Oh my God," said Nikki as she stood up on the sandy beach. She had commanded the UAV to crash into the ship. "I've killed my dad."

Emotions flooded her mind. Involuntary tears came down her cheeks and she started sobbing uncontrollably as the mushroom cloud began to dissipate over the ship. The bow of the ship was all that remained above water and it was sliding rapidly underwater. Oil fires on the water's surface was scattered over much of the bay and garbage, floating cushions, and other debris drifted toward the beach.

Nikki began to replay the last few minutes in her mind. The acoustic transmission by her dad's watch that was relayed to their tiger shark drones, and from the shark drones to her mom on the mini-sub and then to her. The key had allowed her to enter the ship's network through the jammer's wall of silence. The number of computer systems she would have needed to break the code without that transmission would have filled a football stadium. But all she needed was her handheld tablet PC once she had the key. The tender explosion had removed the onboard UAV transmitter, and Shelli had successfully cut power to the mountain transmitter just seconds before the UAV attacked. This allowed Nikki to have full control of the drone. Her mom was ready to send a torpedo to the hull of the ship, so all they needed to do was to get the evidence against the triad and get her dad out of there. It had gone almost perfect, until the end. And the end was horrible.

Her dad had shouted for her to crash the UAV into the ship, and then she saw the explosion, and then his watch cell connection went dead. How could her dad have survived that blast? *I killed my dad. How could I do that? Why did I listen to him? I should have anticipated his situation and called in reinforcements. But no, I directed the UAV into the ship. No one could survive that impact.*

She scanned the scene of the sinking ship and saw Kaleho circling the site in their mini-copter. He was probably searching for survivors. He was talking to her in her earpiece, but she couldn't answer. She couldn't resolve the words or the situation. The **Spearfish** had arrived a few minutes later with officers Kinh Lee and Joe Tyler and two divers. Stephen Chang was also in the boat. They were searching for survivors as well.

She stood with her legs separated a foot apart. The sand was up to her ankles and burned hot in the afternoon sun. The trade winds were lightly blowing strands of her hair, lightly tickling her neck. Ryan was holding her around her shoulders. He was speaking to her – trying to console her. She thought he was saying something like "if anyone could survive, it would be your dad." But she zoned his voice – all voices – out. She had lost her last boyfriend and it still felt as if she had a hole in her heart. It was like part of her soul was missing. But this was different. She felt as if her heart could no longer support the heavy burden of her body and her torrent of feelings. It was going to implode any moment. *Catatonic.* She thought of the word. She never understood how such a state was possible in a person, but now she appreciated the term as never before. The fact that she was mulling this over in her mind made her question her grip on sanity.

170

She finally began to snap out her haze when she heard her sister's voice calling from behind her. She spun around and saw Shelli sprinting toward her and followed by Kai and Stephanie.

Her sister stopped when she saw Nikki crying. "What is it?" Then Shelli looked toward the sinking ship and then back at Nikki. It dawned on her.

"No…Dad…No!" she yelled and started sprinting to the water. Nikki lunged forward and grabbed Shelli's arm and almost pulled her off her feet from the force of momentum.

"You can't go in the water, Shelli. It's got burning oil."

"But Dad's out there. He needs us. He needs us…." Shelli hugged Nikki and they both cried.

Stephanie had her hand over her mouth and was speechless. Perhaps for the first time in her life. She stood back for a moment to let her best friend grieve with her sister. Then she walked up and hugged them both. A new round of wailing began.

It was Kai who broke the mood. "Hey, my dad is moving away from the crash. He's following something in the water to the south of the wreck." He pointed in the direction of the mini-copter as he spoke.

Nikki, Shelli, and Stephanie stopped weeping and looked southward. Ryan reached down in his backpack sitting on the ground and pulled out his binoculars.

"It's the **Stingray**. It's on the surface heading toward the shore. Your mom is kneeling down. She's pumping something. Wait she stopped. She's talking to her wrist. No…she's talking to her watch."

Just then Nikki's watch buzzed. Nikki answered, "Mom?"

Her Bluetooth earpiece was still in her ear, so no one else could hear what was being said. "Yes…OK…we'll be right there," said Nikki.

She wiped the tears from her eyes with her hands. She briefly thought of something her dad had told her when she was a little girl. "Nikki, you're smart and a born leader," he had said. She picked up the tablet, whipped around and addressed her friends.

"Mom's got Dad on the sub. He's out cold and she's trying to resuscitate him. She needs our help. She need's us to get my vehicle down to the beach so we can get him to a hospital. Ryan, go get the vehicle. Yank out all the PC equipment in the back in case Dad has to lay back there on the way to the hospital. Deflate the air in the tires some so it won't get stuck in the sand. Pull the medical bag out of the back seat when you get down to the beach. Kai, you come with us and be prepared to help us get Dad off the sub."

Ryan sprinted northward on the beach. Although he was athletic and frequently worked out, running in deep sand was slow going. When he arrived at the giant rocks along the step bank, he leapt up and then zig-zagged toward Nikki's parked car on the highway shoulder.

Nikki swiped the tablet screen and pulled up the sub's remote control screen. She clicked on "Emergency Dock" and then clicked on a position just off the beach where the water was just deep enough to prevent bottoming out. She tapped her watch. "Mom, I've got the sub docking near the beach. Just hold on, we're on the way."

"The sub's docking; let's go help," Nikki said to her sister with a determined look.

The girls and Kai sprinted southward along the beach. They arrived at the closest point on the beach to the sub to see Danielle giving mouth-to-mouth to Rick.

The water was clear here of oil and debris. Nikki threw her tablet PC into the sandy beach and she and Shelli dove into the water. Kai and Stephanie stood on the shore, with Stephanie unconsciously mouthing "Oh my God." No one bothered to watch Kaleho land the mini-copter on the beach.

The sub was about a hundred and fifty feet out. Nikki could only focus on the moment as she twisted her lithe body and stroked with her powerful arms and legs in the Pacific crystal clear waters. She became aware of everything; like her senses were in some sort of hypersensitive mode. The incongruent sounds of the descending pitch of the helicopter motor, the crackle of the flames of the burning, sinking ship, the sound of her arms splashing with each frantic stroke, and the low roar of the waves hitting on the shore were recognizable and being filed away in her mind. She had her eyes open as she swam – ignoring the sting of the salt water in her eyes. Skies with whimsical cloud shapes alternated with the muted blues, greens, and grays of the ocean bottom. The bulbous shape of the sub finally came into view.

She brought her head up out of the water and was surprised that her sister had just beat her to the handhold on the ship. She stopped and tread water as her sister climbed to the top. Her mom was leaning over her father. She thought she could see tears coming down her mom's cheeks, but she still looked determined as she continued with compressions to her dad's chest. Her sister slipped out the water as fast and graceful as a gymnast swinging her legs over the pommel horse. Years of dance and kung fu training had resulted in incredible agility.

Nikki climbed onto the sub as Shelli came to rest straddling her dad. Shelli repositioned her knees as if she was going to do something specifically. She pushed her mom away and heard her say, "Mom stay back."

Her mom slipped around to her dad's head. As Nikki came up alongside her dad, she gasped at the sight. He was pale, which was rare for her always tanned dad. His face was badly bruised on one side, his lip was cut and blood was oozing from it. She couldn't see the back of his head, but his hair was singed at the sides. His shirt had burn holes and rips in it. There was a small amount of watery blood coming from somewhere under his back. But what was shocking was that his eyes were partly open...open like he was...dead. She felt tears welling up in her eyes.

She started to reach for her dad's arm when she saw Shelli raise both arms above her head. Shelli swung them swiftly downward on the center of her dad's chest. His whole body shook from the impact. Her mom placed her hand on her dad's neck. She shook her head – no pulse.

Shelli raised her arms again, and in a blur brought them back down again to the center of Dad's chest. His body raised up off the deck of the sub from the force of the blow, and a slight cracking sound was noticeable over all the other sounds around them.

Before she could get any feedback from her mom, Shelli raised her arms again. She paused and then raised them even higher before plunging them downward, but this time two hands stopped them before she reached her dad's chest.

Her dad had lifted his own arms and grabbed Shelli's arms mid-swing. He coughed up water and then winced in pain. "No more...," he gasped. He dropped his right arm and grabbed at his chest while loosening his grip on Shelli with his left.

172

Without a thought, Nikki screamed uncontrollably. Shelli did as well. Her mom looked like she was going to faint, but then collapsed down over Rick as if she was shielding him. She gripped his shirt with both hands and started crying tears of joy and relief.

Nikki and Shelli then piled onto their mom and dad in one big group hug. Nikki could hear Kai and Stephanie whooping and hollering, and Kaleho had both arms raised high with both hands twisting with the Shaka signs.

A muffled "off" came from her dad, followed by an extended "owww." They all pulled away giving him some air. Nikki felt as if her own smile was stretching from ear to ear. She suddenly became aware of her heart beating fast, and she felt a warmth deep inside start to well. *I didn't kill him. I didn't kill him.* He was obviously wincing in pain from all his injuries, but he was alive. Water flowed from her eyes as if from a mountain stream.

Shelli leaned over him and softly said, "Welcome back Dad. Are you OK?"

Her dad held his breath in preparation of the pain as he elevated himself up on his elbows. He took a few shallow breaths, preparing to say something. Instead of answering, he looked at each of them for a moment, ending on Mom with a long stare. He smiled.

"Dad, are you alright?" asked Shelli again.

He looked at Shelli. "I feel...I feel ratchet," he said hoarsely.

They all paused a moment, and then burst out in laughter when he followed the comment with another weak grin.

They all hugged him again. He struggled to stop them, but the effort was fruitless.

Their mom finally stood up and motioned to the girls to give Rick air. "We've got to get your dad to the hospital. Shelli jumped up and stepped around her father and reached down into the sub's top portal and pulled up a white nylon braided rope. She knotted one end of the rope to the tie-down on the front of the sub and threw the rope to Kaleho and Kai. They grabbed the end and starting pulling the sub toward the shore.

Ryan pulled up in the vehicle and reached back for the medical bag. He set it down on the beach and then hopped into the water with Kai. The two waded over to the sub and climbed to the top. They each hooked their arms under Rick's and helped him to his feet. They moved carefully to the front of the sub and eased Rick into the shallow surf.

As he emerged from the water onto the sandy beach, Kaleho dropped the rope and swung both arms wide around Rick. "Glad you made it, brah. You had us worried."

"Thanks, Kaleho." He grimaced from the effort. "I got to sit. I feel like I was hit by a truck, and I'm pretty sure Shelli broke something when she was trying to wake me."

Kaleho grabbed Rick's hand and helped him slowly sit on the beach. As Kaleho reached back for the rope, he saw the **Spearfish** ground itself on the beach and Stephen Chang hopped out.

"Mr. Bryant, it's good to see you made it off the ship. Did anyone else make it off?'

Before Rick could speak, Kaleho interjected, "He made it Stephen, but he's badly hurt. Don't make him answer questions. You know as much as we do. But looking at the damage to that ship, I doubt anyone else could have survived that explosion."

Nikki was watching from her position now on the beach. Stephen glanced at the ship and then back at her father. Nikki suspected he wanted some proof that his brother's murderer was dead, but he respected Rick's situation.

173

Nikki's felt the breeze of her mom as she passed her and dropped to her knees behind her dad. She had picked up the medical bag that Ryan had removed from her car. Nikki could now see small blood spots showing all over the remains of the back of her dad's shirt. *Shrapnel*, she thought, *from the UAV's explosion into the ship*. She almost started to cry again at the site it. Her mom opened the bag and pulled out a white cloth and then set out dressings, antiseptic, and tweezers. Her mom then leaned over her dad and whispered something softly in his ear. She pushed up higher on her knees and reached around and gently unbuttoned her dad's shirt. Gingerly, amongst "ouches" from her dad, her mom removed his shirt. His entire back was lacerated and small bits of metal and glass were visible. She checked down the back of his legs and found a few glass bits there too. Her mom confirmed that nothing was too deep or too big, and used the tweezers to pull out all the pieces she could see. She proceeded to clean her dad's skin with a dressing soaked in antiseptic. Her dad complained, but didn't have the energy to fight off her mom's attention.

Danielle called for Kaleho, who had tied off the sub to the bumper of Nikki's vehicle. "Kaleho, he seems fine on the outside, but I don't know if he sustained a concussion or has any internal bleeding. And I don't know how much blood he's lost from his cuts. We need to get him to the hospital. Did you call an ambulance?"

"Already done," answered Kaleho. "You were probably distracted and didn't hear me calling from the helicopter. I made the call when I saw you surface with Rick. They should be here any minute. In fact, I don't know why they are not here now."

"Because they are hung up on Kamehameha Highway in Hale'iwa," said Officer Kinh Lee. "There was a big accident as all the beachgoers were high-tailing it out of here when the action started. It's so clogged that the ambulance can't get through. Apparently they called up for another ambulance to come from Kaneohe."

"Kaneohe? That's going to take them at least 45 minutes to get here," said Kaleho.

Kaleho looked at the helicopter. "I'm not convinced there's enough fuel to get him and me back on the mini-copter."

"We have fuel in the **Stingray**, but there's too much gear on the mini-copter to carry two people anyway," said Ryan.

"Kaleho, can we get Rick in Nikki's car and meet the ambulance coming from Kaneohe?" asked Danielle. "I don't want him to wait an hour-and-a-half to get treatment."

"Yeah, sure," said Kaleho. "Ryan, Kai, help me get Rick up in the car. Kinh, get hold of Dispatch and have them get us a direct line to that ambulance. Tell Dispatch the situation and that I'm driving."

"Sure thing, chief." said Kinh as he reached for his radio.

Nikki stood watching it all, but her eyes kept going back to her dad. Her mom was still resting on her knees behind him, and Shelli and Stephanie were sitting to his right.

She was wandering what to say. *Sorry I almost killed you, Dad* wasn't something she ever thought she'd have to say in her life. As the men prepared her vehicle to take her father to the hospital, Nikki walked up beside her dad and knelt with her legs under her. She held his left hand.

"Dad, I'm really sorry about what just happened," she said a little choked up. "I...I...."

"Don't worry about it, honey," said Rick. "It's not your fault. I told you to crash that drone into the ship. I actually yelled at you to do it. Don't let this get to you. If you hadn't done it,

174

innocent people might have been killed. Including you, or your sister. And in case you didn't know, I was about to be killed by them before the UAV crashed. So thanks for doing what was needed."

Tears flowed freely down Nikki's eyes and she reached and hugged him as she both cried and laughed. "I love you, Dad."

"Ooouch," said Rick as he lifted his shoulders and arms. "That's enough Nikki. I love you too, but it hurts."

"Sorry," said Nikki. "But you're just going to have to suck it up." And she continued to hug.

"Nikki dear," said Danielle. "You're going to open up his cuts again. They're ready to get your father into the vehicle."

Nikki let go of her dad and leaned back. He smiled at her and then contorted his face in pain when Ryan and Kai each grabbed an arm to lift him. She stood and followed behind him as he was being half carried to her car.

As they reached the vehicle, she heard a loud beeping. It was coming from her tablet PC, which was half buried in the sand. It was closest to Stephanie, who walked over and picked it up. She stared at it a moment.

"There's a red dot thingy moving away from the ship." She pointed at the map. "It's going out to the sea. And there are two green dots following it."

Everyone stopped, including Rick and his two human crutches, and looked at her. Shelli took a few steps toward her and reached out her hand. Stephanie handed over the tablet.

"The two robotic tiger sharks picked up motion and they are now following it," said Shelli. She tapped on the screen. "It's moving quickly in deeper water and it just turned southward. It's going fast, but the sharks are having no problem keeping up with it. But their batteries are low – down to about fifteen percent."

Nikki thought for moment. *There's blood in the water, so it could be a real shark. Or maybe a curious dolphin that came for a closer inspection. Better make sure.* "Enable the sharks' sonar and have them run a side pass by the object."

Shelli tapped on the display and the slid her finger twice on the display. "Done," she said. "They'll make a pass on each side of the object."

"That will allow us to get a side-scan image from it," said Nikki.

No one moved – they all stared at the tablet in Shelli's hands. Seconds later the screen beeped and Shelli's eyes widened. She flipped the tablet around and held it out in front of her. On the display was a tear shaped three-dimensional object with a turbulent water trail behind it. "Someone is escaping from the ship," she said.

"We've got to get them," said Kahelo. "Kinh, get on the ra—"

"Stop right there," interrupted Danielle. "You are going to do no such thing. Rick needs to get to the hospital."

"Kai can drive you and Rick, we've got to stop them. We don't know who is in there or how many," said Kaleho with passion. "For gosh sakes, Danielle, the person could have killed Leilani and almost killed Rick!"

"It's got to be Fu Shan Chu, the Deputy Dragon Head," said Rick. "She was farthest from the impact site. And based on the size of that vessel and the speed its moving, there could be room for only one or maybe two at most. You've got to let him go, Danielle."

"Both of you shut up right now. I will have none of this!" she screamed. She stood firm in an akimbo stance. Her eyes were thin slits. "I am not ready to lose you yet, Rick Bryant. But you are sorely testing me right now. Kai will drive. Kaleho, you will ride shotgun. Rick and I will be in the back. We have no idea if someone else from the triad might attack us before we get to the hospital, but I want you there Kaleho to protect us." She emphasized *you* by pointing her finger at Kaleho. "You can also get Kai out of trouble if he's stopped for speeding. You've got two men right here, Kaleho. You can send them after that ... that woman."

She spun around to face her children. "Shelli and Stephanie..." She pointed at them. "...you will ride back with Nikki and Ryan to Hono....lulu" She stopped mid-sentence with the word partial word 'lulu' barely audible when her eyes came upon Nikki. Nikki was standing with her arms folded and shaking her head.

"No, Mom," Nikki said. "I am going after that she-devil." She pointed with her arm in the direction of the open ocean. "I don't want to live the rest of my life looking over my shoulder – wondering if she will be there to kill me, or Shelli or any of us. I almost killed my father because of her, Mom. Look at Dad will you." She aimed her open hand dramatically toward Rick, who was now leaning against the door. "Do you see what she did to him?" Her eyes went wet and mouth trembled.

Danielle's eyes immediately teared. She walked to Nikki and raised her arms and grasped Nikki's shoulders. "Honey, I do not want to argue with you. We don't have the time to debate this. But I will not permit you to go after her. I can't take anyone else getting hurt."

Nikki took a deep breath and felt her body relax. "Mom, you can't stop me."

She pulled away and walked up to her father and hugged him, then went to the front bumper and untied the rope to the sub. She carried it to Officer Kinh and said, "Hold this please." Without another word she waded in the water and climbed up the sub.

Danielle stood motionless for a while, then turned back to her husband. "Rick, tell her to stop. She'll listen to you."

Rick gazed at Danielle for a moment and then held out his hand. "Come on, honey. Let's go."

Kai opened the rear door and helped her ease Rick in. Danielle looked back at Nikki, who kept her head down as she readied the sub. "Ryan, would you please take care of Shelli and Stephanie...get them back to the ship or the hotel?"

"Sure thing, Mrs. Bryant," answered Ryan.

"She's dangerous, honey," said her dad in weak voice. "They are smart and tech savvy. Be prepared for anything."

Nikki nodded in acknowledgement and waved goodbye.

Kai got into the driver's seat and started up the vehicle. Kaleho slid into the front passenger seat. They pulled away and drove about twenty feet and stopped suddenly. Kaleho jumped out and ran down to the water's edge.

"Nikki," he shouted.

"Yes?" she answered.

"I know you're going after the triad leader, but I can't let you go in there alone. Take my two officers with you."

"I'm going too," said Stephen Chang.

"I don't blame you and Stephen for wanting to go after that bitch. But you have to allow my officers to take her down if it comes to that. And they will go with you." He emphasized the word "will." "You're not policemen and we can't let you jeopardize an arrest or your lives."

"Can't you deputize them?" asked Stephanie. She stood on the beach with her hips half-cocked to the right. Her face was one of pure innocence.

*Despite her seemingly superficial attitude, she was smart*, thought Kaleho.

He looked back at Nikki and Stephen. "Raise your right hand," he said. The two complied. He proceeded with the rest of the oath, to which Nikki and Stephen said "I will."

"Go get her," he said in conclusion and then ran back to the car and they sped away.

Nikki watched them leave. She walked to the water's edge and addressed the group. She had the tablet in her hand now and was studying it. Assuming correctly that all eyes were on her, she spoke. "The sharks are still following the craft, but their battery cells are down to twelve percent charge. At five percent charge, they automatically surface and we can't override. If we don't intercept that mini-sub before the sharks run out of juice, then we have lost the Deputy Dragon Head for good."

"The DDH," interrupted Shelli. Puzzled stares was the group's response. "Come on, aren't you guys getting tired of calling her the Deputy Dragon Head?"

"Shall we continue?" asked Nikki without smiling. As she spoke, Ryan, Stephen, Shelli, Stephanie and the two officers gathered in an approximate semicircle. They listened without any further interruption as Nikki continued her faultless, determined elocution.

"First we must catch her, then we stop her and then we...we arrest her," said Nikki as she acknowledged the two officers with a nod. "I'll take the mini-copter and head her off from the south. Stephen, you ride in the *Spearfish* with the two officers. It's fast and can protect you, but you still need to be wary. Ryan you promised to take care of Shelli and Stephanie, so guard them with your life."

"What! Are you kidding!" yelled Shelli. "I'm not staying here. I'm coming too."

Nikki looked down at her feet and tried to think of something clever to say, but then realized that the same determination that compelled herself to go after the witch, was a trait shared by her sister.

"I don't have time to argue about this, and quite frankly I need all the help I can get."

Shelli glanced at Stephanie and high-fived.

"Shelli and Stephanie...you will get onboard the sub and monitor the sharks. They have solar panels on their dorsal side, so take turns allowing them to surface for a little while to recharge. You'll stay in communication with the *Spearfish* once you're underway. Be ready for underwater rescue if it becomes necessary. Ryan, you pilot the sub. And go inside and open the side hatch. We need to pull out a diver sled."

"What if the shark batteries die, though?" asked Stephanie. "What are we going to do? Should we get the Coast Guard to help?"

"I've already called them," said Officer Tyler. "They're on the way now on their cutter. And they are also preparing one of their choppers to assist as well."

"Shelli knows our equipment and capabilities. If you don't mind, Officer Tyler, Shelli will link communication through the sub to the Coast Guard once they get here."

Nikki tightened the last strap and continued. "And I've got three sonobuoys on the copter," said Nikki. "I'll drop those ahead of the mini-sub for triangulation on its position in the event the sharks surface for good."

Shelli was the first to move. Stephanie did a palm-out salute and then followed Shelli to the sub. Ryan retrieved the rope from Officer Kinh and also waded out to the now drifting sub. Stephen and the two officers leapt on the *Spearfish* and prepared to start it.

"We'll communicate on the cell phones," Nikki continued. "The sub will stay on the surface as it follows, unless there is a necessity for it to dive. Stephen, power up the display on the boat labeled S.A.D. It will show a map with all our positions, and the Fu Shan what's-her-name's mini-sub."

"Fu Shan Chu," said Stephen.

"The DDH," shouted Shelli from the sub.

"Whatever," replied Nikki. "Let's go."

Stephen gave a thumbs-up, and powered up the *Spearfish* motor. It pulled away slowly from the shore, and pivoted toward the open ocean. When they cleared the mouth of the bay, the motors throttled to a low roar. The front of the boat tipped up and a ribbon of white trailed as it turned southward.

Nikki saw the side hatch open on the sub and she jumped into the water. A davit arm extended from the interior of the sub with an underwater sled suspended on the end. Ryan stepped out of the portal with the remote control in his hand. He pressed a button and the sled lowered to the water. It was buoyant and Nikki easily unhooked it from the davit. Ryan retracted the davit arm and then jumped in the water and waded next to Nikki.

The two of them held the sled and carried it up to the mini-copter. The diver sled had two handle bars that protruded over an elliptical yellow plastic body. At the back was a propeller surrounded by a wide ring, which protected the diver from being sliced by the prop blades. The sled was a bit heavier than most sleds due to its noticeable armament. Nikki attached it to the edge of the payload rack so that she could push it in the water from the air when she was ready.

Ryan ran back to the sub and fetched a can of fuel while Nikki retrieved a small rebreather for SCUBA diving. He fueled the mini-copter as Nikki buckled in the rebreather, and completed the mini-copter system check. She pulled on her neoprene booties with rubber soles. She put on black diver's goggles, which would also protect her eyes while she flew. She slipped on the wireless earphones, which had two small whips standing up to receive the radio transmissions. Her last gear was a diver's weight belt, to which she attached the remote control for the onboard winch.

When they were done, Nikki climbed into the small helicopter and started the engine. The blades spun slowly and then accelerated to a black spinning blur. Ryan said "Audio check," to which Nikki replied "Check."

Just as she was about to lift off, Ryan darted up to the pilots chair and leaned in and kissed Nikki square on the lips. "Be careful out there, Batgirl" he said. "Come back to me."

Nikki gave him a puzzled look and then gazed down at herself. Black bathing suit, utility belt. She saw her reflection in the glass of the control dials. Mask, and pointed antenna ears

... *Batgirl*. Nikki smiled and then nodded to him, which was the signal for him to step back. The mini-copter lifted or rather slid upward and over the open ocean.

She leaned to the left and the helicopter banked to the south.  A loud static squelch came over the earphones, which made her flinch. It was followed by music.  Nikki recognized the lyrics right away.

*You shout it out*
*But I can't hear a word you say*
*I'm talking loud not saying much*
*I'm criticized but all your bullets ricochet*
*You shoot me down, but I get up*

*I'm bulletproof, nothing to lose*
*Fire away, fire away*
*Ricochet, you take your aim*
*Fire away, fire away*
*You shoot me down but I won't fall*
*I am titanium*
*You shoot me down but I won't fall*
*I am titanium*

*Titanium*, was the name of the song, by David Guetta.  Nikki glanced back toward the Bryant sub that was now maneuvering away from shore.  Her sister was on the deck of the sub making machine gun gestures as she mouthed the lyrics.  Nikki smiled, and pushed the yoke forward to propel the copter faster southbound. She found herself humming the chorus.

Nikki watched the map screen on the dash of the mini-copter.  The display showed the position of the mini-sub, the robotic sharks, her position, the **Spearfish** with Stephen and the policemen, and the **Stingray** – all lined up and parallel to the shoreline heading southwest.

Minutes later she was closing fast on the sharks, when she saw one of them surface.  It was recharging its batteries.  It immediately started losing ground due to the turbulence on the surface of the ocean.  They had been swimming close behind the mini-sub.  But at the rate of their battery consumption, they would eventually run out of power.  The slow charge from the solar panels would fully recharge the batteries if their motors were stopped.  But with their motors running, the panels would at best add a few extra minutes to the chase.  The sharks were her eyes on the target, giving both position and underwater imaging of the mini-sub.  They had cameras in their eyes, but at depth their range was too limited to be useful.  She needed to act quickly before their batteries expired.

Nikki was flying at about a 500-foot altitude.  The town of Hale'iwa was now more than four miles off to her left.  She glanced over her shoulder and saw the **Spearfish** was about half a mile behind her bouncing on the wave crests at a high rate of speed.  She couldn't see the **Stingray**, but the display screen showed it miles behind her.  Although ant-like in appearance, the Kamehameha Highway was lined with cars.  The traffic jam was due to the incident at Waimea Bay, and the ensuing accidents on the road would take hours to clear.  If the Deputy Dragon Head made it to shore, she might be able to blend in and escape.

She watched the display and saw her symbol on the map approach, then merge, then pull ahead of the symbol for the mini-sub.  A label next to the mini-sub symbol popped up – 'DDH-sub.'  Undoubtedly Shelli was at the controls in the **Stringray**.  Nikki needed to get at least a mile ahead and then drop the sonobuoys in a triangular pattern. She clicked on the "Deploy Sonobuoys" menu button on the display and then clicked on the position of the DDH-sub. The next click was a mile ahead. The nav computer calculated a second and plotted three positions for the buoy. As long as she dropped the sonobuoys on those positions or farther apart, she would be able to monitor the position of the DDH-sub over an area greater than three square miles.

Nikki reached the first drop point and released a sonobuoy within feet of the intended position. The sonobuoy position appeared on the mini-copter map display instantly as it hit the water. A series of concentric rings emanated from the buoy's map icon. She repeated this at the second and third drop points. As each buoy hit the water, their symbol appeared on the screen and concentric rings were plotted. The symbol for the DDH-sub, which was still being tracked by their robotic shark, passed the outermost rings of the sonobuoys. Three rings overlapped on its position and tail formed behind the symbol. Nikki's dad had explained this was the object's "track" when he was training her on the equipment.

It was good to see the DDH-sub's track form on the display. The sonabuoy data readouts were showing a strong signal. The second robotic shark icon blinked on her display. It had reached a five percent battery condition and was surfacing and shutting down for recharge on the surface. The first shark was still charging on the surface. Now that the sharks were out of commission, she had about three square miles of open ocean or two linear miles on its current course to stop the DDH-sub.

Nikki lowered the mini-copter to about twenty feet off the water. That was dangerously close to the water's surface and too low to recover from a stall. But she couldn't risk a broken limb from an accidental fall.

She released the buckle of the strap around the diving sled and pushed it off. It fell and made a big splash and simultaneous "thump" sound when it plunged in the water. It bobbed back up on the surface a few seconds later. She notified Stephen and Shelli that she was going in. The earphones were pulled off and Nikki adjusted her goggles to ensure they fit snuggly. She strapped the rebreather on her back and dangled her feet off the side of the helicopter as it hovered. She reached for the carabineer of the winch and attached it to a metal loop on her dive belt. With her hand on the winch remote, she pushed off the helicopter.

Nikki heard the high-pitched whine of the winch as cable played out. She rushed to the water surface and then hit the brake button on the winch remote. Her weight belt tugged at her waist as the resistance of the winch brake kicked it and slowed her drop. When her feet touched the water, she was descending at the rate of thick syrup. She pressed the "stop" button when her chest reached the water's surface. She grabbed the cable above her head and pulled herself up enough to unbuckle herself with the other hand. She slid completely underwater a few feet after unbuckling.

She was neutrally buoyant in the water with the weights on her weight belt perfectly countering the buoyancy of her body, wetsuit, and rebreather. She reached for her regulator, which hung just behind her on her left, and placed it in her mouth. A quick purge of air forced the water out of the mouthpiece, and a light inhale of air into the mouth from the rebreather confirmed it was working properly. She had selected the rebreather because it was small and lightweight. But it wouldn't last long, so she had to find the Deputy Dragon Head and ... end it.

Nikki swam easily to the drifting sled. It had an air bladder, which allowed it to float. A push of the button released the trapped air in the bladder, and it sank underwater slowly. She pushed the start button and then throttled the sled forward. Once underwater, she quickly lost her perspective of her bearings relative to north and south. A couple of pushes on the control panel and a smaller version of her helicopter display came to life. It received all information from the buoys using acoustics. She was pointing westward, so she banked right. She turned wide until she aligned herself for a collision course with the DDH-sub.

Nikki began to think as she moved quietly along. Underwater diving is not a fun experience for everyone. Those who relish the experience often comment on the tranquility, or peacefulness. It took some time for Nikki to get used to it. The sense of being completely alone and at the mercy of her equipment made her uneasy from the start. Its muted and unusual sounds, which are masked by the strikingly loud sounds of breathing in a regulator, added to the alien experience. In her first few dives, the fear that something large enough to eat you, or sting you, poison you, or rapidly and brutally attack you was difficult to overcome. The restricted peripheral vision from the mask itself only added to her anxiety. The other-worldliness of being deep underwater still haunted her somewhat, even after years of experience. It helped for her to think that at least she wasn't on a lone spacewalk – the muted distant sounds of the ocean had to be better than the complete silence of space. Her determination to succeed at everything she attempted, which helped her out of many troubles in life, won out in the end. She acknowledged the fear as an annoyance, and shifted it away from her mind like a file of bills on one's desk.

Nikki had reached the final step of her quickly devised strategy to capture the Deputy Dragon Head. If the Deputy Dragon moved out to sea, then she'd eventually have to surface. If she headed to shore, then Nikki would surface, notify the police, and watch as the DDH was quickly captured. The **Spearfish** and the **Stingray** were behind her and Nikki was in front of her. So Nikki and her team only had to close in and capture. It sounded simple.

But the Deputy Dragon Head didn't get the title she had by being passive; on the contrary she was probably truculent. And she most likely had as much determination as Nikki herself. She couldn't communicate a "halt and desist" message. Should she fire one of her two torpedoes across the bow as a warning shot? What if Deputy Dragon Head retaliated? What if the Deputy struck first? And with what? What did the DDH-sub have onboard and what was Nikki's defense? These issues stirred her thoughts as she sped forward.

The sled had a molded seat and two foot peg metal extensions on the lower side to permit the rider to sit on the sled like a bike. But Nikki was riding it like a snow sled, except with her body hovering above it instead of touching it. This was more streamlined and allowed her to move faster through the water. It made her a smaller target too. The sled had a tough belly made of carbon fiber with two side ridges spaced about two feet apart. The ridges allowed the sled to sit on the deck of a ship without rolling. The carbon fiber resisted gouging from sandy bottoms and coral when the sled was "parked" underwater.

Nikki looked down at the display on the sled. She shifted her grip of her right hand to the center of the handle bars, and with her left hand clicked on the screen button that said "Defense" next to the map display. The screen showed a plan and side view of the underwater sled. The sled was a project of her dad's company. Her dad had projects with a number of alphabet soup U.S. Government agencies, and she didn't remember if he said this

181

was a DARPA or NSW-something-or-another agency project. The Seals and the U.S. Coast Guard MSST were to be the first to use it. It was still considered an experimental system.

To each side of the sled was a torpedo, which were powerful enough to sink a shrimp boat and could punch a hole in a metal skinned ship. Nikki could select programmed, acoustic, or wake homing trajectories. According to the manual, the default program was a straight-forward trajectory. She could "nudge' any trajectory left, right, up or down with keypads. The torpedo range was one nautical mile at top speed, and they were powered by propellers. They detonated either on impact or with a proximity fuse. The torpedoes had to pass close to its target to do any harm using the proximity fuse. There was a single small hole under the belly of her sled that was used by the repeating spear gun. The spear gun propelled up to six spears using compressed gas cartridges. A hidden rotating cylinder that resembled the old Gatling guns held the six spears within the body of the sled. There were three ink dispersal portals at the backside belly of the sled. The propeller blades of the sled pushed the ink outward to offer a nice screen. Nikki joked with her dad that he still needed to add a depth charge launcher before James Bond would use it. He told her that if he added any more gadgets or weapons, it would have to sit still in the water because he barely had enough room for the motor and batteries. The only addition made to the sled since then was the ability to control the sled remotely by detaching the display panel or by using one of their waterproof tablets. A camera mounted in the nose of the sled made remote aiming of the weapons easier.

She had made up her mind what her plan of attack would be by the time she saw a glimpse of a dark figure in front of her. Shoot first and ask questions later. If she hit the DDH-sub, it would at worst case kill the person that tried to kill her dad. No loss there. But thinking back at what her dad had said as he was leaving, she suspected that the DDH-sub had defenses. Her sled was meant for incursion and covert surveillance. Its only defense was offense. So she figured shooting first was her best defense.

Nikki selected one of the two torpedoes and then click on the icon of the Deputy Dragon Head's sub as the target. The **Spearfish** icon showed it had caught up and was just behind the DDH-sub, but on the surface. A distant V-wake and the hull was visible as she was only fifty feet underwater. She selected "Acoustic Homing," which meant that if the DDH-sub moved, the acoustic ping of the torpedo would follow. One last look ahead showed a dark and more defined shape. Nikki pressed "Launch." The torpedo propeller whizzed to life, the attachment lock clicked as it released, and the torpedo shot forward at more than twice Nikki's speed.

When the torpedo reached half the distance, Nikki saw a stream of bubbles release from the DDH-sub, and a few seconds later she saw the explosion of her torpedo. Countermeasures had made her torpedo ineffective. Then she saw another series of bubbles. It took only a few moments before she saw the nose of a torpedo coming straight at her. With little time to think, Nikki pulled hard over to her left and rotated the belly to face the oncoming torpedo. It passed a few yards away from the sled and detonated. The torpedo's nose was just passed the sled's propeller, so the explosion sent shards of metal shrapnel toward the rear of the sled. The pressure wave of the explosion hit the sled, and its sideways acceleration caused the sled to slam into Nikki's chest and the handle bars into her goggles. She saw stars for a few seconds and got her wind back shortly thereafter. She was spinning in a barrel roll, which made her briefly disoriented.

As she jerked her arms to the right to stop the roll, she suddenly felt a burning sensation in her right foot. She glanced back and saw a small dark trail following behind her foot. *Blood. Hit by the torpedo shrapnel.*

Just as she was thinking how lucky she was to have survived the blast, she glanced up to see the DDH-sub looming directly in front of her. It was a two-man sub, with a large glass panel in the front. Two props, protruded out of the aft sides of the sub. Stabilizers came out of the sides near the front of the sub for steering, and it had a large rear rudder similar to the tail of an aircraft.

In the right seat was young man, maybe Nikki's age, and on the left seat was a woman. She appeared to be in her forties and was a mess. The right side of her face was badly burned – to the point of disfigurement. Her hair was short on one side, which was likely due to the fiery explosion of the UAV. Her right arm was discolored with dark patches of brown and red. The woman's dress was torn and blackened. The man was disheveled, but there was no sign of burns. But he was profusely sweating, and the woman appeared to be yelling at him. Nikki had a good look at both of them right up to the point it plowed into her sled.

The sled pushed into Nikki as it took the brunt of the collision in its belly again. The sled must have caught something, because it jerked and spun rapidly to the left. That caused the right handle bar to hit Nikki in the face on her right side. She fell off the sled stunned and immediately drifted downward. She barely missed laceration by the DDH-sub's propeller blades as they passed by, but unfortunately the propeller guard of the DDH-sub hit the propeller guard of her sled. The force broke her sled's guard and bent one of the propeller blades.

Dazed, Nikki drifted downward. She felt like she had been hit by a bulldozer, and made no effort to correct her decent. As she rolled facing up, she saw the DDH-sub continuing to move southward. She followed the small stream of dark fluid still coming from her foot. It meandered upward in the water currents, which led her eyes up to the **Spearfish** as it passed her overhead on the water's surface. It was still following the track of the DDH-sub.

Her first thought was that she had failed. But then she became aware that she was grasping an object in her left hand – just outside her peripheral vision. Diving masks, no matter how much technology they seem to introduce, always reduced one's peripheral vision. Her old diving nemesis – anxiety –struggled briefly to surface, but was quickly submerged by determination. Nikki held up her hand to her face. In it was the control panel of the sled. She stiffened her body, and with a few hand and leg movements, she righted herself in the water. She saw her sled's stabilizers were positioned as opposites of each other. That coupled with the bent prop was causing the sled to both flip end-over-end and wobble like a child's spinning top.

Nikki looked at the remote control. She was almost sure the sled was faster than the DDH-sub, even with a bent prop. Maybe she could stop the out-of-control spin? She studied the controls for a couple of seconds, trying to figure out what to do, when she realized that she had seen the DDH-sub appear twice in the video display on the control. That video was streaming live from the nose camera of the sled. She glanced back at her sled. Its end-over-end rotation was in almost perfect alignment with the DDH-sub's trajectory.

Nikki clicked three buttons on the remote control display, just as she had done before. She held her finger just above the Launch button and then watched the sled's nose rotate. It would require guesswork on her part to launch it just right. According to her Dad, the nudge function was just that – sort of like the spin of a bowling bowl just before it hit the pins. When it reached about ten degrees from being in-line of the mini-sub, Nikki pressed the Launch button. The second of the two torpedoes came to life, detached from the sled and thrust forward. From the remote control display in her hand, Nikki saw the view of the stern of the DDH-sub passed by and the tail of the torpedo heading parallel and to the left of the sub. She pressed on the right key of the control and saw the vertical stabilizers of the torpedo shift to the right. The trajectory seemed to continue unchanged at first, but then slowly started to curve toward the DDH-sub.

The torpedo hit the DDH-sub in the left rear stanchion that held one of the two props. The explosion ripped off the entire prop and punched a hole into the aft section of the DDH-sub. A giant release of air bubbled out of the hole and the sub pitched hard to the right and went into a steep dive.

Nikki watched it in awe. She couldn't believe she'd hit it. Just as she began to think of her next step, she saw a side hatch open. The woman emerged from the hatch seconds after a release of air bubbles. The woman followed them towards the surface, a trick used by divers to minimize the chances of getting the bends.

Nikki saw the Deputy Dragon Head had something dark in her hand. It was most likely a gun. The *Spearfish* was still moving southward and it appeared to be following the original trajectory of the mini-sub. She hadn't seen the man leave the sub, and given the amount of air released he was probably dead. A person in the water would not be detected at this distance by the sonobouys, so the guys on the *Spearfish* could be shot if the Deputy made it to the surface.

Nikki decided to go after the sea monster that was now heading to the surface. She could stop the Deputy before she had a chance to harm anyone else. Nikki unclipped her helicopter winch control from her weight belt and tucked it inside her neoprene top. She unbuckled the weight belt and let it begin its rapid decent to the ocean floor while she started her accent. She blew out bubbles to judge her speed of accent – it did no good to race to the surface and then die of an aneurism.

As she rose toward the surface, Nikki saw the Deputy's silhouette above her. The Deputy paused to take in some fresh air and then immediately started swimming to the shore. The Deputy had no tank to aid her escape from the DDH-sub, so she had taken the direct route to the surface. Nikki's tank still had a few more breaths of air left, so she corrected her accent to intercept the Deputy yards ahead of her course to land.

Nikki was within ten or so yards from the surface when she made one last correction to her accent. She had no weapon, so Nikki had to breach directly in front of the Deputy and grab her before she could fire her weapon.

Nikki lunged forward once the force of buoyancy that had propelled her upward gave way to gravity. The Deputy gasped in surprise and brought her hands inward to protect herself before realizing that it was Nikki, and not a shark. This gave Nikki an advantage and she was able to grasp each wrist of the Dragon. In the Deputy's right hand was a Glock – black and shimmering as the bright overhead sun gleamed on the film of seawater on its surface.

Nikki knew from her training on firearms that a Glock will work just fine after immersion in fresh or saltwater. Since she was facing the Deputy, her left hand was grasping the right wrist of the Deputy.   And even though Nikki was left-handed, a quick rotation of the wrist would bring the barrel directly toward Nikki's face.   If the Deputy knew about this weapon, she would know she would have a good chance of straining, if not breaking, her wrist if she fired it that way.   But Nikki couldn't risk it, and released her grip on the other wrist and grabbed the weapon with her right hand.   Although this effectively neutralized the threat of being shot, Nikki knew she was now potentially facing a more lethal threat.   The first blow across her right cheek triggered a galactic pattern of stars in her vision.   The Deputy's free hand was just as deadly as the gun.

Even with the badly burned face, Nikki could see the hatred in the Deputy's eyes.   She was fearsome.   Nikki couldn't let go of the gun, but she couldn't take a beating.   As the constellations in her vision subsided, Nikki backhanded the Deputy with her right hand into the fresh burn on her face.   She squealed and Nikki felt the Deputy's grip on the pistol loosen.   Still holding the gun in her left hand, Nikki chopped with her right hand on wrist of the Deputy so hard that she thought she heard a snap of the bone.   The Deputy released the pistol, and Nikki flipped it in her hand and held it on the Deputy.

The Deputy, still treading water, was holding her left wrist.   Blood from the hard slap to the face was trickling from her nose.   Her lip was beginning to swell.   But her eyes had no expression -- they were deep black holes.   The pain in her wrist and the burns on her face must be severe, but there was no sign of it visible to Nikki.

Nikki was years younger, well trained thanks to her Dad's insistence, and she felt strong. But her right cheek hurt and she was sure the numbness she felt in it was accompanied by swelling and maybe bruising.   Nikki knew she had the upper hand with the pistol in her possession, but no matter how much she hated what the Deputy had done to her father, she couldn't kill in cold blood. But did the Deputy realize this?

As if she was reading her mind, the Deputy reacted swiftly.   She had evaluated her chance and the few seconds of indecision on Nikki's behalf told her volumes.   With her injured hand she grabbed at Nikki's left hand and shouted something unintelligible.   Nikki unconsciously glanced to that hand and tensed her entire body.   The Deputy then took her good hand and thrust it to a spot on her neck below her left ear, and then applied great pressure to the soft tissue below Nikki's left collar bone.   The pain from the attack shot down her left arm and she felt her grip on the pistol weaken.

Although the Deputy's right wrist was hurt, she reached for the pistol.   The surprise move was painful, but Nikki's training taught her to see through the pain.   Being 'blinded' by pain was not just an expression.   Although she had no control over her left arm and hand, she had plenty control of her body and her right arm.   She rotated her body to the left and downward and punched her right fist into the side of the left elbow of the Deputy.   This caused her left numbed arm to plunge into the water.   The pistol slipped from Nikki's hand and was quickly lost to the depths.   The momentum of the punch partially spun the Deputy away and slightly right of Nikki.

Now without the gun, Nikki knew her fighting skills were her only defense to the wild and undoubtedly desperate foe.   She felt the numbness in her left arm subside.   Instinct told her to put a little more distance between herself and her enemy and prepare for her defense. She arched her back and reached both arms back to take a big forward stroke, which would push her away from the Deputy. What she didn't catch was that when the Deputy spun to the right, the Deputy lowered her left arm into the water and tilted her left shoulder.

The Deputy turned her head toward Nikki, and followed it with her left arm emerging from the water fully extended holding a metallic blade that reflected the bright sun. She was swinging a diving knife in a wide arc toward Nikki's neck. At the same time, Nikki pushed her arms forward and also tilted her head back in reaction to the deadly sweep of the knife. The blade caught her just below her right collar bone. Blood seeped through the cut in her suit and ran down her chest.

Without checking her wound, Nikki saw an immediate opening for a counter-attack. She arched her back and pulled her right knee out of the water and then extended it in a quick flat-footed kick to the nose and lips of the Deputy.

It was an impressive kick, and the full extension of her leg and right hip forward would have broken a 2-by-4-inch stud. And the sound of crunching bone was a good indication of the effectiveness of the kick. The Deputy's head flung backward and when her head leveled, Nikki saw that her nose was completely broken and was pushed flush to her right check. Her eyes were tearing and her swollen lip was now deeply split. Blood welled up through the split in the lip and ran freely down her chin. Her broken nose was also bleeding and was flowing to either side of her lips. Had it been hair, it would look like she had a goatee.

The Deputy was dazed and momentarily stopped treading water. That caused her to slide down into the water until her mouth and nose were underwater. Breathing is involuntary, so sucking in seawater caused an immediate cough reflex. The Deputy's dazed eyes jolted open and she kicked her feet to propel her head above water. She continued to cough for a few seconds. And to her amazement, Nikki saw the Deputy still had the knife in her right hand.

Disheveled, a broken or at least fractured wrist, broken nose, split lip, severe burns and cuts from the UAV explosion, choking on saltwater, and a probable concussion would have stopped most people. But Nikki was guessing that she had just upset the Deputy. She wouldn't stop until she or Nikki was dead. The Deputy howled and shook her head as she looked to the sky.

With the knife still in her hand and the intimidating appearance, Nikki's mind momentarily went blank and flight was the only clear feeling that surfaced. Nikki kicked with her feet hard and backstroked from the Deputy. Hearing the splashing, the Deputy stopped her wailing and started after her.

Swimming with a knife in her hand was slowing down the Deputy. And Nikki, being a good swimmer since she was a child, could tell that the Deputy was not a strong swimmer. But the Deputy was lethal with her hands and she might actually decide to throw the knife. Nikki rolled over and took a series of solid strokes in the classic American Crawl swimming technique. She then slid for a few seconds to a side stroke to check out the Deputy. She was swimming in a mixture of techniques with a poor breast stroke occasionally to get her breath. The saltwater in her lip, in her broken nose, and on her face was most certainly painful too. Nikki had gained almost 10 yards on her with just the few good strokes, so she pushed hard again in the Crawl for half a minute or so. She stopped and treaded water and judged her distance now at more than twenty-five yards from the Deputy. So she knew she could escape if she had too. Maybe she could keep swimming to shore and if the Deputy made it that far, she could fight her on land. But given the amount of blood lost by both Nikki

186

and the Deputy, they were going to attract sharks. She peered to her left and saw that the **Spearfish** was still way off in the distance.  They would soon realize that the DDH-sub was no longer a threat, but they would not be able to get back in enough time to help her if she re-engaged in a fight.

*What to do...attack now...try to slow her down?*  She watched the Deputy swimming straight toward her. She still had watery blood flowing down her chin.  *Maybe if I can outlast her, she'll eventually bleed to death.*

Nikki then became aware of the sound of her helicopter.  She spun around toward the direction she had been swimming, which was toward the shore.  She saw it still hovering at a ten o'clock bearing from her position.  She also became aware of the feeling of the remote in her top.  She started to take it out, but thought how it would slow her swimming strokes down.

Putting her head down Nikki swam straight for the mini-copter.  As she swam she continued to glance up at it.  It slowed her progress, but she didn't want to overshoot.  She stopped directly under it and turned back to the Deputy.  The Deputy had apparently noticed the mini-copter too and had picked up her stroke speed.  She was still not efficient, but she was moving faster.

Nikki reached her arm into her top and pulled out the winch remote control.  The cable had automatically retracted, as she knew it would, not long after she had gone in the water. She pressed the appropriate button and heard the winch start to whine.  Without any weight, it would lower the cable slowly to prevent backlash.  Nikki watched the slow progress of the cable and the fast progress of the Deputy.

As the seconds ticked by at the rate of Hawaiian lava, Nikki switched her gaze back and forth between the Deputy and the winch.  The winch had a big carabineer on the end, which would have attached to her weight belt.  But she had dropped the belt underwater so that she could race to the surface to meet the female devil now just yards from her.  Her first thought was to wrap the cable under both arms and attach the carabineer back onto the cable itself. But that would just tighten painfully around her chest as gravity pulled against the upward lift. The best bet would be to create loop in the cable and put her foot in the loop.  That way she could grab the metal frame of the mini-copter and pull herself up quickly once she got near it.

But this was going to be close.  The cable end was swinging back and forth in the wind as it lowered.  When the carabineer got within her reach, she kicked her feet to raise herself out of the water.  She grabbed and missed.  She was too distracted by the closeness of the Deputy.  She watched the pendulum-like motion of the cable and kicked her feet again.  She got it.  The cable continued to lower and coil on the surface for an extra few feet until she stopped the winch with the control.  She looped the cable and tied a loose knot about two feet from the end.  She resisted the urge to look at the Deputy, but could hear the splashing strokes approaching.  She put her left foot in the loop and clenched the cable with her right hand.  Then she hit the "UP" button.

The winch reversed and began to reel backwards.  The cable pulled taut when the weight of her body first tugged against it.  The whine of the wench changed pitch. The splash from the Deputy's strokes were almost upon her, and when Nikki looked she saw the Deputy was clenching the knife in her teeth so that she could stroke more efficiently.  And she was three strokes away when Nikki's torso began to lift out of the water.  Nikki tensed for the encounter.

Stroke one and Nikki's chest was out of the water. Stroke two and Nikki's waist was out of the water. *Surely she would pull the knife out of her mouth. Kick.* As Nikki's left knee cleared the water she snapped her right foot to the Deputy. The Deputy, with the knife in her mouth, anticipated the kick and twisted her body so that the kick hit her as a glancing blow. Then, as fast as the strike of a snake, clasped her arms around Nikki's leg.

The Deputy's body was mostly in the water, so the added weight and extra surface tension of her body more than doubled the resistance on the reel. The ideal placement of the winch on the mini-copter would be directly below the blade shaft. This would reduce the chances of lateral movement of the helicopter when a load was raised or lowered. But that would put the winch behind the pilot, which would make it difficult to see it. So the winch motor sat to the left of the centerline of the mini-copter. When the pilot was not in the pilot's chair and the mini-copter was hovering, the onboard digital compass automatically kept the mini-copter flying level even when the winch was deploying. But the response was not instantaneous – there was a lag in response to keep the autopilot from overcompensating. This caused an immediate problem for Nikki.

The added weight caused the mini-copter to tilt to the left of its position, which resulted in a sudden drop of three feet in height before the autopilot compensated. Nikki dropped into the water to chest level, and at the same time the Deputy let go of her leg and latched on to Nikki's top with one hand. And in a swift move, the Deputy grabbed the knife from her mouth with her free hand, arched backward, and then plunged it downward at Nikki's chest.

Surprised by the drop and the groping by the Deputy, Nikki's released an audible gasp. But she recovered instantly and thrust her free arm upward at the same moment the Deputy plunged. The block was effective – just below the wrist. She knew it had to hurt, since it was clearly swollen from the crunch she had heard from the same wrist earlier. But the jolt caused Nikki to drop the winch remote, and when she did the reel on the winch stopped. Nikki glanced quickly to see where it dropped. It did float, but that didn't mean it would stay put.

Nikki turned her attention to the Deputy. From the block, she hooked her fist and caught the Deputy on the left side of her face. Even though the pain of the punch on her burned face clearly caused anguish, the Deputy's counter move was already executed. The release of Nikki's block permitted her to slice downward and the knife caught Nikki's swinging arm. Due to the speed of Nikki's punch, only the tip of the knife caught Nikki's arm. But a one-inch deep cut appeared on her arm and filled immediately with blood.

Nikki screamed at the pain from the cut at the same time as the Deputy howled from the punch. Nikki had the presence of mind not to dwell on the pain, and quickly punched the Deputy's face in the same spot just as she had recoiled from the first one. Then she repeated it for a third time.

Dazed, the Deputy let go of Nikki and fell back into the water. Nikki took the opportunity to reach for the winch remote, but instantly discovered that it had drifted beyond her grasp. She released her grip of the cable, dropped her foot out of the loop, and swam the short distance to the remote. When she turned, Nikki saw the Deputy was now holding the winch cable. Although the Deputy still appeared dizzy from the punches, she still held the knife firmly in her other hand. Blood was still flowing down her face.

Nikki soon smelled the copper scent of blood, and was surprised at first that she could smell the Deputy's blood from that distance. But then she saw a dark cloud around her own body. It was her own blood she smelled. The cut in her arm was hemorrhaging at a fair rate. Nikki had been blocking the pain from her mind, but the sudden awareness of the blood made her alert to the stinging of saltwater in the wound.

Nikki had the winch remote, but the Deputy was at the cable and she had a knife. Both of them were bleeding, but Nikki knew the Deputy had to be completely exhausted from the fight. Nikki struggled with her next move, but decided she couldn't let the Deputy regain her strength. She closed in on the Deputy.

"Give it up," yelled Nikki. She now heard the **Spearfish**. They had realized something was happening at the helicopter. "Our boat has police officers on it and they're coming for you. You don't have a chance."

The Deputy was seething. Nikki was swimming in a tightening circle around the Deputy. She lunged at Nikki and swung her arm with the cutting edge outward. Nikki arched her head back, but continued to close the circle.

The Deputy swung again, and shouted some sort of Chinese slur at her. Nikki again dodged the knife and kept swimming in the circle.

"I will kill you, and when I get on shore I'll find the rest of your miserable family and kill them as well. Starting with your father."

The Deputy said the last sentence with a hoarseness in her voice. Her chest was heaving from exhaustion. Nikki kept up with the tightening circle.

"You're going to jail, if you're lucky. But that is if I let you live."

The last statement caused the Deputy to breathe even heavier, and she kicked and pushed herself out of the water and lashed out with the knife. But the cable prevented her from reaching Nikki.

"You know nothing of us. I will never live to see a courtroom. The Shan Chu ... the Dragon Head as you call him... will have me executed long before then. But I will get my revenge on you, on the Bryants, before I die. I will regain honor before I die."

Nikki was swimming smoothly in the water among the maelstrom created by the Deputy as she tried to keep the cable from wrapping around her and the knife between herself and Nikki. It was then she saw the first fin break the surface of behind the Deputy.

Nikki went rigid at the site and stopped all unnecessary movement. She gripped her hand over her wound and applied as much pressure as she could.

"You're not good enough. With all your money, guns, and knives, just look at you now. You've lost your beauty, you've lost your ship, your men, your power, and your honor. You're nothing now. Give up and help us stop the triad. We can protect you."

The Deputy was furious and splashed her arm with the knife in the water. "I am going to take great pleasure in killing you ...." Her sentence was shortened as her whole body jerked sideways in the water. She glared at Nikki with her eyes wide. Her mouth moved, but she said nothing.

"Stay still," said Nikki. "You know what it is, right?"

The Deputy nodded.

The water to Nikki's right mounded. Something was moving toward her and its bow wave spread and the subsequent turbulent wake left a trail on the surface that was deceivingly calm compared to the wind-driven ripples everywhere else. Nikki held her breath and moved the bare minimum to stay afloat. The thought of what she might face if she slipped underwater was causing goose bumps to spread across her skin. Any more nervousness, and she would start to quiver, which would be like a homing beacon for the shark.

As the bow wave came within a body's length from her, she saw it veer farther to her right. It was often a behavior of sharks – pass by the object to inspect it first before attacking. It passed a mere two feet from her and the dorsal fin tip breached the water. Nikki could see the dark shadow of the body…she could see its eyes fixed on her. *The eyes.* It passed, and Nikki turned only her head to watch it. The fin slid slowly underwater.

She knew what she had to do. "Drop the knife," she shouted to the Deputy. The Deputy was making frantic movements. It was as if she was attempting to keep the knife and the shark in front of her. As if the shark would know it meant danger. Since she didn't actually see the shark, she was jerking to every small slap or slosh of the water. And there were plenty given the substantial down draft from the helicopter above them.

"Drop the knife," she shouted again. "I'll come over and we can both get out of here. I have the winch remote, but I'm not coming near you with the knife in your hand."

Without looking at Nikki, the Deputy shouted, "No…no. You'll try to push me away and then go up yourself. You will leave me here."

"No, I won't do that. Listen…we can't keep splashing, it will only attract them more. Just throw the knife and we can both live." Nikki moved slowly toward the Deputy as she talked.

At less than ten feet away, the Deputy sensed something near her and appeared startled to see Nikki. She withdrew for a second, and then slashed out with the knife while still holding on to the winch line. Nikki flinched, and moved back while another slashing put the blade within a couple feet of Nikki. The Deputy tried again, but the winch line went taut as she made a stabbing lunge at Nikki.

"Stop, you're going to kill both us," yelled Nikki. "Look behind you."

The Deputy turned to see a fin pass by where she had just been. She squealed and immediately started her knife dance with the shark's last seen position. After a few moments, it was like Nikki wasn't there again.

Nikki checked her watch. She had only minutes of fuel left in the mini-copter. As it was now, she'd have to land on the beach to fuel up. She twisted in the water and within seconds saw the mound again. It was heading on a course that was off to her left by maybe five to ten feet. This was it – she had to get the timing just right.

The Deputy was still spinning in the water; reacting to every plop and splash of water. Nikki switched from treading water to a slight side stroke so that she could keep an eye on the shark bearing down on her. She stuffed the winch remote back into her swimsuit. First the tip of the fin showed, and in another few seconds the entire dorsal fin was out of the water. As the shark got with a few body lengths away, it picked up speed and turned straight towards her. Nikki took one more side stroke just as the shark arrived. Nikki arched her back and the shark skimmed her body as if it was deflected off of it. As the nose passed her, she placed her hand in its snout and was jerked forward. The push of water from the shark's maneuver effortlessly pushed Nikki's body out of the water, which reduced drag. She let go of her grip of the snout and let her hand slide along the slick body of the shark until it rested on the front of the fin. She grasped the fin and rolled behind it. Her other hand came around now and also gripped the fin.

190

The Deputy finally perceived the shark as it plowed into her. She let go of the winch line and screamed. Nikki was able to grasp the winch line with her right hand, and with her left hand she reached the winch control and pressed the Up button. As the winch pulled her upward, she spread her legs and then rolled off the shark, trying to stay clear of the rear caudal fin. When her legs cleared the water she managed to rotate her leg around the cable. She allowed a little slippage of her hand, which caused the cable to pull tightly around her leg. The burn from the cable on her leg and hands was excruciating, but it was better than pulling her arm out of the socket. As Nikki rose in the air, she could still hear the Deputy's desperate shrieks in the ocean below her.

As her hands neared the winch, she stopped it by releasing the button. She stuffed the remote in her swimsuit and then reached for the tubular frame just inside one of the two side floats. A quick rotation around the frame put her belly down on the deck of the helicopter. She kissed the metal frame of the mini-copter and scampered over to the pilot's seat. She saw the fuel gauge needle pointing to empty.

She clicked the autopilot button off hover, and banked the mini-copter to the shore. As she banked, she glanced over her shoulder and saw the **Stingray** surfacing nearby. She clicked the side button on her watch to call her sister. "Thanks, Sis."

"No pro-ble-mo," said Shelli.

"I think I can make it back to Hale'iwa," said Nikki. "Or at least to the beach. I'll get some fuel and then call you to rendezvous."

"Roger that, Big Sis. The **Spearfish** is pulling up now.

Nikki glanced over her right shoulder and saw the stern of the **Spearfish** before it passed out of her peripheral view. She knew Stephen Chang and the officers would pick up the Deputy and arrest her.

She scanned the horizon for the nearest point of land. She just had to make it to the beach. She could always walk to the nearest gas station if necessary.

She reached for the first aid kit as she flew. The cut on her arm was still bleeding, but had started to clot. She used her teeth to open the alcohol, and she doused the wound. She poured what was left over the less deep cut at her collar bone, on the shrapnel wound on her foot, and over the cable burns on her leg and hand. Then she tore open the single-dose of antibacterial cream with her teeth and squirted it on her arm cut. She held the end of the gauze from the kit in her teeth, then wrapped the roll tightly around her arm several times. She managed to loop the ends of the gauze together and tie it tight.

Now less than a mile away from shore, she thought of the events that got her where she was. It would help keep her mind off the pain. She would need to give her sister a proper thanks for keeping her alive. Shelli had done it just right. She had allowed the fins to pass out of the water just the right distance. The Deputy had no idea. Only when the shark passed closed enough for Nikki to see the glow in the shark's eyes did she realize that Shelli was controlling the robotic sharks. During the fighting, the sharks must have recharged.

The mini-copter motor chugged and the speed flickered slightly. The fuel light flashed red, as she crossed the shoreline. Seconds later the motor was dead and the craft auto-rotated gently to the ground. She hopped off onto the beach and gazed back to the ocean. At four miles out, she couldn't see the **Spearfish** or the **Stingray**. She'd know soon enough how easy, or not so easy, it was for Stephen Chang to pull the Deputy into the boat.

# Chapter 39: *I am Shelli*

Hale'iwa is the largest town on the north shore with about 4000 residents, and claims it is the surfing capital of the world. The town consists mainly of one-story, plantation-style businesses, parks and marinas lining its two main drags – Kamehameha Highway and Hale'iwa Road. Tourism swells in the winter with the coming of giant waves and surfing competitions. The summertime, however, returns the town to a sleepy haven.

The **Spearfish** and the **Stingray** had met Nikki at Hale'iwa Marina. The **Spearfish** and the **Stingray** were each in a slip of their own and the mini-copter rested on the beach near the entrance. Beyond the mouth of the harbor, the **Amphitrite** sat moored. Nikki, Shelli, Ryan, Stephanie, and Stephen were sitting on the hull of the sub. Nikki had her wounds professionally dressed by the paramedics that had arrived. They had used surgical tape instead of stitches at her request. The paramedics left her with an icepack for her bruised face and said to follow up with a doctor's visit.

Police were gathering on the dock as the coroner and his assistant walked up to Officers Lee and Tyler. The assistant had an expensive camera around his neck.

"So where's the body?" asked the coroner.

"What's left of it is in the **Spearfish**," answered Lee as he pointed toward the boat.

"If you can, please let's wrap this up quickly," said Tyler. "We need to get back to the Honolulu. Chief wants us to give him an update ASAP."

"Take one of the cruisers back," said the coroner. "This case has got every CSI team member on the island involved. The beach and Waimea Bay is littered with evidence. We've got this scene and the one four miles out where the triad mini-sub ended up. We're going to be scrutinized by the press and lawyers. We've got to do this right."

"The chief wants us to take the Rick Bryant's kids back to the **Amphitrite** before coming back. And he said to use the **Spearfish** to take them there. He wants to make sure everybody is safe from any triad members that might be seeking revenge."

"I repeat, I do not want to be rushed."

Officer Lee's phone rang. He excused himself and walked away while the partial remains of a half-eaten woman were photographed by the coroner's assistant. On the sub, Nikki asked questions.

"So let me get this straight," said Nikki. "When I left, you guys closed in on the Deputy Dragon Head. She was busy stabbing the robotic shark as you approached her. Then she went under."

"Correct," said Stephen.

"And you saw lots of blood rise in the water," continued Nikki.

"Correct," said Stephen.

"She surfaced and yelled help," said Nikki.

"Correct," said Stephen.

"When you got up next to her and grabbed at her arm, she still had the knife in her hand and she lunged at you with it."

"Correct."

"And you just missed being cut. So you tried to get her to throw the knife away. And she wouldn't."

"Correct."

"And she was pulled down again.   After Ryan took over control of the robotic sharks, he was able to drive off the real sharks. And the remains of the body floated up. Is that right?"

"Yes," answered Stephen.

"There were no real sharks when I was in the water with the Deputy.  Where did they come from?

"Actually I saw them on our sonar scope," answered Shelli.  "They were approaching your position pretty quickly.   And there was a lot of them.  Although I figured you could beat the DDH, I didn't want you to have to fight off real sharks too.  That's when I thought about sending in the robotic sharks."

"Why did Ryan take over the controls when the real sharks attacked the Deputy?" asked Nikki.

"Remember we were underwater," said Ryan.   "We could see everything in full Technicolor.  Shelli and Stephanie started to puke as soon as the first shark bit the Deputy. Body parts started dropping all over. I had stop piloting and take over the sharks at that point."

Shelli and Stephanie went pale at the mention of it.   Stephanie had a little gag reflex.

"When I went over to the boat to examine her, I noticed she had a hole up under her armpit. It didn't look like a shark bite," said Nikki.

"Remember that she killed my brother," said Stephen without expression.   "She died pretty quickly after the first limb was bitten off.   By the time the real sharks were driven back, what was left of her was just floating there upright with her eyes to the sky.  I used your gaff to spear her and pull her up."

Stephanie leaned over the side of the sub and emptied what was left in her stomach.

"Hey, I'm not cleaning that up," said Ryan.

They watched Officer Lee hand his phone to the coroner.   The coroner jerked it away from his ear after saying "hello."   After a few "yes Sirs," the coroner handed the phone back to Officer Lee.  "I was told to clean this up now," said the coroner with an irritated look on his face. He and several other lab technicians pulled out a body bag and put the remains inside. All heads on the sub stayed down, except for Stephen.   With the body and other evidence removed, a marina deckhand hired by Nikki brought out a hose and starting washing down the *Spearfish*.

"You hear from Mom?" asked Shelli.  "How is Dad doing?"

"Yeah.  Sorry I should have told you," said Nikki.  "Mom texted me.  Dad's resting in a private room at Queen's Medical Center.   Mom said they gave him something to make him sleep.  He pretty much hurt's from head to toe, but with the exception of some burns, cuts, and cracked ribs, he'll be fine.  They are going to observe him overnight and will probably let him go tomorrow."

"Poor Dad," said Shelli.   "I broke his ribs, you know.  But I did it to save his life," she said with a smile.

Nikki smiled.   She knew what was next.

"And I saved your life too," said Shelli.

Nikki nodded.

"I am Shelli, hear me roar."

"How 'bout that shark attack?" said Nikki.

Shelli's face went pale.

# Chapter 40: *Grey Stone*

Two days after the return of Leilani and the disaster in Waimea, Kaleho stopped by the Ali'i Towers where the Bryant family had checked in again after Rick was released from the hospital.  It was morning and Kaleho had a tray of Kona coffee in his hands as he rode the elevator up to the penthouse.  He knocked on the door and Danielle answered.

"Coffee delivery," said Kaleho with a smile.

"Good morning, Kaleho."  Danielle reached for the tray and then tip-toed up to give Kaleho a kiss on the cheek.  "Thanks for the coffee.  We just ordered some breakfast from room service.  Can you join us?"

"Don't mind if I do," said Kaleho as he stepped inside the room.

"Rick is out on the lanai.  Go say hello, and bring him a coffee please."

"Sure thing."  Kaleho pried two coffees out of the big to-go tray and walked out on the patio.

"Aloha," said Kaleho as he extended his hand with a coffee in it.

Rick was sitting on a deck chair with cargo shorts on and a pale green palm leaf aloha shirt.  He had bandages on much of his body, and many were still visible.  He wore dark reading shades and had a tablet PC in his lap.

"Mahalo," said Rick as he took the coffee.  He popped the lid off the coffee and took a deep sniff.  With no worry of etiquette, he slurped the coffee to get the full enjoyment of the full flavor.

"Ahh that's good," said Rick.  "Have a seat and enjoy the view."

"It is a good view for sure," said Kaleho.  The waters progressed into deep blues from the bright sandy beach that was, of course, full of people taking morning walks and enjoying the water.  A storm had passed yesterday, and the waves were a bit too high for the newbie surfing students that frequented the waves in Waikiki's waters.

Rick took another sip of coffee and grinned.  "You know I never had Kona coffee when I went to school here.  In fact, I rarely had coffee.  I couldn't afford it.  It wasn't until I left school and got a job and came back years later that I discovered it.  You probably know this, but you can buy it everywhere now."

"Coffee has been grown here for two centuries.  Used to be large plantations of it here on O'ahu.  My mom always had a pot brewing in the morning.  I'd grab a quick mug before running out the door with my surfboard.  Now Leilani puts a pot on for me on a timer the night before she knows I'm going out surfing."  Kaleho paused for a moment and the cleared his throat.  "And thanks to you, brah, I had some of hers early this morning before I hit the waves."

Rick nodded and looked down at his cup.  "I won't take credit for that.  Leilani is safe because of you and my family.  Enough about that though.  How is Leilani?"

"She's had a policeman for a husband for 30 years.  She's tough.  You'd never know anything ever happened.  In fact, that's partly the reason I came by.  She wants all of you to come by for dinner tomorrow."

"Glad she's doing well, and we'd love to come over."

Danielle stuck her head outside the glass door.  "Breakfast arrived...time to eat."

The large room soon filled with the sound of laughter and conversation as the Bryants, Stephanie, Ryan and Kaleho sat around the big table.   Papaya, mango, pineapple, eggs, bacon, baskets of croissants and rolls, mini-quiche's and a variety tray of pupu's were quickly consumed.

Shelli was quick to ask about Kai.  "He was torn about whether he should come or go surfing this morning.  And I have to say that surprised me.   Never seen Kai ever consider anything or anyone over surfing.   I wasn't sure you girls would be here, and I told him that. So he decided to go surfing.  But I wouldn't be surprised if he doesn't call you Shelli."

Shelli blushed and then looked at Stephanie and started giggling.

Danielle finally broke the casual conversation and asked, "Kaleho, how is Stephen? And was his grandfather found?"

"Stephen is doing well and his grandfather is back.   Actually, word got out that we had taken down the triad, so his grandfather basically found us.   He would never say where he was hiding.   He probably thought it would be best to keep it a secret in case he had to do it again in the future.   Stephen is searching for a place now where he and his grandfather can live together."

"That's so nice.  They've been through so much.  It's amazing what greed coupled with a hidden treasure can do," said Danielle.

"Speaking of treasure," said Kaleho.  "The chest of coins you gave the Deputy Dragon Head was recovered.  I tried to get it released, but the DA insisted it remain as evidence until there are convictions for remaining triad members.   Sorry about that.  I know there's a lot of money in there that isn't fake."

"No problem," said Rick.  "I suspect it will only go up in value after this is all over anyway."

"Wonder what happened to the rest of the treasure?" asked Ryan with a mouth full of food.  "I mean, it had to go somewhere."

"That is if it ever existed in the first place," said Rick.  "We never found real proof that anything was ever stolen or missing from the royal family in the first place."

"Actually that is not entirely true," said Danielle. "It took a while to loop around the island in the **Stingray**.   To pass the time, I decided to do some research.  I had borrowed a few books from Barbara Stallings on Hawaiian history.   I also checked out the records online from the Hawai'i State Archives. I'm not an historian and didn't read everything available, but I learned a lot about Hawai'i in the late 1800's in that submarine."

"When the USA annexed Hawai'i, the possessions of Queen Liliuokalani, were taken and auctioned off around 1900.   Many of the furnishings, dinnerware, clothes, jewelry, and other artifacts have never been recovered.   There has been significant effort to return all these possessions back to Iolani palace.   But they have had to use replicas in many cases. Many items have been returned, but many more are still missing."

They were quiet for a few seconds trying to absorb what Danielle had said. "So what are you trying to say, exactly?" asked Rick.

"Well a good number of the items that were taken in the story of the pirate raid are the same items that are still missing today.  Who knows if they all were actually auctioned off, or if they had been missing because they were stolen in 1884?   We already discovered that many of the Hawaiian coins were not melted down by the U.S. Mint.   And Shelli established in her search for real coins to use in the chests we assembled, that those missing coins are not being held by collectors.  So where are they?  And what of the American money?  Rick you guessed that the pirates may have taken all of the American currency with them, but we don't know that for sure, do we?  And the story talked about the pirates stealing from others in town.  What happened to all those things?  We didn't even check with family descendants about lost heirlooms or collectables.  Although there are some minor errors in the story, the majority was factual or at least plausible.  So what I guess I am saying is that there is nothing to disprove the raid. "

Again there was quiet after Danielle spoke.    They looked at one another as if they hoped someone would say what they all were thinking.  Finally Stephanie couldn't take it any longer.

"Mrs. Bryant, do you think that the pirates may have buried it?  Or maybe hidden it?"

"It's widely known that pirates did not actually bury their treasure.  That's folklore.  Besides, much of the shores of Hawai'i is lava rock."  She paused and stood up.  "Did they hide it?  Maybe, I don't know.   But it would have been a big embarrassment to the royal family and to the Hawaiian government.   Since there was a U.S. Navy presence back then, I would guess they would have been notified right away for help if this actually happened.  And what if the pirates had help?   What if the local businessmen, such as those with the Committee of Safety, had actually hired them like Barbara Stallings offered?  They could have arranged for the treasure to be dropped off like Rick suggested.  It could have been hidden somewhere else until things cooled down."

"Let's go find it!" burst out Stephanie.  "That would be so much fun."

"Stephanie, don't be silly," said Ryan.  "If the story was true, that was in 1884."

"But it is still missing!" came back Stephanie.

"There's no other mention of it since that time other than that printed newspaper article in California," said Ryan.  "If it were true, don't you think someone would have talked by now?"

"Not necessarily.  You heard Mrs. Bryant.  It could have been taken to hurt the royal family.  Maybe the Committee of Safety took it and hid it.  And maybe the location of it was forgotten.  It's possible."  Stephanie said it all without breathing.

"If the story is true, and that's a big if, and if it is still out there somewhere, we don't know where to even begin to look," said Ryan loudly.

It was clear to those listening that Ryan and Stephanie's discussion had the signs of becoming a brother and sister spat.  Sensing this, Danielle spoke calmly.

"I believe we do know where to start searching for the treasure."   Stephanie, Ryan and everyone else turned around and stared at her.   "That is, if it exists," continued Danielle.

She turned and walked to the side table of one of two couches in the penthouse living room.  She glanced back at them as she picked up her tablet and started walking back to the table.

"Rick had made a great start with a logical analysis of what might have happened.  So I continued looking at possibilities."

She stood up in front of the group to summarize what Rick and Barbara Stallings had discussed days ago.  "So basically the whole thing could have been the Committee of Safety's way of getting back at the royal family.  If they didn't spend all the money in financing projects like the Honolulu Rifles, then they would have likely hid it somewhere on O'ahu.   The local restaurant and store owners were mostly Chinese, so they might have gotten suspicious of the source of the money and treasures being traded in for supplies or even ammunition. It's possible that over the years the local Chinese businessmen, or even the tongs that we know existed back then, got hold of the treasure. And thus, we have the story that Stephen heard from his grandfather. And remember he talked of the fires in Chinatown. Those fires took place in 1886 and 1900. So if the treasure survived, it had to be someplace safe. Not in Chinatown. Somewhere that was safe, or at least seemed safe."

She paused and looked around the table at the eyes glued on her. "Think back to the 1800's. What are the oldest buildings in Honolulu from that time?"

"Iolani Palace," said Nikki.

"True, that is old," said Danielle. "But it wasn't the oldest building around, and why put the treasure back into the building from which you stole it?"

She swiped her tablet, which opened the screen to a digital photo from the Hawai'i State Archives.

"Here's a picture from the 1880's. Of all the buildings in Honolulu, the Iolani Palace, and the prominent building in this picture have stood the test of time and exist to this day. Chinatown burnt down twice. Most of downtown buildings and Waikiki structures were built in the 1900's. If you were going to hide something that couldn't be blown down in hurricane winds and would likely be around for a long time, then where would you hide it?

"The grey stone church downtown," said Shelli. "The name starts with 'K'."

"Kawaiaha'o Church," injected Danielle. "The church was completed about 40 years before the Iolani Palace. The king himself went there."

"But that's a Christian church," said Stephanie. "The Chinese immigrants were Buddhists, weren't they?"

"Buddhism was one of three primary Chinese religions. The other two being Confucianism and Taoism," answered Danielle. "But you have stumbled on my dilemma, Stephanie. The palace couldn't have been used for hiding. The logical place is something lasting. The church makes perfect sense, but how did the Chinese gain access?"

"Maybe they worked at the church," said Nikki. "After all, some of the Committee of Safety people would have probably gone to that church. And some of them were plantation owners. The Chinese immigrants were brought to Hawai'i to work on those plantations. Maybe some of their Chinese workers also helped at the church."

"It's possible," said Danielle.

"But Stephen's grandfather said his ancestors had the treasure," said Ryan. "And he said that after the fires, no one alive knew where it was hidden. I don't understand how it could be lost if it were hidden in some place like the church. And I still don't see how it wasn't found by someone else by this time."

"Maybe the treasure started out in the church and then was moved by Chinese immigrants somewhere else," said Shelli.

"I might be completely off by thinking of the church, so we shouldn't just focus on it. We should probably check out all the buildings in the area that have survived from that time," said Danielle. Nods of agreement came from her family.

*(Honolulu in 1880's)[2]*

Kaleho had been sitting quietly for some time. Finally he interrupted the conversation, "Hey, listen. This is been an interesting conversation, but I've got to head into the office. We've had the FBI, CIA, Interpol, and you name it calling us about this case. With the information we pulled from the sunken yacht, we've been able to round up triad members from around the globe. So I've got to go. Danielle – I know Rick will forget to tell you, so I'm going to relay the message to you too. Leilani wants the whole family to come over for dinner tomorrow night.

"We'd love to!" shouted Shelli. "Is Kai going to be there?"

"Yes," said Kaleho with a chuckle.

Shelli clapped. "And could you ask him to invite Tim over?" She looked to Stephanie, who nodded her head rapidly.

"Shelli Bryant," said Danielle. "We're guests… you're not supposed be inviting people."

"Not a problem Danielle. Leilani was notified by Kai that Tim would be joining us too."

"Please tell Leilani not to fuss," said Danielle. "And I will be happy to help."

[2] From the Hawaii State Archives.
http://archives1.dags.hawaii.gov/gallery2/main.php?g2_view=core.DownloadItem&g2_itemId=23223&g2_serialNumber=2

"She'll be glad to hear it," said Kaleho. "See you all tomorrow then."

Kaleho left the room. The dinner party sidetracked the treasure discussion. As the dialog began to shift to shopping for the event, Rick decided it was time to return the discussion to the treasure.

"The dinner party is tomorrow, so there's plenty of time to go shopping. Should we start researching where this treasure might be?"

"Yes," said Shelli and Stephanie simultaneously.

"How about I call Barbara Stallings and see if we can pass this by her?" asked Danielle. "She might have more insights. She certainly knows the local history better than we do."

"No kidding," said Shelli. "She is amazing."

Danielle pulled out her phone and called Barbara. The table immediately plunged into more hypotheses as she waited for Barbara to pick up. She walked away from the table holding her finger to her other ear. After a couple of minutes, she hung up. "Barbara said she's off today and would love to talk with us. She suggested we meet her at Kawaiahaʻo Church in about an hour. Who wants to come?"

There was unanimous show of hands, and 25 minutes later they were piling into their car and on their way to church.

# Chapter 41: *Honolulu Burning*

The Bryants, Stephanie, and Ryan arrived at the front steps of Kawaiaha'o Church right on time. Waiting there was Barbara Stallings from the Bishop Museum and another young woman.

The tall clock tower centered high above them showed the correct time, which was a few minutes after 11 AM. The large arched doorway sat in the center of four 3-story white columns. Even from the outside, the scale of the grey color coral blocks was impressive. The August sky shown blue above the building and strong trade wind breezes helped make the heat and humidity bearable.

"Hello Barbara," said Danielle. "Thank you so much for agreeing to meet us on your day off."

"Oh it's my pleasure," said Barbara. "It's so good to see a family so interested in Hawaiian history. Plus it was an excuse for me to spend some time with my good friend and fellow researcher, Rachel Ma. Rachel has a Bachelor's degree in Religion, and is currently working on her Ph.D. in Pacific and Hawaiian History at U of H."

Rachel was tall with black shiny hair with brown highlights, an infectious smile, and fair colored skin. She could have passed for *Kristin Kreuk's* sister.

"Hello Rachel," said Danielle as she reached out her hand. She then made the introductions to the rest of the Bryant gang.

"Given what you told me on the phone, Danielle, I thought Rachel's background was perfect," said Barbara. "Plus she's gone to this church all her life. I hope you don't mind."

"Not at all. We're glad you're both here," said Danielle. She turned to Rachel. "I'm not sure if Barbara told you what we've been researching. If you noticed Rick's and Nikki's bandages, you can see the results of that research thus far. Fortunately HPD has rounded up all the criminals involved. That closed the criminal investigation, but we still have a lot of questions about what happened since 1884."

"Barbara spent the last half-hour giving me the highlights, so I think I'm caught up. And from what I gather, you think that if the 1884 newspaper story was true, the treasures would have been brought here for safekeeping."

"Correct," said Danielle. "We don't know exactly when or if it would have been brought here or who was involved in hiding it. We know the location of the treasure was known before the Chinatown fires given the stories we heard that were passed down through several generations. And given that this was oldest building still at the time and the most secure, other than the palace itself, it seemed like a good place to hide it. If it wasn't the church, then maybe it was another building or structure from that time. We know at some point that Stephen Chang's ancestors took possession of the treasure and that the knowledge of the hiding place was lost. But we don't know how much access Chinese immigrants would have had if it was hidden here. And even if we assume everything about the treasure was true and if it was hidden here, would the treasure still be in the church or on the grounds?"

"Ok, I think I understand the hypothesis. It explains why Barbara wanted my help. My Ph.D. thesis is focused on the religious history of Honolulu." There were a few scattered "ahhs" after that comment. Rachel continued.

"It makes sense to hide it at least temporarily at this church. We're not sure if this was the oldest building at the time, because it was only 42 years old. The city was already thriving when this was built, and there were some wooden structures still around at that time that were older. But except for the palace, this was the most enduring building at the time. Only the church has the title of the oldest today."

"The walls you see are over two feet thick and the blocks were up to 1500 pounds in weight. So if you wanted protection against storms and even invading forces, this would certainly do the trick. And in 1884, the number of Chinese immigrants in the area numbered over 18,000. The church welcomed anyone to its doors. And after the Chinatown fires, the church took in and cared for many displaced Chinese families. What many people don't realize was that there was a growing number of Chinese arriving that were converts to Christianity. So much so, that they opened their own church in the 1880's. Basically, what you are saying was feasible. But I am certain the treasure, if it existed at all, is not in the church or anywhere on the grounds."

"The Bryant group looked stunned with the last sentence. Unfazed by that, Rachel started her lecture. "Before we continue, let me say upfront that I do not believe there is any treasure. I have not read the newspaper article that has been referenced, but I have never read about or heard of any pirate raid on Iolani Palace or anywhere else nearby at that time. Barbara confirmed to me that she had never seen any record of this either. I admit that it is entirely plausible that the matter could have been hushed due to the embarrassment and potential threat to the nation's security. But to have no record or proof at all makes me doubt the existence. Newspapers routinely printed stories, whether true or not, to improve circulation. So just because it was printed in a respected paper, it doesn't mean it was true. Was there ever a follow-on to the story or any other documentation or evidence found?"

They all traded glances to each other and several blushed from embarrassment. Finally Rick spoke. "We did not find any other article. Shelli, Barbara and Danielle searched the archives for a period around that time. But no, we did not do an extensive search. We were more focused at the time on finding who was murdering people and why. And when the kidnapping occurred, it really didn't matter if we believed the treasure existed or not. The triad believed it was real, so we had to continue as if it was a given ... that it did exist."

"Oh my gosh, I didn't know someone was kidnapped," said Rachel. "I knew that your family was roughed up, but I didn't know the details."

"Sorry," said Barbara. "That's my fault. Thirty minutes was not enough time to cover all the details. The Bryants were able to rescue the woman taken by the triad. That was no small feat. You probably heard about the big explosion and ship sinking in Waimea Bay. That was the rescue effort. And 'roughed up' doesn't hardly cover what they went through. The details are being kept confidential until the trials are all over. I only know what happened because I was helping them."

Rachel scrutinized the group, and nodded her head slowly. "Well then. Let's assume that the King decreed that no one should speak of the pirate raid ... similar to what our judicial system has done with this most recent case."

They all remained quiet and absorbed her last words. Rachel continued. "The unfortunate truth; however, is that there is no way the treasure is still here in this building or on the grounds."

"Why?" asked Stephanie.

"Let's go inside, Stephanie and I'll give you my reason," said Rachel.

They all walked inside and took a seat in the front pew of the church. Rachel stood in front of them – the future professor in her was beginning to shine.

"The church has been around for a long time, but it hasn't escaped the ravages of time. They turned on electrical lights here in 1895. But when they began wiring for electrical lights in 1893, they found that termites had eaten away much of the roof support beams. They had to condemn the church and it was closed from 1894 to 1895 while the interior and roof were repaired. In 1925, the church was condemned again. Termites had wreaked havoc throughout the interior wood, and they stripped out everything until it was just the coral walls. It was definitely an extreme makeover. They rebuilt the interior to be more in line with its original New England style and simplicity. Most of what you see today in here came during that remodel. Birds were constantly pecking the exterior, so they put a coating of concrete over the outer wall. Imported slate was added to the roof. New insect resistant redwood pews were added. A new organ was installed and new concrete rooms were constructed to house the organ mechanisms. Then in 1965, there was another round of refurbishment. Painting and repairs to the wood and roof were made at that time. The concrete coating on the outer walls was removed. So there is no way a hidden treasure inside the building could still be here."

Rachel paused for a few moments to see if anyone had any questions. There were none so the lecture continued. "There were a number of changes on the grounds over the years. In 1899, the high wall surrounding the church was pulled down, an artesian well was dug, and a lawn and a line of royal palms were planted. In the 1925 remodel, the grounds were replanted. And a new fountain pool was built to commemorate the church's name, which means 'the water of Hao.' Between the 1925 remodel and the 1940's, a Sunday school building and a social hall were added. And in the 1965 there was another replanting, and the fountain was rebuilt. So again, if there were something buried it would have likely been found well before today."

"So if the treasure were ever stored here, it was likely removed before the interior work in 1893 or the 1886 Chinatown fire," said Barbara.

"I would guess so," said Rachel.

"That's not much time to be stored here," said Rick. "And if you think about the size of the treasure, it would have been difficult to hide it in such a public place. Look how many chests it took to hold all of our coins, and that was just a fraction of the size of the treasure that was taken."

"What chests?" asked Rachel with a surprised expression. Rick explained what they had done. "That's so clever," said Rachel.

"This seemed like such a great place when we were talking this over this morning," said Danielle. "But given what you just detailed, there is no way it could have ever been stored here. Where else could a treasure have been stored?"

Rachel thought a minute and then said, "The Cathedral of Our Lady of Peace was built just after Kawaiaha'o Church. And there were other churches and religious centers, like the Chinese church and Kaumakapili Church built in the 1880's. But for the reason Rick mentioned, they were not likely places to hide such a big treasure."

"There were other buildings at the time, like the Wo Fat restaurant," said Barbara.

"Hey I saw that building when I was in Chinatown," said Nikki. "That had a closed sign in the window. So that was around back in the 1880's?"

"No," answered Barbara. "Wo Fat is the oldest restaurant in Honolulu and was built in 1882. But that original building was burnt down in 1886 in the Chinatown fire. It was rebuilt and burnt down again in the 1900 Chinatown fire. It was rebuilt again and that lasted until 1937. It was torn down and the current building, which was a new location for the restaurant, is the one you see today. The restaurant finally closed more than ten years ago,"

Nikki pulled out her tablet PC from the purse she had on her shoulder. "I'm marking these locations on Google Earth. We can take a look at them when we leave here."

"Given the regular shipment of food and supplies to a restaurant, it would have been easy to get the treasure in and out of there," said Rick. "But if the treasure were stored in Chinatown, all artifacts except the coins would have been destroyed. And with the kind of heat that probably existed, even the coins may have melted."

"Were there any other places that escaped the fires in Chinatown or in downtown Honolulu where the treasure could be hidden?" asked Stephanie.

"There are a number of buildings that were built prior to 1880's that still exist today. Those include the post office and downtown Bishop properties. No way would the post office be a place for treasure, and I am well aware of the history of all the Bishop structures. Any treasures," Barbara said with fingered air quotes, "were well documented historical artifacts. There was a lot of new construction in the 1880's and 1890's. The Royal Saloon Building and The Pantheon Bar, both on Nu'uanu, started construction in the late 1880's. The Royal Saloon still exists today. But the Pantheon was rebuilt around 1911. Barbara paused a second as she was scrolling through her mental file cabinet. "Oh, and there is The Encore Saloon Building. That was built in 1886. I remember because it opened just before the first Chinatown fire. It survived both fires and it still exists today."

"That could be a place they could have hidden it," said Stephanie excitedly.

"Got it," Nikki. She turned her tablet around and held it high. The black and white picture was from the Hawai'i State Archives. Everyone except Nikki stood up and crowded around the 10-inch screen.

"What does it look like now?" asked Shelli.

Nikki turned the tablet around and quickly clicked on it with her index finger. Seconds later she dragged her finger over the screen. She smiled and then flipped it over for the group to see. "The sign is gone, but you can clearly see this is the same building."

"That's sounds like a good place to check out," said Ryan.

"I was walking all over Chinatown when I was looking for Stephen's grandfather. But I don't think I went in here though.

"Let me see that," said Shelli.

"Why?" asked Nikki.

"I'd like to Google the place to see what we can find out about its history."

Nikki jumped a bit and then felt her purse. She reached inside, pulled out her phone, and reached inside. "It's Stephen Chang."

*(Encore Saloon)*[3]

"Answer it," said Shelli. She reached out with her hand open. Nikki gave her the tablet and answered the call. Shelli clicked away on the tablet with Stephanie looking over her shoulder.

"Hi Stephen, what's up?" asked Nikki. She listened for his response and then asked him to hold a second while she told her family. She clicked mute and spoke. "Stephen was at the police station giving more of his statement. After he finished, Kaleho pulled him aside and told him we were talking about the treasure. So he called us."

"The poor kid lost his brother," said Danielle. "And he almost lost his grandfather. I think he should come along with us. Maybe he can get some closure."

"Ok," said Nikki. "Let me get him up to speed and then I'll tell him to meet us down in Chinatown." She pressed the mute again and started relaying the information they had up to that time.

While Nikki was talking to Stephen, Shelli burst out, "Holy mackerel. I found something fantastic about The Encore Saloon Building."

"What is it?" asked Danielle. Nikki excused herself from her conversation and listened too.

"The Encore Saloon Building was renovated in 1980," answered Shelli. "And during the renovation, the workers found a hidden passageway. They said they believed it to be a hideout for shanghaied sailors. But what if they were wrong? Maybe it is where they had hidden the treasure."

---

[3] *From Hawaii State Archives Digital Collection. http://archives1.dags.hawaii.gov/gallery2/main.php?g2_view=keyalbum.KeywordAlbum&g2_keyword=Honolulu&g2_itemId=5877*

Nikki didn't give anyone a chance to speak. "Stephen, we got to go. We're heading straight to the corner of Hotel and Nu'uanu. Meet us there. Bye."

"We don't have room for all of us," said Rick to Barbara and Rachel. "But you're welcome to come along."

Barbara looked Rachel. Rachel nodded to her. "We'd love to. We'll follow you down there in my car."

An hour later the Bryant gang were standing in front of what was The Encore Saloon Building, with Barbara and Rachel in tow. Stephen Chang was waiting for them.

"So we're back in Chinatown...again," said Stephen to Nikki.

Before Nikki could respond, Ryan grabbed her hand in his and held it up. "Sorry dude, but she's holding my hand this time."

Nikki blushed. She knew Ryan had seen the quadcopter footage of her holding hands with Stephen as they pretended to be dating college students a week earlier.

"I know, I know," said Stephen with a smile. "And after seeing her take down two triad members here in Chinatown and the Dragon Lady, you are definitely the safest walking man on the island, brah."

Everyone laughed at the statement. Rick then followed it up with a couple of moans from his injuries.

"So I got part of the story on the phone, but why are we meeting here?" asked Stephen.

Nikki told him about the article Shelli found from 1980. "And we came down here to search for clues about the treasure. We didn't know if we'd find anything, but I don't think any of us expected this."

They all turned to view at the new Encore Saloon Building. There were new restaurants lined up in the first floor suites, with the exception of a new bakery. The aromas of food drifted from each.

"I didn't know this had been all rebuilt," said Nikki. "I guess in this case, Google Streetview is out of date."

"Yeah, some guy from California came in and bought the place out in 2014. He put up these new restaurants. The top floors are small offices for startups," said Stephen. "There have been more than a dozen new restaurants that have come in over the last few years."

"Returning the town hotspot to as it once was in the 1880's," said Barbara.

"I'm kinda hungry," said Rick. "The lunch crowd's thinning and I think we need to discuss what's next. These are all recently hired restaurant workers here – no shop owners. With this new construction, there's nothing left for us to investigate here."

They all agreed and walked into one of the restaurants in the building off of Hotel Street. It had a big table surrounded with chairs, which was perfect for their large group. They all took a seat. After lunch orders were taken, they continued their discussion.

"So if we stay with the premise that the story of the pirate raid is true, and we take the information from Stephen's grandfather that the treasure moved hands to the Chinese immigrant population..." said Danielle. She took a breath and continued, "... and that the location of the treasure was last known to be held in Chinatown, but the location of that treasure was lost after the great fires at the turn of the century, what do we do next? We don't know how it got from the pirates hands to the Chinese immigrant hands. But we're what, five blocks from Iolani palace, so it is likely that the Chinatown merchants would have known about the raid and had seen the coinage being spent in their stores. Somehow they acquired the treasure. Perhaps it's not important knowing how or when they got it."

"Wait a minute," said Shelli with an excited expression. "Remember when we were at Barbara's office doing research?" Except for Rachel, they acknowledged with nods. She turned to her father. "And Dad, you remember when I told you what I found?"

Rick said nothing, looking like he had just taken the last cookie in the cookie jar. Crickets would start chirping at any minute. Shelli's expression was easily readable. It was one of those *oh-my-gosh-dad-you-never-listen-to-me* looks.

"Well to remind you, Dad, I told you that a secret society of 23 Chinese immigrants were arrested. They had knives and were planning something, but no one knew what it was. That was in 1885."

"That's before the great fires, and after the raid," said Nikki. "They could have seen the money being spent and were planning to take it. Steal the stolen treasure."

"If the secret society was a tong, then that knowledge was probably passed down to the triad we just took down," said Rick.

"And they probably never tried to find it because they thought it was just a made up story, a legend," said Stephen. "Until my brother used those coins. My grandfather's old Hawaiian coins was all that was needed to make the triad believe it was real."

Stephen put his head down.

"Stephen, your brother was killed," said Danielle. "The triad was to blame. He was just like any other college kid. And he did what he did to help a friend. Remember that...he did nothing to deserve his loss of life."

Stephen nodded. Rick sensed the tension and decided to turn attention away from Stephen. He cleared his throat, which drew everyone's glance. "So let's create a timeline. Pirate raid in 1884. Tong discovers the treasure exists and steals it. Hide's it until 1886 when the great fires cause the knowledge of the treasure's location to be erased. Only stories of the treasure are passed down over time. We know that in 1980, they found a secret room in this building. So if the treasure was in this building, it was assuredly moved before then."

"And who knows if it was even stored here at the Encore?" said Danielle. "There were the other buildings Barbara mentioned – the other bars."

"There was the Royal Saloon, Pantheon Bar, and the Encore Saloon. They were all on Nu'uanu. Why so many bars?" asked Shelli. Shelli was not drinking age, so the concept of a bar was foreign to her. And to have so many in what she considered paradise was clearly perplexing to her.

"There have always been a constant stream of ships coming to this island since it was discovered," said Barbara. "By the early 1800's, there were about a hundred ships a year pulling into Honolulu. With that long voyage, the sailors were thirsty for a drink and good times. Nu'uanu was called Fid Street by sailors back then, which was their term for spirits.

"Ghosts?" asked Stephanie.

"No," chortled Barbara. "Spirits as in alcoholic beverage."

"Oh," responded a blushing Stephanie.

"By the 1880's, there were thousands of sailors a year visiting Honolulu. So between locals and the constant stream of sailors, the bars had a thriving business."

"So a group of pirates, which looked like any other sailors at the time, walking through the streets of Honolulu at night was not so unusual," said Rick. Barbara nodded. Rick continued. "And there was a good chance that some of the original crewman ended back up here. " Rick then sang, "and…

> What shall we do with a drunken sailor?
>
> What shall we do with a drunken sailor?
>
> What shall we do with a drunken sailor?
>
> Early in the morning.
>
> Put him in the long-boat and make him bail her.
>
> Early in the morning.
>
> What shall we do with a drunken soldier?
>
> Early in the morning.
>
> Get him to tell us where is the pirate treasure.
>
> Early in the morning.

The group all laughed. "Do you know the whole song?" asked Danielle.

"Sure, you wanna hear it?" asked Rick.

"No!" said Shelli loudly. The group laughed again.

"Did you learn that when you were a kid?" asked Nikki.

"Yes, from *The Wild Wild West*," said Rick.

"What?" asked Shelli with a confused look.

"*The Wild Wild West*," said Rick. "I used to love that show when I was growing up. It was about the first Secret Service agents back in the west. There was this evil genius, Dr. Loveless that sang the song. I was about nine or ten years old at the time. I repeated it around the house one too many times and my mom put an end to it."

Laughter broke out again. "But in context to the treasure, there was no reason not to think that the treasure survived the great fires. Stephen's grandfather had evidence of those coins. He wasn't a collector, correct Stephen?"

"He was not a collector," answered Stephen.

"And I can assume that there are few, if any, family residences that survived all this time?" asked Rick.

Barbara paused a moment. "I can't think of any."

"The palace, churches, the post office, and all the other buildings that did exist back then have been renovated," said Rick. "Correct?"

"That's incorrect," said Rachel. In unison, all heads turned to her. "The Kuan Yin Temple was built in 1880. Its architectural history is not well documented, but has been a mainstay for the local Chinese people since it was constructed. I do not think it has changed much since it was built."

"That just brought back some memories," said Stephen. "I know my grandfather has gone to that temple in the past. Once, when I was a boy, we visited him and he smelt strong of incense. I asked him why he smelt that way, and he said he had gone to the temple. So

207

whenever I saw him and he smelt of incense, I always assumed he'd been to the temple. When I was older, I found out it was the Kuan Yin Temple that he was visiting.

"You didn't mention that when we were looking for him before, Stephen," said Nikki.

"I know," said Stephen. "I forgot all about it until Rachel mentioned the name."

"Why don't we eat and then head over to the temple?" asked Ryan. "Maybe someone can there remembers something of the treasure."

As if on cue, the food started to arrive at the table. While everybody else started to dig into their meals, Shelli took the tablet PC out that she had borrowed from Nikki earlier. "That's not good."

"What is it?" asked Danielle.

"I looked up the Kuan Yin Temple and it closes at 2 pm."

Ryan checked the time. "It's one-twenty now."

Rick grabbed their waiter and asked for the check. Then he turned to the group and said, "I hate to rush lunch, but grab whatever you can and let's go. It's not far away, but it will take us at least twenty minutes by the time we park."

Rick paid for the lunch. They had all ordered sandwiches, so they grabbed their food and ate as they made their way back to their vehicles.

Parking was not available on the street in front of the temple, so they had to park in the Foster Botanical Garden next door. It was 1:50 pm as they walked through the temple gate. The gate was framed with red columns and a green roof. A hanging black sign with gold letters said they were at the right place, the Kuan Yin Temple.

Rachel spoke as they entered. "Be quiet and respectful in here. This is a working temple. There are occasionally monks here, and people worshipping. There will be incense sticks to light if you wish. People leave food and flowers as offerings. No photos should be taken."

The place was not large and was actually surrounded by the Gardens. The temple had a few steps leading up to it. The structure had an ornate two-tier roof. A wrap around lanai with bright red columns was accented with green and yellow cornices. The rectangular building's roof had corners turned up like many classic Asian structures.

They walked inside and saw neat settings of fruit and bouquets of tropical flowers lined up along the three gold statues. Rachel said, "Kuan Yin is known as the Goddess of Mercy. She is worshiped most often by women, and is known to help women bear children. But the goddess also comforts the troubled, the sick, the lost, and the unfortunate. She also protects seafarers, farmers and travelers, so she was a perfect fit for the Chinese immigrants in a new land."

A smallish man appeared suddenly to the group. He looked at Stephen and spoke to him in Chinese. Stephen turned toward the group and said, "Closing time, folks."

"Ask him about the treasure of 1880's and the pirate raid, Stephen," said Stephanie. "We'll lose a whole day if we don't ask him now."

"I'll try," said Stephen. He began an animated discussion with the man. Rachel, who apparently also spoke Chinese, joined in some of the discussion. The man was quiet for a moment, and then held his hands out as if he was saying stay. He said a few quick words to Stephen and walked around them toward the main gate.

"He said wait here while he closes the main gate," said Stephen.

The man corralled the few remaining other visitors to the main gate and quickly locked the set of modern green bars behind the gate. He then passed by them again and just motioned to stay without a word. He disappeared behind the building.

A few minutes later, an older Asian man with white hair came from the direction the other man had disappeared. He walked slowly, and somewhat feebly. He seemed alert; however, and never took his eyes off of Stephen as he approached.

"No way," said Stephen.

"What?" asked Shelli. "Do you know him?"

Stephen turned around to the rest of the group and said, "That's my grandfather."

As Stephen's grandfather approached, Stephen stepped forward. His demeanor changed noticeable. He stood with his hand out. His grandfather shook his hand and the traded the greeting "Nin hao." Then Stephen stood to the side of his grandfather and introduced each person slowly, and his grandfather nodded and said "Ni hao" to each.

Afterwards the two began an exchange. It was mostly Stephen talking with his grandfather listening. Everyone else stood back a ways in a semicircle. Rachel listened intently, then said quietly, "Stephen is telling his grandfather why we are here. He is giving a detailed account of the treasure history as we know it."

Stephen's grandfather motioned for the group to follow him. He walked to the rear of the facility. The property of the temple was separated from the Foster Botanical Gardens by a few tall palm trees and plantings. The vast lawn and a greenhouse lay beyond the trees. No one else could be seen walking around the Gardens at the moment.

Grandfather led the way and they moved on to the lawn of the Gardens. He motioned for them to sit and he spoke to Rachel. "He wants us to sit," said Rachel. "Mr. Bryant, please sit closest to the front followed by Mrs. Bryant. Barbara you next and the children in descending age. Rachel was the last to sit and completed the semicircle at a respectable distance from the grandfather. Stephen started to sit as well, but his grandfather stopped him and they walked a few steps away from the rest of the group. There was some quiet discussion followed by some much louder words by the Stephen's grandfather. But Stephen kept his tone hushed. He pointed to Rick and said a few words, Nikki and a few words, and repeated for Shelli and Danielle.

"What's he saying?" whispered Stephanie to Rachel.

Rachel put her finger to her lips and shook her head.

Shelli turned the tablet PC in her hand and swiped it a few times. Danielle softly cleared her throat to get Shelli's attention. Danielle's shake of her head related a clear message to Shelli. She blushed and rested the tablet in her lap.

The discussion finally ended. Grandfather looked directly into each person's eyes around the circle. Then he sat down in a fluid motion and crossed his legs. He sat close to Rick and his grandson sat simultaneously to his other side.

"Grandfather is ready to tell us a story," said Stephen. "He will speak in Mandarin and give us the whole story. He asked that I relay the story back to you in a private place where no one can hear us talk. And Rachel, if you would, please listen carefully so that you can help me repeat this later on."

"I am honored to help."

Grandfather talked in short bursts. He looked directly at Stephen as he talked. He occasionally closed his eyes when he paused, as if he was remembering details. Stephen interrupted him several times with what appeared to be questions, but not to the point of annoying his grandfather. Rachel said nothing, but sometimes nodded at the same time as Stephen.

Grandfather slapped his kneecaps lightly and stood at the end of his long story. Everyone else stood, except for Rick. His legs had gone numb from setting with his legs crossed. Danielle saw the pain in his eyes as he rose slowly and reached to help him. Stephen walked and talked with this grandfather as they all came around to the front gate. The man they had met earlier was standing at the gate waiting for them as they approached. Grandfather spoke a few more words to the group and followed it with "zài jiàn" to each person as they passed out the gate.    Rick and Stephen were the last ones to the gate. Grandfather reached out and shook hands with Rick.

"Zhù nín jiàn kāng cháng shòu," said Stephen's grandfather,   Rick looked to Stephen for translation.

"He wishes you a long and healthy life," said Stephen.   Rick asked him to please relay the same message back, and Stephen did.   Rick nodded and followed his family to the right toward the Foster Botanical Gardens parking lot.

"Míng tiān jiàn," said Stephen. He trailed Rick to the parking lot, turning once to waive to his grandfather.

The group huddled tightly in the parking lot behind the Bryants' vehicle. "Grandfather is being cautious for good reason.   We need to talk about this somewhere private.   Do you mind if we meet back at your ship, Mr. Bryant?"

"No, of course we can meet there," said Rick.

The Bryant gang was followed by Barbara, who had Rachel and Stephen with her, to the **Amphitrite**. Danielle was the first to welcome Barbara and Rachel on the vessel, since it was the first time for both of them.   She gave them a quick tour and met in the conference room when done.    It took a few minutes for the shock of all they had seen on the boat to wear off for Barbara and Rachel.   Shelli and Nikki were at the normal places at two of the command stations.    The Situation Awareness Display glowed blue on one wall.    After everyone was situated, Rick cleared his throat and spoke.

"Stephen, you have the floor."

"I'd like to stay seated if that's OK. I'd feel more comfortable."

"Perfectly fine, dear," said Danielle.

"Rachel, please pipe in if I screw anything up or if you want to add anything."

Rachel smiled. "Let me say before you start, that I'm still in somewhat of a shock. First to hear of all this family has been through over the last week or two; secondly to hear what Stephen's grandfather said.   And finally, to see what you have on this ship.   It's like being in a movie – truly unbelievable." She paused a second, then said to Stephen, "And of course I'll help you."

Stephen started the story.   "The raid was real.   It took place in December 1884, and there was a substantial treasure taken by the pirates."

A small roar burst out from the group around the table.  Smiles and relief on people's faces accompanied laughter and a number of "*I told you so's.*"

"Quiet please," said Danielle. "Let him continue."

"Just as we thought, the treasure did not leave the islands. The pirates seemed to have been paid part of the American currency for their effort, but not all of it. The head pirate also demanded some of the silverware, and some of the loot that they had stolen from the other homes in the city."

"The actual raid was known throughout the Chinese community before the pirates ever left. And the appearance of coins for all kinds of supplies in Chinatown stores early in 1885 just made it common knowledge. But no one would speak of it openly to outsiders because they worried about deportation, jail, being beaten, or death."

"Rachel, grandfather started talking about some United States act or law that was passed, and some historical events following it. Do you know what he was talking about?"

"Yes, I do," said Rachel. "In 1882, the Chinese Exclusion Act had stopped the immigration of Chinese into the USA. That effectively stopped immigration into Hawai'i as well. Wives and families that were supposed to eventually come over, were not allowed. Then in 1885, the Japanese immigrants started to arrive. A *hui*, or secret society formed. It was basically a branch of the local tong." She looked at Shelli. "That was the group of 23 that you found in your research, Shelli." Shelli beamed with the acknowledgement.

"That was December 1885 that they were arrested by the Marshal at the time -- Marshal Soper," continued Rachel. "The hui members never told what they were planning, but according to Stephen's grandfather they were planning on stealing the treasure. Apparently they had figured out where it was by that time. Stephen's grandfather said that wherever its secret hiding place was back then, it has long since been forgotten. In January 1886, twenty-two of the society were tried and convicted."

"What about the one person that didn't get convicted?" asked Shelli.

"It was believed that he was an informer," answered Stephen. "And he was found murdered a few weeks after the trial. The tong was undoubtedly bigger than the twenty-two tried and convicted. There was probably some payback dealt to the traitor. Rachel, can you tell them what he said about the first fire?"

"Sure," said Rachel. "I'm going to add a little background to what he said, which should give a little more context to the story." She paused until she saw nods from Stephen and others around the table. "King Kalākaua was well liked by the Chinese. Mostly local workers and craftsmen, many of which were Chinese, were employed to build the palace. A well-known Chinese woodworker at the time casted the Hawaiian coat of arms and made the panels on the ceilings of the verandas of the palace. And two enormous bronze vases were given to Kalākaua for the palace by the Chinese community at his 1883 coronation. In April 1886, the great Chinatown fire took place. According to Stephen's grandfather, that event effectively stopped all planning for the treasure. During the fire, the King himself came to Chinatown and helped direct the firefight. And after the fire he convened a meeting with his Ministry and set up a fund to help the displaced immigrants. Temporary shelter, clothing, and food for several months were provided to the Chinese. That was something unheard of to the immigrants. It actually took more than a week after the help was available before the Chinese families took advantage of it in any numbers. They were too skeptical at first. Although the Chinese families were industrious and benefited from the trade brought in by members of the Committee of Safety, the kindness by the royals aligned many in the Honolulu Chinese population with the monarchy."

Nikki had started typing on the computer station while Rachel spoke, and pulled up a picture of Chinatown after the fire on the Situation Awareness Display. It looked like a nuclear bomb had hit the place.

"Thank you Nikki," said Rachel. "The Committee of Safety was gearing up by this time to act against the monarchy. They had plenty of money now with the pirate treasure, which reduced the need to dip into their own pockets to fund their efforts. In 1887, and under threat of gunpoint, King Kalākaua was forced to sign the Bayonet Constitution. This new constitution basically stripped the King of most of his powers. It also took away the right to vote from most of the native Hawaiians. Only rich Hawaiians, Americans and Europeans could vote."

"Although the overthrow of the monarchy did not occur until 1893 with the help of the U.S. militia, the Bayonet Constitution was the pivotal point for the Hawaiian monarchy."

"Grandfather said that these events planned by the Committee required substantial expenditures prior to the event. The local Chinese began to realize that something was going to happen whenever there was a spending surge using the Hawaiian coins and American currency. By this point in time, the old tong had regrouped and secret meetings had resumed. Discussions of stealing the treasure became increasingly supported by members. And many of the members were Chinese business owners. It was also decided during the meetings that they should approach loyal native Hawaiians to help, since their right to vote and their king's power had been removed. That turned out to be a good decision. Rachel?"

"In 1888, some of the Hawaiians that were close to the king reported that a rebellion was being planned. It wasn't until 1889 that Robert Wilcox led a rebellion. He was a native Hawaiian that wanted real reform for his people. You probably know this better than me, Barbara," said Rachel

"Robert William Kalanihiapo Wilcox, a.k.a. the Iron Duke of Hawai'i, was not loyal to the King, but he did not like the new political party formed by the Committee of Safety. They cut spending on some of his programs. He wanted to force the King to sign a new constitution. The King got wind of the rebellion, and made sure he was absent when Wilcox appeared at Iolani with his force of men. Wilcox was finally met later that day by the *Honolulu Rifles*. We know the Rifles were being directed by the Committee well before that point," said Barbara.

"Grandfather said that while the Rifles were going after Wilcox, the Chinese tong made their move to steal the treasure," said Stephen. "He doesn't know how they did it, but the entire treasure was confiscated. The treasure was divided up between the Hawaiian's that helped and the Chinese tong. The Hawaiian's took about a quarter of the money, but they seemed more interested in the sacred items, like Kamehameha's cloak. My grandfather said that it was learned later that many of those artifacts were secretly returned to Queen Liliuokalani after she was inaugurated. But my grandfather also said they were later sold off with a lot of her possessions when she was forced to abdicate the throne."

"That explains a lot," said Barbara. "In 1966 the Friends of Iolani Palace was formed, and one of their primary missions was to reacquire all the auctioned items. They've had great success thus far. They found items spread over 30 states and several countries."

"Mrs. Bryant told us about that earlier today," said Stephanie. "She was wondering what was actually sold off and what was missing before the auction."

"They used a list of palace inventory made prior to the auction, and pictures of room layouts," said Barbara. "Many of the items had an official seal on them from Queen Liliuokalani and the Hawaiian kings that preceded her. I was able to get that list while researching for the Bryants. The list had some of the items that were mentioned in the Daily Alta newspaper article. So it made me question how they could have been stolen. But if they were returned to the Queen, then that would explain the discrepancy."

"And history shows that Queen Liliuokalani was also well liked by the Chinese," said Rachel. "She heavily supported the Buddhist and Shinto priests. Her support of the two prevented them from being banned by the Territorial government. And she often appeared in newspaper articles in China and Japan due to her support. So that confirms the claim by Stephen's grandfather that they conspired with the native Hawaiians to get the treasure. They all wanted to see the monarchy reinstated."

"What happened to the remaining treasure?" asked Stephanie.

Stephen began to answer, "The treasure was taken to the Empire Saloon Building and hidden ...."

"Wait, I know...in a secret passageway that no one else knew about!" burst out Shelli. "I found that in an article, remember?"

Stephen laughed at her exuberance. "Yeah, that's right. Grandfather said it took a full team of horses to move the Hawaiian coins, the remaining American currency, jewels, silverware and other valuables. The tong assigned my great-great-great grandfather and his son to take care of the treasure. It was to be used to support the community and to help the Chinese families in need. My ancestors also apparently helped start the Kuan Yin Temple."

"Remember I mentioned that the Kuan Yin comforts the unfortunates and protects seafarers, farmers and travelers. Well that treasure certainly helped that mission," said Rachel.

"According to Grandfather, they decided to split the treasure after the Chinatown fire in 1900. The Empire Saloon Building made it through both fires, so they thought it was a sign that they shouldn't keep it in one spot."

"They must have thought the treasure was lucky after surviving all that time," said Ryan.

"On the contrary," said Rachel. "The treasure was considered to be unlucky."

"But the treasure has helped lots of people," said Shelli. "Why would they think that?"

"First off, the coinage was mostly minted in 1884 even though it was imprinted with 1883. And secondly, the treasure was stolen in 1884. The year of both of those events ended in a four. 'Four' is considered the worst bad luck number of all numbers."

"Why is the number four considered unlucky?" asked Stephanie.

"Chinese culture considers homophonous words to be connected," said Rachel. She saw the puzzled looks on the kids and Rick. Only Danielle and Barbara nodded with understanding. "Homophonous words are words that sound the same but mean something different. The number four sounds like the word 'death' in Chinese. We think of thirteen as being unlucky. Four is considered even more unlucky than thirteen. Elevators and buildings in Hong Kong often do not have any floors with the number four. So you'll find 4, 14, 24, 34, and the whole range of 40's missing on the elevator button panel."

"Grandfather said that some Chinatown residents considered that the treasure was so unlucky that they blamed it as the cause of the second fire in 1900. And Grandfather agreed that it was unlucky. He pointed out that the 23 tong members were caught when they planned to steal it." He paused a moment like something spurred a new thought in his mind. "And just realized that was 23 and not 24 members – they would have avoided that number of men. Grandfather said that some people believed that their capture was a warning sign. Then the fire and the plague. Our family volunteered to take care of the treasure, and we have had our share of tragedies with the latest being Paul." Stephen choked up as he said his brother's name.

Rachel gave Stephen a moment to recover and picked up the story. "Stephen's grandfather said that they split up the treasure into one big lot and one small lot. The bigger lot made up about three-quarters of the treasure and it went to the Kuan Yin Temple and the other quarter remained at the Empire. Stephen's ancestors took responsibility for dispersing the treasure from the temple. Another family took possession of the other treasure. The family names were kept secret to protect each other, and only the priests and Stephen's family knew their treasure was at the temple."

"The Kuan Yin Temple is not a big building," said Rick. "How did they manage to hide that much treasure for so long?"

"Grandfather said that they found out that the U.S. Government was going to melt the coinage. They were collecting it at the local banks in 1901 and 1902. My ancestors knew that they would no longer be able to spend the money, and some families that needed help wouldn't accept the unlucky coins. So they decided to get rid of it. My great-great-great grandfather began spending the coins all over Honolulu. They bought anything made of pure silver and gold, but mostly gold. Buying gold helped reduce the volume of the treasure. To keep suspicions down, he had his son take several large chests of the coins to Maui to buy silverware and jewelry in Lahaina. They focused on the larger denominations."

"Dad that agrees with the coin chart we put together" said Nikki. "Most of the coins melted by the Mint were the dollar and half-dollar coins." Rick nodded in agreement.

"By the time the coins were melted in 1903, they had gotten rid of all but a few thousand of the bigger denomination."

"But there were over forty-six thousand coins of just the dollar coins left after the meltdown. If only a few thousand were left in the remaining treasure, and they are not in coin collections now, where did the other coins go?"

"My grandfather didn't say, but I would bet they were part of the treasure that remained at the Empire Saloon. Maybe they didn't do what my ancestors did. Maybe they melted their coins instead."

"What happened to your ancestors treasure after that?" asked Stephanie.

"My great-great-grandfather, the one that went back and forth from Maui, decided it would be easier to hide all the gold and silver if it was melted down. That took a few years, but they had it done before World War One."

"But how did they manage the distribution of gold and silver bars? I mean if a family needed financial help, wouldn't it be strange if they showed up to a store with a big hunk of gold or silver?" asked Danielle.

"My grandfather didn't explain any of that to us. I didn't think to ask. He said the gold and silver were a safe way to save during the great depression – they didn't lose anything in

214

failed banks or the stock market. But he did say they had to get rid of all their gold in the 1930's."

"Ahh," said Barbara. "The Great Reserve Act of 1934. After the stock market crash in 1929 and in the middle of the Great Depression, President Roosevelt had to do something to get the economy moving. The U.S. Dollar was tied to the gold standard, which made it hard to increase its value and thereby increase its buying power. So he passed an executive order in 1933, which was passed into law in 1934 that made it illegal for US citizens anywhere in the world to own gold. They had to turn it in for paper currency. The Act increased the price of gold, which in turn caused gold to flow into the country. Fort Knox was built to house all that gold. The Act worked brilliantly to stimulate the economy. It wasn't until 1975 that US Citizens could own and trade in gold again."

"1975?" said Stephen. "Grandfather said he took over the management of the treasure in the mid-1960's. He said their resources had greatly dwindled by that time. They had about three hundred thousand dollars left. He said he sought ways to try to make the money grow without risk, but he said that the best that he could do was to spread it across a number of banks. He said in 1977 he decided to convert it back to gold."

"Wait a minute Stephen," interrupted Rick. "Nikki, can you look up the history of gold prices for me?"

Nikki quickly located a graph that showed the price of gold since 1900. The chart showed it flat until 1934, which then bumped up to a plateau until the 1960's. It jumped around a little bit in price for the next decade, but after 1975 the price made an incredible jump in price.

"According to the chart, gold was about $135 per ounce in 1977," said Rick. "It may not have been available to him at the time for that price. Let's say he paid $140 per ounce. Gold now is well over $1200 per ounce. So that's a great return on his investment."

"Well he said he didn't keep it," said Stephen. "Rachel, do you remember what year he sold it?"

"He said 1980 to 1981. He sold half of it then. To minimize attention, he sold over the period of a year," answered Rachel.

"According to the graph, that was at its 20 year high," said Rick. "That's incredible luck. That sale doubled his cash reserves to over six hundred thousand dollars. Plus he still had half the gold. What did he do with the cash?"

"He said he put some money back into the bank and then bought one hundred thousand shares of stock," said Stephen.

"Did he say what company or companies he bought stock in?" asked Rick.

"Apple."

"Apple? Holy cow, Stephen. Was that 1981 that he bought it?"

"I think that's what he said. He said he thought it was a mistake and it worried him for many years," answered Stephen. "He said he just sold all his shares. That's why he wasn't around. He got one of his fisherman friends to take him to Maui. He made sure my family was safely in hiding and then took a flight to New York. That's why we didn't see him leave the Honolulu airport when we were searching for him. He said it was the first time he had ever flown."

Rick laid his head down on the table and shook it.

215

"What's wrong, Rick?" said Danielle.

Rick lifted his head. "Nikki, check the number of stock splits that Apple has had in its history. Shelli, what is the current price of the Apple stock? And what was the price in 1981"

Shelli answered first. "The stock was $2.71 per share when it went public, whatever that means, in 1981. It's going now for about $115 per share."

Then Nikki answered. "It has split 4 separate times, Dad. The first three times was a two-to-one stock split, but the last time was a seven-to-one split."

Rick looked pale at the numbers.

"Rick, please what's wrong?" said Danielle.

"You don't understand. Nikki just told us if you bought one share of stock in 1981, the stock split a total of 56 times since then. Stephen said his grandfather bought one hundred thousand shares. Nikki, do the math."

Nikki typed *56 x 100,000 x $115.00* into the calculator on the Situation Awareness Display. Then she hit "=," and instantly the value *$644,000,000.00* appeared on the display.

"Understand? Do I need to explain that number to anyone?" asked Rick in a monotone voice. Everyone was stunned. Someone moved in their chair and the tiny squeak it created echoed as if it were a train emergency breaking.

"Did your grandfather explain how he knew to make these choices?" asked Rick.

"He said he prayed to the goddess Kuan Yin for guidance," answered Stephen with his eyes still glued to the Situation Awareness Display. "And he said she gave him visions in his sleep."

"Do me a favor, Stephen. The next time your grandfather decides to invest in something, give me a call," said Rick.

"Think what the triad would have done if they knew about this…treasure," said Nikki.

"I shudder to think what they would have done," said Danielle.

Stephen finally took his eyes off the display. "That explains my grandfather's last comment to me today. He told me to ask that you never tell anyone about the treasure."

"You have our word on that," said Danielle without hesitation.

"Don't worry, Stephen" said Rick. "I don't think anyone would ever believe us anyway."

Rick took the precaution to erase the last hour of video and audio data that were automatically recorded in the conference room digital archives. He made a point of showing Stephen it was deleted so that he could feel at ease that no record of their discussion was made.

As the team stood up and started saying their goodbyes, no one noticed the tablet that Shelli had placed at the far end of the conference room table when she had entered the room. It was the one she had taken from Nikki – the one she had at the temple. And as any teenager with a limited attention span, it was the one she had completed forgotten about. The mp3 recorder app blinked on and flashed 'DISK FULL, RECORDING STOPPED.'

# Chapter 42: *Ohana*

It was night and Rick leaned against the largest of several coconut palms in Kaleho's back yard. The concrete slab lanai stepped down to his right onto the green lawn that had a few flat lava stones that led to a big outdoor stone grill. The cool grill would soon be the resting place for the pig that was cooking slowing in the large *imu* next to the grill. Banana leaves covered the roasting pig and smoke was occasionally working its way out, which caused Rick's stomach to growl in anticipation for the morsels that would fall off the bone.

Kaleho moved back and forth between the pit and the grill. He grabbed another water bottle and took long pulls from it, then returned it to the end of the row of empty ones he had created. Sweat was running down his brow and the side of his face from the effort the cooking took. Even though he had a permanent dirt pit for such occasions, the all-day effort of roasting a pig was normally undertaken by several people. Rick's cuts and burns ached with each passing moment, so he couldn't help like he did during their days at college.

Danielle and Leilani were busy talking while making leis for Leilani's hula class that she held for seniors once a week in Kapiolani Park. Each woman had a single pink, white and yellow colored Plumeria flower in their hair and light cotton dresses.

Stephanie, Shelli, Kai, and Tim sat at a big picnic table at that back of the yard along the hedge of bougainvillea that grew taller than the rock wall that surrounded the yard. As the table was a permanent fixture to the yard, grass couldn't grow well under it. So the teenagers sat with their shoes off and toes moving in the beach sand beneath. Both Shelli and Stephanie had purple and white colored Plumeria flowers in their hair, and orchid leis around their necks. The boys had board shorts and dress Hawaiian shirts on. They were laughing at something Stephanie was showing them on her phone.

Gas powered Tiki torches lined the yard, and Nikki and Ryan stood by themselves near one. The gentle trade winds caused the light from the torch flames to dance across their faces. Nikki was smiling as love-struck Ryan talked to her quietly. Nikki looked radiant with her long hair pinned back to one side with a purple Plumeria flower above the ear. She had on her new off-the-shoulder Hawaiian print skater dress that she had picked out earlier in the day with her mom, and sported a dazzling Maile leaf necklace that Ryan had just given her before heading to the luau. The fading bruise covered now by makeup, and the bandage on her arm were the only visible reminder of the brutal confrontation with the Deputy Dragon Head.

Above the wall of bougainvillea, Rick saw the peak of Diamond Head backlit with the gentle glow of Waikiki lights on the reverse side of the dark, dormant volcano.

Traditional Hawaiian music coming from the stereo inside the house was just loud enough to prevent Rick from hearing any conversation or the city noises still audible in the darkness that enveloped the ancient volcano. And that was just fine with Rick. This was indeed paradise – family and friends … and roasted pig.

He was still looking up toward Diamond Head and received a pat on the shoulder from Kaleho. It was just to enough of a pat to send searing pain through his ribcage. The pain combined with the slosh of his sweet tea made him jerk his arm forward. The quick reaction caused the tape to pull on several of his burn bandages, which sent another flash of pain all along his back and shoulder.

"Oowww," said Rick in low voice.  He did the best to keep from reacting the way he wanted and looking wimpy in front of his buddy.

"Oh, sorry man," said Kaleho wide-eyed. "I forgot about the sore ribs."

"No problem. I had almost forgotten about it too until I tried to move too fast, or to slow, or breathe, or eat, or laugh, or … well you get the idea."

They stood quietly beside one another gazing up at Diamond Head.  Then finally Kaleho spoke.  "So, Danielle have that talk with you?"

"Yeah, I knew it was coming.  Didn't make it any easier."  Rick looked back at his wife. "But she's probably right.  I dove head first into this…this detective, crime-stopping, mystery solving…

"Life saving," interrupted Kaleho.

"Well whatever you call it.  I didn't consider the consequences to the family.  I mean I worry about them, but I just figured I could protect them.  But these two cases have taken a toll on Danielle.   Seeing people die and the near-death of family has been pretty rough on her.  I thought she was all cried out over my injuries, and then she saw Nikki.  Needless to say she didn't speak to me for a few hours after that."

"I know how you feel Rick.  It's hard to leave it – believe me I know.  Even when I take a day off, I feel like I might be abandoning someone that needs help.  Fortunately I have Leilani to keep me sane.  And I still have her because of you and your family, Rick.  And for whatever you might be feeling now about leaving this business behind, you should feel good that you have kept this family and many more alive.  And I'm eternally grateful for what you guys did.  If you had any doubts before, you know you're Ohana for sure now."

Rick smiled and shook his head.  "Thanks.  You and your family have always felt like family to me.  And I know you would have done the same for me."

"You got that right," said Kahelo.  "So you've acquired all that equipment.  What are you going to do now?"

"My first love…science.  My company, Marine Science Systems, focuses on maritime related technology.  It's been sort of on autopilot since I've been working on these mysteries.  I've got a great group of employees, and I'll keep helping out with port and harbor security with local police forces and the Coast Guard.  I'll also continue research with HIMB out on Coconut Island, and with Mote Marine back in Florida. Plus Danielle will continue to work with Ringling Museum in Sarasota and with Bishop here.  So we'll be back to see you guys regularly."

"That's good, brah.  We don't have a big place, but we always have room for you as long as you need it.   And looking at those kids of ours, I suspect neither of us would get complaints about cramped quarters."

Rick laughed and then winced from the pain it caused.  "You know, Shelli even mentioned something about going to U of H when she graduates.  She's never, ever talked about colleges before, but I think this trip has been eye opening for her."

"That would be kinda cool for our kids to be going to the same school we did," said Kaleho.

"It would be. And it would give us a reason to visit even more. And speaking of visiting, you guys need to come visit us in Florida. We could go out fishing for tarpon down at Boca Grande Pass, or head up to Homosassa to snorkel for scallops, or maybe even go out on the *Amphitrite* and cruise down to the Bahamas."

"That sounds like a plan my man," said Kaleho. A searing sound from the imu drew his attention. He nudged Rick. "You too sore to help me with the pig? It's ready. You used to always love to help back in the day."

Before Rick could answer, Danielle spun around in her seat and shouted, "Ryan, help Kaleho with the pig. Rick, don't you even think about lifting that pig. You'll rip your bandages and get your burns and cuts bleeding again."

"Kai you help too," said Leilani.

Kaleho turned to Rick and spoke quietly, "Super-human hearing is still good even into their fifties."

Rick smiled as he nodded. "No comment," in fear that he might be overheard.

They both chuckled. Then Kaleho and the boys removed the banana leaves and lifted the pig from the bed of still warm rocks in the ground pit. Chicken wire wrapped around the pig kept the tender meat from sliding off the bone. They hoisted it onto the grill, which allowed for easy pickings.

Leilani changed the music to some traditional Luau tunes. She had a nice setting of island delicacies and a bountiful tray of pineapple, mango, papaya, kiwi, starfruit. Laughter, oohs and aahs from the pig roast were the main sounds for the next few minutes.

No one talked about the events that led them up to the blissful evening. It was behind them and it was time to rekindle the long friendship that had simmered over of the years since Rick and Kaleho's graduation from the U of H. Their lives had gone in different directions. Neither one of them could have ever envisioned where they were now. Rick did know one thing for certain. He knew there was nowhere on Earth that he would rather be at this moment in time.

# Chapter 43: *Unfathomable*

The sun was now high in the sky and the breeze was strong from the Northeast. Darker clouds were hanging tight to the ridgeline of the southern Ko'olau Range, so Rick was pointing the **Spearfish** southwest. They were past Barbers Point and about eight miles off the coast.

Rick was watching the map display closely, while Kaleho was sitting on the bench seat behind him rigging the bait. The higher pitched roar of the engines dropped to deep, slow quavers.

Kaleho set his rod aside and swayed as he walked up to Rick. "We there yet?"

"Yeah, I think we should start here," answered Rick without acknowledging the kid pun. He pointed to the display. "We are near the 1,000-fathom line, and we are going to follow that line northwest. We should have a chance at some Mahi Mahi, Ono, and Ahi. If we don't have much luck, we'll try go back in closer to shore and fish around some of the offshore objects just beyond the 100-fathom line."

"Sounds like you know what you're doing," said Kaleho. "I didn't know you knew that much about fishing O'ahu waters."

"I don't. I asked the older guys hanging around the marina." They both laughed.

They were silent for a few minutes, absorbing the tranquil setting.

"I talked to Danielle one more time before she left for Florida on a commercial flight. She made it pretty clear that she expected me to get back to my company or retire. So I'm going to have a little more free time to fish when I get back home."

"I'm sure that once you get home and dive back into science you'll soon forget about the detective stuff," said Kaleho. "Why did Danielle go back anyway? Kai's having fun teaching the girls how to surf on the tiny waves down at Waikiki. The two of you could have relaxed and hung out with Leilani and me."

"Danielle had to go back to prepare for the *Seafair* art show," said Rick. "The Ringling museum is managing the event, and they put Danielle in charge. It's no small show, and it's a big deal to be managing it. Danielle's super excited to be given the responsibility."

"She definitely knows her art. I couldn't tell you a Picasso from a Rembrandt."

They cut the motor and started fishing. Rick volunteered to fan cast the chugger bait to bring in the Mahi Mahi toward the boat, and Kaleho cast with the live bait. They pulled in their first nice catch when the phone rang. Rick stopped casting and pulled out his phone. He expected that Danielle was calling from home, but noticed it was Sheriff Steele's number.

"Hi Mike, I'm out pretty far offshore. So I apologize in advance if I lose you. I'll call you back if I do."

"Then I'll talk quickly Rick." He cleared his throat. "We were able to track expenses and examine tax records for William Hawthorne. He listed his occupation as security consultant. He made more than seven figures annually, which would be exceptionally high for that occupation. He was paid through mostly shell companies based overseas, so Uncle Sam can't probe into their finances. Not the IRS, at least. But the FBI believes these are front companies for the Mafia and other organized crime syndicates."

Rick remained quiet, but his stomach began to tense as the Sheriff spoke.

"We also reviewed more of the footage and location data for our man over the three weeks he was watching your family. At first it appeared the patterns were random, but then we realized that the majority of the time was spent when Danielle was around. He did spend some time on you and on Nikki, but the interest was by far more focused on Danielle."

Rick started to walk in circles as the Sheriff continued. He was squinting as if he was looking at something in the distance, but he registered nothing of what he saw.

"And we finally got back the analysis from the FBI crime lab of Hawthorne's last words. They said the video your cars recorded was quite helpful. They matched the lip movements with the sounds. We thought he had said 'arda.' But what he actually said was 'art da.'"

The Sheriff stopped talking. *Art da...they were following mostly the family, and particularly Danielle. Art da...we own lot of art, all of which was made or purchased by his wife. Wait a minute. Art...Danielle. He was warning me that this was about art and Danielle.*

"Art, Danielle," he finally said out loud. "You knew that of course," said Rick. "You wanted to see if I had the same conclusion. But why spy on Danielle?"

"Rick, I know you know the answer to that question. You're just trying to convince yourself that it is something else. Whatever Danielle is involved in the art world, it must have gotten the wrong kind of attention. Hawthorne was a hitman, plain and simple. His background showed that he once had a wife and young daughter. They were both murdered. We think that drove him into his trade. You saw ... he killed without a moment's hesitation. But maybe he was having second thoughts about killing when he started watching your family. Thank goodness he didn't succeed."

"But the people that hired him are still out there."

"Yes, so when you get back we're going to put your family into protective custody. But while you're there, you should be safe with your Honolulu police friends."

"Mike, Danielle is not here with us. She took an early flight home by herself. She's either just walked into the front door or will do so shortly."

"Holy cow," responded Sheriff Steele. "I'll get someone over their right away."

"Please do, Mike. We'll be wheels up within two hours. Please let me know when your officer is there. I'm going to try calling her now."

Rick hung up and turned to Kaleho. Kaleho was standing there looking concerned.

"It's Danielle. She's in danger. Please call the kids. Tell them it's an emergency and they are to head to the airport immediately. No stops at the hotel before – just go straight to the airport private terminal area. I'll meet them there."

"Roger that," said Kaleho. "They'll have a police escort the entire way to the airport." Rick was glad to see that his friend had instantaneously switched to policeman mode.

"I'm going to try to reach Danielle and our pilot." Rick's instinct was telling him to call Danielle first, but he knew it would take time to get the private plane prepped and clear for take-off.

Rick quickly dialed the pilot, who answered on the second ring. Within a minute he explained the urgency and the pilot confirmed he'd be ready in an hour and a half to take off.

Rick then took a deep breath and dialed Danielle's number. The phone range, once, twice, three times, and then after the fourth ring... **"Hello, this is Danielle. Thanks for calling. Leave your name and message after the beep and I'll call you right back."**

# Message from the Author

It has been more than four years since the first installment of The Bryant Family Chronicles (TBFC) was released. Running a science and technology company keeps me busy. I also published a technical book and number of technical papers since the first TBFC. I had fun writing this book, but it took much longer than I expected. The research was time consuming, and led me down many dead ends before coming to the final storyline printed in this book.

I stumbled upon the Daily Alta California story when I read tidbits of it from a treasure hunting forum back in 2012. I was looking for a follow-on storyline to TBFC book 1 that would take place in Hawaii. I ended up spending about three years of research during my spare time on the story and on Honolulu in the 1880's -- partly to understand the facts, and partly because I was just enjoying it too much. I'd like to thank the great resources at California Digital Newspaper Collection where I found the full newspaper article, and the Hawai'i State Archives, which is a division of the Department of Accounting and General Services for the great State of Hawai'i. I found the pictures in book 2 and some historical data for the story at the Archives. If you really want to know about the period, use the book: _The Hawaiian Kingdom 1874-1893_ by R. S Kuykendall. It is a phenomenal work that was years in the making, and it was a great help in understanding the period. I'm not a historian, so it took a great many nights of reading to feel comfortable about writing the 1884 passages, and I still feel like somewhat of a newbie on the subject. _The Origins of the Tiandihui_ by Dian H. Murray, and a number of useful websites gave me insights into the tongs. I purchased _'Iolani Palace_ by Friends of Iolani Palace from the Iolani Palace bookstore. This little book of pictures and short chapters, and the tour of the palace were great inspiration for the storyline from 1884. These sources and a host of web links are found on The Bryant Family Chronicles webpage at www.deepseapublishing.com.

I went to school at the University of Hawai'i at Manoa in the early 1980's, about a hundred years after the time the raid supposedly took place. Besides my physics and math courses, I took courses in the Hawaiian geography, geophysics, and received a certificate (similar to a minor) for my studies in the Marine Option Program (MOP). It was while earning my MOP certificate that I had the opportunity to work on a funded research project at the Hawaii Institute of Marine Biology. I took up scuba diving as well when I was a student, and have gone on many fantastic dives in the crystal waters of the Pacific in years since.

Although I had spent years in Hawai'i as a student, and had come back with my wife several times since then, I felt my experiences were a little too dated when I started writing the parts of the book that take place in present day Honolulu. So I took my family to Hawai'i to research some of the sites found in this book during the summer of 2013. It was a wonderful trip and it renewed my love of the Hawaiian people and culture. I was so enthralled by the pirate story and the history I dug up, I will be releasing a second book about the raid that examines the facts of the day, the characters, and more pictures of the time. It was truly an incredible time to be living in Honolulu.

I'd like to thank my family for putting up with me over these long years of writing book two. Nikki and Shelli are exceptional children, but they don't compare to my two real kids. I especially thank my school-teacher wife for the long hours she spent in editing, making suggestions, and helping me with all aspects of getting this book to print. I thank my parents again for the encouragement and love they've always given me, and for allowing me to make my first trip to Hawaii as a student more than thirty years ago.

I'd also like to thank the hundreds of great ideas provided to me by friends and family. My wife's parents are a great source of information about Florida, and regularly send me newspaper clippings of interesting events or people. And some of the names of characters found in this book were borrowed from supportive friends and family.

The science and technology in this book are real, and many of gadgets and sensors are either built by my technology company or by companies we work with – including the acoustic hailer, the radar and camera technology, and the self-driving cars. I had a great visit to University of Parma and was given a ride around the town in a driverless car, where I rode in the backseat directly behind where the driver should be seated. The surf boards, **Dolphina**, and robotic sharks are all produced in the USA; however, I did add some additional capabilities that would be easy modifications to them. The **Amphitrite** and its deployable submarine were modeled after a real ship that was built just after TBFC book 1.

Believe it or not, the gambling ring, the Chinatown fires, the discussions around the dinner table at Iolani Palace, and even the discussion of the mongoose brought to Hawai'i were based on real events and facts. I encourage future visitors to Honolulu to check out the Bishop Museum, Chinatown, Iolani Palace, Kawaiaha'o Church, the Hawai'i Maritime Center at Pier 7, the ship *The Falls of Clyde* built in 1878, Punchbowl, the University of Hawai'i at Manoa, and the waterfront instead of baking in the sun at Waikiki beaches each and every day. Maybe take a hike out to the top of Diamond Head from inside the crater or take the walk down to the beach at Diamond Head Beach Park. The other islands, which were barely mentioned in this book, have a wealth of cultural, historic, and entertaining sites and activities too numerous to list here. Hawai'i should be on everyone's bucket list.

Book 3 of The Bryant Family Chronicles is being written now and is expected out in 2016. No more waiting for four years for the next book. The story has the same complex turns, cutting-edge technology, and family dynamics.

One last comment…the Suntanned Merluza is a long-time favored fish sandwich at *Cha Cha Coconuts* in St Armands Circle, Sarasota. The restaurant was enjoyed by my kids each time we visited their grandparents in the greater Sarasota area. Also mentioned in TBFC book 1 and 2 was one of the best places to get fresh fish and oysters -- *Phillippi Creek Village Restaurant and Oyster Bar* on Route 41.

# About the Author

Eddie Hughes is the President, Co-Founder, and Co-Owner of Detection Monitoring Technologies (DMT), which primarily builds security radars and integrated mobile monitoring systems. Mr. Hughes graduated from Lynchburg College with a B.S. in Physics, and the University of Hawaii at Manoa with a B.S. in Mathematics.

Mr. Hughes is an avid fisherman and kayaker, certified scuba diver, and loves the outdoors. His travels have taken him around the world and his stories capture the sights and local flavor of these exotic locales.

Mr. Hughes, his wife, and his younger daughter live in northern Virginia, but frequent southwest Florida several times per year. His youngest will be heading for college soon. His oldest daughter graduated from college and is making a name for herself. Both daughters have published children's books of their own. His wife, formerly a school teacher, stays active in the community and manages book shipments.

*The Bryant Family Chronicles: Death and Gold in Zara Zote* was Mr. Hughes' first novel in a series of novels that are planned about the Bryant family. We hoped you enjoyed the second installment of the series. The Bryant family will return in book 3 expected to be released in 2016. Mr. Hughes also published *Site Surveying Guide for Radar and Cameras* and has other radar-related books planned for 2016.

# Upcoming Books and Information

The Bryant Family Chronicles book series is published by Deep Sea Publishing (DSP), a Florida limited-liability company. We welcome you to our website where you can read more about our authors, check out news about book releases, look up book signing events, and shop. DSP books can be found on Amazon.Com and at many other book resellers and sites. Any bookstore can also order our books using the ISBN number or the title and author's name.

## www.DeepSeaPublishing.com

New books to be released in 2016:

- Book 3 of *The Bryant Family Chronicles*,
- Honolulu Pirate Raid of 1884,
- New young adult books and children's books,
- New books on sensor technology.

People that have bought *The Bryant Family Chronicles* have also purchased Hardt's Tale (by Gwendolyn Druyor) and The Good Fight (by Ophelia Hu). Young adult readers have enjoyed Capria Rodalia (Sidney McPhail), The Gallivan Legacy (Sable Lewis), Twisted (Brittany Hawes), and Ty Burson's series of books -- *Modern Dragon Chronicles*. Let Sleeping Dragons Lie and It's a Dragon-Eat-Dragon World were the first books by Burson. His short story and teacher's guides are also available.